SHARDS OF CRIMSON

LIZ MAVERICK
PATTI O'SHEA
CAROLYN JEWEL
JADE LEE

LOVE SPELL

NEW YORK CITY

LOVE SPELL®

January 2007

Published by

Dorchester Publishing Co., Inc.
200 Madison Avenue
New York, NY 10016

ISBN 0-505-52710-3

CRITICS RAVE FOR THE *USA TODAY* BESTSELLING *CRIMSON CITY* SERIES!

LIZ MAVERICK
CRIMSON CITY

"Shocking revelations, danger, and intense heat are ever present in *Crimson City*. For a fast-paced rollercoaster ride to hell and back, run—don't walk—to your nearest bookstore and snatch up a copy."

—*Romance Reviews Today*

"Maverick provides an intense tale with complex characters to kick off a new series set in an original, dark and fascinating world."

—*RT BOOKreviews*

CRIMSON ROGUE

"This is the powerhouse conclusion to the exceptionally creative *Crimson City* series, launched by the versatile Maverick.... With nail-biting suspense and fast-paced action, this novel is a spectacular finale!"

—*RT BOOKreviews* (Top Pick)

"*Crimson Rogue* ends the *Crimson City* series with heartstopping action, danger in every dark corner, adventure, and explosive characters in volatile situations. Once you start reading it, you just can't put it down."

—*Romance Reviews Today*

PATTI O'SHEA
THROUGH A CRIMSON VEIL

"This adventurous thriller is searing hot and filled with passion, treachery and danger. It's paranormal adventure at its ultimate! O'Shea has definitely found her calling."

—*RT BOOKreviews* (Top Pick)

"Danger is around every corner; demons and otherworldly creatures lurk in the darkness, and passion comes alive in Patti O'Shea's *Through a Crimson Veil.*"

—*Romance Reviews Today*

Other books in the *Crimson City* series:

CRIMSON CITY by Liz Maverick
A TASTE OF CRIMSON by Marjorie M. Liu
THROUGH A CRIMSON VEIL by Patti O'Shea
A DARKER CRIMSON by Carolyn Jewel
SEDUCED BY CRIMSON by Jade Lee
CRIMSON ROGUE by Liz Maverick

SHARDS OF CRIMSON

TABLE OF CONTENTS

A TIME TO HOWL
    by Liz Maverick   1

DX by Carolyn Jewel   101

SCHOOL BITES
    by Jade Lee   183

DARK AWAKENING
    by Patti O'Shea   281

To the fans waiting for Jill and Marius…we'll get there.

A Time to Howl

by
Liz Maverick

Chapter One

The doorman at the ground level of Dumont Tower touched his earpiece, his leather-clad index finger delicate against the metal. His coat looked as it did every afternoon, as if he'd removed it from a sea of unwrinkled tissue for just this one day. He wore his top hat perfectly straight; his face exhibited a kind of blank confidence that never let on that the archaic accessory might be slightly bizarre in the context of the current century. Across the street, from a perch atop a mailbox fused shut back when postal service ended, Tajo Maddox mused that it hadn't seemed bizarre for some time now.

Yes, even the humans understood that with immortality came tradition. The styles, philosophies and behaviors of earlier centuries infused this latest incarnation of Los Angeles, blending modern and old-fashioned in a pastiche that made the place unlike any other; that made it Crimson City. And as the humans lost ground to the vampires and werewolves and found themselves in jeopardy from the other races they themselves had helped empower—the demons from the plane of Orcus, the mechs from the humans' own military labs—the present borrowed an ever-increasing number of elements from the past.

One thing hadn't changed for years: The richest and most powerful group in Crimson City was still the Dumonts, one of the pureblood vampire clans collectively referred to as primaries. They'd had centuries to perfect their operations, and it showed. From this doorman at the bottom of Dumont Tower to whatever the hell went on in the penthouse war rooms at the top.

Tajo's own group had not enjoyed the luxury of time. The Rogues were new players in Crimson City. Glancing down at Hayden Wilks, Bridget Hathaway, and Jillian Cooper sprawled along a concrete riser beside him, he had to marvel at how far they'd already come. Especially for a bunch of mercenaries and freelancers used to working alone.

They hadn't organized into an actual team until recently. It wasn't easy surviving as a rogue in Crimson City. You had no backup, no clan or family to run to for an army of help. People assumed the worst—that you had no sense of honor, no sense of mercy. People who wouldn't dream of killing a primary seemed perfectly able to justify killing a rogue. What really talked in this town, what safety really demanded, was power.

So a bunch of rogues teamed up. The idea of thumbing their noses at the rigidity and insularity of the purebred clans by forming a mixed species superpower appealed to the rebel in all of them. They'd even chipped in and bought an underground club to turn into a headquarters. They'd dubbed it the Rogues Club, and just like that the city was put on notice. Except, not everyone had noticed. Yet.

Tajo jumped off the mailbox and sat down next to Hayden. The two cased the area in mutual silence, waiting, wondering, wary. Without turning away from her surveillance, Bridget stuck her hand out; Hayden took a last puff and gently laid his cigarette in the V of her fingers.

Jill leaned back as Bridget took a drag, coughing and waving away the smoke even as she darted nervous eyes to the dove cooing on the overhang above her head.

Yeah, this was a solid bunch, a good team. In time, they'd be great. In time, they'd be ranked right up there on the Crimson City power scale alongside the Dumont vampire primaries, the Maddox werewolf clan from whom Tajo had long ago exiled himself, and most certainly the human government that had once seemed so indestructible.

"Time?" Hayden asked.

"About three minutes since you last asked. Maybe you could ask Jill to get you a watch for your birthday," Tajo muttered.

Hayden turned back to Tajo. "I'm holding out for something more personal," he said with a cocky tip of his head.

Tajo followed the gesture to Jill, who was sitting by Bridget on the end. She fiddled with her field glasses, then pointed them up the façade of Dumont Tower for the umpteenth time. Two seconds later, she lowered them and looked down, a wounded expression darkening her face. Jill was supposed to be thinking about the Rogue job, but it was obvious it was her doomed bond with Marius Dumont making her search the Tower so intently.

Tajo kept his mouth shut this time, wishing he hadn't joked about it. Hayden had been circling Jill since she joined the Rogues. So far, his interest seemed to be as much about revenge against the Dumonts as it was about the girl herself.

Tajo's gaze shifted to Bridget. He and she had tried out a thing, had some fun together, and decided they were better suited as friends with the occasional benefit. Tajo still admired her and her bad-ass fearlessness, but like Hayden, the girl had something truly dark inside of her and Tajo wasn't sure her allegiance to the Rogues would hold. Especially since she'd once worked inside the human species' headquarters.

Bridget leaned forward and looked both ways down the street. "Anyone else starting to think no-show?"

"Like, they forgot? Impossible. We just set this thing up a day ago."

"Do you hear escort sirens?" Hayden asked, cocking his head.

Jill and Bridget were human; they wouldn't be able to hear anything from too far away.

Tajo frowned. "I hear 'em. Jill, did you check the press slate before we left?"

The former newspaper reporter still made full use of her old contacts. She pulled a folded paper from the pocket of her hoodie and scanned the document. "If there's anything going on with the Dumonts this morning, they aren't advertising." She looked down the street. "Now I can hear them. And see them."

Four heads swiveled as the cadence and sounds of everyday street activity abruptly changed. Tajo's watch ticked loudly in the silence. The hour turned and a chorus of horns blared out in four-part harmony.

Several blocks away, a caravan turned the corner and started toward Dumont Tower. The Rogues watched slack-jawed as a set of guards jumped from security runners fused to the chassis of a white limousine to block regular traffic and push back pedestrians on all sides.

The caravan inched toward them, first a set of black,

smoky-glassed cars, then a choreographed mass of white horses, red plumes and shiny brass horns. The white limousine came next, the runners still carrying a set of guards on one side. And then the bookend, a second set of black cars.

The guards continued to hold the traffic; the pedestrians strained forward to get a better look.

Tajo narrowed his eyes, trying to get a read on the miniature flags fluttering from each side mirror on the limousine. "Jill, can I borrow your field glasses?"

Jill pulled the set from her neck and passed them down. Tajo flipped off Night Vision and focused on the flags, whistling low as he made out their provenance. "New York, New York."

"Really? Is it someone for the Power Summit?" Bridget tried to grab the glasses, but Tajo darted out of the way, shifting the sights over to get a peek at the limousine's side window, cracked a third of the way down.

"Zoom?" he asked.

"The long thingy on the right," Jill said. "It's a new model."

Tajo zoomed in. A strand of blond hair fluttered out the small window opening and a row of delicate fingers curled over the glass, one sporting a delicate gold royal crest. "No kidding!"

"What?" Bridget asked. This time, Tajo let her take the glasses.

"East Coast werewolf royalty is what. The Dumonts must be serious about this werewolf alliance."

"That's not exactly news," Jill said bitterly. "Except, I thought the lucky girl was already living at Dumont Tower."

"There were three princesses born to New York's werewolf House Royale if my memory serves me right."

"Three werewolf brides for three vampire brothers,"

7

Bridget said. "Almost poetic—if it didn't smack so badly of cheap mail-order bride."

"Something tells me this one doesn't come cheap," Tajo said. "She's probably worth a lot in political currency."

Jill took the glasses. "All three pairs plan to marry? It just doesn't seem . . ."

Tajo guessed she wanted to say "fair." Instead she said, "Necessary." "There's no question matching all three of them would make a bulletproof alliance stretching coast to coast."

Hayden folded his arms across his chest, one of his fangs curling over his lower lip as the cavalcade continued forward. "East Coast style. Nice. Can't say I've ever seen the Crimson City dogs show up the Dumonts like that."

Tajo nodded, his gaze fixed on the limousine door where the crest of House Royale shone fresh and bright. Seeing it there was something of a shock, the way it trumpeted the superiority of the pureblood werewolf in a kind of splashy, overdone way Keeli Maddox's primary clan would likely have eschewed.

Though Tajo hadn't allied himself with Keeli's clan for years now, he felt a strange pride at seeing a werewolf crest displayed so blatantly in the streets of Crimson City. Note to the Dumonts and everybody else, it seemed to say: Wealth and power are not the domain of only the primary vampires.

Werewolves and vampires were naturally distrustful of one another. It was why the alliance between the primaries of the two species always seemed so fragile. And so susceptible to external pressures like rogue interference.

Across the street, the doorman leaned out to watch

the limo move easily forward in the empty, blocked-off street.

"This does beg the question," Tajo said, looking up at Dumont Tower. "Pureblood werewolves en route to an engagement party with pureblood vampire primaries . . . so what the hell are a bunch of mutts like us doing in the mix? Our rendezvous point is less than five yards away from kiss-kiss-will-you-marry-me, and we happen to get a no-show on our job. Anyone else smell a setup?"

Hayden nodded. "Not my favorite smell," he growled, his bared fangs sparkling under the white light of the moon.

"Who's our client?" Bridget asked.

"Humans. Needed a solid mercenary team to handle some quick business, but wanted to meet the team first."

"Anyone I know?" she pressed.

"I got the gig through a middleman—a human middleman I'm going to have to beat the crap out of next time I hit Bosco's." Tajo sighed. "I should have known the money was too good to be true. Sorry, guys."

"No biggie." Bridget picked up her messenger bag and strapped it across her chest. "It happens. And we have to take some chances. God knows our team needs the funding. So, I guess we're outta here?"

"Yeah." Tajo whistled and rotated two fingers in the air. "Round it up. We're out of here."

Everybody except Jill stood. "I want to see her," she blurted.

"No, you don't," Hayden said, pulling on her shoulder. "Come on."

"I'll catch up with you at the clubhouse," she said, her shoulders squared.

Tajo sent Bridget a pleading look, and she squatted down next to Jill. "Marius's fiancée is already up there, Jill. This is just one of her sisters." She dropped her voice and added, "Don't torture yourself."

Jill's cheeks suddenly burned red. She mumbled an apology and began gathering her equipment.

In the street, the first set of black cars passed them by, then the horses, and finally the limousine pulled up at the tower entrance. To Tajo's surprise, a trio of vampire security men moved around the chaos and headed directly toward the Rogues. Tajo looked in the direction of the main camera mounted by the front door of Dumont Tower and waved.

"We're leaving," he mouthed.

The vampires pulled their weapons and changed course to help secure the perimeter of the area, while support personnel moved in to receive the royal guest. Bridget let out a breath. "I thought they were coming at us."

"Ready," Jill said.

But Tajo didn't move. Frozen in place, he watched a small, blond female step out of the white limousine, almost fairylike in her wispy, delicate looks. Two body-guards closed in on either side. The doorman spoke into his microphone, then bowed deeply to the were-wolf princess as she looked around curiously. Her handlers tried to hustle her inside, but she flung their hands away, pointing at an adwriter hovering low. Maybe they didn't use them in the New York City skies yet.

The guards were pulling at her now, their fingertips barely grazing the princess's elbows, trying to move her without really touching her. She wasn't having it, her head swiveling from left to right as she took in the surrounding sights and sounds. Tajo smiled just watching her.

And that was when he smelled it. The stink of imminent danger separated itself from the dark scent of unrest normally lying thick over the city. Trouble was, the smell of the tools of war had become so pervasive in Crimson City that it was often hard to distinguish remnants of a prior event from those yet to make their mark.

"Tajo?" Bridget asked.

The smile disappeared from Tajo's face as the odor of danger clogged his nostrils. Beside him, Hayden flinched.

"Don't hurt her," Tajo murmured to no one in particular, his eyes fixed on the princess's lovely face. Unaware, unafraid, her eyes wide with excitement.

The dove above Jill's head cooed softly. Dumont Tower's lobby exploded in a storm of fire.

The Rogues dove for cover, the lot of them immediately covered by a fine layer of silt and shattered glass. The pedestrians who'd stayed to gape at the princess ran in all directions, making it impossible to see who was who, what was what . . . and who had fired shots.

The alarm system blared. Smoke billowed into the street. The horses in the caravan went crazy, rearing and bolting, their plumed handlers abandoning their brass horns as they tried to secure their charges. The sky filled with the shadowy forms of vampires taking flight off the balconies rimming each level of the skyscraper.

A gust of wind cleared the air in front of Tajo long enough for him to get a read. Residue peppered the white limousine; the head of a gargoyle from the building's façade lay in a crater on the hood.

Tajo collected himself enough to climb to his knees and crawl to the nearest body in the street. No pulse. He looked around. The princess was nowhere in sight. His chest still heaving from the shock, it was all he could do to focus on the lives of his teammates. The ground and the dead bodies were riddled with shrapnel, and he could smell that the metal had been dipped in silver nitrate. He was the only werewolf of the group, and while the shrapnel could have wounded them all at this distance, the silver itself could kill only him. Leaping to his feet, Tajo quickly checked his exposed skin and confirmed his armor had not been penetrated. He'd been close enough to the concrete barrier to miss the worst. Lucky. Very lucky.

Jill was the next to get up, in spite of Tajo barking orders to stay down. Her hand shielding her eyes, she looked upward. A trickle of blood wound down her cheek as she robotically patted the pocket where her reporter's pad had once lived.

"Tajo!"

He swung around, trying to see through the haze. Evacuations were already in full swing as the alarms continued to sound. Already, a squad of vampires attended to the flames at lobby level, a second group shoring up the infrastructure. Vampire medics raced to their injured; werewolves went for their dead. And nobody, it seemed, had found the princess yet.

"Tajo, over there. Get her!" Hayden shouted, pointing at the pile of bodies in the street. The vampire himself was busy tending to a shrapnel wound in Bridget's thigh, a wound, from what he could tell, caused by a bronze plaque blown off the side of the building. Bridget was pounding her fist against the pavement and swearing a blue streak—something about yet another scar, which had to mean she was okay.

Tajo called out to Jill and gestured to the bodies. Her eyes half closed against the filth in the air, she leaned over, grabbed one of the dead bodyguards' legs and helped pull several corpses away. The princess lay facedown against the concrete, her forehead pressed into the cushion of her bloodied left hand. Tajo and Jill looked at each other and nodded, then slowly rolled her over on the count of three. She opened her eyes, looked up at Tajo and smiled the sweetest smile he'd ever seen. Then she passed out again.

"Can I get some help over here?" Hayden yelled, struggling to lift the thrashing Bridget to her feet. "We gotta get her to medical, ASAP."

Tajo nodded at Jill. He could smell the Dumont guards bearing down on him; a glance up showed they were already ringing a circle around him and his friends, waiting for one of the Dumonts themselves to arrive. Once Marius showed up, Jill would be useless.

"Go help him," he said.

"Are you thinking what I'm thinking?" Jill asked, gesturing to the unconscious princess. " 'Crimson City, we'd like to introduce you to the Rogues—capital R.' "

"You'd better believe it," Tajo agreed, lowering his voice a notch. "An asset like this drops in our laps, I think we run with it. In this case, with her. Go on and help Hayden. This isn't her blood. It's her bodyguards'. I think she just knocked her head."

Jill reached up to the utility belt slung low around her waist, unclipped two cartridges, tossed them to him, and moved on. Pocketing the ammo, Tajo bent to his knees and swept the hair from the princess's face with his free hand.

She was the picture of innocence—all milky white skin and a smattering of freckles across her nose. But she was on her way to being a pawn for the primary vampires and the other dogs, and it was only a small detour to being a pawn for the Rogues instead.

Letting her bruised cheek fall gently against his shoulder, Tajo gathered her in his arms and stood, nearly falling backward with her in the next moment as Marius Dumont, Fleur Dumont, and Dain Reston careened down through the swirling dust and slammed to the pavement in front of him. Framed by the backdrop of Dumont Tower smoking and sparking in the dark, they formed an impressive front.

Tajo held his ground. With the princess held in one arm, he pulled his pistol from its holster and pointed it directly at Marius's chest. The gun was ridiculously tricked out to look impressive and deadly, which, of course, it was when it worked properly, but this seemed to have no impact whatsoever on Marius. The vampire fixated on something—or someone—over Tajo's shoulder.

No one said anything. Tajo, Fleur, and Dain followed Marius's gaze. Jill looked up from where she helped Hayden hoist their injured teammate to her feet. Her eyes seemed to lock with Marius's, though the expression on her face remained blank. The cut on her cheek oozed a line of blood, razor-thin and hardly noticeable with everything else going on. Or so it would seem.

A smile twisting his lips, Tajo looked around at the three vampires. "Um, anybody gonna give me shit here, or can I go on my way?"

Fleur and Dain exchanged looks. Fleur glanced impatiently at her cousin and said, "Marius, go check on the war room."

Marius looked at her in surprise, but without saying another word, took himself away.

"This mess your doing, Tajo?" Dain asked.

"Fair question. But, no. My team got set up."

Fleur stretched out her arm to touch the princess's face.

Tajo stepped back out of range. "She's fine. As you can see, I'm busy saving her."

Dain snorted.

"Hey, man, we had nothing to do with it. Somebody obviously wanted the princess dead, and they wanted it to look like we were involved. I mean, how idiotic would it be for us to sit and watch our own assassination attempt like it was a fucking musical?"

Fleur gestured to the princess in Tajo's arms. "If you were set up, you had no plan to take her. So, why don't you give her to me and we'll call it a night?"

"You've got bigger things to worry about than me." With the tip of his boot, Tajo flipped the doorman's top hat up in the air. Fleur caught the singed accessory. "You've got a helluva security breach in there."

Dain snarled, the kind of uncontrolled reaction of someone who hadn't been used to controlling his vampire state for very long. Fleur murmured something and he reluctantly backed down.

"She have a name?" Tajo asked.

"Her Royal Highness Princess Gianna Asprey," Fleur answered tightly. "But I'm sure when she wakes up and stops screaming she'll let you call her Gia."

" 'Gia.' Nice."

Fleur took a step forward, reaching for the girl once more. "You leave here with her, understand you'll have House Dumont, House Royale, and even Keeli's werewolves all over your case."

Tajo stepped back out of her reach again. "Aw, c'mon, Fleur. Did you even look at my gun? It's a really big one." He hoisted the slipping princess up again as best he could and brandished his weapon, pointing it straight at Dain. "That's the thing with women—they just aren't interested in our toys. How 'bout you explain that this is a really big gun and it's going to hurt a lot?"

Dain snarled again, the veins in his neck throbbing, but Fleur held him by the arm.

Once he could overlook; twice was asking too much of an alpha. Tajo narrowed his eyes at Dain, with a rough flick of his wrist switched the cartridge on his weapon to liquid silver, and pointed the gun at the princess's head.

"Don't piss me off, Dain. You think I wouldn't do it? You forget that there's still honor in fair payback. We know about the rogues you've picked off. And I don't mind putting a bullet in *her* to set things straight."

"A mercenary's sense of honor," Dain muttered. But neither he nor Fleur made a move.

"Well, this has been great, but Gia and I need to get going," Tajo said, his gun still pressing into the princess's temple. "Oh, and Dain . . . you should think about getting those hair-trigger reflexes looked at."

Tajo kept moving backwards until the darkness of an alley enveloped them both. Then he turned and picked up his pace, moving as fast as he could with the girl a dead weight in his arms. She was getting really heavy.

The others had undoubtedly taken the transport to get Bridget to medical. Tajo wended his way through the city streets until he felt secure enough to slow down. The Rogues kept a number of safe houses scattered around the city. They'd originally pooled their resources and bought them because most of the members still worked freelance mercenary jobs; it was nice to have somewhere to go when you were on the run and needed to disappear. One of the perks of membership. But as the Rogues became increasingly involved in city politics, those same safe houses were literally becoming critical to their survival.

In the silence of a deserted alley, Tajo sheathed his weapon, shifted the girl into both of his arms, and walked the rest of the way at a more reasonable pace.

The walk gave him an opportunity to get a lead on what exactly he'd just gotten himself into. And with whom. One thing was for sure. A lot of white, lacy fabric kept getting tangled in the zipper of his jacket, and some feathery accessory tickled his arm. The purse hanging from the crook of her elbow banged against his ribs.

As he passed under the gasping wattage of a faulty streetlamp, she came to a little, turning her head, burrowing into his neck. He could feel her mouth against his throat, the damp of her lips burning like a brand into his flesh. Struck by the oddest sense that he'd just been marked in some way, Tajo tightened his grip around her and hurried toward the building entrance.

Focus, Tajo. Focus.

"Hello, knight," she murmured.

Oh, you're kidding me. "Hardly," was all he managed to say. The perfumed scent of her hair mingled with the dirt and the blood on her face and dress.

She either didn't hear, didn't care, or had a serious head injury not visible to the naked eye. All she did was exhale a warm throaty "Mmmm" against his cheek and snuggle closer.

"Hello, knight" was essentially how fairy tales started. But this princess was caught in the open in

Crimson City, outside her castle. And Tajo wasn't anybody's hero.

Hopefully, she'd catch on quick to the whole kidnapping thing and would keep her screaming to a minimum. At least until he'd had his first cup of coffee.

Chapter Two

Gia was awake before she opened her eyes, but she didn't need to see to know that she wasn't at home; this was undeniably the most uncomfortable bed she'd ever slept on in her life. Keeping her lids lightly closed, she noted the lack of scented linens, flowers, and customary full English breakfast, though she knew immediately that poor quality coffee was present. Most unsettling of all, what *was* there and wasn't supposed to be was 100 percent male. She hadn't ever had *that* in her bedroom at home.

Slowly, Gia opened her eyes and blinked to clear her vision. The gauzy shadow of a man tightened into focus. He sat across the room with his boots propped up on a table and a steaming mug clutched in his hands. He was staring at her. Just staring with a slight smile that set his mouth off-kilter. More alarming, even, was that he seemed to have misplaced his shirt.

Granted, the sliver of light that escaped the closed blinds suggested the night had long since ceded to the morning and it was much warmer than it had been when she'd first arrived in Crimson City, but all the same it was just Gia, herself, alone with one scantily clad male. A rare event, to say the least. One should, it seemed, make the most of the moment.

Tatiana and Folie would absolutely die when she told the story. They all said nobody spun a story like Gia. *Let's see. He was one of those big, strong types. Muscles all over and stubble on his jaw. He looked so very dangerous. And he was wearing next to nothing. So much skin! The way he looked at me was positively . . . electric. As if we both knew—though, of course we were strangers and hadn't even spoken yet—that there was something special between us. It all started when he swooped in and rescued me from the disaster, like a knight riding in on a white horse . . .*

Wait a minute. The disaster. Where are my minders?

Gia sat upright, the details of the explosion at Dumont Tower flooding back into her memory. Her bodyguards would have swarmed her at something as benign as the buzz of an insect, and that had been some kind of bomb.

Though she could sense he was werewolf, Gia knew without a doubt that the stranger in this room wasn't one of hers. And if he wasn't one of hers, he wasn't anybody she was supposed to know.

"Good morning," he said, raising his mug.

"Good morning." Gia cleared her throat. "I beg your pardon, but where are my bodyguards?"

He tipped his head to one side, wincing a little. "Your bodyguards are dead. They died doing what they were supposed to do."

Gia's eyes welled up with tears as guilt flooded her, that peculiar guilt that came with not having known enough about someone who worked for you to mourn their loss in a personal way. She slumped against the headboard and looked away.

"I'm sorry," the stranger said. "Someone planted a device in the lobby of Dumont Tower."

Silence stretched out between them as Gia collected herself.

"Someone tried to kill you," the man finally added, studying her face so closely Gia had to wonder what it was he hoped to see.

"I said that someone just tried to kill you," he repeated.

"Yes, I heard you. It's happened before. The trying part of it anyway." Gia ran her arrival at Dumont Tower through her mind one more time. "Is there a reasonable explanation why I'm here with you?"

"I'd say that I pulled you out of the danger zone. The Dumonts would say that I kidnapped you." He took a big swig from his mug. "If you're going to scream, now would be your moment."

"How long have I been here?" she asked, choosing to ignore his suggestion.

"Overnight."

"And you're not one of the Dumonts?"

"We both know you know that I'm not a vampire, much less a Dumont."

She smiled broadly at him. "Yes, I can smell it. You're not a vampire. You're a werewolf."

"Yeah. Tajo Maddox."

Her eyes widened. "You're related to Keeli?"

"Cousins. But we don't run in the same circles."

She wrinkled her brow. "But you're in the same clan, aren't you?"

He shook his head. "Only by birth, a fact I consider nothing more than a technicality. The Rogues are my family now. I'd die for them and no one else."

"Are you a friend or an enemy?"

"To you? Neither, really," he said with a shrug. "Something in between."

"Something in between," she echoed. "What were you doing at Dumont Tower?"

"Just happened to be in the area for a job—"

"Like planting an explosive device in the lobby, perhaps?"

"*No*. We just happened to be in the area for a job."

"Then what? And who's we?"

He opened his mouth to answer, then gave her a quizzical look. "I don't owe you any explanations."

Her eyes opened wide; nobody ever spoke to her like that. "Do you know who I am?"

He crossed his arms over his chest. "Clan Asprey, New York's House Royale. Werewolf royalty. Princess Gianna-fuckin'-Asprey—and I can hardly believe it."

"Technically, it would be 'Your Royal Highness Princess Gianna-fucking-Asprey,'" she said, meaning to challenge him. "But you can call me Gia. So, you know who I am and you don't give a damn, is that it?"

"Not in the personal sense."

"What does that leave?"

"The political sense."

"I see. What are you going to do with me?"

"Use you as leverage to gain power for my team. You're going to give us a much higher profile in this town."

She moistened her lips. "Should I be afraid of you?"

"I'm not going to hurt you."

"No?"

"Not a hair on your head."

"What about the rest of me?"

A look of annoyance crossed his face. "You're not in any danger now. Obviously, I can't vouch for what happens when the primaries catch up with us, but you're not in any danger from *me*."

"I've offended you."

"Well, yeah."

It was almost funny. "You *did* kidnap me," she pointed out. "And I expect you've killed before."

He blinked rapidly, as if trying to figure out how to explain that there was a difference. "Well, I'm not going to hurt you."

"Excellent. Then, I apologize for suggesting it."

He looked at her like she was crazy. "You understand what I'm saying, right? That it wasn't our intention to take you away from them when this all started. It was just that once you were there, and we were there . . . we decided to make the most of it."

"And now things are getting a little out of control?" she suggested.

"No," he snapped. "Things are not out of control. They're very much in control. I have teammates handling the political strategy while I handle . . ."

"Me."

He shifted in his chair. "Exactly. So, you get that I'm not going to hurt you but that you are, by default, kind of my . . ."

"Hostage?" Gia suggested brightly.

Tajo chewed his lower lip. "Right. In the sense that you go where I tell you to until I let you go."

She nodded and clasped her hands in her lap. "I understand."

He seemed to be expecting something more. Something more dramatic, perhaps. Gia just played it cool, more comfortable having him off balance than herself.

He felt compelled to continue. "Look, no worries, okay? All things being equal, I'm pro-werewolf. I may not subscribe to clan politics, but I'm still a dog."

She flinched at the term. "We don't say that where I come from."

"It's just you and me. We can say it about ourselves. We're both werewolves."

They looked at each other and maybe had the same thought, that they were the same yet completely different. She waited as he stared at her for a moment, opened his mouth to say something, closed it again, and finally said, "Huh."

"What?"

"You seem . . . young."

"I'm older than I look."

"Sheltered, then," he said.

"Embarrassingly so."

"And they're just going to marry you off? Just like that?"

"Goodness, don't look at me like that. I've been legal for some time now."

"I get that." He cocked his head. "Maybe it's just that you seem . . . so . . ."

"So?"

"So . . . fresh."

"Fresh?"

"Yeah. I mean, you're . . ." He gestured sort of randomly to her person. "Fresh. Yeah, I think that would be the word. Not a word I find myself using much in this town, either. So, you're going to be married off to one of the Dumont boys. *Man.* Have you ever even been kissed?"

His laugh followed, and it was positively mortifying. Gia felt the heat in her cheeks, and knew exactly where the two spots of color would be burning. The curse of such pale skin.

She sighed crossly. "No. I don't get out much, as they say." He smiled, and Gia couldn't help but smile back, suddenly shy as his glance flickered between her eyes and her mouth.

"You know, I have to say . . . you don't seem very scared."

"I thought you told me not to be," she replied. "Should I be?"

"Not of me. Maybe of whoever set off the explosives, but not of me." Tajo suddenly put down his coffee and, before she could even think about protecting herself, came at her with an enormous knife he'd slid from his boot. His hands pressing all over her legs, he began sawing at a rope tying her ankle to the bedpost. She hadn't noticed it. She hadn't noticed much of anything but him.

His arms were spattered with blood and muck from wrist to elbow. His hands were clean, though, and Gia wondered if he'd washed them just to touch her. She was never, it seemed, allowed to be dirty. Never allowed to be tainted. Certainly not by the likes of him, a dirty commoner.

Of course, Gia was not the model princess her family would have liked her to be, and the thought of a dirty, common werewolf touching her body had certainly excited her in theory more than once. She would be happy to report to her sisters that it had been just as good, if not better, in practice.

Almost as if he guessed what she was thinking, a slow, simmering smile spread over Tajo's face. Unnerved by the unmistakable glint of sexual attraction in his eyes, Gia blurted, "You won't need to tie that again. Savage, really. And not necessary. I'm not going anywhere."

He gestured to her hands. "Well, I'm thinking you'll want to go to the bathroom and get cleaned up."

Gia followed his gaze to her broken fingernails, muddy palms with fingers covered in a dirty reddish brown, and the crimson-soaked hem of her delicate lawn sleeve. Goodness; she looked at herself and saw almost nothing she recognized. "That would be . . . lovely."

With her grimy hands held stiffly in front of her, Gia slid off the bed and went into the bathroom, nearly dying of embarrassment when she saw the rest of herself in the mirror. She turned on the water let the basin fill up, then began working soap into her fingernails to get the blood out.

At least two people she knew of, likely more, had just died protecting her life. She'd missed the whole thing. So typical, that she should never see the bodies, never see them bleed. Never actually witness one of countless sacrifices it seemed people were always making for her and her sisters.

The stains on her summer dress were dirt and somebody else's blood. If she'd been at home, the maids would have stripped this off her within minutes and she'd never see any evidence of it again. She might even begin to wonder if it had all really happened.

Wiping her hands on a limp, grayish hand towel, Gia glanced out the window and did a double take. She saw Crimson City for the first time, really—without filters, without blinders—without protection.

The world was close enough to touch; freedom, experience, adventure . . . real life was only a single pane of glass away. Gia reached out and unhooked the brass lock, pushing the window up. She wanted so badly to go out there, to experience life in all of its good and bad. She'd led her whole life according to an anesthetic palace-sanctioned list of acceptable experiences. It was a world where suitors in white gloves and plastic smiles escorted her to garden parties and recreations and musicals. A world of hushed tones and polite clapping.

Marrying one of the Dumonts wouldn't change a thing in that respect, and what was more, she wasn't sure she could tolerate the idea of one of those stiff, reserved vampire types pretending at emotions that didn't exist between them.

Her eldest sister, Tatiana, had told her all about her fiancé. She said Marius Dumont rarely touched her, and when he did it was with an intensity that suggested he was trying to force something into his heart that wasn't and could never be there. Their youngest sister, Folie, was only seventeen, and would be given to whichever brother was left next year. Gia herself was the only one who had a choice: Ian or Warrick Dumont. As if it really mattered.

Maybe Folie should be given the preference for one of the men, and Gia would simply take whoever was left. No way out of it, really, without letting the family down. Of course, it had occurred to her more than once that maybe they wouldn't accept her if she wasn't pure. But she was as pure as they came. All three Asprey daughters were. It was hard to get dirty if they never let you out to play.

Gia glanced behind her and listened to make sure Tajo Maddox wasn't just beyond the door. He'd have to be really good to be undetectable, but there were so many competing sounds and smells coming from outside the building. Gingerly she stepped forward and leaned out the left side of the window: metal clanging, voices, a smoky current of peppermint and thyme from a grubby little window box hanging off the ledge next door.

Barely able to contain her excitement, Gia swung

around to the right, gasping as she caught a man staring at her intently from a balcony across the way. She immediately pulled back into the bathroom, her heart pounding.

There was nothing and nobody between her and the real world with all its good and bad. And there was bad out there. She wasn't too sheltered to understand that much. She might be two steps away from experiencing her ultimate fantasy, but she couldn't forget that with reality came danger.

Turning and gripping hard at the rust-stained sides of the porcelain sink, Gia gazed in the mirror and thought about the blood on her dress, the dead bodyguards killed by silver meant for her, and the too intense look of a stranger who couldn't have known or cared that she was supposed to be untouchable.

You can't not go out there. But you can't go out there alone.

"I don't hear running water. Everything okay?" Tajo's voice pierced the thin door so easily he could have been standing right next to her. A slow smile spread over Gia's face. *You don't have to go alone.* "I'm quite all right," she called out. "Thank you. Mr. Maddox?"

A pause. "It's Tajo."

"Tajo?"

"Yeah?"

"Have you a change of clothes for me?"

A short laugh. "Nah, sorry. We're not that well stocked yet."

"Oh. So I'll have to wear my soiled things again?"

"Hopefully not for too long."

"I see." She fluffed up her dress, brushed off some of the dirt and grit still clinging to the lace, and walked back out into the living space. "If I may ask, how long will it take for this to all play out?"

"Not long. My pals are working on getting the most from your disappearance and then it's done with and I get you back home."

Gia tried not to look too disappointed. "Well, then, we don't have much time."

"Time for what?" Tajo asked, looking confused.

She glanced at him and suddenly couldn't contain herself. With a laugh she bent down to slip her shoes back on. "To really live, of course. Oh, you should hear them. 'Gianna, sit still. *We* don't do that. Gianna, watch your temper. *We* don't do that. Gianna, stop that! Stop experimenting with the change. *We* don't do that. You're better than that. You're a royal princess, Gianna. You must behave like one.' On and on, they go. You'd think after so many years they'd let us alone."

Tajo's face looked incredulous, as if the idea of repressing one's animal nature was a completely foreign concept.

"You get used to it after a while," she said. "It becomes second nature to stop yourself from turning animal. Eventually, you can't remember what it was all about anyway. For all intents and purposes, it makes us more like humans."

"And that's the goal?"

Gia leaned against the table. "The goal is not to succumb to werewolf stereotypes. The goal is to behave as an upper-class lady should."

"But what about during a full moon? What happens to you then? People must see you in wolf form at some point."

"Nobody sees me," she said simply. "They lock me in."

Tajo shook his head and started to laugh . . . until a casual knock at the front door wiped the smile off his face.

Dain Reston paced the length of the war room at the top of Dumont Tower. Marius wished the man would sit down. The ache in his head felt like an ultraviolet burn.

"Tajo Maddox is not a murderer," Dain was saying. "Okay, well, he wouldn't murder an innocent girl. At least . . . being a mercenary doesn't make him necessarily cruel. I know this guy. Womjep is just not his m.o."

The man finally took his seat next to Fleur, and Marius managed to relax his shoulders a little, settling himself down next to his brothers and across from the couple who served as the leaders of the House of Dumont. Though he himself was usually at the forefront of decision-making for the primary vampires, lately he'd felt neither entirely capable nor even desirous of such a role.

Fleur looked around the table. "I don't think the Rogues are consistent enough yet for us to determine what *any* of their operational patterns might be."

"That's one good thing about being entirely disorganized," Warrick Dumont noted.

Marius tapped his fingers on the table, forcing himself to engage in the conversation. "We cannot tell House Royale yet."

"Marius!" Fleur blurted.

He held up his palm to silence her. "The alliance with the East Coast was about our political survival. And now so is this. We must get control of the situation—at least get our facts straight and locate the princess first. I don't want to have to say we don't even know if she's alive."

"Tajo's not going to hurt her," Dain repeated.

Everyone went silent for a moment. Marius ran his hand over his face and closed his eyes. "This can't happen again."

"It won't happen again," Warrick said. "I'll order a full review of our defense procedures."

"Fine, but what are we doing to get the princess back now that we've lost her?" Fleur asked.

"We're in contact with the Rogues," Marius said. "Cyd and Finn are the go-betweens on their side."

"Good," Dain remarked. "That's something."

"Let's not make assumptions," Ian said gently. "Allegiance is a funny thing."

"Indeed," Marius murmured. "But Warrick and I reviewed the surveillance tapes. I think Tajo was telling the truth. Which means the Rogues didn't mean to take her in the first place and they have no reason to want her dead."

Warrick swore. "Damn humans."

"They're falling apart," Dain said almost apologetically. Perhaps he was ashamed of his previous species. "They're probably desperate for any leverage they can get."

"Killing a werewolf princess from House Royale doesn't seem like something that would endear them to us," Fleur commented.

"I don't think they want to endear themselves. I think they want to thwart our power play with the East Coast werewolves since they can't really make any plays of their own."

"Well, look who has control of the board now," Fleur said with a grimace. "I wonder if their plan included having the tables turned on them by the Rogues. The humans' loss of power might just turn out to be the Rogues' gain. And I don't see what benefit there is in that for us. We need to find a way to end this thing quickly and quietly." She turned to her husband. "Well, let's work your old human contacts and see if we can get some facts."

"My thoughts exactly," Dain agreed. He gave a sad smile.

Marius glanced down at the documents on the table. The pair's easy smiles sometimes grated on his nerves. It was jealousy, pure and simple. He'd tried to manufacture at least a little of the same rapport between himself and Tatiana Asprey, but she gave him nothing to work with. Losing her sister—letting her sister slip out of their hands and into harm's way at that—wasn't going to do much to improve matters.

"We need to find out if there is anything specific Tajo and the Rogues want out of this," he repeated. "And then we need to think seriously about just giving it to them. The Power Summit is a week away, and we cannot afford to go to the podium with an unhappy ending. Not with Keeli's people and the humans and the Rogues and the entire East Coast watching."

"Nicely played, Tajo," Ian Dumont muttered.

"That is, unless Gianna Asprey winds up dead," Warrick said bluntly. "That's something neither he nor we can necessarily control—not if humans still plan on carrying out this assassination. Tajo may have made a hell of a move . . . but he might live to regret it at the end of the game."

Marius nodded. He was a Protector vampire, born and bred to protect house interests at all costs, not intended to stalk and kill. That task was for others. But this princess was someone entrusted to the Dumonts' care, someone his fiancée loved deeply. And sometimes protection required a kill. If it came to that, he was ready.

"He might regret it at that," he said. "Tajo must

know that eventually we will answer his action with one of our own. It's a matter of saving face and saving our alliance. Warrick, please make a note to send a personal message to him on behalf of the House Dumont at an appropriate time."

Warrick sighed. "Fair payback. He'll definitely regret it at that."

Chapter Three

"That's not the right knock. That's not Rogue code. Shit." Tajo pulled Gia away from the door in case whoever was outside tried shooting through. "Someone must have tailed us from the explosion," he whispered. "I'll bet they went back and got backup or they would've tried to nail us by now. Gia, is this everything you came with?"

Whoever it was knocked again.

Gia stared at him, her hands tangled in her hair as she paused in the middle of trying to pin back the mess that had just slumped into her face. Her hands floated to her sides and she looked in confusion at her dress. "Yes. Well, this and my reticule."

"Where is it?"

She pointed to the bag in the corner on the floor. "That's all I had with me."

"Good." The knocking came again, this time punctuated by the ominous thud of someone's shoulder against wood. Tajo grabbed Gia's bag, shoved it at her, grabbed her arm and turned her around. He marched her into the bathroom and locked the door behind them.

Taking a moment to secure his comm earpiece, he dialed up the Rogue's Club, cursing under his breath at the busy signal. He made a note to get another phone line and some extra administrative help for the headquarters, then pulled up the window.

Ducking his head out for a second, he scanned the area. Nobody shot at him. There were no obvious plants. He climbed through the window and tested the strength of the spidery fire escape. Satisfied, he stuck his hands back through and held them out to Gia.

She didn't protest. She didn't struggle. And she didn't do anything to send a heads up to the bad news at the door. If she wanted to be saved from Tajo, she clearly had no idea how to go about it.

No, she just looked at him with those big baby blues and smiled as she put her delicate hand in his, her silly handbag all feathers and tassels hanging from the crook in her elbow. With her spare hand, she pulled up the skirt of her dress, placing a dainty satin shoe on the toilet seat as Tajo stood on the fire escape outside and prepared to help her through.

The long layers of her skirt got tangled in the slats of the radiator. Tajo gave her a look, then leaned back in the window, ripped off a giant swath of fabric and tulle, which he stuffed into the top of her bag, and unceremoniously hoisted her through. She perched on the fire escape along with him, gripping the metal, looking over the side with a mixture of horror and excitement.

"Sorry about your dress," he mumbled.

She dismissed his apology with a regal wave of her fingers. Standing on the rusting metal slats with both hands clutching the railing, she glanced down with her cheeks flushed and her hair floating all around her. Truly a sight to savor.

This isn't the time, Tajo admonished himself. He put his arm around her waist to guide her down the escape, and to his surprise felt her heart beating about a million miles an hour. Scared little rabbit, but too proud to admit it.

No sooner had they made it to the ground when someone whistled and followed it up with a fervent shout.

Tajo cursed under his breath. "We've got to get moving."

"I know." Gia pointed up, and Tajo followed her gaze to a stranger poking his head out the window from which they'd just fled, pointing down at them with a weapon.

Before the shooter could fire off a round, Tajo took Gia's hand in his, ducked her into the shadows, and ran her behind him through the alley leading to a common courtyard for the adjoining buildings. She slipped on some damp moss covering the bricks, her knees hitting the ground, green muck smearing the fabric of her gown. Pulling her to her feet, Tajo shoved her again behind his body. He pressed her back into the wall while he double-checked the ammo in his weapon and redialed the Rogues Club.

"Have you a spare?" Gia asked from behind, her voice muffled and her breath so hot and damp between his shoulder blades that it seemed to burn a hole through his shirt.

"I don't want you to hurt yourself," he said, surveying the tops of the surrounding apartment complexes. "Weapons are trickier than they look. It's not just point and shoot."

He heard a small "Hmph," and then, "What do you think I do with my time? Needlepoint?"

"Well . . . *yeah.*" Tajo hung up on the persistent busy signal and set his comm to automatic redial.

Gia wriggled against his back; then her hands came up and she shoved fruitlessly at him. "Give me your spare and tell me what to shoot."

"*Who* to shoot," he said matter-of-factly, thinking that would shut her up.

"Oh!" She stopped squirming—thankfully, because her hands all over his back were beyond distracting—and brought up a point as if it had just occurred to her. "Are we sure they're trying to kill us?"

"You. They're trying to kill *you.*"

After a pause she said, "Well, then, fair is fair," and she stuck one hand out through the gap between his waist and his arm. Tajo laughed and let her free.

She looked flushed and bedraggled, her hair falling down around her face again, her dress about as damaged as it could get and still be recognizable, but her dignity transcended the circumstance of her appearance, and she simply lifted one imperious eyebrow and princessed him until he melted and turned over his spare. She expertly cocked the trigger and tipped the gun sideways, pointing it at Tajo's gut as she looked the weapon over.

"This is rather large."

"Hey, hey, hey!" He moved the muzzle of the gun away from his body. "How about you point that thing up and about forty degrees to your right?"

"Yes, yes," she said impatiently, training it upward. "I've got it."

Tajo rolled his eyes. "Right. So, okay. If you see a sniper or whatever, just . . . go ahead and shoot 'em.

So far we've got one shooter. I think he climbed to the roof."

He turned back to search above them—

Zing!

Gia squealed in surprise as a bullet ricocheted off the wall between them. Tajo swung his weapon around, but too late—

Bam!

—Gia already had them covered. She pulled her smoking weapon back toward her, and she and Tajo watched a second shooter fall backward off a building forty degrees to her right.

"Damn," Tajo muttered as he grabbed her hand and continued moving down the alley. If memory served correctly, at the end of the alley was an outlet to the other side of the city block. "How's your hand-to-hand combat?"

"They wouldn't train me for that. A few defensive tips, but really just shooting. They hated the idea of any of us fighting. All that physicality, too much like a werewolf."

"You *are* a werewolf," Tajo said. He gestured for her to flatten herself against the wall of the next building as they continued toward the next open space.

"Yes, but God forbid I act like one," she said bitterly.

Tajo glanced over at her in wonder. How could you possibly ignore the werewolf inside? Talk about repression.

"Besides, when you have an endless supply of bodyguards to fight for you, it doesn't come up much."

The notion of him being one of an endless supply of expendable protectors didn't sit quite so well with Tajo. Nor did the fact that the outlet he'd counted on was blocked by new construction. They could either go up and risk being open targets for the snipers already at rooftop, or backtrack about halfway and try to find a gap between the buildings that would dump them back out on the street. What he really needed was a little backup to provide cover.

"Something wrong?" Gia asked.

Zing!

A second bullet followed the first, pinging off the metal plates riveted into the street below them. The trajectory suggested the shooters were all on the rooftops. They'd downed the one, which left at most two shooters from what Tajo could tell.

Zing!

"Okay, that's it!" Tajo shouted, furious now. He pulled Gia behind him once more, shielding her with his body as he led her down the alley coming off the opposite side of the courtyard.

Someone high up on the fire escape of one of the adjoining buildings caught Tajo's eye. There wasn't a clean shot. Looking around for an easy out, he found the next best thing, an enormous Dumpster. They were made of the strongest materials around.

Still blocking her with his body, he moved Gia to the side of the garbage can and swiveled around, pressing the front of his body into hers as he reached over her head and lifted the massive lid. She didn't move, just stared up at him in a kind of wonder, lips parted, cheeks flushed, the ripped bodice of her gown revealing a hint of the pale curves of her breasts.

"Get in," he managed to say in spite of the hoarseness of his voice.

She stared straight into his eyes. "I'm sorry?"

"I'm sorry, too," he said. "Now get in."

Comprehension set in; Gia narrowed her eyes. "I don't think so."

"Are you wearing armor under your dress?" Tajo asked.

"I'm not wearing anything under my dress."

Oh, Lord. "Then get the hell in this garbage can."

She pressed the back of her hand to her nose at the stench that rose from the bin. "There is not even the remotest possibility that I will get in that," she said calmly.

Zing!

Tajo reached down, grabbed Gia by her ankles, and tossed her over the side and into the stench-laden sog. He slammed the lid, the reverberations ringing off the concrete sides of the alley. Gia was displeased, of course, and he had to keep pushing the lid back down with one hand while he tried a different number on his comm.

Zing! Tajo ducked, fired off an entire cartridge of shots at the rooftops, and then all went silent.

Finally, his damn call went through. "Can I get some goddamn backup already, Hayden? What the hell kind of strategy are you working on back there?" Tajo shouted into his comm device, as he paced in front of the garbage can, monitoring the lid.

"It's Jill."

"Well, *hell,* Jill! Where's Hayden? I need some backup. And is anybody at the club working on this thing at all?"

"We're working on this thing," Jill said, clearly trying to keep the annoyance in her voice to a minimum. "And Hayden is already in the field. I'll reroute him to you."

Tajo took a calming breath. "Okay. Good. Tell him I'm in that inner courtyard area behind Safehouse C. Where they dump the garbage. The outlet is blocked and I need cover to get Gia out safely. Oh, and the shooters are at rooftop."

"I got it," Jill said.

"And sorry I yelled. It's just, you know. Dead royalty is never a good thing." Gia took the opportunity to bang her fist against the lid.

"No problem," Jill said. "Be careful and wait for Hayden before doing anything else if you can."

"Got it. Bye." He clicked his comm off and listened carefully while he scanned the area for danger.

Gia banged on the underside of the lid again. "I can't breathe!"

Tajo finally cracked the lid on the Dumpster and found her sitting atop an upturned Budweiser case, her arms wrapped around her torso. She inhaled deeply. "This is absolutely revolting. I hardly think—"

"Can't you smell the silver in the bullets?" Tajo asked pointedly. "It's too dangerous. There are still a couple shooters out there."

"But—"

"Breathe," he said.

Gia looked confused, but took in a gulp of fresh air. Tajo slammed the lid of the garbage can back down.

"Tajo Maddox!"

Tajo let her bang away, trying keep his body hidden from view of the rooftop. Calling in Hayden would not have been his first choice. He didn't usually call in the cavalry; usually, he *was* the cavalry.

Gia stopped banging on the lid and silence reigned over the alley. Tajo surveyed the rooftops and listened for any giveaway sounds. All was still completely silent.

"Please, Tajo!"

Gia's voice actually sounded pained this time. Tajo weighed his options, but it seemed pretty clear the shooters were waiting for them to realize there was no way out.

With a sigh, Tajo opened the lid, pressing his finger to his lips to keep her silent. "Put your hands on my shoulders," he directed.

She stood and did as he said, and he wrapped his arms around her and lifted her out of the bin. He didn't let go when he should have, just sort of lost himself for a moment, indulging in the feel of her body against his, enjoying the quick heartbeat and her breathlessness though he knew it had to be fear as much as anything else.

The staccato sound of rapid-fire weaponry echoed down the alley, followed by the sound of boots pounding on pavement. Gia clung to him as a figure bolted toward them. Hayden. Halfway there, the rogue vampire stopped suddenly in his tracks, flung himself against a wall and unloaded a thunderous round of bullets up to the rooftops. There was a pained cry. Hayden relaxed, turned to where Tajo was still holding Gia tight, and strolled toward them.

"Uh, is this the emergency? Jill made it sound kind of . . . important." The vampire stood with his legs braced wide, a massive gun in either hand, and a wad of gum in his mouth.

Tajo practically shoved Gia off him.

"Aw, don't mind me," Hayden said. "I can wait around if it's a quickie."

"You must do well with the ladies," Gia said dryly.

"I do just fine," he replied, looking her up and down. "Maybe you'd like a taste."

"Hayden," Tajo warned. His blood was beginning to boil, though he knew Hayden had an issue with upper-class women. "This isn't a good time for me to kick your ass."

The vampire didn't take the hint; he cocked his head

and looked at Gia. "You know, you were supposed to die in that explosion. If you hadn't taken your sweet time getting out of that limo, you'd probably be third-world cuisine by now."

Gia's eyes narrowed. "You must have a really dreadful backstory to say such a thing."

"Don't we all?"

"No," she replied softly. "No, we don't."

" 'Scuse me a moment," Tajo interrupted, gently pushing Gia away from the rogue vampire. He turned to Hayden. "No offense, buddy, but you give her the respect she deserves or I'm going to blow your fucking balls off right here." He heard Gia suck in a gasp, but he didn't take his eyes off Hayden for a second, and the three of them stood there in tense silence.

Finally, Hayden's jaw started working his gum again. "Then how about *you* give *me* the respect *I* deserve?" he said.

Tajo blinked, caught a little off balance.

"I heard you on the comm. You don't like the way I'm handling things at the club, maybe we should switch places," Hayden went on. "I'll take the girl, you take the lead back at the club."

"No," Tajo said—so quickly that even Gia looked at him in surprise. *Nobody touches her but me.*

"No *what,* Taj?"

"No, you're handling things fine," he said through gritted teeth. The two men sized each other up for a moment longer; then they both nodded, de-escalation complete.

Tajo looked at Gia. "We just need to a have chat here for a moment," he said, putting his hand on Hayden's shoulder and steering the vampire to the side. Safely away he told the vamp, "An asset drops in our lap, we make the most of it. That's what we agreed and I'm still with you. So, if you want to tell me what our plan is, I swear I'm all ears."

Hayden seemed placated. "We've got Cyd and Finn with the Dumonts trying to get everything in order. The primary fangs are bloody pissed. They know we have her, they want her, and best of all, Cyd thinks they haven't told the family she's still AWOL."

"No shit?"

"Shit. We all know that if House Royale thinks the Dumonts lost their daughter, particularly when she's the humans' assassination target in a city where they don't have the reach to protect her, I don't think that alliance is going to hold. But who knows? 'Cause with Marius already committed and the humans turning out to be fairly useless allies these days . . ." He gestured with his head toward Gia. "She shed any light on things?"

"You ask me, she's barely seen any light her whole life," Tajo said. He immediately regretting the comment.

"Nice. Virgin territory." The vampire nodded, absently rubbing the tattoo on his palm.

Tajo bristled. "I just want to make it clear that I haven't so much as touched a hair on her head."

Hayden's mouth quirked up in a smile, and Tajo rolled his eyes. "Okay, so I touched her hair. Big deal. I was carrying her. So . . . um, how's Bridget?"

"Took some shrapnel, but she'll be fine."

"Good. Now what's the plan for turning the princess back over to her family?"

"Not quite yet."

"Why?"

"Things are just getting juicy."

Tajo forced himself to hold his tongue. The Rogues

didn't have a leader, per se, but he often found himself in that role, calling a lot of the shots. It was incredibly disconcerting to be stuck out in the field while major shifts in strategy took place without him. "Did you confirm it was a setup?"

"Third-party intel says absolutely. The humans were planning an assassination. They get a broken alliance between some really unhappy werewolf parents and some sloppy vampires, and everyone points the finger at us. The new power structure breaks down and the humans have a chance to rise again. But the plan doesn't work if she doesn't get killed. This couldn't be more perfect if we'd done it on purpose," Hayden said. "Can you imagine how bad the Dumonts look to House Royale right now? The longer we have her, the better it gets."

Tajo looked over at Gia, who was trying to remove a bit of rotten lettuce from the sole of her shoe with her gun, her nose wrinkled and her hair falling messily around her face. "We just had a close call. Keeping her to create chaos in the primary houses is one thing. Her dying in our custody would be something else entirely." He couldn't manage the words dispassionately.

"No argument there. We're just looking for the right timing."

Gia waved her gun in the air, the piece of lettuce now stuck to the muzzle. Hayden stared at her without even trying to hide his disbelief. But he didn't know anything; all Tajo could do was watch her and think she was the most adorable thing he'd ever seen.

"What's with the shit-eating grin, Taj?"

"What? Oh, nothing. It's just . . . she's a rare one." When Hayden just stared at him blankly, he let it go. "The thing is, she's a total innocent in all of this, and I think we've got all the play we're going to get. The longer we have her out here in the field, the more dangerous it is, and the more we risk overplaying our hand. I'd like to send her home."

Hayden's jaw clenched. "Umm . . . no. We're not going to send her home just yet. Which head are you thinking with?"

Tajo bristled, his hand moving to his pistol, and the rogue vampire threw up his palms, laughing. "Down, boy. Think about it. This is the play that's going to put us Rogues as a city power on the map—East Coast and West. The primaries won't be able to step all over us anymore, picking us off one by one with no repercussions. Just keep her out of sight and make sure nobody kills her. That shouldn't be so hard."

"Well, maybe if the rest of you did a better job running interference!"

Hayden pulled a key from his pocket and tossed it to Tajo. "Feeling a little out of control, Maddox? Fancy yourself the boss-man? Looks like this gig will give you a whole new perspective on things."

Tajo rolled his eyes. "Whatever." He gestured back to the alley from where they'd come. "Can you cover us?"

"Yeah. I missed the one at the mouth of the alley. He was on the roof."

"Waiting for us to come back out."

"Probably. I got the other guy, but I don't know if there's anybody else. Did you see the space between the green and white buildings on the left side? It's about halfway back down. It'll kick you right out."

"Perfect," Tajo said.

"Well, I'd like to get on with this so I can get back to the office," Hayden said with a grin. "Oh, and the key is for Safehouse B."

Bullets suddenly ricocheted all around them. Gia squealed and raised her gun in the air.

"Gia, get down!" The girl had already dived back behind the Dumpster, though to Tajo's chagrin, she was still wielding his spare, blasting off rounds into the dusk.

All went silent again. Crouched behind a block of concrete, Hayden looked at Tajo. "I guess there are two left," he said with a shrug.

"You sure you want to handle this alone?" Tajo asked, choosing his words carefully.

"Number one, they're humans. Number two, they're shooting silver bullets at a vampire. Give me a break."

"They could switch cartridges."

"Not soon enough," Hayden said, adjusting his armor. "I didn't fly in. They have no idea."

"You sure about the strategy? Is more time going to make or break things?" Tajo yelled over another burst of gunfire. "She's already nearly died twice in as many days."

"Week's not over yet," Hayden called out. He readied both his weapons and raised the guns up as he walked boldly out and down the center of the alley. "But we'll have her home soon enough."

A *pop* and a *zing*, and another hailstorm of bullets rained down. Dodging the field of fire, Hayden leaped into the air and took flight. Tajo heard the vampire laughing as he unleashed a double-barreled response.

Talk about a death wish. But Hayden was as good as his word. As Tajo crouched with Gia in the alley, it wasn't long before the shots became more sporadic, and then completely died out. The alley went silent and Hayden's voice came over the comm device with a terse, "All clear."

Tajo looked back at the garbage bin. Gia crouched there, her tongue sticking slightly out of her mouth as she squinted up at unseen targets. Then she put the gun down and wiped her hands on her skirt, ridiculously unfazed given what had just transpired. He could only do so much to keep her safe; she just didn't get how dangerous this all was. Her people had shielded her from everything, kept the really difficult things in life out of her sight. She understood that those bodyguards had died for her, but at the same time she'd managed to shake their deaths off pretty quickly. As if someone had told her a frightening story but then closed the book so she could pretend it had never really happened.

But what if it was somebody she was close to who died, or at least somebody she knew? Would she understand then how serious things were? Would she understand then how deadly those bullets could be? Maybe she just needed to be taught a lesson. Suppressing a smile, Tajo holstered his weapon and fell back on the pavement.

Gia sagged back against the brickwall, woozy from adrenaline. Her reticule remained hooked on one elbow, her spent weapon lay on the ground next to her. She stared in fascination at her gown and shoes; they looked draped on someone else's body.

Slowly she pulled the reticule onto her lap and fished out a tiny jeweled compact. She touched her dirty, sweaty face with a hand that sported two broken fingernails, and let her fingertips draw a wide line in the filth caked on her face. And in the reflection of the mirror she smiled, almost shyly, though it was for herself alone. She might end in a tower high up in the Dumont complex, but she'd go there having lived a little.

A moaning sound snapped her out of her reverie. "Tajo?" she whispered.

He didn't answer. Gia dropped the compact into the

bottom of her purse. "Tajo?" She crept to the side of the bin on her hands and knees, and stuck her head around the corner. Tajo was writhing on the concrete.

"Oh, goodness." She remembered to look around for dangerous people and then scuttled to his side. He wasn't moving now. Gia put her hand on his cheek and tried to figure out how to feel for a pulse.

"Please don't be *dead,*" she fretted, touching his face. He couldn't be dead. That was ridiculous. But he was so still.

Suddenly, Tajo took an immense breath, exhaling on the words "I'm dying, Gia. I'm dying."

She narrowed her eyes. Something was . . . off. Tajo clutched at his chest, exhaling another gravelly declaration of certain doom.

"I think you're making fun of me," she accused.

"No, no, I'm serious. Only you can save me." He paused, then the corner of his mouth twitched as he tried not to smile. "Kiss me, Gianna. I'll die if you don't kiss me."

Now he was *definitely* making fun of her.

"You have to kiss me, or I swear to God, my blood will be on your hands."

"What blood?" she asked.

"It's under my armor," he hissed dramatically.

He was such a bad actor, Gia almost burst out laughing. But the fact of the matter was that she *did* want to kiss him. Very badly. For a first kiss, it didn't seem right that she should be the one in charge, but there it was. Now or never. *Time to live, Gia.*

"Well? What's it gonna be? Death or the maiden?" he asked, again writhing in mock-agony on the ground.

She tucked a lock of hair back behind her ear and studied Tajo's mouth. The corner quirked up in amusement as he assured her of his imminent death.

"Well?" he rasped.

"Do be quiet."

"What?" He'd just realized she was calling his bluff, and he clearly didn't know what to do next. He hadn't really expected her to try and kiss him.

"Shut up," she said nervously as she climbed atop him.

He was clearly shocked. He watched her watching him, unconsciously wetting his lower lip with his tongue. Gia gazed at the damp streak left behind, her pulse racing so fast that she'd have mobilized an entire cadre of doctors had she been back at the palace. Of course, they also would have pulled her off him.

Tajo went still, lying below her as he was, just staring back at her with a strange kind of agony clouding his face. "Gia," he mouthed more than said. "I was just kidding. Don't do—"

Gia lowered her mouth to his, her heart beating loud in her ears. As she touched their lips together, Tajo's hand came up, perhaps to push her away, perhaps to bring her body closer. The movement was arrested as she slipped out the tip of her tongue.

The warm, damp shock of his mouth seared every nerve in her. And it seemed to do the same to him. Tajo reacted like a man electrified, surprise and lust arching his body up hard against hers. A gasp lodged in her throat as their bodies met. Tajo's hands were suddenly slipping under the fabric of her dress, his fingers feathering across her bare skin. Gia closed her eyes to experience the sensation—and the feel of his erection pressing up between her legs with just a layer of fabric between them.

But in the next moment, Tajo was pushing her off him, pushing her away from him. She stumbled backward and he quickly stood. "That's enough. I don't know what the hell you're thinking." His tone was angry, though the look in his eyes was still hungry.

"I—I . . . I just . . ." She didn't know what to say. The yes men in her life didn't dare look at her like that. *I'm thinking that you're exactly what I want.*

"You don't even *know* me," Tajo said, as if he could read her mind. He still looked stunned, and he cut short as suddenly as it came the laughter that burst from his mouth. He turned away, his shoulders lifting as he inhaled, then he shook out his combat cargos.

Gia wanted to look and see if the evidence of his arousal was gone, but she didn't want to embarrass him, curious though she was.

"Hey!" Tajo turned back to her, his quick strides closing the gap between them. "You're hurt."

"It's nothing," she said, her mind spinning all over again as his body closed in on hers.

"It's not nothing. I know the scent; you're bleeding. Let me see."

She sighed and turned her head to show him her cheek, which was stinging.

Tajo focused completely on the cut; whatever tension remained between their two bodies had to be all on her side. A sliver of disappointment pierced Gia. Her sisters always said she was too drawn in by the fantasy of what could be rather than what was. But as she stared into Tajo's eyes while his fingers trailed like flame across her face, she accepted that there was such a thing as simply knowing. She believed in things of fantasy and fairy tales, like love at first sight and taking chances—and simply knowing that something was meant to be.

Gia's eyes captured Tajo's for a moment, and she knew he might be struggling with the spell between them but that it was present nonetheless. He dropped his hands to his sides and took a step backward.

"It wasn't a bullet," he said softly. "No silver. Just a splinter or something. You'll heal."

Gia just stared at him.

"We shouldn't have opened the door," Tajo said.

"What?"

"Nothing." He tipped his head up toward the sky, staring up with a kind of disbelief that brought a smile to Gia's face. But all he said after that was, "Let's get to the new safe house."

He led her down several blocks to a manhole; they climbed down and he led her farther still along a maze of tunnels. The sound of a nearby subway rumbled the earth around them, and dislodged crumbs of dirt from the walls and ceiling. Tajo was totally unfazed by the falling silt. Gia forced herself not to complain as the stuff settled into her hair and skin and dress.

A solid twenty minutes later underground, Tajo nodded and pointed to a ladder leading up.

"Could I have a moment?" Gia asked, struggling with a bit of dust in her eye.

"Sure. Hey, let me see." He tipped her chin up and, with the inside of his sleeve, wiped the silt away and off her eyelashes. Then he took her filthy hand and wiped that as well.

"Thank you," she said, studying the way her hand fit against his. Pulling back, she managed to clear her eye of dust and then looked up at the ladder. "We're not staying underground?" she asked with more than a little relief.

"Nope. These tunnels belong to Keeli. I'm not looking to have a run-in with any werewolf primaries."

"But they're your clan!"

"I don't know if you can understand this, but I don't give a damn." He cocked his head and looked at her.

"Or maybe you can, considering you seem to enjoy being my hostage more than being a princess."

"But I would never turn against them," Gia said, flustered by his suggestion mostly because it was true.

"But you would disobey them."

"It's not the same."

The werewolf nodded. "If you *knew* you could never go back to them, would you leave in the first place?"

"I—I don't know. Is that what happened with you?

"Yes. And I'm better off with the Rogues than I ever was with my clan."

"What was the problem?"

"The problem was that I'd just as soon shoot Keeli Maddox in the head as shake her hand." He laughed darkly. "I might still get around to it someday."

Gia just stared at him, unable to imagine turning on her own kind like that.

Tajo shrugged. "It was an issue of loyalty and honor. We disagreed. And I wasn't going to sit there and walk the clan walk and talk the clan talk just because those are werewolves of the same flesh. I think that's a point of view the rest of the Rogues can relate to. I would rather be alone."

"But you didn't have to be. The Rogues are your family now."

"Yeah. Not to mention they give me the freedom to do what I want, and backup to help me do it. Show me a clan that will really allow that much latitude."

Gia couldn't, that was for sure.

"You ready?"

She nodded, then headed up the ladder and into yet another complex pattern weaving them in and out of an endless array of passages. Finally, Tajo pushed through another manhole to the surface street and brought her to the next safehouse.

Inside, Gia dumped her reticule on the floor and headed straight for the bathroom to clean up. Tajo was rummaging through her bag when she returned.

"I would have let you if you'd asked," she said, trying to dampen the edge of irritation in her voice. "I don't like it when people presume things."

"Sorry, Princess," he said without looking up. "Just being careful." He tossed her a food bar which she bobbled awkwardly, then gestured with the paper in his hand. "This was supposed to be your itinerary?"

She glanced at the silver-edged folio. "Yes, well, I expect some of the events have been canceled on account of my absence."

He grinned. "I expect so." He tapped on the page with his index finger and stuffed a bite of his own food bar into his mouth. "Your sister Tatiana is already here. What about your other sister?"

"Folie. She was en route. I begged them to let her come, but it took extra time for her to get the quarantine visa. She should have landed by the time you and I met."

"Why did you beg her to come?" Tajo asked. "You actually seem like you could hold the fort on your own." He meant it as a compliment, and that didn't escape her. Gia looked down into her bag to hide her embarrassment.

"I just wanted my sisters with me." She looked up again into his eyes. "I don't even know Ian Dumont."

Tajo held her gaze for a moment, then looked back down and scanned the itinerary. "You and your sisters were supposed to spend the day at the Getty-Dumont Gardens. You think that shindig's still on?"

Gia shrugged. "I don't know. I think it was supposed to be an opportunity to take the air and such, get to know the Dumonts in one of those idyllic country settings."

Tajo raised an eyebrow. "That's what you do? 'Take the air'? Jesus."

"Among other things," she replied. "When I'm not learning to shoot or doing needlepoint."

"Well, I would guess both sides would still be eager to try and prevent the marriage alliance from falling through. I'll have one of the Rogues figure out a safe time to make contact with your sisters."

"All right," Gia said, trying to sound more like someone who hadn't just implied she couldn't get through a weekend without her sisters around.

Tajo stuck the itinerary back in her bag and yelped in pain. "What the hell?"

Gia glanced up from the spot where she'd curled on the couch. She studied the sparkling mass in his hand, then went back to reading the label on her food bar. "It's my tiara."

"These are real?"

She cocked her head and laughed. "Of course. I'm a princess. There was supposed to be a big ceremonial party when I arrived. For Tatiana and Marius."

"And you've just been . . . carrying this in your purse all this time?"

"You aren't suggesting I could have let it out of my sight."

"No." Tajo held the gem-encrusted headband in his hands, then went to the wall mirror and tried it on. "Heavy."

Gia burst out laughing. "It doesn't suit you."

Tajo walked over to her and knelt down. He placed the crown gingerly on her head, and the look on his face was silencing. "But it suits you."

"Not as much as you'd think," she said softly.

"You'd miss the life, if you chose something else."

"I'd miss having a life if I didn't." Gia studied her frayed cuticle. "You know, I could easily have escaped through the window in the bathroom, if I'd wanted to go back."

"I know you could have tried. Why didn't you?"

"I wanted a little time to live. I just wanted a little time to live. And I wanted you to help me do it," she added, raising her chin defiantly, half expecting him to laugh at her.

Tajo didn't laugh. He just looked at her the way he had when she'd first kissed him.

Gia sat on the sofa, tucked her legs up close to her body and rested her chin on her knees. "Tajo, can I ask you something?"

"Uh-huh."

"When we first met, you said we were somewhere between friends and enemies."

"Yeah," he said softly.

"Show me," she said simply, with a smile that had regularly charmed even the most difficult courtiers to their knees.

He flinched. "Show you what?"

"Show me what's between friend and enemy."

Tajo stared at her in disbelief, but she just sat there patiently, looking what she hoped was at least a little seductive. "What are you doing, Gianna?" he asked, his voice hoarse.

"I want to know. Before I do all the things I'm supposed to, I want to know what it's like to do all the things I'm not supposed to. Is that so wrong?"

"What does that have to do with *me*?" he asked. "Look, that thing back there, the kiss—I was just messing around. I wasn't trying to get you into bed or any-thing, okay? It was just a joke, a misunderstanding."

She looked up, feeling her cheeks flame. "It didn't feel like a misunderstanding to me." She glanced pointedly at his cargos.

"Okay, yeah, well, I'm a guy, you know? A . . . guy. That stuff happens. I'm just a guy who picked you up out of the street. That's where I operate. I'm on street level, you know? I'm getting my hands dirty. You're so far out of my league, it's not even funny."

"I'm not laughing."

"Gia, don't. I'm serious."

"You don't understand, do you?"

"I understand. Poor little rich girl looking for some excitement and a bad boy to rebel with. Maybe I'm just not bad enough. And you know, the Dumonts aren't bad guys either. My complaint against them is purely about power. Either Ian or Warrick, they'd treat you well."

"Ian is the one I'm supposed to fall in love with."

Tajo's face clouded over. The unconscious jealousy there gave Gia a thrill.

"You wanna know why Hayden's in such a bad mood all the time?" he asked abruptly. "He fell in love with a primary vampire. Fleur Dumont. She's cousin to the Dumont brothers."

"I *know* who she is," Gia said.

"Hayden was still human when he fell in love with Fleur and begged her to make him vampire."

"And then they broke up," she recalled.

"You could put it that way. I think he'd use a term a little stronger. Fact is, he was ruined. He couldn't adapt. He's never forgiven her for not refusing when she knew what he would be facing. Damn it, Gia. Why the hell would you ask me something like that?" he muttered.

"Why are you getting so angry?" Gia felt a bit insulted. "I don't mean to be self-congratulatory, but most men would jump at such a proposition."

"Why am I getting so angry? *Why* am I getting so angry!" Tajo stalked the room, fury written across his face. "This isn't some game . . . this isn't a movie . . . this isn't *Roman*-fucking-*Holiday*."

"Of course not," she said sweetly, just to make him crazy. "There weren't any automatic weapons in *Roman Holiday*."

Tajo was not amused. He wheeled around. "You may be naive, but you are not a child."

"Then let's have an adult conversation."

"An adult conversation." He laughed helplessly and ran his hand over the stubble on his chin. "Okay. Here it is. I am angry with your proposition because obviously I would like nothing better than to crush you into that bed in the other room and fuck you like the dog I am."

Gia swallowed hard, shocked, but she was definitely aroused by him—by his language, by the pure animalistic sensibility behind it.

He watched his words register. "I get it. I totally get it. You know what your problem is? Your problem is that your family has denied you your basest instincts. Ironic, because you're about as high up in werewolf hierarchy as they come, and your upbringing seems designed to crush the animal right out of you."

Gia reeled back, unnerved by words she couldn't easily deny. When she said she wanted freedom, she didn't simply mean she wanted to run freely outside castle walls, be they brick-and-stone replicas built on the East Coast or the monolithic towers of the Dumont world. When she said she wanted freedom, she also meant she wanted the freedom to act like the animal she was. Like a werewolf.

She gazed up at Tajo's face in wonder that he could know her so well.

"I get it," he said again.

The sudden note in his voice felt like pity. Gia couldn't stand that. That wasn't what she wanted at all.

"I get what's going on here," he continued. "You don't want to go up there and marry a stranger and have polite sex every month to try and have an heir. But you have to. So before you go, you want . . . you want me to . . ."

Gia moistened her lips, stared him in the eye and never let herself look down even though her cheeks were on fire. "I want you to fuck me like the dog you are."

Tajo's fingers curled into a fist. He exhaled slowly and let them unfurl. "If it makes you blush to say it, maybe you should think twice about asking for it."

"I'm not embarrassed by what I said. The exact words might be a bit foreign, but I'm not truly embarrassed . . . because that's what we are, Tajo," she said softly. "We're werewolves. We're dogs. We are who we are. What's so wrong?"

He knelt down in front of her and slid one finger under her chin, tipping her face up to his. Gia closed her eyes, savoring the touch.

"Gia," he said, his voice hushed to a whisper, as if he were tasting her name. "There is nothing about what you want me to do to you that goes against nature. Except for one thing. I'm not going to be the guy who sullies you. I'm not going to be the guy who messes up your life, your dreams, your destiny. Not the way Fleur messed with Hayden."

Gia opened her eyes, confused and annoyed. "This

isn't about Fleur and Hayden. And besides, we are both already werewolf, you and I."

"But you are pure—and you're an important political asset," he said, sweeping his thumb across her lips. "And I'm not jaded enough to ignore that combination." His hand moved to caress her cheek. "It's making me crazy, just crazy, the way you walk around with your head in the clouds like you can get away with whatever you want—like this is some kind of fairy tale we're living in."

"In a way, it is," Gia said, moving to press her lips against his fingertips.

"Well," he said tightly, "every fairy tale has an end." He snatched his hand away and reached past her to grab a throw pillow. "I'll take you to see your sisters tomorrow."

Then he took the pillow to the chair by the window, put his gun and comm device on the windowsill, and settled in for some rest, turning his face away from her.

Gia went into the bedroom, lay on the bed and pretended to fall asleep, her throat oddly tight, and the faint sensation of tears pricking at her eyes.

Chapter Four

Morning came too soon. Tajo rechecked his watch, trying not to think in terms of his minutes remaining with Gia. He unfolded her Crimson City itinerary and double-checked the arrangements, keeping one hand on his comm earpiece. The Rogues were finishing up aerial reconnaissance; the report indicated that the Dumonts were still struggling with defense and had bunched security out today.

The Getty-Dumont Gardens covered an area of the former downtown like an enormous bandage. The bombed-out city blocks had been replanted in a kind of homage to New York's Central Park; Gia's sisters might well find some comfort in the familiar while they awaited word of their missing sibling. Besides, the Dumonts probably didn't know what else to do with them, and keeping them away from headquarters as the crisis unfolded would seem logical enough.

Tajo dialed in and asked for confirmation of security coordinates. Nothing much had changed. With their bodyguards, the two sisters were slowly making their way through an enormous rose garden in the center of the park. Tajo and Gia waited much farther out, inside a dense stretch of trees in the garden forest that went on for blocks.

Gianna impatiently shifted her weight from one foot to the next. "Are you coming with me?" she asked.

"No."

She swung around. "No?"

"Of course not. What the hell do I want to talk to your sisters for?" he asked gruffly. "This isn't a social visit. Just . . . go tell them you're alive and okay."

Gia got a funny look in her eyes. She'd be a fool to come back and they both knew it.

"There they are." Tajo pointed across the field to a splash of color and two dots of white that were moving into view.

Gia sucked in a quick breath. "I didn't realize how much I've been missing them until now."

Stopped several feet behind, the Asprey bodyguards watched their charges while they lit up a couple of smokes. The two sisters kept walking.

"That's right, keep coming," Tajo muttered to himself. The girls looked like dolls. Each had one hand twirling a gaily colored parasol over her head and the other lifting the hem of an impractical white skirt. Their dresses looked like old-fashioned costumes against the sleek, metallic backdrop of Crimson City.

Tajo put his hand on Gia's back and gave her a gentle push. "Okay, this is our moment. The guards are far enough away. Try and get them to come closer without giving us away."

Gia nodded. "Tati," she hissed. "Tatiana!"

The taller girl swiveled around and looked straight into the grove of trees in which they hid, the brilliant blues of her parasol brightening with the sun. She squinted, chewing on her lower lip.

"Tati, it's me." Gia immediately put her finger to her lips to signal not to give her away.

Tatiana Asprey gasped, then called out to her younger sister, who was walking several steps behind. "Folie, come here and look at the buterflies!"

The younger sister hurried over. Tatiana leaned down and whispered in her ear. Folie's head snapped up. She looked straight into the grove.

Tajo could feel the excitement in Gia's body as her sisters looked behind at their guards. "We're going to look at the flowers at the edge of the garden!" Tatiana called out over her shoulder.

One of the men raised his hand in understanding. "Don't go into the trees," he warned.

"We won't!"

Tajo shook his head in disgust; the Dumont security team must be thinner than he thought. He watched the sisters move quickly now, practically skipping toward them. They stood on the edge of the glade, staring into the forest with wide eyes. He saw they'd each been fitted out with white utility belts that would have blended into their dresses were it not for the silver pistols tucked into the holsters.

Gia looked at him, and it struck him right in the heart. Her reluctance to leave him was gone. "Go tell them you're okay," he said grimly.

Gia smiled, then ran out and fell into the arms of her sisters. Tajo began to ease back into the forest as she disappeared from view, trying to ignore the swirl of clean white and girlish voices. The wound in his heart seemed to spread across his chest. Maybe he didn't deserve her, but then, neither did the Dumonts. If he didn't give her back now, he would never be able to stop himself from making her his own.

No, no matter what they could get from holding on

to her, he had to give her up, Hayden and the rest of the Rogues be damned. She'd never come to harm while he could help it.

He glanced back. Gia had one arm around each sister now. He could hear her laughing. The guards would be all over her in a moment. Tajo held on to the scent of her skin for a moment longer; then he stepped back into the trees and forced himself to walk away.

The princesses Tatiana and Folie Asprey pulled away from her embrace and stared at Gia as if she were a ghost. They were standing in the shadows of the two woods.

"Everything okay?"

Gia froze at the guard's question, her finger once more pressing against her lips.

Tatiana and Folie frowned in confusion, but they didn't give her away. "We're fine, thank you! Just collecting leaves," Tati called. She slipped the gauzy shawl from her shoulders and wrapped it around Gia's. "Why are you hiding? They're just trying to protect us. You must be in shock. We must get her home, Folie," she said to her sister.

Gia lunged for the comm device in Folie's hand. "Don't!" she cried.

Folie looked frightened. Gia instantly relaxed her fingers clutching her sister's wrist. "It's just . . . don't," she repeated.

"Have you gone Patty Hearst on us?" Folie asked.

Gia laughed. "It's not what you're probably thinking."

Folie gazed at Gia's dress and shoes, running her fingers over the gray stains and bald spots on her reticule. "It's *filthy* out there," she remarked.

"I know," Gia said. They locked gazes for a moment.

"I smell a male on you," Tatiana said softly. "Are you all right?"

Gia couldn't help but blush. "I'm just fine."

"Really?" Tatiana looked her sister up and down. "Because you look unspeakably dreadful." She pulled Gia's hand up and studied the damage. "Always the rebel, Gia. You're supposed to be saving yourself for an alliance through marriage. I'm almost afraid to ask what you've done."

"I haven't done anything . . . yet," Gia said, trying not to show her annoyance at the implication. As if anything she'd done was wrong! How was yearning for experience wrong?

"Are you still saving yourself for that cold fish, Marius Dumont, Tati?" she countered.

Her sister gave her an emotionless smile, an empty shell of a thing. "He's not a cold fish, just in love with someone else."

"And that doesn't bother you?"

"Of course it bothers me. But that's the way it is."

"That's the way it is, is it?" Gia reached down and plucked a tiny orange poppy from a patch of green at her feet and twirled its floppy leaves in her hand. "If I have to sacrifice the rest of my life for the royal cause, I at least want to know, just once, what I'd be missing."

Folie looked flushed and nervous. Tatiana looked numb, as if expectation and duty had worn her down.

"Everything okay?" the guard called again.

Gia flinched at the sound of his voice. The sisters all looked at each other.

"We're fine, thank you!" Tatiana called. She frowned. "Everyone thinks you've been kidnapped. Or did you just run away?"

"I was kidnapped. And now I'm running away."

"You know you must come back, don't you?" Tatiana pushed. Her voice was gentle, though her eyes were not. "I know you, Gianna. You must come back."

She knew it was true, but the bond she'd developed with Tajo Maddox was unlike anything she could hope for in the stuffy confines of Dumont Tower. A short time with Tajo . . . a short, brilliant time with Tajo was all she was asking for.

"Oh dear," Folie said. "What are you thinking?"

Gia felt something ignite in her very soul, and she answered, "Well, I'm not coming back yet."

The three of them stood in silence, each looking at the others and understanding the significance of what was happening. One of them was stepping out of the box.

Folie took Gia's hand and gave it a squeeze. "Well, then," she said, "what shall we tell Mum and Dad?"

"I'm not sure we have to tell them anything," Tatiana said, the anger in her voice just barely detectable. "They've already made plans to send out the cavalry, if you will."

Gia sucked in a quick breath. "Have they?"

Tatiana rolled her eyes. "Of course. They're under the impression you've been kidnapped, and are a bit upset," she added. "We all were. Just thinking of you being manhandled by some dirty, rogue werewolf."

Gia smiled at the description. Somehow, it had gone from a disparaging remark to a compliment since she'd met Tajo.

"For what it's worth, the quarantine visas are a problem again, so you have a little time," Tatiana admitted. "But don't take this much further. Try to imagine how much we've all worried about you already."

Gia nodded. "I know. I'm sorry. I will come back. I swear it. But swear you won't ruin this for me, either."

Folie and Tatiana looked at each other. "Gia always gets her way," Folie said.

Tatiana managed a snort of laughter. "Gia *always* gets her way," she repeated. She pulled her sister into a hug along with Folie and took back her shawl. Their good-byes needed no words; the three parted with a kiss and Tatiana and Folie began to make their way back to the rose garden.

Folie looked back once before stepping out into plain view. "Oh, and, Gia?"

"Yes?"

"We expect details." She winked, linked arms with Tatiana, and they both turned away.

Gia slipped back into the wood, farther from sight. She watched until her sisters disappeared from view, safe in the care of the guards, and then she turned to run into the darkest shadows of the trees.

"Tajo, I'm done," she whispered, taking a delicate step forward. The leaves were thick and spongy under her feet. A chill breeze crossed her bare skin, fluttering what was left of the skirt of her dress.

"Tajo?"

Something wasn't right. She couldn't find his scent. She lifted her face to the sky and tried to concentrate, but the city smells bombarded her even in the park. His presence wasn't strong enough, just remnants, really. He'd left her. He'd left her here alone.

She whirled around, hurrying back to the tree line. "Tatiana! Folie!" But they were far, far away driving off in a trolley, taking the guards with them, nothing but white dots and colored parasols in the distance.

Gia stumbled backward, too conscious of that helplessness which wasn't in her nature, but was in her breeding. And it was as much that she wanted to see him again as it was her fear to be without a guard when she whispered into the dark, "Please come back."

A fresh scent did come her way, then, but it wasn't werewolf. She knew the human was present before she ever saw him. Before his arm swiveled around her neck, the blade in his hand curling under her chin.

Her assailant tugged her backward, cutting off her air in the first instant that she would have screamed; she heard a funny little *ting* as the blade knocked against her earring. After a struggle, Gia screamed Tajo's name, but the silence that answered her was of no help.

The human shifted his grip, digging the tip of his blade into her flesh, and Gia felt herself turn cold as her body and mind shifted to automatic. With all the strength she could muster, Gia drove her elbow into her captor's gut. He gasped and staggered back.

She twisted around to face him as his surprise gave her some slack. A finger to his eye, and he doubled over, his hands up to his face. Gia screamed Tajo's name again, even as she lifted her knee to her assailant's chin. The crack of bone sent his arms flying wide. He bellowed in pain. Gia's screams died out to a hoarse gasp as she pushed the man backward, then slammed her shoe as hard as she could into his groin.

She backed away, but she could smell more humans coming closer—probably this one's backup. Dashing through the trees, she ran as fast as she possibly could.

No further sound came from Gia's raw throat. Silent tears streamed down her face as someone grabbed the back of her dress, lifting her off her feet. She crashed headlong into the dirt, struggling and fighting with every bit of strength she possessed.

A hand barreled toward her face. Gia rolled to avoid the blow. Not fast enough. The human latched on to the back of her neck, pulling her to her feet, choking her with the collar of her own dress. Once more she faced a knife, the silver blade hovering a fraction of an inch from her neck.

Trying not to lose her balance and fall onto the weapon, Gia pulled at her assailant's arm, but her sweaty fingers slipped on his meaty hands. She'd reached the limits of her training. Panic set in. *Tajo, please come back. I know you can tell I need you.*

And then, as if she'd summoned her white knight and he'd heeded her call, Gia knew that she wasn't alone anymore. Tajo filled her senses before she ever heard the cock of a trigger confirming it.

Without daring to move anything else, Gia slowly shifted her gaze upward. Tajo Maddox held a massive gun to her human captor's temple, the fury contained in his taut body and the look of death in his eyes saying everything that could be said between them. All Gia could produce was a kind of squeak that might have seemed comical in other circumstances.

"If you kill her, you won't be able to move fast enough to avoid dying yourself. Let her go."

"I think you'll kill me either way," the human said, his voice as frayed as Gia's nerves. He twisted the blade in his hand.

As the edge of the knife scraped her skin. Gia whimpered, her feet slipping on the damp leaves beneath her. The blade pushed against her throat. She blinked back tears blurring Tajo's face. He looked into her eyes; behind the controlled rage was something soft, something just for her. A sob stuck in her throat.

Tajo's fingers wrapped tighter around the butt of his weapon. His gaze shifted back to her assailant. "If you let her go, I give you my word that I won't shoot you when you run."

"I have your word on that, Maddox?"

"Yeah. And we both know it's good. Better than yours."

The human managed a tight laugh, then suddenly pushed Gia away. She fell to the ground and scrambled behind a tree.

Tajo and the human reached out for each other, backed off, their bodies primed for a fight. Tajo wasn't fighting his werewolf bloodlust as it bloomed from within him—or wasn't fighting it enough. For the first time, Gia watched his animal nature consume him.

Lips curling, Tajo snarled, low, vicious. His eyes glazed as he raised his weapon.

The human stepped back. Tajo snapped his jaw, snarling again. "Leave while you can," he warned.

Gia clutched at the tree trunk, chunks of bark raining down on her feet. She knew without a doubt that Tajo would have no qualms about killing for her.

The tense silence stretched out until the human finally flinched, backing down. He turned on his heels and ran—but not before sending a shrill whistle into the air.

Tajo turned and stared into Gia's eyes. His hands came up from his sides, his fingers curved and taut, his spine arching as he put his head back and howled. Gia gasped, aroused by the sound—by the sound of the possession Tajo felt for her in his very core. She swooned, falling to her knees while still clutching the tree, unable to quite handle the depth of emotions flooding through her body.

The ground beneath her trembled, and she knew this was not over; the human had summoned his backup team. There were three of them. Three humans against one werewolf. But an alpha wolf in a frenzy to protect his mate.

Tajo's muscles pulsed as he balanced on the edge of his animal power. Gia watched as that pulse became a ripple and his body began to morph. *The change.* She'd never seen it. And to see it *now*, because she needed him . . . extraordinary. His lean, sleek body curved into animal form, a dusting of fur just barely visible. His hands curled in, his fingers gracefully morphing to razor-sharp claws. He snarled, the full intensity of his rage in that sound. And though the points of his teeth sparkled like knives, still the humans came at him.

Wielding his fists like bludgeons, Tajo answered their attack. He rained blow after blow upon them, raking the human flesh with his claws in a fury that seemed to consume his entire being.

A flash of metal arched through air and slashed through Tajo's jacket. He answered with his claws, and human blood spattered across the leaves.

The metallic tang in the air hit her hard. The sight of Tajo nearly all wolf now hit her harder. She reacted as if she were his mate, her body lusting to join his in the change. Struggling against the rules of propriety she'd lived with for so long, Gia tipped her head back with a gasp and allowed the animalistic pleasure she recognized in Tajo to echo through her own body. Then she joined him in battle.

Tajo and Gia fought side by side against the humans. She wasn't graceful, but it could not have mattered less; for the first time in her life, she was able to indulge the glorious frenzy of her werewolf form. Claws sharp as swords, teeth like daggers, the two fended off the greater numbers with a bloodthirsty passion. It all happened so fast. Gia stumbled back from the fight, watching Tajo pressing his boot down on one of the bodies, arms outstretched, baying at the sky.

Unrepressed. Unchained. This was pure. This was freedom.

Tajo lowered his chin, meeting her gaze. As they stared at each other, she watched him slowly return to human form. He had practice controlling this; she had not. He could sense the beast within her still struggling for an outlet.

Self-conscious about the lust she knew was so obvious, Gia turned in confusion and ran.

Tajo ran faster, quickly closing on her. He grabbed her hand and spun her around, pulling her to the ground with him. His tongue swept into her mouth, rough and frenzied. This was nothing like the sweet sampling they'd shared the first time they'd kissed.

Rays of sunlight slipped through the shaggy branches of the trees, throwing a golden glow over parts of the glade. Tajo's body entwined with hers on the fallen leaves, his mouth greedy on her body. He touched her as if had a right, as if he owned her, his hands and lips bent on marking every inch of her skin as his personal territory. Gia closed her eyes, giving in to the passion without restraint.

His tongue flicked at her nipple and his mouth closed around the flesh of her breast. Pulling roughly at her shredded bodice, he tore it asunder with violent abandon. Gasping and bucking with want, Gia arched her back to bring her body even closer to his.

Tajo reared up over her and growled, a thick sound of impatient desire. Throwing her arms back above her head, Gia surrendered completely to his care, savoring the sensations burning through her body as he pressed himself between her legs. She'd never had a man like this, never understood what it was to feel such arousal and the grip of desire.

Tajo's hands pushed under her skirt, his fingers trailing fiery streaks across the delicate flesh of her thighs to a place that had never been explored by another. But there was nothing delicate about him, and Gia wanted it that way. She wanted everything.

She moved her hand down between his legs. He grabbed her wrist, holding her still. Panting, his body taut, skin sleek with sweat, Tajo stared into her eyes and whispered her name.

If he was asking for mercy, she wasn't about to give it to him. Pulling away, she grabbed the front of his cargos, rending the fabric as greedily as he'd done with her dress. His sex sprang free.

Tajo reared up over her, his cock erect and glistening. Instinctively Gia turned her body to face the ground. Raw, natural scent from the grass and dirt and flowers filled her senses, mingling with the musk of their bodies. Tajo's hands pushed her skirt up and his cock pressed hard against the curve of her behind.

She snarled at him over her shoulder—to spur him on. Tajo ignited like flame. There was were no tentative movements, no hesitation, no awkwardness. He was primed; he was an animal. And so was she.

His arm reached around underneath their bodies to finger the damp nexus between her legs. The pleasure of his touch undid her. She wanted more. Needed it. Unschooled, unable to control herself, she jerked back very suddenly, taking Tajo's cock inside her.

"Gia!" he cried out, his voice edged with equal parts surprise and ecstasy. Sharp, sweet pain seared through her body. Tajo didn't move. Panting with exertion, he held his entire frame still. His labored breath warmed her temple where his mouth pressed hard.

Gia gloried in the delicious pressure of his flesh covering hers, the pain floated away, and all she wanted was to be filled by him over and over again. Tajo read her well. Taking control, he moved over her, slowly pumping himself in and out. Gia shivered as his fingers reached for her again, the tips sweeping across her very core. Desire coiled up from his touch throughout her body, and he put one hand on her cheek, taking her mouth in a brutal kiss as he drove himself in to the hilt.

Gia cried out as a strange and wonderful sensation began to build. Cupping the side of her face with his palm, Tajo trapped her gaze in his and eased their rhythm to a slow, intoxicating pulse.

Sheer bliss wound itself around her body, teasing, nearly blinding her. And in the moment when she whispered Tajo's name, climax came like a gorgeous surprise. Bucking with abandon, her breasts cupped in his hands, Tajo pulled her roughly back against him and found his own release.

Holding her for just a moment longer, he finally lowered her gently to the ground and lay down beside her. For a second, Gia wondered if he felt regret, but just then his fingers touched her wrist. He didn't look over at her; he just lay there on his back next to her, staring up at the trees. Then he took Gia's hand in his and held it tight as they rested side by side in the grove.

Chapter Five

Gia seemed so at home here at the Rogues Club, Tajo was almost able to forget she was royalty. She held Bridget's wardrobe contribution—an impossibly short tennis outfit, of all things—up to her body and wrinkled her nose. "A bit odd, don't you think?"

"It's the best we could do on short notice," he said. "But you'd look like a princess in anything you wore." *You look beautiful. And I want you more than you could ever know.*

She just smiled, so Tajo cleared his throat and decided to get the difficult part over with. "So. I was wondering if you wanted to have me set something up so you could have some time with your sisters while we're dealing with the Power Summit. Security will be focused on the dais and it might be a better opportunity than most."

Gia's eyes lit up. "I'd love it. I've been missing them terribly." She was looking at him like he'd just given her a present, and he hated himself for lying.

"They're probably going to go into shock when they see me in this," she added with a laugh, heading into the bathroom with the tennis outfit which she carefully arranged over the towel rack.

Tajo followed her and leaned on the doorframe. "It's dangerous, though. I just want to make that clear."

Gia smiled and let her shredded dress fall to the ground. "It's all dangerous," she said, stepping free of the pool of fabric and tossing it in the trash can.

Unashamed of her nakedness—reveling, it seemed, in the newfound freedom of her body—she let Tajo look his fill, then served up an impish smile and disappeared into the shower. The pale shadow of her body flashed through the smoked glass, and he had to remind himself to breathe as he relived the moment in the glade over again.

Running a bit of change in his pocket between his fingers, he watched the hazy curves of her body undulate as she cleaned off the evidence of their time together. It bothered him that a little soap and water could erase what seemed like a brand burned on their skin. Tajo stared at the discarded dress spilling out of the trash onto the floor. That she could step out of that shower clean and new, and look at him like he'd never been inside her, like he'd never been the first like they'd never created a bond so deep that even after she was gone and belonged to someone else, they'd always secretly know they belonged to one another. . . . On some level, she would always belong to him, and whether she understood it or not today, on some level, he would always belong to her.

The change fell to the bottom of his pocket as he froze, realizing for the first time what it was about the two of them that made their relationship special. This wasn't just a case of love—or even lust—at first sight. This wasn't about fairy tales, not really. It was one simple thing: Gianna Asprey was his mate. His *mate*. The concept was so . . . clannish. He'd shunned every last trapping of werewolf tradition long ago, but there was no denying what he felt for Gia. In his mind and in his heart she was his mate, and he'd go back to the clan system if he ever thought he'd have half a chance at being with her.

Unfortunately, the Dumonts had laid their cards down first, and Gia was part of a political alliance that would leave Tajo and his heart in the dust.

"You're a goddamn romantic, after all, Tajo," he muttered bitterly to himself. "A goddamn romantic."

Lingering for a moment longer to listen to Gia humming in the shower, he knew that if she turned around and noticed he was still there, he'd be in that shower along with her in under a second. But she didn't turn around. Lost in her thoughts, she simply continued humming and running the sponge along one arm.

Tajo got himself out of the bathroom. Closing the door, he leaned against the wall with a tortured moan. It took him a moment to clear his head before he felt capable of meeting the others with anything resembling a clear head.

Candlelight flickered in the catacombs of the Rogues Club. Once nothing more than the most basic underground development, the entire property was now tricked out, thanks to the growing notoriety of the club's members. Far from the somber chic of Dumont Tower up on high, the Rogues preferred a more historical décor. And candles were always good.

Blue flame flickered along the carefully sculpted tunnels leading to the war room, the assembly rooms, and the living suites. Passing under the war room archway en route to his meeting, Tajo stopped short and stared. The bronze plaque that had once adorned Dumont Tower—the one that had cut into Bridget's leg—was now hammered atop the assembly archway.

COME NOT HERE IF YOU DO NOT BELONG

"Kinda like stealing the team mascot," Hayden said from behind him.

Tajo nodded. "Kinda like passing the baton." Power was shifting in favor of the Rogues; this was certainly a metaphorical slap in the face of the Dumonts.

"The Gia thing was brilliant. Put us right on the map alongside the primaries," Hayden said, passing Tajo and opening the door to the meeting.

The Gia thing. It was nothing more than a strategy to the rest of them.

Jill and Bridget looked up as the two men walked through the door. Jill's eyes sparkled with excitement. "We got it," she said. She held up a sheet of paper and read: "The representatives of Dumont and Maddox hereby offer the Rogues a seat at the cross-clan Power Summit. An audience with Her Royal Highness Gianna Asprey is requested."

Hayden looked over Jill's shoulder and took a look for himself. "Nice euphemism for 'Come join us against the humans.'"

Bridget and Jill—the only pure humans in the room—looked at each other and frowned.

"*Primary* humans," Hayden muttered to placate them. "I meant the humans in power. The *bad* ones."

"Nice euphemism for 'Give her back,'" Tajo put in, trying not to let his heartbreak show. "So, that's the plan, then—they let us address Crimson City, we make it clear we're not to be pushed around anymore? We present Gia as proof of our strength then give her back?"

Hayden shrugged. "I'm sure the fact that she's been so well . . . 'entertained' in captivity will work in our favor."

Jill punched Hayden hard in the shoulder, but Tajo didn't rise to the bait. He didn't care what Hayden thought about what had happened between himself and Gia. Hayden couldn't know.

"Are you okay, Taj?" Jill asked.

"Ah . . . um, yeah."

She stubbed the toe of her boot into the ground. "I just want you to know that I'm sorry about how things are ending for you two. I saw the way you looked at her when you came in—"

"I'm fine."

But she wouldn't let it go. "I know what that's like. You taste enough to shatter your heart, but too little to satisfy."

"It's *fine*. Everything's fine."

Hayden laughed. "Uh-huh. Keep saying that, man. But you know what they say: 'The heart wants what the heart wants.' Of course, maybe a little later, the heart wants her dead," he added carelessly. He got up and headed for the door. "It's the damnedest thing, love is."

I know, Tajo thought. *The damnedest thing. But what my heart wants now is the one thing it will want forever. And she has to be with someone else.*

The Rogues approached the power summit the way they would have approached going out for the night together: pointedly casual and ready for a little fun at someone else's expense. They took two transports, Jill driving Hayden, Bridget driving the others. Tajo stared out the window as they drove; he wouldn't look at Gia.

He just held her hand and kept staring out the side window.

"Tajo," she whispered. "Is everything all right?"

He turned and lifted her hand to his lips. "It's fine. Yeah. Everything's . . . as it should be."

"You're not going to try and give me back again, are you?" she teased. "You know that won't work."

He laughed and it sounded all right. Gia leaned back, nestling into the crook of his arm, and Tajo held her tight.

At walking distance from the meeting site, Bridget parked her transport behind Jill's and the group assembled on the landing. A stiff breeze whisked across the plateau where LAX still lay in shambles. The airstrip was closed to everything except copters and other small aircraft. Gia had arrived in Crimson City this way; she didn't intend to leave.

"Why here?" she asked Tajo as they approached the field, buzzing now with all manner of assistants, representatives, and guards.

"The human power used to hold this." He pointed out farther, to where a gleaming white complex rose from the flat terrain. "They still hold that, and they can see us from there, which is sort of the point."

"The point is to let the humans know that it's three against one?"

Tajo grinned. "Yeah. A few weeks ago, they'd probably only consider it two against one. But things are different now. We've got a voice. I'm just sorry you had to be a target to make that happen."

"I'm not sorry," Gia said. "After all, I'm still here . . . and I'm with you."

Tajo's smile faltered a little. Stung, Gia grabbed his arm. "Is there something you want to tell me?"

"Nope. Everything's good. Are you ready?"

"What do you want me to do? Are my sisters here already?"

He didn't say anything for a moment, just looked into her eyes as if he was trying to memorize their color. And Gia suddenly knew he meant to give her back.

"I'm going to go out and talk to some of the VIPs, and then I'm going to come get you and—"

Gia took a step back. "Oh, Tajo, you're lying."

He swallowed hard. "Look up at those posts. Those are cameras mounted there. They already see you, and I think we have about thirty more seconds before they ID you, in spite of that outfit you're wearing."

She couldn't breathe. "I thought you believed in us. I thought you believed in our fairy tale."

He had tears in his eyes. To his credit, the coward had tears in his eyes. "You're a princess, and I'm just a mercenary rogue. You have loyalty to your clan and a duty to perform. So, go. It's the right thing to do. Just go. And don't run back this time," he said. Then he spun around and headed toward the heart of the massing crowd.

Gia stood in shock as she watched him walk away. No touch, no kiss . . . nothing to say he'd ever felt anything for her at all. She stood there in the open with her tiara in a tennis bag as her identity was processed by the security monitors. And that was all it took; she could feel the intensity build around her.

Up ahead, Hayden and Bridget joined Tajo in the inner circle on a podium, preparing to say through the microphone something political and wholly irrelevant to Gia.

Jill came up beside her and looped her arm around Gia's shoulder. The two of them watched as a swarm of security began to form and head toward them.

"They've figured it out, haven't they? My God," Jill

muttered. "I don't think I quite realized what this would be like."

In a kind of daze, Gia nodded. "It's rather something, isn't it? Maybe I should make some official statement." She added bitterly, "Do you think I should wear my tiara? It would look smashing with this outfit."

"Gia, don't."

Gia's heart pounded faster and faster as the mob of security men moved cautiously toward her across the field. She clutched at Jill's hand. "They must wonder if I'm rigged," she said nervously. "Where's Tajo? I can't see him."

"He's with the team," Jill said. "Um, I think I might need to get out of here." She took a step back, clearly unnerved by the ferocity of the men bearing down on them.

Her hand slipped away, and Gia sighed and braced herself. The mass of men intent on saving her life caught up with her.

In the moment when they circled around her, it was all over; any anger or bitterness vanished, and Gia knew that she had no choice but to go. Still, she wanted at least to say good-bye.

But the security detail had official processes and procedures on their minds. They were suddenly all over her, rushing her down the field, jostling and bumping her, nearly tearing her apart it seemed. She wanted to ask them how she could be so important to them, how they could be willing to give their lives for her when she didn't even know their names.

A copter zoomed erratically into the airspace, obviously away from the official landing strip. Documents whirled into the air, tables and chairs collapsed and tumbled as the VIPs took cover as best they could.

The dust and the chaos intensified, and all Gia

wanted to do was scream for everybody around her to stop. This was so damn silly. All of this for a silly princess who didn't want to be saved in the first place.

Craning her neck to see over the chaos, she tried again for a glimpse of Tajo. And it was pure joy she felt as she saw that he'd given up on the pretense that he didn't care enough to say good-bye, that he was looking for her as well. He'd second-guessed himself and was straining against the pull of his friends and peers.

Taking advantage of the element of surprise, Gia kicked and punched herself free from the swarm. Catching Tajo's gaze across the field, she ran straight for him. And just like in a fairy tale, he caught her up in his arms, spun her around and let her down gently only to press his lips against hers.

"Good-bye, Tajo," she whispered.

"Good-bye, Gia."

He stepped back, and this time Gia let him go. A shot rang out, the copter's engine revved. Everyone was shouting. The power summit was falling apart, and Gia didn't care. Walking backward toward her detail, she kept Tajo in her sights, kissing her fingertips and blowing it to him, laughing and crying all at once as he caught it in the air and brought it to his heart.

She should have cared about the shot. Tajo's hand never left his heart. His knees buckled beneath him and he fell heavily to the ground.

Gia froze, unable to believe what she was seeing. One of the Dumonts stood calmly in the center of the chaos holding a pistol, the muzzle still smoking. Gia pushed toward him through the confusion. "A personal message from the House of Dumont," the vampire said, then added to her, "I'm sorry, Your Royal Highness."

Gia ran to Tajo and knelt down beside him. She pressed her hand over his. "It's the old joke, isn't it, Taj? The old joke?"

"Kiss me, Gianna," Tajo said hoarsely. "I'll die if you don't kiss me."

Gia tried to laugh, but the look in his eyes . . . and he wasn't laughing. "Tajo?"

He made a funny little sound then, grunting in pain and the little quirk in his lip wasn't there.

"Tajo, don't tease me like this. It's not funny." Her eyes blurred with tears.

The swarm was coming back; she recognized the sound of pounding feet, the smell of them, the sweat and the adrenaline. Arms reached down, pulling at her—pulling her away from Tajo. "No! Let me go . . . Tajo!"

"Your Royal Highness, let us help you."

"Gia!" a familiar voice screamed.

"Get away from me!" She lashed out blindly, catching one of the bodyguards in the face, her nails drawing lines in his skin. "Leave us alone!"

"Gia!" Her sisters. Gia turned to find Tatiana flanked by two vampire bodyguards, her face nearly white as she surveyed the scene.

"Tell them to give me some time, Tati. I just need some time." She didn't wait for the answer, turned her focus back to Tajo laboring on the ground to breathe.

The quirk in his mouth appeared, though it cost him plenty to keep up the pretense of humor. She could see that plain as the pain written across his face. "You have to kiss me, Princess. My blood . . ."

"What blood?" she echoed, tears streaming down her face.

"It's under my armor," he murmured.

This time, she knew it was true.

She moved to unzip his armored jacket, but his hand wrapped around her wrist. "Don't touch the blood, Gia. It may be tainted. Just kiss me."

Gia gently took his mouth with hers, the sweet, sweet taste of him mingling with her tears. He sighed, and she pressed her lips against his ear. "I love you, Tajo. I don't care if it sounds crazy. I love you."

Tajo's chest heaved erratically. "Not that crazy," he managed to get out. "But every fairy tale has an end, Princess."

He coughed, and Gia pressed her head down on his chest and sobbed hysterically, begging him not to go. "It's not a fairy tale. It's real. We're real, and you know it."

Tajo smiled and his fingers shifted to catch a bit of her hair. "We are a *fairy tale,*" he insisted, in a voice growing fainter by the second. "But it's the best one I ever read."

His hand slipped roughly to the pavement, fine strands of her hair caught between his fingers.

The commotion around her roared into full volume as what seemed to be a million hands tried to pull her away from Tajo's body. Gia fought as hard as she could, but it wasn't enough against the bodyguard swarm. Through her tears she saw Hayden and Jill pulling Tajo's body by his legs, his arms splayed behind him on the ground as they dragged him away.

Chapter Six

For the last half hour, the only noise in the main dining room at Fleur Dumont's suite was that of silver clinking against porcelain. Gia thought it entirely possible that she would go mad if she had to sit at the table much longer.

Her sisters, Tatiana and Folie, appeared to be holding on to their emotions by only the most delicate of threads. It wasn't just the sense of being in the wrong lair; three werewolf princesses trapped in a vampire world. And it wasn't that the Dumonts were unkind. In fact, Ian Dumont was more than attentive to Gia as Warrick was to Folie across the table. Marius seemed to be trying harder with Tatiana than she gave him credit for, touching her hand with his even when she snatched her own away. It was just a general feeling of unease.

Fleur and Dain Reston, the only married couple at the table, sat at the heads exchanging pained glances.

Another course came, the white-gloved servers moving in between the diners to clear and serve and create perfection. Gia already knew perfection, and it wasn't to be found high up in Dumont Tower. It had been a mistake to assume that she could taste happiness only once and that the feeling would last long enough for a lifetime.

No one had mentioned Tajo Maddox's name since she'd been brought in. The only thing she cared about was to know what had become of him; and yet no one had the courage to even say his name. Thank god it wasn't Warrick she was supposed to marry. She could scarcely look at him no matter how many times Folie and Tatiana tried to explain how his action had been strategically justified. Strategically justified? He'd shot Tajo in cold blood!

The teeth of Gia's tiara dug into her skull, the heavy crown weighing her down, pinning her to her chair. She raised her hand and pressed at the sore spots. Across from her, Folie just stared at her plate, scraping the tines of her fork through what had once been a carefully piped mound of butter-laced potatoes, shooting glances up every few moments.

"Your family is arranging the appropriate visas to cross quarantine lines," Fleur finally said to Tatiana. "They'll be here soon, I should think. Of course, if there's anything we can do to make you more comfortable . . ."

"We're fine," Tatiana said bleakly.

Folie managed a tight smile and nodded. Gia just looked between her two sisters and nearly lost it. She'd cried all the prior night, out of her head, hysterical with the lot. And when she slept, she'd dreamt of lying in the grass with her hand in Tajo's after making love.

She'd told herself to maintain composure while in the company of the Dumonts, and so Gia hadn't cried in the morning while the Dumont ladies' maids trussed her in one of the dresses from a trunk of her belongings, nor while they coiffed her hair and tried to paint some life on her face with makeup; the emotion just built up inside her. Now it seemed as though if she so much as opened her mouth to take in food, she would find herself unable to stop sobbing.

She looked across the table at Folie, again reaching up helplessly for the tiara driving nails into her head. "Folie, get this off me," she whispered.

"It's all right," Ian Dumont said. "I've got it." More gently than she felt she deserved, he leaned over and began pulling the pins securing the jeweled rig from her hair, and he removed the tiara from her head.

"Thank you," she said. "You probably would have been lovely if things were different."

The table went silent.

Gia looked down at her lap, her lips trembling. But she couldn't stop the tears, so she pushed her chair back. "Excuse me. I'm just so . . . tired," she managed to say before running from the room.

She made it back to the opulent bedroom in which she'd been lodged, fit for the princess she was, and burst into tears on the bed. "They shot him. They shot him!" Tatiana and Folie came in on her heels, sitting down on either side of her.

"Everything's going to be fine, Gia," Tatiana said. "You don't have to marry him. They really only need one, and it's me. I'll wed Marius and we'll be done with the whole thing."

Another sob slipped from Gia's throat. "It doesn't matter now. It's too late."

Tatiana stroked Gia's hair. "That must be what Marius tells himself about that girl," she murmured. "It will be all right."

"No, it won't. I can't have that moment back. If I

could have that moment back when he told me to go, I wouldn't turn away this time. I said 'goodbye.' How could I have just said 'goodbye' and then turned away?" she asked in anguish.

"Gia," Folie began tentatively. "You really fell in love with that commoner, didn't you? Even in so short a time. You just knew—is that it?"

Gia nodded. "I just knew."

"What was it like?" Tatiana asked.

"A fairy tale," Gia said. "It was like a fairy tale."

The three Dumont brothers had adjourned from dinner into their smoking room. Warrick sprawled on the sofa tracing patterns in the air with a tiny letter opener as if it were a fencing sword. With an elegant twist of a match, Ian puffed a thin, black cigarette into life, trailing clove scent in its wake. The fiery crimson crackling at the end could not have burned as hot as Marius's temper.

"It's a disaster," he said, pacing along the floor-to-ceiling windows. "Hell, send all three of them home if they want to go. Just send them home."

"You don't mean that," Ian said.

"I mean that!"

Warrick and Ian both looked at him in surprise.

"What?" Marius snapped. "I'm not allowed to get angry?"

Ian held up his palms in mock self-defense. "You're definitely allowed to get angry. It's just that it's usually you telling one of us that doesn't solve anything."

Marius rubbed his hand over his jaw. For some time now, he'd been feeling as if something inside him might explode. That the restraint he'd worked so hard at, that he was so admired for, particularly as a vampire, was more in jeopardy than his brothers could guess.

"I don't care if we send them home," Warrick said. "Beautiful. Especially for dogs, I'll say that without reservation. But a hell of a lot of trouble."

"They were supposed to be worth the trouble," Marius said tightly. "An alliance so powerful, so far-reaching, it would take an army of everyone remaining to challenge us."

Warrick sat up. "Make no mistake. I don't like to lose either. But we're not going to win every battle. We just need to win the war. So if you want to send them back and start over at square one, it's fine by me."

Ian cleared his throat. "I spoke with Fleur about it earlier. The thing is . . . Tatiana won't be backing out. She says she will not trade duty for cowardice. Actually, Marius, she sounds very much like you."

Marius winced, almost as much at the sympathy in his brother's voice as from the reality of the words. He was engaged to a woman he didn't love, the two of them tangled in a morass of duty-bound tradition.

Ian and Warrick glanced at each other. "Do you want to break the engagement?" Ian asked.

The long silence revealed the truth, even if Marius himself could not bring himself to say the word. But it would be a wasted word; he'd never follow through. He could never stand up at the Assembly and deliver such news without eroding their personal power. And he could never break a relationship he himself had crafted without damaging his reputation and his self-respect. No matter he'd run the fantasy through his head a thousand times.

"We'll stand by you," Ian said.

Marius looked over. His brother's expression indicated Ian was ready to do as he said; Warrick's less so, though Marius knew both siblings would support him if it really ever came to that.

He stared at their faces, then let his gaze pull back to take in the room and the view of a moon-tinged night through the window behind them. Then he swore on his honor that it would not come to that.

"No."

As he said the word, it was the strangest thing; he thought not of Tatiana, but of the rogue vampire Hayden Wilks. Crossing quickly to the bar he poured himself a shot of liquor, dousing his throat as if the burning alcohol could drown out his searing envy for a rival who knew nothing of honor, nothing of duty, who could live for himself alone. And who could have any woman he wanted—including the one woman Marius wanted.

And it was then that he sensed it. The disaster wasn't what was happening here, this ridiculous muddle, this fairy tale about three princesses which could be fixed as easily as a snap of his fingers; the disaster still lay dormant in the hearts and minds of three others—himself, Hayden, and Jill. They would have to come to some implicit agreement to let it all be. If only they could just let be what already was, they would all be relatively fine. But if every one of them could not let go of the revenge and the desire that consumed them, then the true disaster, the worst tragedy in Crimson City would yet be known.

Jill didn't have the strength; Hayden didn't have the incentive. It was Marius alone who stood as a barrier, a force to uphold what had to be.

"Marius!"

His brothers were standing in the middle of the room. Ian smashed the remnants of his cigarillo into an ashtray and quickly walked over to him. "Good God, where did you just go?"

"What are you talking about?" Marius replied, oddly disoriented.

Warrick laid his hand on his brother's shoulder, gripping tightly. "You had the most murderous look on your face, old boy." He was chuckling, and Marius forced a smile to help keep things light.

"There are three of us, you know," Warrick went on. "Plus Fleur and Dain. You don't have to solve all of these problems yourself."

"And you don't have to take all the blame, either," Ian added sharply.

Marius shook them off and moved to the picture window that divided them from everyone else in Crimson City. "No problems. No blame. I'm interested in solutions. And right now we need solutions for House Royale, beginning with this one: I will marry Tatiana Asprey and we will join East and West, vampire and werewolf, just as we planned."

"We send Folie home," Warrick chimed in.

"We send Folie home," Marius echoed in agreement.

"And what of Gianna?" Ian said.

Marius leaned his face against the cool pane of the window and replied, "Gianna will simply have to stop crying long enough to tell us what she wants."

Chapter Seven

Tajo Maddox sat on the porch of Jill's new apartment, his right leg raised up on a pillow. Bandages encased his chest, and his pals were buzzing around him like a bunch of nurses still in training. But hell, it was the thought that counted. And the view was spot-on. It included a nice slice of Dumont Tower—the eastern facade, in fact.

Once the last of the heavy-duty painkillers had worn off and he'd realized with a reasonable amount of clarity that he was in fact still alive, Tajo's first thought was of Gia making a life for herself somewhere in the building before him. Like Jill, he got something out of being able to see the place where his soul mate now lived. Of course, there was a limit; he'd still asked his pals not to show him any newspapers, not to turn on the television, and not to share any current events.

He might be battered and weak—half-dead, as they'd told him—but the only thing he knew could really kill him was news of Princess Gianna Asprey's engagement and marriage to the House of Dumont.

So when Bridget came in and said that someone wanted to see him, his first reaction was: "No, thanks."

"He won't take no for an answer," Bridget replied. She stepped aside and Marius Dumont appeared through the door.

"Good morning, Tajo," he said.

"It's morning. I'll give you that much," Tajo growled, clearly struggling to remain calm. "I guess I should be glad just to still be around. I thought Warrick would be a better shot."

"I'll just . . . be somewhere else," Bridget mumbled, slipping through the sliding glass door again.

"Come now, Maddox. If we truly wanted to kill you, we would have used silver. What did you expect? Everyone in Crimson City knew you'd taken her from us. I don't like to be embarrassed in front of my allies, and I don't like to be made to look weak. Let's just say it doesn't suit."

Tajo's eyes shone with barely suppressed anger. "And you decided to deliver your message where everyone and their mother could read it. The Power Summit."

"Of course. You would have done the same." Marius pulled up a chair.

Tajo reared back, a sudden fury coursing through his entire being. He smelled Gianna in the air. "I can smell her on you," he said, clenching his fist and wishing to God he wasn't bandaged, trussed up like some helpless kidnap victim.

"I did not come here to get your blood up," Marius said. "And since I already have a fiancée, I can't imagine you would think anything of it. After all, she is—"

The door burst open, framing Jill and Hayden with their arms full of groceries, playfully fighting each other to get through the doorway first. They saw him and everybody froze. Hayden took the grocery sacks and placed them gently on the floor. The crack down the center of Marius's heart seemed to split that much wider as he watched Jill's body language change.

"Hello, Marius," she said boldly, delicately smoothing back the hair along the side of Hayden's temple.

"Point taken," Marius said, trying not to let his hatred for the rogue get the better of him.

"What do you mean?" she asked in mock innocence.

Marius stepped forward. "Don't play games. It's dangerous."

Hayden moved between them. Crowding Marius back against the wall, he brought his lips to the Protector's ear and whispered, "The danger is what makes the game so fun to play."

Marius recoiled. Jill's eyes found his over the rogue vampire's shoulder. Foreign murderous rage pooled where love should have been. "Choose your next words carefully, Hayden," he warned.

The rogue smiled, his face so uncomfortably close, his body closer. It made Marius want to cringe again, but he forced himself to remain steady.

In a voice so low that only the two of them could possibly hear, Hayden went in for the kill: "Look at what you do to her, Marius. She's dying for you. Even humans can't fail to sense the passion you inspire in her. She can scarcely breathe for wanting you. And you know what's going to happen? When you walk out that door, I'm going to encourage her to spend all that passion on me."

Marius moistened his lips, never taking his eyes off Jill. She seemed pinned in place, unable to move. She looked mesmerized, stricken. "Don't you dare turn her vampire," he warned. "Don't turn her. Don't even touch her."

Hayden laughed and stepped back. "Game on, Marius."

Marius nearly forgot himself, but he fought the urge to strike out. Hayden grabbed Jill by the hand and pulled her out and onto the deck.

Marius took a step to follow, his fists clenched. "Don't let him bring out the darkness in you, Jillian!"

Jill didn't seem to hear. She was concentrating on Hayden's face. His hands caressed her cheeks. He stroked her, whispered something in her ear. Jill leaned back on the stone ledge, her neck exposed.

"No!" Marius leapt forward as Hayden brought his head down.

But it was only a kiss. A brutal, passionate kiss that Jill didn't shy away from.

Horrified, embarrassed, hating himself, Marius stumbled back and closed the door on a vision that burnt his eyes without mercy. *Game on, Marius.* Game on, then.

"I'll see you in round two, Hayden," he muttered under his breath.

"What the hell do you want, Dumont?"

Marius spun around.

The werewolf narrowed his eyes. "I can't believe you'd come here to Jill's place as if it did nothing to her," Tajo continued. "If you had a little class—or at least a little common sense—you'd've sent one of your brothers. If you don't want her, then for God's sake let her go so she can get over it."

Marius studied the ceiling for a moment. "I know these are not things you subscribe to, but I felt it was my duty as—"

"Son of a bitch. Save that crap for someone who gives a damn, and tell me what you came to say."

"For your part," Marius spat, in an uncustomary loss of temper, "if you'd let me say what I came to say in the first place, we could have been done with this business before they'd ever returned from buying your invalid's lunch at the corner market. I clearly saw them leave the apartment from the limousine I was waiting in downstairs *with Gianna.*"

The werewolf looked like he might faint. "Gia's downstairs?"

Marius gently pressed the back of his hand against the ache in his forehead. "She refused to come up until I could determine whether or not she was welcome under these rather unfortunate circumstances."

"She's . . . *welcome,*" Tajo said hoarsely.

Marius accepted the answer with a slight nod, then clipped his comm device to his ear and dialed. "Please escort the princess to the door now, Vin. Very good, then." He hung up, turned, and walked to the door.

"The best of luck to you, Tajo Maddox. I hear New York City is particularly lovely around the holidays." And with that, Marius Dumont saw himself out. Tajo Maddox never did get another word out.

Every muscle in Tajo's body tensed as he stared at the door, unable to stand, the anticipation of seeing Gianna's face almost more than he could bear.

The vibrations along the floorboards signaled her arrival in the hall outside. With a smile, Tajo closed his eyes and inhaled her scent as she neared. He heard the twist and click of the doorknob, and when he opened his eyes she was there in front of him.

She'd never been anything less than a princess to him, and her sisters must have done her up to suit the title. A silvery, diaphanous gown highlighted her pale skin. A thin band of diamonds winked in the folds of her perfectly coiffed hair. They'd made up her face; she was flawless.

But it was the memory of her gamely wrestling with a piece of wilted lettuce, her dress and hairdo falling to pieces around her, her smile as bright as ever that flashed in his mind. Princess or not, she was the same. She was his mate.

She must have read his thoughts. With a cry of delight, she fell to her knees before him.

Tajo's heart monitor went on the fritz, and Bridget, Jill, and Hayden were suddenly there trying to run interference. Gia shifted between crying and laughing, then looked horrified as the monitor continued beeping.

Hayden kept trying to push Tajo back down in the chair, when all Tajo wanted to do was get up and take Gia in his arms and hold her forever.

"Gia, I was an idiot. I never wanted you to go. I only said it because I thought it was what was best for you! I love you."

"You've got to calm down, Tajo, or I'm sending her away," Jill scolded.

"If you send her away, I really *am* going to have a fucking heart attack!"

"Taj, I'm the only one who can say what's best for me . . . and I'm not going anywhere," Gia said. She crawled onto the chaise with him and they just held each other.

Tajo looked up at his friends, pleading with them to leave him in Gia's care. And though they rolled their eyes, clucked, shook their heads and did all the things that friends were supposed to do, they finally let the two of them alone.

He and Gia didn't speak for a while, just listened as

his heart monitor slowed to a regular, steady pulse—one that kept time with her heartbeat.

Tajo finally shifted in his chair and took Gia's left hand in his. "No engagement ring," he said.

"No engagement ring," she echoed. "It's lucky I'm just the middle sister—I can do something crazy and marry for love."

"Marry for love? I'd have to go back to a werewolf clan," Tajo repeated, trying the words out on his tongue. "Who'd've thought? Would your family even accept me? I mean, I'm never going to completely fit the mold."

Gia laughed. "My sisters have a saying."

"Yeah?"

" 'Gia always gets her way.' " She looked up, her forehead suddenly wrinkled with worry. "You wouldn't mind leaving the Rogues behind?"

"It'll be nice to know someone here in Crimson City has my back," Tajo said. "But what I need the most is you and me."

Gia smiled and tucked her face into the curve of his neck, trying to be careful of the bandages. "You and me," she whispered, moving her mouth to his, smiling against his lips. "A princess and her knight. A fairy tale."

As ever, thanks to Liz Maverick for such a great series and thank you to all the other Crimson City authors, too. You rock. Many thanks to Megan Frampton, Sherril Jaffe, Colleen Wenker and Kathy Alvarez for reading drafts. Thanks as well to Tom Pierce for information about fancy cars and to the gym elf for doing arm curls right in front of my bike. Inspiring, indeed. Yet another reason why exercise is good for you. Last, but by no means least, thank you to Chris Keeslar for being a great editor.

DX

by
Carolyn Jewel

Chapter One

The way the briefing room went silent, Hell Marshall knew she was on the outside of an inside joke. Jim West, chief division agent for U.S. Internal Operations in the city of Los Angeles—Crimson City—gripped the projector remote in one hand and a red pen light in the other. I-Ops was the intelligence branch of the human government's agency dealing with the city's paranormals. Battlefield Operations was military, the muscle on the streets. I-Ops was pencil-pushers, spooks and a few other things nobody admitted. West signaled one of the field agents to hit the lights. The room went dark. He clicked the remote and two seconds later Hell understood the silence. *Shit.*

"This is from a surveillance camera installed at the Golden Wing Spa and Health Center," West said. The camera had been placed behind the reception desk, so the back of a perky blond head occasionally blocked a portion of the screen. The spa's owner, Tuan Ng, was clearly visible in the right corner of the shot.

Hell didn't move, didn't change her expression. West was looking at her. Everyone was looking at her. She could feel it, but she kept her eyes glued to the screen. She didn't work for I-Ops anymore. They'd fired her ass nine months ago, and that meant her personal life was nobody's fucking business. She was here because Milos Sanders, director of I-Ops in Crimson City, was the only friend she had left. Well, that and the promises he'd made to get her back for this assignment.

She wished she had the nerve to give up L.A. and move to her Aunt Lucy's beach house in Bodega Bay. Her aunt wanted someone she trusted in the house. She could open a little coffee shop and serve killer espresso and sandwiches. At night she could sit on the porch, eat saltwater taffy, breathe fresh air and watch the stars. It was a stupid fantasy, but it was all hers.

In the video she was supposed to be watching, the perky receptionist kept looking in Tuan's direction. Tuan Ng was movie-star handsome and, now that Hell wasn't seeing him, notoriously available. If these jackass agents expected a scene, they were destined for disappointment. Her relationship with the vampire had been doomed from the start because he was a fang and she wasn't.

On-screen, the lobby door opened and one of the most beautiful men Hell had ever seen walked in. He wore loose trousers and no shirt, and he had the pecs, abs, and everything else to pull off the look, plus more. His long black hair was held back by two narrow braids that started at his temples and secured the rest in a ponytail. Silver threads gleamed in the braids. His skin bordered on bronze, and he was ripped. Seriously, beautifully ripped, without looking like he spent all his hours in the gym. What was a guy like that doing in a place like Tuan's spa?

If you had the money, the Golden Wing accommodated any and all consenting adult interactions, regardless of species. Tuan's open-minded attitude cleared him a million and a half a week. A guy who looked like this one could have any woman he wanted with one flex of a pectoral. Flex the other and his beauty of choice would do any kinky thing he wanted. What was he doing here?

Mr. Gorgeous walked toward the reception camera. His eyes were a freakish pale amber. She'd never seen eyes that color.

"Can I help you?" the receptionist asked.

The man gestured and a flash of yellow light filled the screen. When it faded, the blonde was facedown on the counter. Scarlet blood oozed around her head and dripped onto the floor. On-screen, Tuan shouted. Six of his enforcers rushed into the lobby.

West paused the video and pointed his laser pen at the screen. "No need to identify *him*," he said, centering the light on Tuan's forehead. "But this"—the light shifted to the bare-chested stud who was, it seemed, a deranged killer—"is our DX. Demon of unknown origin." Hell sat up. "For the uninformed in the room— Hell—he's been identified as a Bak-Faru."

She was an outsider now that she made her living as a private investigator. She didn't want to be a security guard, walking around some stupid shopping mall waiting for criminals to steal all the panties in Victoria's Secret. Tuan sent referrals as his way of making up for ruining her life, but working for vampires was a dicey business these days, since the recent crises. A woman stuck in L.A. had to have a steady income, and for that she needed her security clearance back. This job, courtesy of Milos, was her ticket to regular rent payments. If she did this for him, she might even get back her old job. She leaned back and clasped her hands behind her head. West stared at her exposed navel.

A self-employed former I-Ops field agent without the security clearance required for lucrative government jobs, and who was also pissed off at losing her job for a lie, could, if called in to consult, arrive at the briefing dressed in, say, tight black low-rider pants, boots, and a hot pink shirt that exposed the ring in her navel. But that would only be if she was bitter. There were perks to her current situation that made up for paying self-employment tax and her own insurance.

"You got your regular demons . . ." West gave her his full attention, speaking as if he thought she was deaf or didn't understand English. True enough, she'd never worked demon detail, and she'd left I-Ops well before anyone knew much about them. But she wasn't ignorant. West was such a dickhead.

Hell rocked her chair back and checked out the only person here besides her who wasn't wearing a suit— Agent Jaden Lightfeather. The man oozed sex appeal, and she was having a hard time not staring. Ever since the fiasco of Tuan Ng, her libido had been on vacation. Whoa. Vacation over. She could feel the guy even when she wasn't looking at him. Agent Incredible Hunk had Native-American features, brown eyes, and skin two shades darker than café au lait. On him, black clothes looked good instead of pretentious. He wore a silver earring. The small yet prohibited body decoration meant he was either undercover or covert. With his short hair, her money was on covert. Agent Incredible Hunk was scowling at West. So maybe he thought West was an asshole, too. Already they had something in common.

West was still talking about demons. ". . . Mahsei, Elismal, Niteh, and so on. Then you have the mean ones. Dark demons. Setonian, Kivernian and the like. And way out here"—West gestured, spreading one arm wide and wiggling his fingers—"you have pure evil like our DX here. The Bak-Faru. They don't get any darker, meaner, or more vicious than his kind. It didn't take many of those freaks to tear this city apart."

"Oh," Hell said as if a lightbulb had gone off. "I get it. Some demons are nice and friendly. Some of them are mean." She pointed at the screen. "And those ones are mean *and* nasty." Somebody snickered. Score one for Hell.

"Take a good look, Hell," West said, shining the penlight on the DX. "You ever see anything like that, it's the last thing you'll ever see."

"Fortunately," she said. "I don't believe in demons."

West snorted. "Didn't you get any smarter after they booted you out?"

"Just a better smart-ass, I guess." Of course she believed in demons. Anybody who'd lived in Crimson City these past months was either a fervent believer, dead, or plain stupid.

"Cut the crap, Helen." Milos Sanders swiveled his chair. He never used her real name unless he was pissed, and the last thing Hell wanted was to piss off Milos. He'd been her mentor, practically a father to her; he'd kept her out of jail and tried to keep her from getting fired. She owed him.

West, the smug dickhead, clicked the remote. "Let's make a believer out of you, Hell."

The video started again. The DX faced his attackers. A yellow flash whitened the screen. When it faded, two of Tuan's vampire enforcers were gone and the demon had another fang by the throat. The DX smiled with anticipation and then his hand blurred. The next thing Hell saw was him laughing, the fang's heart clenched in his fist with tendrils of smoke rising toward the ceiling. Tuan flew straight up, dragged by Fabienne, his primary enforcer. The remaining fangs met gruesome, bloody deaths she'd rather not have seen. The DX never broke a sweat.

West stood in front of the blue screen. One of the field agents, from the looks of him barely old enough to shave, raised a hand. "Sir. When was this film taken?"

"Three weeks ago."

"Impossible," Hell said. "There's no more demons in Crimson City."

"Go on, Jim." Milos, about forty, maybe forty-five, ran fingers through his prematurely gray hair.

West clicked the remote again and the screen showed two men and a woman drinking coffee. It was night, and they sat outside at a battered metal table bolted to a cracked sidewalk. Whenever the camera shifted left, part of a boarded-over window, heavily tagged with gang graffiti, came into view. Two armed men stood behind their table. Probably there were more out of sight. The camera angle wasn't straight on, and every now and then the scene wobbled.

Hell crossed her legs and leaned forward, studying the faces. She was having a hard time forgetting the DX. She'd never seen anything kill like that and smile the whole time. Like he was having fun. During the major demon troubles, she'd been cooling her heels and her heart, suspended from I-Ops but still thinking Milos could pull off a miracle and save her job.

On-screen, streetlights dimmed as a junkie walked in front of the table. One of the guards trained his MP5K on him. The dominant man of the three was Caucasian, about thirty, maybe younger, and handsome if you liked them tall, broad-shouldered, and with sandy brown hair. The second man was Latino and whipcord thin. He had Mestizo features, and he would have been pretty if he didn't look so mean. The woman was Sybil Hu. Lacquered wooden sticks held up her black hair, and Hell would bet good money the ends were razor sharp.

West froze the shot with the junkie in midstep just past the table. The guard still had his gun trained on him. With the penlight, West trained a red dot on each of the subjects in turn. "Elijah Douglas, formerly of the LaRoux werewolf clan"—the red dot appeared on the dominant man—"now a rogue dog inhabiting the Lower." The dot moved. "Per Nielsen of the Skullhand Cazadores, and Sybil Hu, Wang Li Tong."

The Incredible Hunk covert agent moved. Up to now, he'd been about as frisky as a block of granite. He touched his earring. Hell didn't much like what she was hearing. The idea of the Cazadores and the Wang Li Tong getting friendly made her stomach hurt. The Cazadores were a gang. A big gang with big money. They controlled the Lower, the worst section of Crimson City. If it was illegal, the Cazadores had a lock on it in their neighborhood, but their main source of income was illegal hunting. Any dog or fang who wanted a taste of the wild could go to the Cazadores, pay up and spend a night hunting with full denial from the City that anything of the sort went on. Nowadays, the Cazadores were expanding their territory and business. A deal with the Wang Li Tong would get them into gambling, drugs and prostitution in a big way.

"Elijah," West continued, "is considered mentally unstable. However, he's a confirmed Alpha establishing the first known werewolf pack in this quadrant of the city. We estimate he's at ninety-five percent of what's required for stable pack structure."

That was scary. A crazy werewolf in charge of a pack in the Lower? Hand in paw with the Cazadores, who pretty much ran the Lower, *and* the Wang Li Tong? West ticked off the contents of the file Hell had been given after she cleared security about an hour ago. Per had been accused of multiple felonies: murder, attempted murder, accessory to conversion without informed consent, possession of controlled substances. No convictions. None of the charges was more recent than fifteen months. Going by his file, Per Nielsen was an all-around nice guy who paid his taxes.

"Hu," West continued, "is Elijah's alpha female. Thought to have been illegally converted about six months ago." What West didn't have to say was that Hu headed the human division of the Tong. Tuan Ng headed the fang division.

West was done playing with the penlight. He clicked the remote again. The junkie walked past the boarded-up window, and out of the shot, the guard lowered his MP5K, Elijah eyed Sybil's boobs, and the video ended.

"Note," Hell said, bending over like she was writing. "Elijah the dog is a tit man." That got a few laughs and another sigh from Milos. Agent Hunk was deaf to her wit. Damn; her attraction to him was out of hand if she was actually trying to get him to notice her. *Have a little pride, woman!* Did he have to be so freaking hot?

"I hope you were paying attention, Helen," Milos said. "Because I'm sending you after Elijah."

"Oh, goody," Hell said into the darkened room. More like, *Oh, fuck.*

West turned on the lights and sat. He put down the remote but continued playing with his penlight. Everyone slumping on his chair sat straight. Except Hell and Agent Hunk. With cheekbones like that, his profile was to die for. She stayed slouched and crossed one leg over the other. Lightfeather didn't move. "What's the connection between Elijah Douglas and the DX?" she asked.

"We believe," Milos said, with the smoothing of his hair that meant he was not as calm as he appeared, "that Elijah Douglas is constructing a new portal to the demon world."

"Shit," said one of the other agents.

"No shit," Hell said softly.

"And that he has allied himself with certain demons trapped here since the portal was destroyed and the demon attack failed. We believe the assault on Tuan Ng was a test of what demons can do for him once Elijah has a working portal." Milos scanned the room. "I'd say the test succeeded. This city can't survive another demon war. Therefore, it is the job of everyone in this room to take all necessary steps to neutralize the threat. Your job, Hell," Milos added, "is to convince Elijah Douglas it is in his interest to ally with us. Not demons. And not, God help us, to mend fences with Tuan Ng."

West closed his folder with a palm slap. "Sir, once again I protest. She's a fang banger," he said. "She can't be trusted."

Hell leaned forward with both hands on the conference table. "Have I mentioned, *Jim,* how much I hate you?"

"Your relationship with Tuan Ng compromised an ongoing investigation." West directed his penlight to her forehead and left it there long enough to make it clear their feelings were mutual.

"I wasn't the leak, West."

"Bullshit. You were sleeping with the guy."

She slid her hands off the table and addressed Milos. "If Elijah's such a danger, take him down. Eliminate the risk entirely."

Milos was the only one who didn't look at Lightfeather.

"Well, then." She pointed at Agent Lightfeather. Damn, but he was good-looking. The guy must be six four and not a sign of gawkiness. "He's trained to take out humans, dogs, and fangs with a single weapons-appropriate shot. Let him take care of our problem with Elijah Douglas."

Lightfeather mouthed the words "Fuck you."

"Same to you," she said sweetly. She wished. Just her luck: he didn't like chicks with short hair and navel rings.

Milos sighed. "Helen, you may be the one person who can get to Elijah right now."

"And why is that?" she asked, forcing herself not to look at Lightfeather.

"Ng and Douglas are in the middle of a war."

Her affair with Ng had been the stuff of tabloid headlines for far longer than the subject was interesting or even accurate. There wasn't anybody who didn't know about her and Tuan Ng, even mentally unstable dogs and hunky covert agents. She stared at Milos. "If all you wanted was for me to get your assassin close enough to blow some damn dog's head off, you should have said so from the start."

Jaden Lightfeather rolled his eyes. "Is she always like this?"

Crap, the assassin had a sexy voice.

Milos spread his fingers on the table. He wore a wedding band, but his wife had died before Hell even started at I-Ops. "My ass is on the line for you, Helen, so sit up and listen. We won't get a second chance. If we eliminate Elijah, then his Beta or some other dog we don't know takes his place and God knows what happens. If, however, you do your job, as I know you can, then Elijah plays on our side. If you do your job well, Elijah and his demons play with us instead of against us."

"Then why do you need him?" She glared at Jaden.

"Jim, tell Hell who killed your predecessor on this team."

"Tuan Ng." West smiled at her. "Say, are you still dating him?"

"Get beat."

"I heard Tuan is great in the sack." West leered. "That true? Did he do it for you?"

She heard several snickers. "I heard you're an asshole," she replied. "And I *know* that's true."

West clicked on his penlight and pointed it at her head again. "You filing a pair of nice sharp fangs, Hell?"

She pushed out of her chair, shaking with anger. "Guys, it's been an honor, honest, but get yourself another patsy for this job."

"Afraid to smile for us?" West asked.

Milos stood up hard enough that his chair crashed to the floor. "That's enough." The room went quiet. "Step out of line again, West, and you're off this task force." He looked around the room, ending with Hell. "We believe Ng won't be so quick to dispatch you if you succeed in getting close to Elijah. In addition to turning Elijah, we want you to find out who's controlling the DX and where that damn portal is so we can destroy it. Is that clear?"

"Yes, sir."

"And, while Lightfeather is quite capable of wet work, that's a last resort."

"You want him to babysit me? I do not need a babysitter." Hell was far too aware of Jaden's attention on her, and it sent another shiver of arousal through her. Hunk or not, she didn't want I-Ops guarding her back.

Milos righted his chair and sat with his clasped hands atop a black folder. "Agent Lightfeather's job is to keep you alive until you've done what you're supposed to."

"Yeah," said one of the agents. "But if he offs Elijah, Tuan, or the DX, that's a bonus."

"Maybe he'll off Hell," someone said to more than a few chuckles.

Hell gave the room the finger.

Milos glared at her. Like she hadn't been provoked. "You are not to interfere with Lightfeather."

She slumped on her chair. "What if he interferes with me?"

"He won't." Milos's interlaced fingers tightened.

"Hell," West said. "Just do the job you're being fucking paid to do, all right?"

She ignored him. "And for doing this, I get . . . ?"

"Your discharge from U.S. Internal Operations will indicate a voluntary separation retroactive to the date of your administrative leave."

"What about my clearance?" Voluntary dismissal opened the door to reinstatement.

"That, too." Milos licked his lips. "Do we have a deal?"

She waited a beat. "Sure."

Milos smiled. "I hope you like Moroccan."

"Love it," she said.

"Excellent. Because the dog will be at Mimouza tonight." He pushed the black folder at her. It slid about halfway and stopped. She leaned across the table and grabbed the edge with her fingertips. "Bring me Ng, Elijah, *and* the DX, Hell. I know you can."

Her response was automatic. "Yes, sir."

Milos smiled again and for a minute, she was back before her life went down the toilet, when she'd been Milos Sanders's most promising field agent. "I wouldn't be putting my career on the line for you if I didn't believe that," he said.

"Thanks, Chief." She pulled the folder toward her and caught West staring down her shirt. Perv. She glanced at Jaden. He wasn't looking. "Hey, Lightfeather. When do you want to meet up?"

Jaden shook his head. "I stick with you twenty-four-seven."

"Great," she said. "That's really great." She put the black folder on top of the others, looking at Lightfeather while she did. "Come on, then, gorgeous. Let's go bag ourselves a dog, a fang, and a DX."

Chapter Two

With a couple of hours to kill before they were due at
Mimouza, she and Jaden agreed he'd drive them to
her place so she could change clothes and review the
files. From the outside, his sedan looked like no big
deal. Hell was terrible at deciphering automobile lo-
gos and couldn't tell if his was American or an Asian
import, but it was black with shiny hubcaps and a
low-to-the-ground body. Inside was gadget heaven.
She didn't know what half the gizmos attached to the
dashboard did.

When he turned the ignition, the engine thrummed
in her ears and vibrated under her feet. Definitely not
your average car. She settled herself on the seat. Her
bare skin touched leather, and she flashed back to the
first time she rode in one of Tuan's cars. Tuan had a
penchant for Italian sports cars, which he liked to
drive too fast on Highway 1. Their first weekend away
had been in Santa Barbara. She'd worn her bikini on
the way back to their hotel, and she'd never forgotten
the sensation of her skin against the leather seat.

Funny, the things that sparked a memory. She'd wondered at the time if Tuan was *the one*.

In Jaden's I-Ops–issue car, she tried crossing her legs, but her foot tangled in the strap of her bike messenger bag-cum-briefcase. What with a smaller tote containing all the crap she'd taken from her car balanced on her lap, she couldn't untangle herself without looking dorky. She didn't mind having long legs except when she was in a car built for speed over comfort. After Tuan, she'd sworn off men, but if she remembered her ancient history, long legs were a perk when it came to the opposite sex. Jaden the Incredible Hunk looked, but it was when she was flailing around trying to get settled. *Crap*.

He punched her address into the GPS—he knew where she lived, wasn't that unsettling?—and they were off, too fast. Without navigation as a subject for conversation, all there was to listen to was the motor. Or she could watch lights and dials glow on the dash. It was dark out and getting darker. Traffic wasn't bad, not bumper-to-bumper anymore. Jaden seemed happy with silence so she crossed her arms over her chest and stared out the window. His car was frighteningly clean. New-car smell lingered in the air.

He shifted and punched the gas to merge into a gap in traffic. Hell grabbed the dashboard as her tote went sliding off her lap, spilling the contents on the floor. At least six cars hit their horns. When her heart was back in her throat, she exploded. "Clue, Agent Leadfoot! You probably think people are always honking their horns, but they aren't. They're trying to tell you that you drive like a goddamn—oh, Jesus! Look out!" She clutched the emergency brake. Horns blared. "Would you please slow down?"

He shifted again and tailgated a car getting onto the freeway on the expiring yellow. "I didn't want this assignment," he said without looking at her.

She picked up her keys and her cell. Her heart banged against her ribs. "You didn't have to say yes."

"Yes, I did."

"Gee, too bad."

He merged into freeway traffic. "Let's be professional about this."

"Don't worry," she said politely. "I think you're being as professional as you can."

Something on the dashboard beeped and several lights flashed. Jaden punched a button, swore, and pushed another series of buttons. "Take notes, honey."

Sixty-five. "If I live, sure."

"Fuck you," he said as he switched lanes and cut off a truck.

"You wish." *Eighty-five. Ninety.* Her exit was coming up, and he wasn't slowing down.

He merged again without checking the rearview mirror. "Sure."

"Drop dead, you freak. Arghh!" She covered her head with both hands.

"I thought you wanted—"

"Fuck you!"

A killer smile appeared on Jaden's face. "Absolutely."

They got off the freeway and spent the last five minutes of the drive in utter silence. "Street parking only," she said when the GPS gave the last turn. He found a spot within a block of her building and parallel-parked exactly like the maneuver was diagramed. Smooth as silk. Hell couldn't parallel-park worth a damn, and people who could made her feel inadequate. He should at least not be so damn hunky.

"Look," he said after he turned off the ignition. "West is a fucking asshole. You shouldn't let him get to you."

She let her head fall against the back of her seat. "Why are you being so nice when I'm being such a bitch? This just stinks. My life's been in the tank ever since I met Tuan."

His big brown eyes lingered on her face, and she felt the pull, right down to her toes. He looked sympathetic. And totally gorgeous. "I don't give a shit about Tuan Ng."

"Aren't you curious?" Oh God, he was going to turn out to be a nice guy. "Everyone else is."

"Just one thing."

Hell stared at the roof of Jaden's car. She didn't hear any of the usual prurient scorn in his voice. "What?"

"He ever come see you at your place?"

So much for thinking they might actually be friends. She turned her head. But for the glowing dashboard lights, the interior was dark. A shiver of intimacy danced along her spine. Agent Lightfeather was exactly the kind of guy she went for, all dark and dangerous. She'd had the same reaction to Tuan, and for many of the same reasons. Lightfeather would be very bad for her. "Why? You want to know how many times we did it and in which rooms?"

His expression didn't change. "If he did come to your place, he knows the layout, and my job gets a lot harder. I'd like to know before we go in."

"Yeah, he knows the layout." She turned on the seat to face him. Light from the streetlamp struck the side of his face and made his eyes glitter like a cat's. "There's no way he knows about this." She laughed softly. "Unless his mole was at the briefing."

He tossed his keys on his palm and made a fist

around them. He had long fingers. "Anything else I need to know?"

Man, he was gorgeous. And nice. It made her feel sad. "Yeah."

Jaden went into covert agent mode. "I'm listening."

"I wasn't expecting company. Consider yourself warned. My place is a mess."

He laughed, and her pulse skipped. He had a nice smile, and she couldn't remember the last time she'd been anywhere near a guy with a nice smile. She missed that. "That's okay," he said. Man, his smile was pure magic. She could feel the heat all the way across the interior of the car. "I'm a slob, too."

"Kindred spirits, my man." She stuck out a hand. "Friends?"

He took it. "Friends."

Jaden let go of her hand right away, so it wasn't the physical contact that made the car feel like it had just shrunk. Wow. Jaden Lightfeather really got to her. His smile absolutely did her in, and he was sitting there smiling at her and after all those months trying to get over the disaster of Tuan Ng, her libido wasn't on vacation anymore. As dangerous men went, he was a nice guy. He leaned forward. She didn't lean back because if she leaned back, he wouldn't kiss her, if that's what he had on his mind. But maybe she leaned toward him. Whichever way it went, the distance between them disappeared.

At first he didn't do anything except hold her, and being held felt way better than she expected. But then he moved his head and his lips brushed her cheek, and then her lips. Almost like an accident. Only not. She hadn't kissed anybody since Tuan, and she was out of practice, which didn't seem bother him. His mouth opened over hers, and he leaned closer. Much closer.

Jaden Lightfeather, she discovered, was worth kissing. He was a fabulous kisser. Sensational, in fact.

She slid an arm around his neck. He was a much, much larger man than Tuan. His nape was warm, feverish, and very soft. He adjusted his position and continued his slow, soul-stealing kiss; like he had all the time in the world and all he wanted to do with it was kiss her. Hell melted, inside and out. Ignoring the gearshift, she plastered herself against him, bringing his head closer to hers. Tongues met, hands began to wander. He groaned in the back of his throat.

After a while, he leaned back. "Let's go inside."

"Definitely."

He reached behind his seat and grabbed a dark duffel bag. The motion involved a fluid turn-and-snatch, during which his shirt pulled tight across his chest and any number of muscles flexed. While she sat trying to get her hormones under control, a waft of cooler air came at her because he'd opened his door. Damn. She was still staring at his seat when he closed his door.

Hell cradled her messenger bag and tote and opened her side. Jaden was already on the sidewalk. Oh, perfect timing. She had her legs sprawled, one in the car, the other on the sidewalk in that awkward transition required by full hands, heels, and tight pants. He slung his duffel over a shoulder and reached for her bags. Light reflected off his earring. He took a long look at her leg, from her black leather boot to her thigh.

The attack was silent and blindingly fast. One minute Jaden was standing there all gorgeously ethnic poker-faced, and the next, something had him around the neck. Everything in his arms hit the sidewalk. Jaden tumbled backward.

In Crimson City, only one thing moved with that speed and stealth. A fang. Hell scooped his car keys off the pavement and snatched her bike bag by the strap to fumble inside for her gun. Her little .32 wasn't going to do more than slow the vamp down, but a few seconds could make all the difference. The vampire was on his feet with Jaden clasped in a prebite armlock. She pulled the safety and shot the fang in the knee. He stumbled, which gave Jaden the time he needed.

Wham!

Jaden slammed the fang facedown against the trunk of his car. The tactic, taught to every agent at the Academy, put sharp teeth at maximum distance from fleshy targets. A fight with a vampire wasn't about strength or speed, it was about leverage and keeping calm. The fang struggled, but Jaden's defensive lock reduced him to helpless cursing.

Another shape emerged from the shadows. Hell recognized her immediately: Fabienne, Tuan Ng's enforcer, a six-foot-tall Caucasian woman in stilettos, black leather pants, and a black suede bustier. Hell happened to know she was a natural blonde who dyed her hair black. Her full lips were the same cherry red as her nails, she had an iPod strapped around her upper arm and way better eye makeup than Hell's. Fabienne looked twenty-two but she was a lot older than that.

"Good evening, Hell. So wonderful to see you again." The enforcer's warmth was totally fake. Her straight hair fell to her shoulders in a jet river. "Be a love and tell your friend to let my friend go."

"Get in the car, Hell." Jaden had one hand braced on the man's neck while the other twisted the fang's arm alarmingly high up his back. His arm muscles bulged, but he sounded calm.

"Or," Fabienne continued, "I'll have to tell my friend to kill your friend."

"Jaden?" Hell said.

If either fang was trying mind games on him, they weren't working. "Get in the car, Hell."

"Stephano, my love. Go ahead." Fabienne smiled in that ghoulish way she had that exposed one fang in her cherry-red mouth. "Hell, darling," she continued; "Tuan wants a word with you. Why don't you come with me while Stephano and your very impressive friend get better acquainted?"

Stephano was another of Tuan's enforcers and, like Fabienne, favored the black leather look. He also had way better eye makeup than Hell. Jaden jerked Stephano off the car with an ease that spoke volumes for his strength. Stephano looked like he was having trouble breathing. Whatever Jaden was doing to the vamp, it was effective.

"Stephano!" Fabienne snapped.

"You know what?" Jaden said to Fabienne. He looked furious enough to convince Hell he could take down a fang bare-handed. "If you don't get out of here right now, I'm going to kill Stephano and let *you* tell Ng to leave Helen Marshall the fuck alone."

"Jaden," Hell said. "They're vampires. Unless you have a stake or UV, you can't kill them."

"Wanna bet?" he snarled.

Fabienne put her hands on her hips and shook her head. "She's right, handsome."

"I know for a fact a fang can die." He smiled at Fabienne, and Hell discovered Jaden had a nasty smile to counter the nice one. "How about you try and stop me from killing your friend?"

Fabienne moved, and that ought to have been the end of everything. No human could outpace a fang. But it wasn't. With a hiss, Fabienne launched herself at him. Jaden did something with his hands, and

Stephano hit the ground without a hint of self-preservation when he landed. Fabienne's momentum ought to have bowled him over, but he evaded her. Or maybe Fabienne, who never made a mistake, missed. She hit the side of his car instead.

Hell heard a click and there was Jaden, bent over Fabienne with the barrel of a gun making a dent in her forehead. Fabienne snarled, fangs exposed.

"Uh-uh-uh," Jaden said. "UV, sweetheart."

Hell hadn't seen him take out a gun, ultraviolet payload or otherwise, but there it was, pressed to the middle of Fabienne's forehead.

Jaden smiled again, the nasty smile, and said, "Tell Tuan Ng to leave Helen Marshall alone."

Fabienne nodded, a single, cautious movement. "I'd be delighted." With her chin, she nodded toward Stephano, motionless on the concrete. "And my friend?"

"Don't bother," he said, and the way he said it made Hell shiver.

Fabienne rose, hands raised. She had on three-inch stilettos, and Jaden was still taller. The gun barrel didn't waver.

Jaden clicked the safety back on the gun when Fabienne left. "Some days I love this town."

Her heart started beating again. "What are they feeding you over there in Covert?"

"Raw meat." He flashed his killer smile. "Get in the car, Hell." She did. She handed him the keys when he slid into the driver's side. "You all right?" he asked.

"Yes." She still hadn't gotten over the way he'd handled Stephano and Fabienne. She'd never seen anything or anyone make Fabienne turn tail.

"You sure?" He touched her cheek. "You look pale."

Hell ran her hands through her short, dark blond hair. "I'm fine."

"Give me your cell phone." Jaden held out a hand and wriggled his fingers.

She dug the phone out of her purse and handed it to him. "Okay, but what for?"

He opened his door, leaned out, and put her phone on the pavement.

"What are you doing?" Her voice rose. She lunged and clutched his arm, but trying to budge him was like trying to move a boulder.

With the door still open he put the car in reverse. There was a crunch as the car lurched. He leaned out the open door and looked down.

"Hey!"

He threw an arm across her chest, shifted into first, popped the clutch, and ran over it once more. After another glance at whatever was left, he slammed his door.

"Bastard!"

Jaden reached over, put a finger under her chin, and pushed up. His earring sparkled again. "Now nobody can track you via your cell."

"I hate you."

He laughed and leaned in to kiss her, mouth open and not as gentle as before. For half a second she intended to push him away to make the point that phone-destroying covert agents didn't get any, but she never did. *Ohmygod,* the man kissed like a dream.

"Mm," he said after a bit, leaning back to check the time on his comm. "Damn."

Her heart did a little dive, because he looked disappointed.

"Too late now. We gotta go. Buckle up, honey."

She'd barely clicked her seat belt closed when he

pulled out of the spot. In the rearview mirror, she could see Stephano's unmoving body on the pavement. The corpse was already losing shape as the body decayed into ash. He took the corner ten miles an hour faster than was safe. She clutched the dash with both hands.

"Relax," he said, changing lanes and braking hard to avoid rear-ending a taxi.

Her seat belt locked. "I don't want to die."

"You won't. I'm starving, aren't you?"

"No," she said through gritted teeth.

"Mimouza, here we come."

"I hope we live to get there."

Chapter Three

Mimouza was half a mile into the Lower, the most desolate, lawless part of Crimson City. Only half the streetlights worked, the rest either broken or missing. Trash spilled off the sidewalks onto the streets, and before long the GPS became useless. Whole intersections were blocked by rubble and military surplus blast barriers. Gang tags covered everything still standing and a lot that wasn't. To a height of three stories or more, windows and doors were boarded over or behind a metal grill.

Jaden found parking a block from the restaurant. The *rat-a-tat-tat-tat* of automatic weapon-fire drifted over from the next street. Generators hummed from the upper floors of several buildings, but what light there was from the inhabited buildings didn't make it down to street level. How did anybody live like this? Exhaust and garbage gave the air an acrid scent, and the stench of outdoor sanitation was overpowering. Many of the buildings here were fallen down, decrepit hulks scavenged into nothing.

She and Jaden stood shoulder to shoulder on the

sidewalk looking at his car. "You think it'll be here when we get back?" she asked.

"Milos will get me a new one." He shrugged and armed the antitheft system. "Stay close."

"Just so you know," she said, "if we get mugged, I have a black belt in aikido."

His head whipped to hers. He had on his sunglasses so she couldn't see his eyes, but she could see his smile. The nice one. Covert got night-vision lenses. "You promise to keep me safe, Hell?"

"You betcha." She made a phony karate chop. "Bring on the bad guys."

Jaden stopped walking and pulled her hard against his chest. Next thing she knew, she was kissing him back for all she was worth. "Wow," she said when he stopped. Her toes were still curled. She buried her fingers in his short brown hair, and it was a stretch for her to reach. "Where have you been all my life?"

"Yeah," he said softly, his arms around her. One of his hands drifted to her ass, and his smile was just so sweet. "Wow."

They sidestepped a woman sleeping in a doorway and went into the restaurant. Inside, the décor was arched and pointed doorways, with Byzantine patterns painted on the walls in glossy paint. The ceilings were tented with a pleated white fabric. Brass chandeliers with colored-glass lamps hung from the center of each room, and rugs of various shapes and patterns covered the floor.

Music blasted over the sound system—drums, something oboelike, and a stringed instrument Hell didn't have a name for. She recognized Per and Sybil, seated on pillows, clapping in time to the music, while two dark-haired women belly-danced in a clearing. Elijah Douglas was dancing with both women.

Video did not do him justice. On-screen he was striking, but in person, the charisma of an Alpha wolf was overpowering. His shoulder-length hair was lighter than it looked on film. Jeans hugged muscled thighs and a fantastic butt. He wore a crisp white shirt, and he had the greenest eyes she'd ever seen. The werewolf danced with a nervous energy that suggested he was stronger than he looked. He shimmied close to one of the dancers, as sinuous as his partners.

The maitre d', in an ivory caftan, a brown fez, and a sheathed dagger on a thong around his neck, hurried toward them. He did a double take when he saw Jaden. No wonder. Jaden had that close-to-the-bone look a man got when he was more than fit, the flat belly that made the waist of his black cargo pants hit below his navel. Just now, the icy set to his mouth suited him. His Ray-Bans added to the intentional machismo. He looked scary.

"Welcome to Mimouza," the maitre d' said. He bowed low but glanced over his shoulder at the still dancing Elijah. "This way, please, please."

The werewolf saw her. His gaze slid to Jaden and then back to her before he held out a hand, gesturing for to her to join him and the belly dancers. Hell looked to Jaden for some clue to what he expected her to do. He didn't move. Not a twitch. She shrugged and walked across the rugs.

The music vibrated in her when Elijah clasped her hand and whirled her into the dance. She went in close, her head beating with the drums. Her ears pounded; blood throbbed in her veins. Her balance was off because she fell against Elijah's broad chest. Her head whirled, and she stopped dancing.

Her breath caught in her throat. Someone . . . some-*thing* was pushing her aside, in her head. A presence pulsed inside her, in her body. She shouted, but no sound came out. She moved away, stumbling. The presence went with her, encircled her, drew the area in which she perceived the world into an ever-shrinking circle. Sound blared in her ears, words that made no sense. Feelings that weren't hers rocketed through her. Triumph. Joy.

Helen Marshall. You are mine now.

The floor jumped at her, pulsing until she felt sick to her stomach. How had she fallen without feeling it? She fought whatever was in her head, but it had her clamped down, compressed until all she could do was huddle in a tiny corner of her mind.

Another presence slithered inside her, darker, more dangerous and malevolent than the first. Her head exploded in pain and she screamed in the vortex, a whirling, teetering, ripping away from herself. With a physical rebound that felt like a punch, sound and sensation returned to normal. Except, the darkest presence remained. Her stomach curdled at the taint of evil. She shuddered, a full body shiver. Elijah stood arm's length from her and Hell knew this wasn't the same man she'd seen when they came in. Someone else was looking at her through Elijah's green eyes. The DX, she thought. The DX had him.

"Move!" Jaden yelled. The dark presence in her jumped and goaded her. It hoped for a fight. It wanted to kill and rend and maim. "Now!"

She had control of her limbs again. Hell turned for the door, but not before a flash of light blinded her. Behind them, someone shouted. Jaden pushed her down with a hand to the back of her head. Her knees slammed into the floor hard enough that she felt the concrete underneath the rug. Something sizzled in the air above, and ozone and smoke filled her lungs. Jaden hauled her to her feet, pushing her toward the exit. She kept low and headed for the door.

Outside, he grabbed her around the waist, and with her leaning against him, still reeling from whatever had happened to her in the restaurant, they ran. She was more clearheaded by the minute. Across the street where he'd parked was nothing but empty space. An animal howled inside Mimouza. The front window exploded outward in a spray of glass and splintered wood.

They took off running. Streetlights dimmed and went out. A transformer popped, and she smelled smoke and burnt wires. Far away, she heard an explosion and sirens. Two blocks from the restaurant, the city was lit only by the moon.

Hell glanced over her shoulder and saw six men loping down the street, gaining on them with chilling speed. Male werewolves, she realized, still in human form. There were werewolves after them, and they were in the Lower, where the Cazadores carefully regulated illegal hunting. Three of them split off to the opposite side of the thoroughfare. More charged into the street, racing ahead. Werewolves were now in front of them and behind. The few people on the street scattered, giving her, Jaden, and the dogs sole possession of the sidewalk. The streets rang with slamming doors of alternate exits. There wasn't anywhere to go but deeper into the Lower.

Hell lost sight of the dogs in the shadows, but she could hear them. Sweat trickled down her back and between her breasts as they ran. Her throat was raw and parched, her leg muscles streaked with pain, and her boots were killing her feet. The dogs were driving them to wherever it was the others were waiting. Some dead end where escape would be impossible. Over the pounding of her heart and the thud of Jaden's shoes and hers, she could hear the dogs running.

The sidewalk tilted precariously. Moonlight spilled onto the street, casting enough light so she could avoid the worst of the cracks. Jaden kept a grip on her hand, but she was slowing him down. A werewolf howled when they reached a barricaded corner. Every nerve in her body screamed for her to hide *now*. The dogs had driven them onto a street blocked at one end by the rubble of a brick building with an intact rear wall. At least ten werewolves waited there. To the right, the ruins of several concrete blast barriers barred escape. There wasn't any way out but the way they'd come, and there were six more dogs behind them.

She snatched a broken two-by-four off the ground and swung it in the wolves' direction. "I'm not going down without a fight, you furry little freaks!"

"This way." Jaden grabbed her around the waist and boosted her up the pile of destroyed blast barriers. She dropped her two-by-four in order to jam her fingertips into any available hole and hoist herself over the top. Below, the dogs howled in outrage. Jaden vaulted over the top while she was picking her way down the other side, slowed by a wobbling ledge of concrete and rebar. In the dark, Jaden was a shadow moving down the mound of debris. Her pink top seemed a spectacularly bad fashion choice now. At the bottom, Jaden held out his arms, and she jumped. He caught her like Baryshnikov catching the Sugar Plum Fairy. They sprinted into an empty intersection fled by a group of teenagers who left behind the lingering scent of weed.

Wolves came over the barrier and another rhythm joined the pounding of two feet. Four paws. Another howl split the air and was answered from a distance. Jaden's grip on her hand tightened. He came to a stop

at the next corner, wrenching her down to crouch beside him in the concavity created by the bent metal
grill of a long-closed shop. He reached into the
garbage-filled space behind them and swept an armful
of filth onto the street. Hell covered her mouth and
nose against the stench. Jaden wasn't even breathing
hard. She sounded like a bellows. He slid his back partially over her, pressing her against the grill. He drew
his gun, replaced the clip with another one from near
his waist, and screwed on a silencer.

The question was whether all his covert special teams
secret assassin training at taxpayer expense was enough
to overcome half a pack of pissed-off werewolves.

Chapter Four

The first dog came around the corner fast. It missed the trash but shot past their niche. How Jaden could see in this shadow-shifting darkness, night-vision lenses or not, Hell had no idea. He fired and after a soft *popf* from the gun, the dog went down and didn't move. She smelled blood, sharp and coppery, and pushed backward until the metal grill dug into her back. Jaden accounted for the kickback and held steady while the second wolf charged around the corner. This one hit the trash and slid off balance. Jaden's shot sent the dog reeling against the burned-out wreck of a car. The wolf yelped, bounced off, gathered itself, and leapt. A second shot took it down for good. The body lay in plain sight in the intersection, unmoving once it retransformed to human shape.

Across the street a light hissed and buzzed, flared yellow, and died. The flash shed enough light for Hell to see wolves on the opposite corner.

"Elijah wants the woman," said a raspy voice from the near side of the corner. With one body in plain sight, this dog was more circumspect than the first two. Jaden scanned the area, his attention lingering at the spot where the other wolves had vanished into the dark. Hell was convinced every wavering shadow must be one of the dogs crossing the street, setting up an ambush. The last werewolf pursuer still in human form stepped into view. A shaft of moonlight crossed her face. "I promise you, no tricks."

"Tell Elijah I eat weaklings like him for breakfast." Jaden sounded calm and insanely confident.

"This was not the agreement." The woman threw her head back as if she were in pain. A shudder rippled through her. Hell had never seen a werewolf transformation, and she didn't want to now. Or ever.

"Not my problem," Jaden said.

"It is now." The rasping words melted into a howl.

The hair on the back of Hell's neck prickled. Cartilage, bone, and sinew broke and reshaped, morphing the woman from human to canine with a crackling, wet popping that made Hell's skin crawl. Movement flickered at the corner of her eye. A shadow elongated and became a werewolf slipping into the moonlit street. Another stayed corner-side and a third slunk up the sidewalk where earlier the teenagers had vanished. Yet another dark form leapt onto a wrecked car at the corner. One hind leg went through the rusted roof, but the beast moved forward to where the metal was more stable. The werewolf was at least four feet high at the shoulder with a shaggy coat of fur ruffled there. Across the street, the light flared up again. Overhead electrical wires buzzed and sizzled. Jaden muttered under his breath—a prayer, Hell thought, in some language she didn't recognize. The wolf on the car snarled, exposing sharp canines.

That must have been a signal, because the others attacked at the same time. Things happened fast. Jaden pushed her behind him. A flash of yellow light seared her eyes and she could smell something burning. An animal howled in pain. By the time she could see again Jaden had killed the one nearest the corner. A gray wolf streaked through the air, body extended. It hit Jaden hard, slamming into his gun arm. There was another burst of yellow light. Some kind of modified UV, she thought. The streetlights surged and dimmed, then went out. Electricity arced through the air and shot past her head.

Two more dogs attacked. She heard him break one's neck. The other lunged for him and Jaden's weapon clattered to the sidewalk. She scrabbled on the concrete in the direction she thought the gun had traveled. Behind her, a chilling snarl broke short. She squinted, saw a black mound in the darkness, and stretched out her arm. Her palm landed on the handle of the gun. She grabbed it and whirled in Jaden's direction, afraid he might already be dead.

A human man lay on the sidewalk, his neck bent at an impossible angle. A second man sprawled at the curb, eviscerated. Body low and balanced, Jaden launched himself at her. She looked up in time to see the wolf on the car leaping at her, muzzle open, snarling. Her heart about exploded. No way could she get off a shot in time. She was dead. Dead because she hadn't seen the wolf until it was too late.

Jaden collided with her. The gun flew out of her hand and skittered across the concrete. He rolled with her in his arms when the dog hit them, growling and snapping. She ended up underneath, facedown. Covered by Jaden's body, she gasped for breath. Her ribs hurt from the landing. One of the dog's paws hit the pavement, claws scraping by and just missing her shoulder. She could see the gun now. Jaden rolled off her, and she extended her arm. Her fingers closed around the just-short-of-hot silencer. She grabbed it and whirled. "Head down, head down!"

The werewolf's jaws were inches from Jaden's face, but he had one hand around its throat. He ducked, she put her butt on the sidewalk for stability and pulled the trigger. At a range of three feet, she couldn't miss, and she didn't; the silver-loaded bullet dropped the wolf. She scrambled toward Jaden. He lay prone on the sidewalk, pinned by the dead dog. She used her foot to shove the body off him.

In the darkened street, she bent over him, running her fingers over his still body. He was breathing, thank God, but then panic flooded her. He'd been bitten. Badly. Hot, wet blood, full and coppery to her nose, ran down his left upper arm and covered her fingers. She stripped off her shirt and tied it above the wound. When she was done, she sat on her haunches and gathered herself. He'd been bitten by a werewolf. Surviving the bite wasn't the worry. She rifled through his outer pants pockets until she found the canister every field agent carried. She unwrapped it, popped the seal, and slid out a syringe loaded with an emergency dose of SaniLyco. Werewolf antidote had a twenty-four-hour window of effectiveness, but it was a law of diminishing returns. The further out you got, the higher the chances you'd convert anyway. The probability increased by the minute, not the hour.

Overhead, lights came on with a deafening pop. Except for the electrical buzz, the street was silent. She blinked in the bright light.

"Whoa," she said instead of *Thank God*. Her heart skipped a beat.

Agent Jaden Lightfeather wasn't Jaden Lightfeather anymore. This guy was wearing Jaden's clothes, his sunglasses were on the sidewalk next to him. Blood oozed from his arm, and her tourniquet was still in place. But he had long black hair in a ponytail trapped under his shoulders. His skin was a deeper gold and his face was . . . completely foreign and frighteningly wild. And sublimely beautiful. His eyes opened, and his hand clamped around her wrist. He sat up. Hell reached for the gun with her other hand, but he said something that sounded like gibberish to her and the gun melted. Heat from the remains pulsed like a miniature furnace.

"What are you doing, Hell?"

"Jaden?" But that was absurd. Except for his brown eyes, he didn't look anything like Jaden.

"Yes." His face was delicate, ethereally fierce, if there could be such a thing: slanted cheekbones, a straight nose, a mouth that looked as if it could be gentle but wasn't. His body was as perfect as Jaden's, though. Maybe more so. His ponytail reached at least to the middle of his back, and some sort of metallic silver thread was worked through the two thin braids that held back his hair. He took the syringe from her, but didn't let go of her wrist. "That won't do any good."

"Don't tell me." She could hardly breathe. "You're already a dog."

Agent Lightfeather's smile appeared on the stranger's mouth, and her heart dove a million miles straight down. He bowed his head, and using his injured arm because he was still holding her wrist, he took off his contact lenses and tossed them. When he lifted his head his eyes weren't brown. The light was uncertain, so maybe she was wrong about the color.

They looked pale and more yellow than brown. Amber. His eyes looked like faded amber. She knew those eyes.

"You're the DX."

He shrugged his injured shoulder.

"All this time it was you. Not Elijah."

"So." He picked up his shades and tucked them into a pocket.

Fight or flight. And then there was choice C. Paralyzing fright. Right about now Aunt Lucy's place in Bodega Bay seemed like a really good idea.

He examined his wounded arm. Moving it had restarted the bleeding. "Hurts like a bitch," he said.

"No duh." Out of pure instinct, she checked her tourniquet. His fingers clamped around her wrist radiated heat.

"Setonian bastard," he said. He muttered something else and a penumbra of pale yellow gold appeared over his arm. When it faded, his arm was whole. Except for the now dried blood, there wasn't a mark on him.

"Well," she said. "If I'd known you could do that, I'd have saved my shirt."

His attention lingered on her brassiere. She'd done laundry recently and had on a purple silk underwire designed to improve one's cleavage. Judging by his expression, it was helping. A lot. He untied her ruined shirt from his arm. "Thank you," he said.

"You're welcome." She heard sirens far away but coming closer. Of more concern was that two armed men were heading for their corner. The sirens faded. "Shit."

"I promise I will keep you safe, Hell."

She remembered West's warning about Bak-Faru demons. "Oh, fuck," she said.

"Look at me. *Look,*" he growled. He grabbed her

chin and turned her face to his. Fear shivered down her back when she met his amber eyes. "Hell, I promise I will keep you safe."

She swallowed hard. "If you're a demon, you have to keep that promise, right?"

"Yes." He let go of her and frowned. "We need to get off the street."

She nodded. From the graceful way he got up, you'd never know he'd been torn up by a werewolf. Since he still had a grip on her wrist—guess he didn't trust her—she didn't have much choice but to follow him past the dogs he'd killed and down the street to the shadow of a broken stoop where the smell of garbage scented the air.

While she and Jaden plastered themselves to the side of the stucco building, the two new men, both with large guns strapped to their backs, approached the dead werewolves. Beside her, Jaden felt hot. Burning hot. The men were too far away for her to overhear their conversation, but before long, one of them pulled out a cell phone and made a call. His companion scanned the street, said something, and pointed in their direction. She and Jaden were standing on one of those metal doors that lead to a basement. She slid off and pulled Jaden with her so she could yank on the handle. It creaked but refused to budge. One of the men—clearly Cazadores—heard the noise. The man touched his companion and pointed again. Jaden let go of her wrist to open the door, which he made look as if it didn't weigh a ton and a half. Metal stairs led into gloom.

Jaden went down first, keeping her at his back before he climbed up to pull the door closed. At the bottom again, he said a series of words. Her breath about stopped when she heard the Cazadores on the sidewalk above. One of them had a flashlight because electric light streamed through the crack where the halves of the door didn't meet.

"I told you," one said. "I saw something."

Jaden pushed her to one side and stared up. Metal groaned as the men yanked on the handles. The doors refused to open. "Not down here," said a disembodied voice.

"Oh my God," she whispered when they were gone. "I thought we were dead."

"I would not have allowed them to harm you," Jaden said.

She whipped her head around to his, and she knew the minute their eyes met he meant it. "Yeah," she said softly. "I guess not."

Now that she wasn't praying for a miracle, she took in their surroundings. One of the foundation anchor bolts had sheared off, and there were cracks in all the walls. The smell of dirt and dust overshadowed the decay down here. Fist-sized pieces of mortar and concrete covered the floor. She leaned against the wall, but the rough-finished brick scratched her bare back, so instead, she stood by the stairs, a hand on one of the metal rungs. Jaden stripped off his tattered, bloody T-shirt and stood there like some kind of girl's wet dream. Knowing what he was didn't change the fact that he'd saved her life, and since Hell was terminally addicted to dangerous men, it didn't change the way her body reacted to him, either.

"If you're the DX," she said, "why aren't I dead?"

"I promised to keep you safe."

She clasped her arms over her chest, rubbing her upper arms. "For now. What if later I piss you off?"

It was hard to see, but she thought he smiled. "Try not to."

"Mind telling me what happened back there at Mimouza?" She looked into his real eyes, his real face. She ought to be terrified; but she wasn't. Which didn't mean she could reconcile the killer from the video with the man who'd kissed her like nobody's business, not to mention saved her life three times already. She couldn't. "How about why a Bak-Faru demon is masquerading as an I-Ops covert? Or why you saved my life tonight when you should have been doing your demon-fu on me?"

He kept his distance. Just as well. "Ask Milos Sanders those questions."

She drew her eyebrows together, keeping her arms tight around herself, and not for the warmth. "What does Milos have to do with you?"

Jaden walked toward her, and she backed up until she hit the wall. He couldn't kill her; he'd promised. But that didn't mean she wanted him near her. "Milos Sanders has my true name." His voice sounded different, deeper, rounder, and with an edge of darkness that sent fingers of ice down her spine. "Because of this, he was able to summon me from Orcus."

"Milos did what?"

"For more than a year, he has compelled me to do as he wishes."

"You cannot be serious."

"Among other things, I was compelled to attack Tuan Ng. And to pass as human and deceive you."

She went hollow inside. "Milos is my friend. He'd never do that. And he wouldn't have anything to do with demons." He couldn't be summoning demons. He couldn't be. "How do I know you're not lying?"

"Look at me, Hell." He put a hand under her chin and lifted her face to his. She knew she shouldn't look a demon in the eye. If you weren't careful, you ended up obligated to give away your firstborn child. But this was Jaden, and she didn't want him to be evil. Their eyes locked. "On the subject of what I have done in the Overworld, Helen Marshall, I will tell you the truth. And I will answer the question you mean, not the question you ask."

"There has to be a catch." She was in so far over her head it wasn't funny. She stared at his mouth and tried to figure the angles. "With demons, there's always a catch, everybody knows that. So, you'll tell me the truth—in return for what?"

"Listen to what I say." He stepped back two, maybe three feet from her. "Hear what I ask of you."

Oh, Milos, she thought. *What have you done?* "Deal."

His eyes shifted with color, eddies of pale gold. "Helen Marshall," he said, moving closer again. "It is done."

"Is what you've already told me the truth?"

"Yes."

"What else?" She didn't know whether to cry or curse.

He drew a long breath. "Milos Sanders ordered me to give you to Elijah Douglas."

"Give," she said slowly. "Not take me to."

"Yes."

Hell chewed on her lower lip. From her position, she had a distracting view of his shoulder muscles. You'd think pale eyes would seem washed out or unfinished, but his didn't. The color shifted, as if something deep and mysterious floated beneath the surface. "But you didn't. Why not?"

She caught a glimpse of orange in his eyes, a hot and fiery color that settled back to pale amber. A smile flashed over his face, grim and desperate. She felt cold at the sight. "But I did," he said.

"Explain that."

"The werewolf Elijah is no longer in control of his body or his will. I gave you to the Setonian demon who possesses him, as Milos ordered. You felt him, Hell. He took possession of your will." He put a hand on the wall above her shoulder. A demon. She was inches from a Bak-Faru demon. "I did what Milos commanded, and then I took you away from him." He sneered. "I knew the Setonian was not strong enough to keep you."

"What happens when Milos finds out?"

"He will correct the error of his command."

She swallowed hard. "But why?"

"In return for my true name, Milos promised the Setonian a human female." Jaden put a fingertip to her forehead. Her skin reacted to his heat. "Someone close to him. Someone important. Someone he loves."

"That's crazy," she whispered.

"Milos chose you." He leaned closer to her, and she remembered kissing his soft and tender mouth. Except, she'd thought he was Agent Incredible Hunk. All the time, she'd been kissing a demon. "If Milos does not keep his promise, the Setonian will kill him."

"This gets better and better, doesn't it?" She looked at the ceiling. "So this *wow* between us. Was that all pretend?"

"No." The demon's fingertip moved down her face along with a searing glance, tracing a line from her throat to the tops of her breasts. She could have stopped him. She didn't. When he hesitated, when his eyes asked what he should do next, she didn't pull away. He watched his finger moving over her skin and the shiver of arousal that followed. He fingered the front clasp of her bra. His knuckles brushed against her. Hell's pulse raced, and it wasn't with fear.

"There is one more thing you must understand. I do not care if humans go to war with werewolves or vampires or amongst themselves. My only wish is to be free of Milos Sanders." He popped her bra open, and cool air swept over her. His hand moved in to cover her, to gently hold her. She drew in a breath. Her life was out of control and headed for disaster, but she didn't want him to stop. "I would rather die, Helen Marshall, than remain subject to his will."

The tingle in her spine spread to her belly. He looked into her eyes while his fingertips brushed over her nipple. She was wet, ready for him, in need of him. The malign presence from Mimouza probed around her. "I'm sorry. I'm so sorry he did that to you."

He smiled sadly. She watched the pale shades of color shifting in his eyes, knowing there was something more, something she was missing. "I have promised to keep you safe, but, Hell, what Milos tells me, I must do, even if it means breaking my promise to you."

"Then why did you promise?" Their eyes met, and she felt the malignant shadow of him.

"Milos Sanders is a fool," he whispered. He grabbed her wrists and pinned them above her head with one hand, and then he gazed at what that did to her torso. She felt his presence nudging at her thoughts. "He should have fought for your heart. I would have." Jaden bent his head for a moment, eyes closed. Then looked at her again, and she was struck anew by how fiercely beautiful he was. The knot in her stomach eased. His darkness reached into her and touched her until she quivered with relentless longing.

He cupped her, and she couldn't stop herself. She arched into his hand, and he accepted the offer of her body. He pushed aside the halves of her bra, let his fingertips pluck at her nipples. She moaned softly. In her head, the video of Jaden in the Golden Wing played over and over. He had killed easily and with enjoyment. Did it matter that he was forced when he liked it so much? Did it matter that she liked what he was?

"There is a way for me to keep my promise to you when Milos orders me to give you to the Setonian."

She tried to focus on what he was telling her, but it wasn't easy.

"A demon male bonded with his mate protects her with his life. His mate will always come before any promise. Always. There can be no exception." He lowered his head and kissed her breasts, one, then the other with a soft butterfly lift of her into his mouth, a tongue circling her nipple. He raised his head long enough to say, "Let me bond you to me, Hell, and I will protect you no matter what Milos does."

Her thoughts scattered, and she had to draw them back from what his hands and mouth and the blackness of his energy were doing to her. She liked what she was feeling. Liked it too much. "I thought demons didn't have any choice in their mates."

He let go of her wrists. He stopped touching her, too, and it was all she could do to not pull his head down and demand more. Instead, she let her arms drift down until they landed on his shoulders.

"If you don't," Jaden said in a low voice, "I must do what Milos orders. Even if he tells me to kill you." He dropped his head to kiss the underside of her jaw. She angled her head to give him access. He whispered, "I do not wish to harm you, Hell. Please. Agree, and I will keep you safe." Hands sliding down her sides, he leaned against her. His bare chest brushed hers. "Agree, and I am bound to give my life for you, even before Milos."

"Can you undo it afterward?"

He raised his head. The color of his eyes shifted toward golden red. "No."

She bit her lower lip. She wasn't so far gone that she didn't understand how dangerous he was. "There has to be another way."

He shrugged again. "You are human." His fingers touched her arms and stroked gently. "You are unlikely to feel the bond as a demon female would, and demon females rarely feel the bond as deeply as their mates."

"I'm the kid whose Cracker Jacks didn't have a prize." She worked her fingers around to the back of his neck and then underneath the black silk of his ponytail.

Jaden smiled softly. "I can bond you so it is the same as if you are my vishtau mate." He curled a hand around her waist, sliding his fingers downward.

"Why not just do it?"

"To do that, Hell, I would have to harm you." He touched the ring through her navel, tugging gently. "You must agree."

"You're a demon, Jaden. What happens to me if I do?"

He turned his head to kiss her fingertips. "You would become my heart."

"I felt you. I can feel you now. What you are." She licked her lips. "At Mimouza. I felt what you are, and you are dark and frightening. You felt evil, Jaden." Her hands slid over his torso, over his silken skin, the mus-

CAROLYN JEWEL

cles and sinew of his chest. "I wouldn't convert for Tuan and you're a thousand times more intense. You would overwhelm me. Look at me," she whispered, still touching him. "I can't keep my hands off you. You're beautiful." Her hand slid down to his belly and then lower, over his erection. A growl rumbled in the back of Jaden's throat. "If this is what you do to me now, what happens if I let you bond me? What happens if I feel more for you than I do now?"

He tipped his pelvis back and, his ponytail falling over one shoulder, unfastened his pants. What would he look like with his hair loose? she wondered. She slipped a hand lower on his belly and curled her fingers around his penis. Jaden undid her zipper, pressing against her while he pushed her pants down her legs. She ached for him.

Something heavy landed on the metal doors above them. *Boom-kaboom*. They froze.

"Hell?" called a familiar voice.

She closed her eyes. "Shit. He always had the worst timing. It's Tuan." While she put her clothes to rights, Jaden zipped his pants and rebuckled his belt.

"Don't let him see you like this, Jaden," she said. Jaden morphed to his human form. The transition was smooth and nearly instantaneous. She shook her head. "Somebody in I-Ops is feeding him information. You don't know what he's like. He's smart, Jaden. Chances are he's figured it out already. He shouldn't see you at all. Not in any form."

"I will kill him if necessary."

"Hell?" The metal door started to open.

She grabbed Jaden's arm, and decided she'd gone freaking insane. "Can you do what the Setonian did to Elijah? Possess me? So he wouldn't know you're here?" His eyes widened, and her heart misgave her more than a little when she saw his anticipation. "If you can, do it now."

"I know you're in there, Hell."

Chapter Five

Tuan Ng had never been one to embrace the strata +1 look like most vampires. No Armani or Versace for him. He wore his wealth in subtler ways, like the diamond stud in his ear, or the cars he drove. His hair was rough cut and short enough that it spiked across the top of his head. He liked his enforcers to wear leather, and he'd been known to go out for the night wearing leather himself. Right now, however, he was wearing baggy tan shorts that hit midthigh, a pink and gray bowling shirt, and a pair of leather flip-flops. He was tall for a Vietnamese, five ten, maybe five eleven, and had broad shoulders and smoldering black eyes. Hell had always liked the casual beach look on him.

"What are you doing here, Tuan?" she said to him from the basement floor. Tuan had lifted the doors and streetlight and moonlight poured in. Hell gripped the metal railing of the ladder because otherwise she'd have keeled over from the disorientation of having a second person in her body. This possession stuff was wild. Jaden was inside her, experiencing her consciousness, her emotions, and her sensations and his own, too. She felt the malevolence of his energy vibrate through her.

"Hell. Come up here. We need to talk."

There was a moment of confusion while Jaden adjusted to the different physics of her body, and then she climbed the stairs on wobbly legs. At the top, Tuan leaned a shoulder against the wall and eyed her, pausing at her brassiere-clad torso. She liked it better when Jaden ogled her.

"You look good." Tuan spoke with that Southeast Asian slurring around certain sounds that she really, really liked. Then he smiled and reminded her of all the reasons she'd fallen for him in the first place. He was handsome, of course. He had a twisted sense of humor, and she'd believed for a long time he wasn't hung up on his power.

"Thanks."

"I've missed you."

She crossed her arms over her chest. Jaden, she discovered, had a much different take on the world than she did, and it was bleeding into hers. She'd never assessed Tuan as a rival, but Jaden did. "What are you doing here?"

"The same one-track mind as always, I see." He grinned. "Fabienne told me you were in trouble."

"Nah," she said.

Tuan looked at the blasted-out street and tumble down buildings. He pushed off the wall. "What I heard is some goon had you."

"He's not a goon, Tuan." They'd been an un-item for well over a year. Except for one brief but disastrous backslide, she hadn't seen him for months and she still felt an absurd descent into emotional baggage that ought to be long empty of impact.

"Your goon killed Stephano. And left you alone in

the Lower. The Cazadores could get top dollar for you, Hell, don't you know that? Where is he?"

Oops. There hadn't been time for a cover story. "He left to get help. How about you, Tuan? Are you here to help or gloat?"

The vampire sighed. "The car's there." He jerked a thumb toward the street.

With the lights back on, the block looked worse than before. The Cazadores were gone. So were the werewolf bodies. The buildings across the street were more or less rubble and the ones on this side weren't much better. Other than Fabienne leaning on a Mercedes convertible with a Street Sweeper balanced on her shoulder, there weren't any people. Fabienne bared her fangs at Hell and hissed.

"Lose the attitude, Fabienne," Hell said on the way to the car. She could see the seating arrangements already: Fabienne driving, her and Tuan in the backseat. Arguing. Or worse. She turned around. "Hey, Tuan?"

"What, darling?" he said, opening the rear passenger door for her.

"Let me drive." She stood on the sidewalk, hands on her hips. Jaden seemed to enjoy the sensation. "Come on, Tuan, why not?"

"For you, anything." He nodded at Fabienne, who stepped away from the driver's-side door.

In the car, Hell waited for Jaden to realize he had to move the seat forward before she fastened her seat belt. She gave the belt an extra tug and then Jaden took over. And that was a freaky experience. She felt a black energy buzzing in the back of her head, and then she was, gently, shoved aside. Her world turned into a spectator sport, surround-sound and a 3-D movie on steroids. She was an observer in her own body. And

Jaden relished the control. No, he delighted in it, adored it, embraced it. Wanted more.

"Golden Wing?" she asked. She expected Jaden's voice to come out of her throat, but it was her voice because he'd used her body to speak, rather than his power to vocalize on his own.

"Yes," Tuan said. He opened the passenger-side door and slid in. Fabienne got in the back and pouted about it, too.

Jaden was aware of Fabienne, of her energy and strength, and if not her thoughts, then her mental state, which was angry and sulky. Jaden did not see Fabienne as a threat. He also thought Tuan's enforcer was hot. Both vampires were a near match for his physical strength, but little if any for his power. He believed he could kill either of them. More disturbing than Jaden's sexual attraction to Fabienne—Hell wasn't used to feeling aroused by another woman—was that Jaden had access to her memories of Tuan.

He was not a good lover, Jaden remarked in her head. *I would be much better for you. I'd like to do* that.

Shut up and drive.

Fabienne gave directions, but it wasn't clear to Hell that Jaden needed them. He seemed to have an internal GPS of his own. The minute they left the Lower, the enforcer crossed her arms under her chest, slunk down on the backseat, and didn't say another word. Jaden pulled into traffic on the last second of the yellow. Fabienne shouted.

Jaden blocked Hell's reflexive close of her eyes when he cut off an SUV and merged behind a moving van. He changed lanes again and punched the gas to make another yellow light. Horns blared all around them. Three car lengths from the left turn lane, he went left, jamming on the gas when he saw the light for the cross-traffic turn yellow. He steered the Mercedes into the turn to counter the shimmy at the back. Wheels screeched, and he whipped into the right lane without looking.

At the Golden Wing Jaden pulled into Tuan's spot and shut off the engine. For several seconds, the only sound was the cooling engine and the garage HVAC. The quiet was worth every minute spent praying they weren't going to die in a flaming ball of gasoline and engine parts. Jaden opened the door. "Here we are," Hell said brightly because she knew how much that would piss off Fabienne.

Tuan got out and came around the front of the car to put a hand on Hell's elbow. "Where'd you learn to drive like that?"

Jaden mined her thoughts and said, "Traffic school."

Tuan laughed. "I'd love to see what you'd do with a real car, Hell."

"Do you have one?" Jaden asked the question.

Tuan smiled. "There's the Lamborghini I bought for your birthday last year."

"Oh yeah. Nice wheels."

"It's still yours." He stroked the back of her arm. "I know a private road," he said. "You can get as fast and wild as you want. Come upstairs with me, and I'll get you the keys."

"You!" said Fabienne from the backseat. She put a hand on the top of the door and vaulted onto the pavement next to Hell, the Street Sweeper clutched in her other hand. "You are a fucking maniac!" Fabienne put a hand on Hell's shoulder and pushed. Hell didn't budge. "You shouldn't be allowed anywhere near a car!"

"Tuan likes the way I drive." That sounded way too much like Hell was baiting her. She was surprised Jaden could feel Fabienne's jealousy. It was easy enough to guess, but Jaden felt it. He still thought Fabienne was hot.

"Then he's crazy, too." She whirled on Tuan. "Let her near the Murciélago, boss, and the car is toast, guaranteed."

"We got here, didn't we?" Tuan let go of Hell's elbow and slid his arm around her waist. Tuan knew Fabienne was jealous, too, but he liked it. "Let's go inside, shall we?" When she hesitated, Tuan said, "We need to talk, Hell."

Upstairs, Tuan kicked off his sandals and walked straight into the living room. The furniture was still forest-green leather, two couches, some chairs and an ottoman, glitter gold walls and a bamboo floor. There was a koi pond and a waterfall in a corner. Hell sat on one of the couches and felt like she'd never left. Jaden receded enough to let her take the lead. "Keys?" she said.

Tuan snapped his fingers at Fabienne. The enforcer rolled her eyes, but she left the room long enough to return with two sets of keys. She threw them at Hell, hard enough to hurt if she hadn't had Jaden's reflexes to snatch them out of the air. She stuffed the keys in her pocket. "Thanks."

Fabienne flopped down on the other sofa, splaying out her long, elegant legs. The Street Sweeper lay across her lap. Jaden thought that was especially hot. She had a great rack, and with that observation came an image of Fabienne stretched out on the sofa, naked with her—no, Jaden—caressing her breasts. Was that all men thought about? Hell's stare got a puzzled look from Fabienne.

"Fabienne," said Tuan. "A bottle of tequilla and some limes." On their third date, when Hell wasn't even sure they were dating, they'd come here and between them consumed an entire bottle of tequila and then she'd had the best sex of her life. He didn't bite her. He didn't so much as flash a fang, but the sex was fantastic. The pressure for biting and more didn't come until later.

He still wants to convert you, Jaden said.

I can handle him.

We should go. Now.

What, and leave Fabienne all alone?

"Sure, boss." Tuan's enforcer headed for the kitchen.

Tuan sat next to Hell; close, but not too close. Being around him in her bra and pants was uncomfortable to say the least. She leaned back, and then scooted away under the pretext of rearranging her legs. Tuan noticed, and he frowned. "I hear your meeting with Elijah Douglas went badly."

"How do you know?" Hell replied. She knew better than to look at any vampire, especially Tuan, in the eye, and Tuan knew her well enough to understand her distrust. A chill sped down her spine. The rat fink was trying to establish the mental connection needed to lull her into compliance. Then she'd tell all and do all. Her fear roused Jaden. *It's all right.* "Stop it, Tuan."

"Hell, darling." He didn't try to make direct eye contact again, but he did touch the nape of her neck. "I am well informed. You know that."

"Then you don't need to ask me anything, do you?"

Fabienne returned with the tequila and two shot glasses. "You can go now," he told her.

"I wouldn't recommend it, boss."

Tuan shook his head. "I have personal business with Hell."

Her mouth tightened, but she turned on a heel and left.

"What I don't know," Tuan said softly as Fabienne retreated, "is what happened to Agent Lightfeather. Is he dead?"

"I don't know. I told you, he went to get help." She lifted a hand, palm out, when Tuan handed her a glass. "I'm working tonight, Tuan."

"It's your favorite."

"No, it isn't."

"That's not the way I remember it," he said in that soft voice that always got her into trouble. She did like bad boys. "What are you afraid of?"

"Fine." She took it and put it on the teak coffee table in front of her. The guy always had to be right about what was best. He had to be right about what she thought, right about what she remembered, and right about how she remembered it. Her shoulders tensed up. The waterfall in the koi pond burbled gently. She was better off now, way better off without him.

"We were good together, Hell, you know we were."

She shook her head. "No, we weren't."

Tuan slid close enough to her to touch her bare shoulder. "Yes, we were." She pushed away his arm. Inside her, Jaden rumbled his displeasure. Tuan sighed and left his hand on the top of the sofa. "About Agent Lightfeather."

"What about him?"

"I'm interested in talking to him."

She pretended to be astonished. "No shit?"

"I know what he is, Hell."

She damn near looked at his face. As it was she managed to veer off at the last minute and stare at his ear. "You mean a covert agent?" She laughed, but it was a close call. "Trust me, Fabienne is the only assassin you need."

"You can't lie to me, Hell." He was being polite for

now and staying out of her head. Thank God. "I'll know. I'll always know."

Her back was sticking to the couch, and she leaned away from the contact. Jaden ran hot, and she was uncomfortably warm. She shrugged. "Okay, he's not covert."

"He's the demon who attacked me and killed six of my people."

Her pulse jumped but she kept her body still. "Are you sucking crack-addict blood these days, Tuan?"

"Who do you think gave Milos the video?" He leaned forward. "Damn it, Hell, I watched him do it."

"I saw."

"As soon as Fabienne told me what happened to Stephano I knew who he must be." The room was too close and far too warm. And Tuan was about to leave off being polite.

"Don't," she said, lifting a hand. "Just don't, okay?"

"Did you send him?" Tuan gripped the back of her neck.

The instant he touched her, Jaden put himself in control. Tuan set a hand to her chin and forced her to look at him, but she closed her eyes, willing Jaden to stand down. He didn't. Jaden opened her eyes, and she saw, as a spectator, Tuan's deep black eyes and felt the mental pulse of his connection, and what Tuan met was Jaden, not her. Tuan hissed, exposing his fangs, and leapt halfway across the room. Fabienne came into the room at a run, a Ruger automatic ready to fire.

"No!" Tuan shouted.

Fabienne slid to a stop, eyes on Tuan. "Boss?"

Hell stood up, but under Jaden's power, not hers. Her body felt clumsy because Jaden stood like someone who was much taller than she and whose center of balance was different. He adjusted, and she stopped feeling like she was going to fall over. "I'm fine, Tuan. It's fine, everything's fine. Goddamnit, Jaden!"

"Is that you, Lightfeather?" Tuan asked.

"Yes." God, that felt strange, his answer coming out of her mouth in her voice.

"Is she the one controlling you?"

"No."

"I want a deal," Tuan said.

Hell gasped when she felt Jaden leave her. She'd have fallen if he hadn't kept an arm around her. It was a sickening, disorienting stripping of herself from the inside. Fabienne shouted when Jaden appeared in his demon form. God help her, Hell wanted him back. Fabienne would have fired the Ruger, but Tuan lifted a hand, staring at Jaden.

"It really is you," he said.

Jaden tightened his arm around Hell, keeping her steady. "Go on, Tuan Ng."

Tuan's eyes went flat. All his considerable attention was on Jaden. "I want protection for my people against dogs and humans." He stayed close to Fabienne. "Your services," he said. "At my command."

"Why should I enslave myself to you, vampire?"

"Partnership in the Golden Wing." Tuan smiled. "Forty-nine percent."

Jaden shrugged. "And?"

"Show me where the portal is being built," Tuan continued, "and I'll see you get through whenever you want. As long as another one like you takes your place, ready and willing to do exactly as I say."

Hell's stomach felt like a rock. She didn't like the look on Tuan's face. The fang was too certain of himself. "No," she said. "Jaden, no."

Jaden let out a breath. "For that," he told Tuan, "you must protect Hell with your life." He stared at the vampire. "If she dies or is harmed, I promise I will kill you."

"Jaden, no." She swung around in front of him. "No. Don't do this."

He touched her cheek with the side of his thumb. "This way there is a chance."

"No." Frantic, she put her hands on his chest. If he obligated himself to Tuan, he'd never be free. Ever. Tuan would use him the same way Milos had. "I'll do it," she whispered. "Everything."

"Hell," Tuan said. "Please do not interfere."

She didn't look at him. God, was she crying? She couldn't stand the thought of Jaden enslaved to anyone. She swiped a hand over her cheeks and, damn, they were damp. "Forget the Golden Wing, Jaden. I'll do what you said, plus make you a full partner with me. Marshall and Lightfeather Investigations. Fifty-fifty."

Tuan laughed.

"Everything? Are you certain?" Jaden asked.

"Yes."

He bowed, one fisted hand over the other. "Helen Marshall, it is done." He kissed her, and she melted against him. His arm snaked around her waist.

"Hell?" Tuan said. His eyes glittered, but Fabienne rested a warning hand on his arm. "It isn't over between us," he said.

"Yeah," she said, slipping her hand in Jaden's. "It is." For the first time in her life, Hell walked away from Tuan Ng without a shred of regret, and it felt good. Really good.

In the garage, Jaden put a hand on the hood of her silver Lamborghini Murciélago like he'd found paradise. He opened the driver's-side door and slid in. He adjusted the seat all the way back. A grin on his face, he leaned over and popped up the passenger-side door.

When she had her seat belt secured, she looked at him and took a deep breath. She was going to do this. She really was. "My place or yours?"

Chapter Six

"You said you were a slob." Hell stood in a living room without a stick of furniture. The walls were bare. No pictures. No artwork. No curtains. The floor was hardwood with no rugs. No nothing. There was a ceiling light, but the bulb was out because nothing happened when she flipped the switch.

"I am." Jaden walked across the room. Hell stared at his back, unsettled by the shiver of pleasure she got from looking at him. Midnight hair spilled down his naked torso, thick and glossy. He wasn't taller or more muscular, but he felt menacingly bigger than in his human form. Part of her liked the danger. A lot. He disappeared through an open door. A light went on in another room.

"No, see, in order to qualify as a slob, you have to have stuff you fail to put away." She stared at the empty room. "I don't think you have any stuff." He lived in a high-rise with a spectacular view of the city. Not quite the same as looking down from the vampire level of Strata +1, but impressive all the same.

"Come, Hell," he called from the other room.

The clack of her square-heeled boots echoed across the floor. A light was on in an open area that formed a nexus between the kitchen, a small bedroom or office, and the master bedroom. Jaden had just tossed the car keys on the floor. The kitchen was immaculate.

"Don't you have any furniture?" A flight of butterflies took wing in her stomach. Was she really going to do this? Bind herself to a Bak-Faru demon? He seemed so matter-of-fact. Like it was no big deal, what she was going to let him do. Maybe for him it wasn't. For her, it would change her life.

He held out a hand, pale amber eyes fixed on her. "I have a bed."

Yes, she was going to do for Jaden what she'd refused Tuan. She put her hand in his, and he led her to his bedroom. Her throat went dry as Death Valley in midsummer. He turned on the light. For a heartbeat, she thought the room looked onto a desert under a crimson moon, but it was a landscape painted on the entire far wall. Pillows by the dozen, all in brilliant jeweled tones, lay on the floor next to the mural. A cobalt-blue bowl was nearby on the floor. The other walls were stark white. She said, "You don't have a bed."

He wrapped his arms around her and dropped a lingering kiss on her shoulder. "Yes, I do."

"That's a pile of pillows, not a bed."

Jaden let go of her and walked to the pillows. "This is where I sleep; therefore, it is my bed." He bent to unlace his boots and take them off. She shrugged and took off her shoes and socks, too. The heat of his smile about combusted her right then and there. "Come here."

When she did, he put his hands on her shoulders and leaned toward her. The air smelled clean and sharp. A faint scent reminded her of sandalwood, but she couldn't tell if the odor came from the pillows or something else. He was close enough for her to see his eyelashes were black as soot. A tingle spread outward from her spine. He had the most incredible eyes she'd ever seen. She wasn't doing this for his eyes, she reminded herself; she was doing it because no one deserved to be enslaved.

He knelt at the side of the bed. As he did, his hands slid down her body, leaving heat in their wake. He reached for her hand and tugged. "Sit."

She lowered herself to the pillows, nerves fluttering at the edge of panic. Jaden touched her cheek at the inside corner of her eye. "I understand you do not want this." He traced a line beneath her eye, then spread his fingers over her cheek. "I will be a good mate for you." His voice caressed her ears. "You will be safe with me, *tes*." At her puzzled expression, he smiled. "*Tes* is what a demon male calls his beloved."

"Let's get this over with, okay?"

He reached behind his neck and untied his ponytail. Long, black-as-midnight hair fell past his shoulders. Silver threads glittered in both braids. Seeing him with his hair loose felt shocking and more intimate than if he were nude. His cheekbones looked even more angled, his mouth soft, and Hell couldn't help the reaction of her body. He drew a short dagger from a sheath fastened to his belt. "Your arm."

She eyed the knife. "Will this hurt?"

"A little." Facing her, he tucked her wrist between his side and his upper arm. Their eyes met again and she swore she could feel the mental pulse of him. "Thank you, Hell. For my freedom."

"Do it. Before I lose my nerve." She rose up on her knees to relieve the pressure on her shoulder and turned her head so she couldn't see her arm or the knife. "I'm a wimp when it comes to pain."

"There are words you must say." Hell was grateful for his matter-of-fact voice. "I will give them to you at the proper time."

He began to chant, a low sound that threatened at every moment to make sense, but never did. The words gathered around them, pushing at the heated air, pressing in on them. She flinched when he made a cut in a vein at the inside of her elbow, a quick, sure slice. Pain blossomed and then evaporated. She looked despite her queasiness. Blood welled and ran along the crease in her elbow to land in the cobalt bowl he'd set beneath her arm. He released her and fisted his hand. With the other, he nicked his arm in the same fashion and collected his blood in the bowl.

His chant was in her head again, beating in time with her heart. Picking up the bowl, he tipped it over the cut in his arm. Bright droplets hit his skin and flowed toward the wound, and all the while he was chanting nonsense words. His body radiated heat. The air around them glowed amber. Her head throbbed, and a presence curled inside her. He stretched out her arm again and held the bowl over her cut. "Say these words, Helen Marshall."

Blood dripped onto her when, with his help, she repeated the sounds. Her skin sizzled and a trickle of warmth entered her arm and flowed into her. She stared at his face, watching his mouth move as the trickle heated and thickened. The shadow coalesced inside her and became an awareness that wasn't her. She swayed. That dark presence was Jaden. She knew what he was. And everyone who'd ever said *they're not like us* didn't understand the half of it.

He let go of her arm and reached for one of the tiny braids at his temple. Hell took a breath and tried to find some place in her where Jaden was not. Her lungs wouldn't expand, and she wondered if she would suffocate. Fear uncurled in her belly. Jaden touched her chin, lifting her face so she looked into his glowing amber eyes. Her panic receded, and she could breathe again. He separated one of the silver strands from his braid. With a low, dark word, the material changed in his hands, becoming a small braided circle that did not quite close. Smiling, he pushed her back against the pillows and replaced the ring in her belly button with the one he'd just made. Another word preceded a flash of amber light. She gasped at the sensation of heat through her piercing, a sharp burst of fire. He tugged once on the ring and whispered, "It is done, Helen Marshall."

She couldn't tell if he was whispering in her ear or whether his words had worked their way inside her head. The sensation of his being inside her hadn't stopped but was settling down, working through her and twining with her being. He'd said he didn't think she would feel much of the bond, but he was wrong. Her awareness of him was physically and mentally visceral. There was a blackness to her sense of him that came from him having the sort of power that made his world one with few limitations. The reality of what he'd done took her breath. He'd entrusted her with his life. For as long as they lived, there would be no other women for him. *Wow.*

"You are mine now, Hell," he whispered. He touched his lips to her forehead, and desire roared through her, overwhelming and uncontrollable— emotions foreign to her: his bitter satisfaction at having taken the one action that could see him free, resignation that the solution was permanent, remorse that he had acted, and the conviction that his predicament had given him no choice but to tie himself forever to a human. And there was his desire for her. Her, and no one else. He'd known all along it would be like that for him.

She put her hands on either side of his face, tears burning behind her eyes because if not for Milos, he would never have done this. "I'm sorry, Jaden."

He pulled back to stare at her, and as he did, his black hair brushed the backs of her hands. "You have no need to feel sorry."

"I still am," she said.

"But I am not. Not now." He spread his fingers over her belly. Her skin shivered, a delicious sexual charge. "Are you all right?"

"I think so." She reached for the ring he'd put in her navel and met his fingers, still splayed over her belly. "What is this?"

"A gift. A mark every Bak-Faru male gives his mate." He ran his fingers through her hair. "It is more usual to put this in a mate's hair, *tes,* but yours is too short."

"Too bad."

He laughed and stroked a finger across her forehead. "You will always feel me, but with this—" He touched the ring, and she bowed off the pillows with the flood of sensation through her. His feelings, his desire, his darkness. "You will know me and be able to touch me as I touch you."

She sat up and was immediately woozy.

"If you need my strength, Hell, use it." He reclined on the pillows and put his palm on her back, a warm and solid contact. Her dizziness lessened.

She turned around, looking down at him, and found

his eyes wandering her body. Not even Tuan had
looked at her like that, as if she were the most beautiful woman he'd ever seen. "What if you need mine?"

"I could use it." His palm continued sliding over her
skin. He placed her on the pillows next to him. He
leaned over her, his hair a veil of black. His body lowered over hers, and he kissed her gently, tenderly, as if
afraid of hurting her, as if she were the most precious
thing in the world. One hand moved from her belly to
the waist of her pants. Her breath hitched. They'd
talked about her being his mate, and she'd realized
that must encompass a sexual relationship, but she
hadn't equated that with his wanting her like this. It
scared her, the depth of his feelings.

The thing was, she'd wanted him long before this.
Her desire wasn't anything new. He was dark, she felt
his otherness, qualities she happened to like in a man,
and now he was driving her out of her mind with longing. He wasn't just in contact with her body, either. His
mind and his will, the dark and maleficent essence of
him, was inside her, feeding her and taking her inex-
orably toward pleasure.

He slid down her zipper. One tug, and her pants
were halfway off. His fingers brushed her bare skin on
the way down her legs and again on the way back, a
slow, languorous upward caress. The entire time he
was doing that, he kissed her, and his mouth was soft
and gentle. This wasn't like before when they'd been
headed for sex, back there in Lower. This time, he was
going to make love to her. Jaden, a Bak-Faru demon,
darkest of the dark demons, was going to put his body
inside hers, and she was going to welcome him.

Jaden hooked a finger in the waist of her panties.
Her white cotton low-rider briefs went sailing off to
wherever her pants went, and Jaden touched her there,

a gentle brush, an electrifying flick. Her breath came in ragged huffs. She was trying to catch up to what had just happened to her, but sensations she didn't understand flooded her, thoughts that weren't hers, alien feelings that caught her up; and then there was his skin, hot beneath her fingers, the scent of him, something dark and mysterious and beyond arousing. His fingers curved around her hips and his chest slid along her skin, his thigh brushed her legs. With nimble hands, he unhooked her bra. She watched his eyelids flutter closed while he touched her. His mouth was hot on her breast, her shoulder, her belly, and then between her legs, his tongue slow, the pressure almost unbearable. She tangled her fingers in his hair, urging him on. With Tuan, she'd never been able to entirely lose her restraint, but with Jaden, she had no restraint at all. She shattered within moments.

His mouth came off her to be replaced by his fingers, and a moment later his arm went around her waist, moving her farther up the mound of pillows. His body followed. Black hair fell around her, onto her shoulders and against her cheeks. "Beautiful," he said, but once again, she didn't know if he'd spoken out loud or in her head. "You're beautiful, Hell."

He rolled to one side and worked at his pants. Golden-bronze skin stretched over muscle, and she felt weak when she saw his naked body. She put a hand to his chest, and he stilled while she touched him. Inside, she quivered with desire. Heat centered in her belly and between her legs. His body was perfect for her; everything about him aroused her. His penis was erect, and she was dying to touch him there, dying to have that inside her.

As if he'd read her mind, and maybe he had, Jaden pulled himself over her, naked, his fevered skin sliding over hers like warm silk. "Beautiful Hell, you're the first," he said.

Her heart did a jitter step. "What?"

"I have never mated with a human female." He kept one hand propped on the pillows while the other slithered down her side to her hip and then to the back of her thigh, lifting her leg so he was cradled closer to her body. "I have heard many things about human women." His penis strained against her belly, and she pressed against him. Jaden's mouth curved in a whole new smile. "I have heard you are cold inside and that because you are small, a demon male feels more pleasure. That you like to ride a male without mercy, and I have heard that your tongues are deformed so you are able to drive a male out of his wits with pleasure. Can your tongue do that?"

"Uh, I could try."

His smile turned wickeder yet. "I have heard that because human men are weak and cannot change their form to please their females, human women are eager to mate with a Bak-Faru demon."

She threw her arms around him and pulled him close. "Jaden, what are you waiting for?"

"You," he said. "Only you." He adjusted his pelvis and slid inside with a groan of pleasure rumbling in the back of his throat. Just like that, her world changed. He was inside her body. Jaden was inside her, moving, touching, his body sliding against hers, his hair so dark around his face his eyes looked like fire. He was hard and stretching her. He slowed, waiting for her body to adjust. She arched against him, needing to take as much of him inside her as she could. Their connection stopped time. A growl rose in his throat, an unhuman sound that thrummed between her ears. He put his weight on his palms and pushed his shoulders up and his hips inward and forward.

He was as much inside her head as he was inside her body. She found a world expanded into heat and emotion. She could feel his magic, could practically touch the malevolent source. He drew her into him, his emotions, the cresting urgent instinct to mate, and she met him without reservation. He was inside her head, sharp blackness in a maelstrom of darkness and heat, and he was feeding her his reactions, taking more and more control of her body because he needed the dominant role. He was holding back because he was afraid of hurting her when, in fact, he wanted rougher sex and more control.

"You're not hurting me," she said. And he wasn't. Her mouth traveled down his throat to his shoulder, and she bit him. He growled. The rhythm of their love-making increased; the edge of Jaden's need to dominate rolled through her. She responded to the rawness. Moments before she would have come again, he pulled out of her and turned her onto her stomach. One of his hands slid around her stomach to her belly button to tug gently on her navel ring as he entered her. Hell's body went taut. He cupped her hips. He knew she wanted to touch him, to explore his body, but he denied her because he had no intention of allowing his first mating with her to be anything other than what his nature demanded from them both.

He fed her images of her pale spine and the fit of her backside to his pelvis, his hands holding her hips. He gave her the coolness of her skin under his palms, the slick pressure of her around his cock, the tightness of his balls. She was cooler than a demon female, and he found that arousing. She felt different to him, physically and mentally. Foreign and exotic, and he liked that, too. His belly was hot against her backside, his penis sliding in hard. She felt a shift in the distribution of his weight, the scrape of his skin against hers.

"The Bak-Faru are shape shifters," he said into her head. He propped his weight on one hand, and through half-open eyes, through a mind drugged with arousal, she saw a hand that wasn't human. He leaned back on his haunches, taking her with him, one arm tight around her waist. An unhuman hand traveled the length of her thigh while his hot breath scoured the back of her neck. He'd made his penis thicker and his body gave off enough heat that her skin was soon covered in a layer of reactive sweat. She was beyond any edge she'd ever thought existed. Jaden turned her to face him again, settling her against the pillows. He'd taken a monstrous shape, an unwordly, snouted, be-clawed creature. She held out her arms. The beast morphed into the form she knew as Jaden, her beautiful, bronze-skinned, black-haired demon.

Jaden took her in his arms again, and she embraced him. He came inside her and growled, and she convulsed around him. She felt him take her orgasm and ride it, pushing her beyond anything she'd ever experienced, and then he joined her, his climax roaring through her until she fell at last into the malevolent embrace of his mind.

After a while, he said softly, "Are you sorry to be bound to me?"

"No." And it was the truth. She wasn't sorry.

"Another time," he said, keeping her in his embrace, "another time you will do with me what you will."

She rolled onto her stomach and rested a hand on his belly. "Is that a promise?"

"Always." He kissed her again, and she was ready to

start all over, but he sighed and pushed himself upright. Her heart fell because she knew what he was going to say before he said it. "It's time to find Milos, Hell."

"Give me your comm, Jaden. Or a cell, if you have one. We're not going to meet him without some backup." When he gave it to her, she punched numbers on the comm. "West?" she said when he picked up on the other end. "Hell calling."

Chapter Seven

The offices of Marshall Investigations—make that Marshall and Lightfeather Investigations—consisted of a rented room in a cruddy upstairs space she shared with palm reader and seer Madam Lakisha. An insurance agent had another office and a conversion counselor who seemed to lose more clients than he saved these days took the third. They shared the restroom and a windowless conference room/seance parlor, which was where she and Jaden were when Milos walked in with Elijah Douglas. Jaden, in human form, was leaning against the wall, arms crossed over his chest. He had on a fresh shirt and his Ray-Bans in order to hide his eyes.

Hell wore one of Jaden's black T-shirts and sweat dampened the back. She felt Jaden's presence. He was part of her now, and she was a little freaked to realize that wasn't going to change. Ever. Her pulse kicked into double time when Elijah and Milos sat at the battered table. Hell tried to figure out how to tell if Elijah was possessed, but she couldn't. Not from looking at him. She tipped her chin toward the werewolf. "What's he doing here?" she asked Milos.

"He . . . contacted me after that unfortunate incident at Mimouza." Milos had dark circles under his eyes, and the lines at the corners of his eyes and mouth seemed deeper than she remembered. But maybe that was the lighting: a cheap, underwattage chandelier for evenings when the conference room hosted a seance. His attention fixed on Jaden. "I don't know if I can save your deal, Hell," he said. "This hasn't gone as planned."

"You have Elijah. And you know I can get you Tuan Ng. Let's start talking." She reached for the pitcher of water and poured a glass. Her hands shook. Milos must be feeling pretty confident because he hadn't done even a cursory sweep for bugs. He should have. In the back of her head, Jaden was a presence, a constant awareness. His hatred for Milos was dark and edged with fire. She felt, too, the compulsion Milos had over Jaden and Jaden's resentment. She shared his outrage. "Water, Milos?"

"No, thank you."

She avoided looking into the werewolf's eyes. "Mr. Douglas?"

The werewolf shook his head. His body stayed in motion, a finger tapping the top of his thigh, a foot shifting on the floor, never still for a moment. Like Milos's, his attention was on Jaden. The room felt like it was going to combust.

"You will do nothing to interfere, Jaden," Milos said.

Jaden's hatred burned in her head. Hell leaned toward Milos. No more pretending. "Why not?" she asked. "Say, want to know what I found out about the DX? Oh, but here's a better question. Why'd you sell me out? I trusted you, and all the time you were handing me over to a demon."

"So that's how it is," Milos said after a quick glance at Jaden.

"That's how it is." She knew Milos wasn't sure which demon she meant—Jaden or the Setonian.

He shook his head. "Humans aren't at the top of the food chain anymore. If we're going to survive, we need allies who can protect us, and they aren't dogs or fangs."

A few scattered pieces clicked into place. "What have you done?"

"We're giving them the Lower, Hell." He smoothed his hair. "As soon as we get the portal working, and trust me, we will, we'll have enough demons to pull this off. They get their own playground up here, and in return, they protect us humans from the dogs, fangs, and rogues. It's practically a done deal."

"Are you crazy?"

Milos threw up his hands. "We lost control of the Lower years ago. Look at them. They live like animals. It's anarchy. If we don't do something, the whole damn city will be in chaos and the only people left will be prey for the monsters. Why not let the demons have the Lower while the rest of us save what we can of Crimson City?"

"Sounds great," she said. "Unless you happen to live in the Lower."

Milos slicked back his hair, then reached for the water. "There's always collateral damage."

"That what I am? Collateral damage?"

Milos stared at his hands. Perspiration trickled down his temples. "They wanted a gesture of good faith before we negotiate in earnest."

"In other words, me."

He bit his lower lip. "We can't let them run loose, not without a solid contract. I'm sorry, Hell. You don't know how sorry I am, but it had to be someone I care about. Someone I loved." He looked at Elijah and trembled. "For God's sake, this is killing me! Fucking take her, will you?"

For once, Elijah went still. "No," he said. Within the single word, the werewolf's voice shifted from smooth to rough. His head jerked, then stilled.

Milos paled. "She's there. All yours, Elijah. I've wanted her for years. Years! You know it's the truth." His voice broke. "She's exactly what I promised."

Elijah shook his head.

Milos drew his sidearm. The click of the safety going off sounded like an explosion. "I'm sorry, Hell," he said. He pointed the weapon at her forehead, aim steady. "We need to seal this deal, or there won't be any such thing as humanity."

She felt energy gathering in Jaden. He was still compelled to do nothing, but his obligation to protect her built to an unbearable pitch. "You're insane, Milos."

"Hell, get your ass over there or I'll shoot you. I swear I will." He smiled. "I doubt Elijah wants to kill you. Not right away. I wouldn't if I were him." His voice lowered. "But if he does, isn't it worth it to save the rest of us? Now move! Jaden. Get her over there."

Jaden morphed to his demon form and stepped in front of her. His refusal to do as Milos ordered was tearing him apart. With a shock that wrenched her soul, Hell realized Jaden had known this would happen. He expected to die.

"Get out of the way, Jaden," Milos shouted. "Do you hear me? What the fuck do you think you're doing?"

Energy boiled in him, malefic and searing hot. If she

didn't do something, this was going to kill him. She reached for their link, and it was like turning a faucet from a trickle to full blast. The air around him started to glow.

"Take her!" Milos cried.

"The Bak-Faru has bound her to him." Elijah twitched again and Hell wondered if that meant the demon was having trouble controlling the werewolf. It was, after all, a full moon. "He will not allow me to take his mate without killing him first."

"Bullshit!" Milos shouted. "He isn't going to interfere. He can't. I told him he can't." His attention shot to Jaden. "Whatever the fuck you did, undo it. Now! Or I'll kill you. And then it will be my pleasure to hand her over."

"You will not harm her, Milos Sanders."

Milos pulled the trigger just as Hell pushed every ounce of herself into Jaden. The surge of power from her to Jaden knocked her to her knees.

The bullets melted in the air, raining down like metallic hail.

Amber light boomed through the room, blowing Elijah off his chair. Milos tumbled backward, knocking over a chair. The pitcher of water exploded in a hiss of steam. Milos ejected his empty clip and scrambled for another. He shrieked as the gun melted in his hand, and he dropped to his knees, screaming. Hell felt the drain on her energy, but she refused to stop. The flow remained a torrent.

With a smile of malign joy curving his mouth, Jaden whirled on the wolf. His ponytail arced through the air. He uttered a single word, and something foul gathered in him and shot toward the dog. Elijah convulsed and hit the wall, mouth open in a howl that shattered the air. The dog slid to the floor. A second shape appeared, standing on werewolf's feet. In a blink, the form became the physical manifestation of the Setonian demon. From head to toe, the demon was the color of new blood; hair, eyebrows, skin and even his eyes were crimson.

"You cannot survive," the Setonian told Jaden. "Your female will be mine."

On the floor, Elijah's body twitched. A wet, crackling sound rippled through the room. Cold fear rushed through her, but she continued to push herself into Jaden, letting him draw on her reserves. He couldn't die. She would not allow it. Elijah's transformation completed. Less than a foot from where Milos knelt, the werewolf quivered in a four-footed stance, head down, muzzle open, saliva dripping. The dog lunged.

Shit. Jaden remained bound to protect Milos. Sooner or later there wouldn't be anything more of her for Jaden to draw on, and she knew without a doubt that when they reached that point, he would either be killed by the Setonian or Milos or the strain of his competing promises would end his life. She launched herself at the other demon, toward the embrace of his scarlet arms. Jaden whirled, and the room exploded with amber heat. Milos screamed. Only once. When she opened her eyes, all that remained of the Setonian was reeking ash, and Elijah, in werewolf form, stood over Milos's unmoving body.

"Goddamn!" Jim West stood in the doorway, gun drawn. His eyes were wide on the smoking ashes of the Setonian. He swapped out his clip and aimed at the dog as he walked around the room to Milos's body. His eyes shifted between Hell, Milos, Jaden, and the werewolf. "Goddamn fuck me, Hell. I thought you were lying. Milos *was* behind it."

"Uh-huh," she said.

"What the hell did you use on the DX, Light-feather?" West asked, nodding toward the ashes. Hell didn't correct his conclusion that the Setonian was the DX.

Agent Jaden Lightfeather smiled. "Classified."

A shudder went through the werewolf. Hell closed her eyes when she heard the first wet *pop*. Elijah as a wolf was terrifying. Elijah as a fully clothed human was impressive. Elijah as a naked human was a plain uncomfortable sight. She stared at the werewolf's bare feet, splattered with red droplets. With a nod at Jaden, Elijah said, "I owe you. You ever need help, you let me know."

West pressed two fingers to Milos's neck. "Shit." He hit his comm and called for a cleanup team. When he'd given their location, he put his back to the wall and slid down, gun arm balanced on his upraised knee. "For the next five minutes, I don't see anything. Anybody here when I get up takes the blame for this whole fucked-up night."

Elijah wasted no time. But on her way out with Jaden, Hell paused at the door. "Thanks, West. Maybe you're okay. For an asshole."

Hands clasped behind his neck, West stared at the floor. "Get out of here, Hell."

She grabbed Jaden's hand, and they headed for the street and her Murciélago. As she and Jaden approached the car, she stopped him with a hand to his arm. She pushed his chest, but he didn't budge. "What?" he said.

"You're stuck with me now, you know."

"Yes."

"So, don't you ever try to die like that again." She

ruined her big scene by breaking out in a sob. "I don't think I could live if anything happened to you."

Jaden pulled her into his arms and kissed the top of her head. "Hell. *Tes.* You are my heart." She put her arms around him and held him close. He growled. "My place," he said in a thick voice, "or yours?"

"Mine." She swiped at her nose. "Because I have furniture." But once they were in the car, Jaden kept his hand on the ignition. "What?" Hell asked.

He looked at her, and said, "How about we go someplace else?"

Hell stared back at him and thought of Bodega Bay and Aunt Lucy's empty house and a sky full of stars. She remembered the mural in his apartment, with its dark, open sky. "Like where?"

"I don't know." He shrugged, but she knew he wasn't feeling as casual as that. "Someplace far away."

"Someplace we can see the stars at night."

"Yeah. Someplace like that."

"Is four hundred and fifty miles north far enough?"

Jaden grinned. "Let's find out."

She said, "I've heard this place is so pretty, we might not want to come back."

"Sounds perfect to me."

And Hell screamed as Jaden hit the gas and her Lamborghini Murcielago shot into traffic amid a screech of brakes and blaring horns.

My thanks to the Crimson City team and especially to Liz for her wonderful vision. But special thanks go to Jackson and Baxter. If I hadn't spent nights frolicking with you, I could never have written this story, you two hairy macho hunks of doggie luv muffins!

YES! ☐

Sign me up for the **Historical Romance Book Club** and send my THREE FREE BOOKS! If I choose to stay in the club, I will pay only $13.50* each month, a savings of $6.47!

YES! ☐

Sign me up for the **Love Spell Book Club** and send my TWO FREE BOOKS! If I choose to stay in the club, I will pay only $8.50* each month, a savings of $5.48!

NAME: _____

ADDRESS: _____

_____

TELEPHONE: _____

E-MAIL: _____

☐ **I WANT TO PAY BY CREDIT CARD.**

☐ VISA   ☐ MasterCard.   ☐ DISCOVER

ACCOUNT #: _____

EXPIRATION DATE: _____

SIGNATURE: _____

Send this card along with $2.00 shipping & handling for each club you wish to join, to:

**Romance Book Clubs
1 Mechanic Street
Norwalk, CT 06850-3431**

Or fax (must include credit card information!) to: 610.995.9274.
You can also sign up online at www.dorchesterpub.com.

*Plus $2.00 for shipping. Offer open to residents of the U.S. and Canada only.
Canadian residents please call 1.800.481.9191 for pricing information.
If under 18, a parent or guardian must sign. Terms, prices and conditions subject to change. Subscription subject
to acceptance. Dorchester Publishing reserves the right to reject any order or cancel any subscription.

JOIN NOW!

School Bites

by
Jade Lee

Chapter One

To a wise man, every day is a new life.

The screams reached her first. Toni Freedman was just putting the chalk swoop into the last letter of her morning inspirational quote when she heard teeny-bopper squeals become alarmed jeers. Within moments a full-out riot of noise crashed into her little special ed classroom on the second floor of Ben Franklin Middle School. She was already running down the stairs when her walkie-talkie sounded "Cafeteria incident" in its garbled, dark tones.

She slowed briefly as she waded through a crowd of lunchroom staff and kids. As she was only five two, many of the onlookers were larger than her, but what she lacked in stature, she made up for in attitude. She was the adult here, the teacher, and the woman trained to take down either of the three boys mixing it up on the floor. Of course, a little backup would be nice, but when had that ever arrived on time? In truth, she was supposed to wait for help. Her training told her to "monitor the situation" until at least two other staff members helped her take control—one for each kid. To hell with training. She wasn't going to sit on her hands while two children were pummeling a third.

As she pushed through the last of the crowd, she mentally categorized the incident. Gang-related: the somebodies against the somebody-elses, spurred on by some girls with affiliation to whatever. The particulars didn't really matter. Here at Crimson City's most challenged middle school—right next to the newly created Wolftown district—violence happened when preteens jockeyed for social position. Add in hormones and post-holiday malaise, and tempers ran hot.

She entered the fray as two black kids took aim at a mixed Latino/black: Victor Somebody—a relocated victim of the recent hurricane down South. The lunchroom teachers were doing their best to clear the room, but like her, they were vastly outnumbered. And everyone—including herself—had been trained to *not* step into the middle of a fight. It was just too dangerous, especially in vamp, werewolf—and recently, demon-infested—Crimson City.

She blocked a blow from the nearest kid, only to watch as the big one—Kumars Gray, aka hoodlum trash—planted a fist in Vic's face. Blood spurted from Vic's nose, and he howled in pain as the impact knocked him onto his butt. Toni lunged forward, body-checking Kumars before he could draw back for another blow. Ugh, was Kumars wearing body armor or something? It was like ramming into a solid wall, and no way could that pudgy body be that solid.

She bounced off Kumars, but still managed to throw off his attack. He stumbled backward with a whoosh of Cheeto-laced breath—yuck!—and caught a flash of commando-like body armor beneath his tee. Great.

Hoodlums with body armor. Just what was called for in middle school.

Kumars's cohort was moving in. Toni could tell from his angle that he was getting ready to kick, and she pivoted, trying to block the blow. She already knew she was too late, but hope springs eternal in a fight. She saw the kick land on . . . nothing.

Vic wasn't there. He'd leapt up from the floor with an unholy roar. Thankfully, she was already in position to block him from the others. So long as she kept herself between Vic and the thugs, things would de-escalate. She took a knee in the belly, but had been braced for that. Same for the blow to her shoulder. At least she was larger than little Vic and he didn't have any armor on. Plus he was off balance, so she could press him back down onto the floor, pinning him on his back with all her slight weight. It was safest for everyone if she kept her body on top of his because Kumars and company wouldn't hit her.

Vic didn't understand that, of course. All he knew was that someone else was flattening him, and the kid released another bellow—damn, he was noisy—while he squirmed like the very devil beneath her. Out of the corner of her eye, Toni saw her backup arrive, quickly restraining Kumars and his buddy.

"Calm down!" she grunted. Vic was just slippery enough to throw her off, and . . .

She felt the sharp pain of a bite on her arm. Her reaction was automatic. The only way to break a bite was to shove your arm deeper into the kid's mouth. It forced his jaw open enough to break free. Except, damn, this kid's mouth was big.

Only then did she realize that his body felt longer than before, leaner and hairier. She turned to look at

Vic's face, her heart dropping straight into her stomach. Aw, hell.

Werewolf. And her arm was dripping blood from his bite.

Toni's nose twitched as the nearly overpowering scent of garlic permeated the school nurse's office. It came from the foul, burning SaniLyco cream that nurse/health teacher Linda was roughly kneading into the bite on her arm. Toni sat as still as possible, having gone through this routine more than once in her career.

"Drink lots of fluids," Linda was saying, her pasty-white skin looking especially pale as she worked with the salve. Really, the woman should take an outside shift every now and then—except she and a few other teachers were practically maniacal about taking only indoor hall duty. "Stay out of the moonlight, and make sure someone—"

"Someone with a silver bullet gun sits with me all night. We'll know if I'm converted within twenty-four hours." Toni sighed as she pulled away from the powerfully muscled nurse. "Yeah, I know."

Linda carefully stoppered the SaniLyco tube, then impulsively thrust the entire container at her. "Here, take this. Use it all night long if you need to."

Having already swallowed the pill form, Toni was unsure what more cream would do for her, but she accepted the medicine—and the gesture—for what it was: true concern for a fellow teacher. They both knew that the pill and cream forms of SaniLyco worked less often than the manufacturer reported. There was a higher success rate with injections, but that stuff was military-grade and not distributed to schools like this. She smiled and was about to say something reassuring when a deep male voice interrupted.

"God, that stuff smells awful. You'd think for what it costs, they could give it a nice lemony scent or something."

Toni looked up, strangely mesmerized by the broad-shouldered sight of Principal John Wayne Wong. Yes, his name really was John Wayne Wong, thanks to his Hong Kong immigrant parents who mistakenly believed the name would make their son more American. In truth, his name was the only hokey part of the large-boned, granite-skinned man with dark, intense eyes. Rumor had it that on weekends he rode with a motorcycle gang and went by the name Dread. Toni could believe it. One tended to forget he was supposed to be a baby-faced Chinese amid the overwhelming size of the clearly mixed-race man.

Linda wasn't tongue-tied. She took a deep whiff, then wrinkled her nose. "Most people find the smell reassuring. You know, garlic wards off the evil."

Principal Wong stepped into the room. "That's vamps, not werewolves."

Linda shrugged as she pulled sterile gauze out of a drawer. "Whatever. They're both just infections."

Toni felt her boss's gaze sink to the goo-covered puncture wounds on her arm. "So, did he know?" she asked.

Principal Wong's gaze leapt to her face. "What?"

"Did Vic know he was a werewolf?" Parents were legally required to report potential health hazards like AIDS, vampirism, and lycanthropy, but no one did; the prejudice was just too great. Then again, maybe the family didn't know. Since the inner wolf rarely manifested before adolescence, most parents didn't realize until something set their child off. Something like getting his face pummeled.

"Claims he didn't know a thing," answered Principal

Wong. "Mom, too. Either way, it's B-Ops problem now." B-Ops—the street-level paranormal-watching unit of Crimson City's human government. Wong squatted down in front of her, his focus disconcertingly powerful. "How do you feel?"

"Like I'm going to get really tired of that question." He didn't respond, merely waited in silence for a real answer. "I'm glad I applied for that position in Santa Monica," she finally confessed.

He nodded, understanding mixed with panic in his expression. "Let's not make any major decisions right now, okay?"

Translation: *Please, please don't quit.* SPED teachers were damn hard to come by, and she was one of the best. Given that Ben Franklin Middle School sat right next to a newly created werewolf neighborhood, hiring any teacher was hard. Keeping a good SPED teacher was nigh impossible.

She shook her head, feeling the movement in every single one of her bruises. "Sorry, John. I've stayed this long because you let me run ED how I want. Well, my program works. I've proved that. Now it's time for me to take the show on the road."

He reached out a hand, but stopped short of touching her. "You know the stiffs up north are never going to give you the freedom I do. They'll never support you like I do."

"They'll never leave me alone to take down a werewolf by myself, either."

"Howie and Juan were stopping another incident in the sixth-grade girls' bathroom." He sighed. They both knew that there just wasn't the money to provide enough support. A full B-Ops SWAT team wouldn't be enough protection. "This population needs you," he pressed.

"This population bites me," she retorted. Then she abruptly felt bad for her ill-temper. It wasn't his fault that she might wake up tomorrow morning as a plague-infested outcast. "I think I better go home now." She stood, but moved too fast. The room spun and she banged her wrist as she tottered. But then he was there, holding her still, his large hands gentle where they cupped her arms. She felt his breath feather across her cheek, and she felt . . .

Fire. *Oh. My. God.* Fire like she'd never experienced before. Burning through her blood, roaring through her mind. A chemical heat just beneath her skin that began where he touched her and rapidly whooshed through her entire consciousness. She crumpled, gasping out shock in a desperate need to cool the flame.

"Whoa!" he said, his hands rapidly tightening. She fell against him, her chest against his abs, her face pressed to his pecs. He smelled of some spicy, musky, amazing scent that completely smoked her brain. Her muscles tightened as she fought to regain control, but then her vision began to throb and her mouth began to water. What was happening to her?

"She's having a reaction," Linda was saying. "That SaniLyco stuff can do weird things to the blood." She twisted for her phone. "I'll call for an ambulance."

"No!" Toni gasped. Didn't the nurse know how much an ambulance cost? Even with insurance, it was well outside her price range. "I'm fine. I'm fine." And she was . . . sort of. She was standing, kinda. The fire still raged, but at least it was manageable. If only he didn't smell so damn good.

What?

"I need to get home," she murmured. She shoved a hand in her jeans pocket and pulled out her keys. It was a huge wad of metal plus a silver charm in the shape of an apple that pissed her off for some reason, and she stared at it, a growl building in her throat.

"I think I'll drive," he said. Who said? *He* said. The one who smelled so good.

"What about the after-school program?" the other one asked.

"Kieera can handle it." The man turned back to her. "It'll be okay, Toni. Just try to rest."

Her keys were lifted from her hands, and she made an off-center grab for them. "Give them back!" she growled again.

Meanwhile the human woman was speaking. "Sani-Lyco has side effects. This isn't really unusual, and I did give her a big dose. . . ."

"I'll take her home," the man responded.

Home. She felt herself smile against rippling chest muscles. Home with the good-smelling one would be *very* nice. Then she lost her footing. She gripped his arms with all her strength as the world teetered around her. His chest was moving. Her face was rolling up to his shoulder and neck. She was cuddling close.

He was holding her? He'd picked her up and she was snuggled tightly in his arms. She grinned. *Yes.*

"Still with us?" he asked.

"Home," she purred as he carried her out into the hallway. The class bell rang—a loud clang that cut through her brain and made her whimper—and the hall suddenly erupted into a cacophony of movement and sounds. Normally she loved the business of children, but it was too much. Especially as kids kept touching her or bumping her or assaulting her brain with stuff.

"Look at Miss Freedman! She don't look so good."

"Is she sick? You gonna be sick, Miss Freedman?"

"She going wolf, Mr. Wong? Want me to bullet her for you?"

Toni buried her nose against his throat and closed her eyes. Then he spoke. His voice was a deep rumble that shivered through her body and she flattened her ear tight to his chest just to hear better.

"She'll be fine. It's just a reaction to the SaniLyco. Let me through here, kids. She's not as light as she looks."

She growled at him.

"You taking her home, Mr. Wong? You gonna drive her?"

"She's got a white Honda Civic, Mr. Wong. She parks—"

"I know, Miss Miller. Thank you."

"My word, is that Toni? Will she be all right? Is she a . . . a . . . ?"

"Just the SaniLyco, Georgette. Shows it's doing its job. Nothing to worry about."

And so it continued as he took her down the sixth-grade hallway, past the band room, and out the door—outside!—to the teacher parking lot. She lifted her head, trying to sniff past garbage and exhaust to the green things in the nearby park. Near. So near . . .

But not him. She dropped her head and put her nose right back to his neck. *He* was better than any green thing. Until he ruined it by setting her down.

"I've got to open your car door. Can you stand?"

Of course she could stand. Her legs felt strong and vital. Her feet hit pavement and she pushed against it, straightening herself into . . . well, right back into his chest, which was exactly where she wanted to be.

"How 'bout we just lean back a bit?" he murmured.

She did. But she took him with her. Her arms were

wrapped around his neck and she pulled him close enough to nip at his ear. He yipped in surprise, and she extended her tongue, licking in a long leisurely stroke around and inside that very nice . . .

"Okeydokey *Miss Freedman*. Just try to hold still." His voice sounded tight, but she heard a ripple of pleasure underneath all that sternness, so she did it again.

He jerked away, and she moaned in disappointment. At least he kept one arm wrapped around her hips, holding her steady. She tested her balance, wiggling against the warm pressure of his arm. Shifting slightly. Letting her groin rub—

He hauled the car door open, dislodging her position. She proved she could hold her balance by neatly sidestepping through the door in order to rub herself completely against him: hands to shoulders, chest to chest, knee slipping between his thighs to wiggle—

He grabbed her waist and roughly pushed her backward.

"Hey!" she cried.

"Miss Freedman, please, try to listen to me. You are having a reaction to the SaniLyco. You are not yourself right now."

He might be holding her belly away from him, but her hands could still reach his thick, hard biceps. They could slide over the rather boring sports jacket to snuggle into the amazingly soft refined cotton shirt underneath, burrowing into the heat—

"Toni! Christ!"

She loved the feel of his voice as it rumbled through his chest. There was hair underneath his dress shirt, and she wanted to touch it. She wondered if it was silky or springy, straight or curly. She started to unbutton his shirt, only to have herself abruptly spun around by her hips until she faced the interior of her car.

She arched her back, lifting her tailbone and pressing backward—and hit pay dirt. Thick, hard, it was straining against his trousers. She growled in welcome.

He leaned forward, his arms lifting to surround her as he braced himself against the car door. He was trying to maneuver her inside, but she wasn't having any of it. Especially as she wiggled and arched back harder.

"Toni, *no!*" he said against her neck. "Home. We've got to get you home!" But he didn't move. Then she felt it. The tiniest wet touch—his tongue as he tasted the side of her neck. She began keening deep in her throat.

"*No!*" The word was explosive, but not nearly as rough or angry as his abrupt shove to her knees. She buckled, and her head dropped low enough for her to fold forward into the car; her backside was still lifted, her legs straining in invitation.

His fist shot between her legs, sinking deep into the seat. Then he swept it sideways, probably intending to lift her and settle her into the car. But she had her balance. Better yet, she felt an amazing strength fill her body. Her legs didn't move. Instead, she tightened her thighs around his arm and sat. With his fist caught on the seat, he couldn't move away as she dropped onto his forearm. It was hard and contoured with a special ridge where his fisted thumb lifted and pressed into her.

Hunger rippled through her belly. Her jeans were thin there, but not thin enough. And she twisted her head around to find his neck, opening her mouth, trying hard to find skin—*his* skin. She heard him moan, low and deep, and for a brief, wonderful moment, she felt his fist open, his hand shift, and he cupped her. Large, hot, and so completely embracing—

He lifted her up and roughly deposited her on the seat. Then he ripped himself away, grabbed the seat belt, and strapped her in. She reached for him, but he was relentless. He pulled her knees up and pushed her legs inside the car. Then, as she tried to grab his hands, he shoved them away and slammed the car door.

It wasn't until he'd stalked around the vehicle and gotten in the driver's side that she realized he'd locked her in the backseat. Not that there was a police divider or anything, but still . . . she couldn't even fondle him from back here. Not unless she unbuckled—

He roared the car backward hard enough that her hands flew off the seat belt. If she hadn't been strapped in, her forehead would have been through the windshield. Who knew her little Civic could move that fast? Then he slammed on the brakes, throwing her back against the seat before he shifted the car into gear so hard her head drove deep into the headrest. Deep enough to expose her throat.

She growled in anger.

"Just hold it together," he rumbled from the front. "Just a little while longer. Hold. It. Together." Was he talking to himself?

She closed her eyes, letting the sounds of his fury roll about in her head. She liked his voice, but she liked even more the harsh rasp of his breath. Short huffs, almost like pants. Scent rose from his body like steam, filling the small, closed space of the car. She felt her heart speed up to match his, her heat rising to mix with his. In her mind's eye, everything about them had merged, twined together, fused—*mated*—over and over. Bodies heaving, hips pumping—

The driver's window dropped, blasting the car with exhaust fumes. She gagged on the stench.

"Where do you live?" he demanded. "Toni!"

The car lurched again, hitting the freeway at top acceleration. The air from his open window came hard now, slamming her in the face with a myriad of confusingly sharp scents. She pushed her nose toward the wind thinking it would cool the fire that still roared through her body. It didn't. The air was hot and sticky, and the scents would not blend in her mind. Instead of smelling normal Los Angeles air, she smelled diesel fuel and car exhaust, eucalyptus and hot tar, salt air and burning tacos. And all of it was hot, hot, hot.

She couldn't stand it anymore; she kicked out of her sneakers, annoyed when the laces knotted and she had to reach down and rip them open. Her socks went off next. No way could she get out of her jeans. The best she could manage was to pop the button and lower the zipper. But they weren't coming off her hips. Besides, she couldn't breathe. The blouse and bra had to go.

"What are you doing?" John Wong's panick-stricken voice easily overrode the wind.

"I'm hot," she muttered.

"You're having an allergic reaction. SaniLyco does weird things to the body. It triggers things. It . . ." His words ended on a strangled gasp as she gave up messing with her minuscule blouse buttons and just ripped the whole damn thing open. "For God's sake, Toni, fight it!"

"I'm hot!" she repeated. Then she hauled the ends of her blouse up from beneath her jeans, relishing the rough pull of fabric against her hips. Free! Or nearly free. She struggled against the fabric arms trying to get out of the polished cotton. Why had she ever thought this was *comfortable* clothing?

"Toni! I'm serious. This isn't real!"

She glanced up at him in the front seat, strangely

fascinated by a coarser tuft of hair near his collar intermixed with the silky black strands.

"Do you remember when we first met?" she asked as she tugged down the starched cotton of his collar. Odd, how she'd always thought of him as perfectly neat, every hair in place. And yet right here were these longer black hairs, not so shiny and kinda ragged, right along his collar.

"Don't do that," he snapped as he jerked away from her. But that made him jerk at the wheel, which lurched the car, which created a whole series of swerves and corresponding honks. Toni ignored it all, pleased that she was getting better at managing her balance through it all. What was most important was that his attention was riveted back on the freeway—his body naturally straightening as he fought with the steering—which brought his neck back in reach.

Yeah, she could touch his neck and hair again. Sure enough, he had coarse and fine hairs all mingled together. She pulled back on his collar and peered down his back only to be vaguely disappointed. No hair there. She hauled his shirt sideways trying to see his chest. Surely even Asians had some hair on their chest. Meanwhile she kept talking, her mind and her mouth and her hands all moving in different directions, all at top speed.

"It was at that Meet the New Principal thing. You know, with the horrible Gatorade left over from the year before because Kim couldn't find the lemonade mix? And those really good cookies that were gone in like a second flat because Georgette was such a pig. Then you walked in all big and dark, and we'd been talking about how you transferred from Tomas High because you wanted a bigger challenge and we heard your motorcycle—how many do you have? Hey, lean back. I can't see your chest."

He caught her right hand with a muttered curse, imprisoning her fingers. Fortunately, her other hand was free to roam. Unfortunately, it couldn't quite wrap around far enough to release the lever on the seat, what with him swerving all over the road and everything.

"Hey, let go! My bra itches. I'm gonna take it off."

His grip tightened. "Tell me more about the lemonade," he urged. "Think about that."

"It was lime Gatorade mix, and you drank it like you were really, really thirsty, and I just kept watching your throat bob up and down as you drank and all I could think was, Damn, were you as huge all over—like, *everything?*" She paused and tried to peer down at his pants but couldn't get the angle. "Well, are you?"

"What?"

"I'm gonna jump you in a minute. You know that, don't you? I mean, I've been fantasizing about it forever. I love a man with big hands and you've got huge ones. And you already know about my job and stuff, so you're not going to freak when I get a call at two in the morning because Laniqua has run away again or—"

"You're having a reaction!" he cried.

"Yeah, whatever. Turn on the air. I'm hot." She twisted her free hand behind her and managed to pop the clasp on her bra. "God, that's better," she said. But then the elastic started rubbing her in all the right ways—except that it wasn't his hands. The touch was too light, both irritating and erotic at the same time. She licked her lips. "I really love your hands, you know. And the kids talk about you all the time. About how you straddle that big hog—"

"It's a Yamaha!"

"I watch for you every morning. I drink my coffee and stare out the window and just wait for you to ride on up. It's my morning ritual."

"We cannot do this, Toni. We cannot! You are not yourself."

She paused a moment, a flash of reality burning through her brain. He was right. She was not herself. There were a zillion reasons to haul back on whatever was going on right then. But she couldn't think of a single one. Ah, she got her bra off one side. He still had her right hand imprisoned such that her bra dangled from her elbow. But her breasts bounced free, free, free in the steamy air.

She shrugged, loving the way it made her breasts dance. "Whatever," she said. "Pull over so I can go down on you."

Chapter Two

Mistakes are the portals of discovery.
—James Joyce

John's blood left his brain. What little he'd been using to drive drained straight south. The thought of Toni's perfect lips and mouth and tongue sucking. . . . His hands spasmed on the wheel as he jerked too hard toward the exit. Another car horn blared, and he glanced in the rearview mirror to make sure he hadn't just killed someone.

No! No! Don't look back there! Too late. He saw Toni's perfect breasts gleefully displayed for his viewing pleasure.

A few more minutes. He had to hold it together for just a few more minutes. Then he could . . . what? Drag Toni's naked body inside and. . . . *Don't go there! Don't even think it!* And yet, how could he not? Especially as she continued to talk in the most graphic terms about exactly what she was going to do to him. With him. Oh God, who knew this awesome petite blond SPED teacher had such a dirty mind? Sure, he'd noticed her before; she was an attractive woman in a warm, loving, nicely athletic, excellent-at-her-job sort of way. She brightened a room whenever she entered it. It was something in the way she bounced—*no! No thoughts about bouncing!*—something in the way she *warmed up* a room. Everyone responded to her joyous manner. She could motivate a room of angry children or contemptuous adults like no one else. And yet, she was a tigress when defending her kids.

Who wouldn't admire such a dynamo? What man wouldn't notice the way her jeans hugged tight curves or fantasize about just how energetic certain activities could be in bed, on his desk, under the bleachers or in the teachers lounge . . . ?

He spun into the first parking place he could find. He'd taken her to his house, since she wouldn't tell him the location of hers. Glancing into the backseat, he was both relieved and disappointed to see that she hadn't been able to pull off her jeans, though her fly was fully open. Unfortunately, the view of a white Victoria's Secret panty made his brain sweat, especially when he caught sight of the pink stitched dog just below her right hipbone. Imagine taking a big ole bite of that doggie and pulling it down with his teeth—

"Oh, thank God," she gasped as she managed to release her seat belt. Only Toni would strip half naked in a car and yet still be safety-minded enough to keep the belt on. And why did he find that so incredibly sexy?

Stay in control! He jerked off his jacket and threw it around her shoulders. She immediately tried to shrug out of it, but he held it firmly on her shoulders. "Just until we're inside," he urged.

She stared at him, and he could tell her rational

mind was making a valiant effort to regain control. Then her eyes dropped to his mouth, and oh hell, she pushed the tip of her pink tongue out to slowly wet her lips. His hips jerked in automatic response. Her eyes dropped to the movement and . . .

"Inside!" he ordered, bodily hauling her out. "And keep the jacket on!" The last thing he needed was someone seeing him drag a naked teacher into his house. And God forbid if any one of them had a camera phone.

"This isn't my place," she murmured as she sniffed the air.

"It's mine. You didn't tell me where you live." He should have taken her to a hospital. He should have, but he already knew what was going on. No way could they keep the situation quiet if she went to a hospital. He just had to help her ride out the conversion process, wait until the SaniLyco was thrown out of her system like the big damn, useless dose of alcohol it now was.

The problem was, *her* conversion was creating one in *him*. The more aggressive *she* got, the more lustful he became. He couldn't hold out much longer, but he had to. He simply had to. But all his blood had long since drained straight to his groin.

She tried again to throw off his jacket, but he kept a firm grip on her shoulders, both keeping her covered and steering her all at once. At least that was the plan. Until she abruptly reached out and gripped him right where his blood pounded the hardest.

"Dominate me," she said, her voice a low, throaty growl. "Throw me down and do me hard."

He didn't answer. He hadn't the control, especially as he shoved her against the wall beside his door, pinning her with—*No! No! Keep it zipped!* He rolled away from her, keeping one arm out to hold her steady while the other fumbled with his keys. But he couldn't do it all, and he couldn't do any of it well.

She threw off his jacket, wrapping her arms around him enough to pull her mouth to his neck. He let her. Inserting the key in the lock required all his attention. "You're a teacher," he said firmly. "I'm your boss."

"I've never been this wet before."

The door opened and they stumbled inside. He held her upright just long enough for her to scrape his jaw with her teeth while he slammed the door shut behind them. Then she shimmied out of his arms and her jeans in one smooth slide. A bare second later, she was down on all fours before him with her luscious bottom lifted in invitation.

He could not, not, *not* do it doggie-style with a teacher! he railed at himself. Then the scent hit him: hot, musky, a spice that slid straight past his brain to grab hold of his gut. He lost all restraint and all his good intentions. His pants didn't make it past his knees before he grabbed her. Every iota of his consciousness was centered on that sweet, hot, wet. . . .

He plunged into her. She reared back against him and howled. He heard both ecstasy and pain in the sound, but his senses were overwhelmed with the tightness, the slide, and waves upon waves of pleasure. He grabbed hold of her hips, dragging her hard backward. Their flesh connected with a smack that echoed sensually in his brain, each impact pounding a frenzied tempo through his body. His belly contracted, her heat built, and the power roared behind his eyes.

He released with the fury of a rocket launch. Fire burst over his skin and roared through his blood. His consciousness exploded out of him and into her. Wholly and completely into her. And he kept going, kept pouring, kept being in her while she writhed beneath him.

"Hard," she gasped. "Harder."

He reached down over and around her, forcibly spreading her knees, lifting her higher against him. He heard his pants rip and didn't care. It gave him more room to thrust. He let his right hand slide upward—God, was she wet!—and he cupped her with no skill at all. His fingers delved clumsily around her until they found her cleft and rolled into it. The weight of her body increased his pressure. The thrust of his hips gave the friction. Her climax pulled the last of his sanity from him.

More. Harder. More!

Her hands slipped on the carpet and she went down face first. His knees buckled and he followed her down, but not before he slid out. He cursed and flipped her over. She lifted her legs, urging him back. Again the slam into her.

Breasts and teeth, legs and orgasm. Over and over. Twisting and biting, howling and hard, harder, hardest!

Yessss—ooowrrrrr!

Toni came awake slowly. Her entire body hurt, and yet she felt strangely aware. Even with her eyes closed, she could catalogue sensations with amazing clarity. She could smell pine and lemon furniture polish, plus chicken and rice with asparagus done in a creamy basil sauce. Her knees, left forearm, and upper rear had rug burn. One of her hips ached from a deep bruise, and her hair lay across one cheek. A light cotton blanket lay across her shoulders—across all of her except for one foot—and she was lying on a velour futon mattress that was definitely not in her apartment.

Someone added bacon to the chicken, and her stomach rumbled. In the back of her mind, she knew exactly who that someone was, but she decided to focus on her body instead. She was already standing, blanket wrapped around her nakedness, before she opened her eyes. When she did, she catalogued basic furniture along spare contemporary lines, a jade Kwan Yin statue on a table next to family pictures—she would not look at those just now—and a well-stocked bookcase.

She moved quickly past the pictures, closing her mind to any thoughts but food. She would absolutely not wonder why her muscles were sore. Unfortunately, the food was being cooked by the someone-who-would-not-be-named. "Good morning, Principal Wong," she said just as she did at school every morning. So much for the not-naming part.

He looked up from his stove, his expression exactly like her neighbor's Boston terrier in headlights. "Uh, call me John. And it's evening." Then he blanched and looked down at the pan. With amazingly efficient movements, he pulled out a couple of plates from the cabinet, carefully scooped food in equally huge portions onto them, dropped the pan into the sink under running water, and slid her plate to her. "Dinner," he grunted. Then he cursed under his breath. "I mean, I made dinner. I hope you like chicken."

"Love it, and I'm famished. Thank you. But, uh . . ."

"Silverware. Right. And drinks." He fumbled underneath the countertop, then pulled out two forks, three spoons, and a knife. Then he reached behind him for glasses, hesitating in front of the refrigerator. "I've got the basics—milk, juice, water. There's beer and wine too, but . . . um . . . I'm not sure you should—"

"Actually, I was thinking about clothes."

He blinked, obviously taking a moment to process her words.

"My clothes," she clarified. "Any idea where . . . ?"

"Oh! Right. Um . . ." She hadn't thought his skin could go any whiter, but it did, giving him a real Caucasian cast. "I . . . um . . ." He looked around. "Your jeans are next to the futon, but . . . um . . . I've got a tee you can borrow. That should work for now. The rest of your clothes are . . . um . . ."

"In the car," she answered for him. Her memory had returned. The floodgates could not be held shut any longer and reality rushed through. She had slept with her boss. She had done the nasty—wow, at least a few hundred times—in the wildest, most explosive sex she had ever experienced. Double wow. At a less awkward time, she was going to look back on this afternoon and try very hard to remember all the exact details. Every single one.

In the meantime, she had to think about saving her job. "So, you've got a clean bill of health, right? No STDs?"

"No!"

"Good. I'm clean, too. And I'm just finishing my cycle, so no babies likely. Which means that there's no reason for this to be awkward." She forced out a laugh. *"I'mgoingtogetdressednowwhere'sthebathroom?"* She said it in a rush.

He blinked. Dumbly pointed to the hallway. She nodded, whipped past the futon for her pants, then dove into the bathroom. She didn't take much time in there. Yeah, there were the basics, but mostly she had no wish to see the rosy flush to her skin that might or might not be rug burn or scratch and bite marks. She knew from memory that she had given a great deal more than she got. And wasn't that just putting a cat-that-ate-the-canary grin on her face. Who'd've thought Principal Wong was so very, very, very uninhibited? Who'd've thought she was?

Knock, knock. "Um, everything okay in there?"

"Yeah!" she returned too brightly. "Just coming out now." She hauled open the door to stop cold as he filled the doorway. Damn, he was big. In more ways than one. Her lips started to quiver with nervous anxiety or hysterics, she wasn't sure which.

He hastily stepped back, holding out a Franklin School basketball champs tee in Go Team! crimson. "Um . . . there's dinner. And . . . well . . . we've got to talk."

She shook her head, whipping on the huge tee-turned-dress. "No. Really, John." The Principal title just had to go. "No, we don't."

"Actually, we do."

"No, no, I don't think so. I'll just get my . . . um . . . keys and—"

He grabbed her arm, and she stiffened, the skin on her back prickling with energy. "Toni. We do."

"Let go, John." Humor had disappeared. Suddenly, she was filled with a raw, dark anger. "Now."

"You're a werewolf."

She frowned. She tilted her head and frowned again. And yet, he did not go running from her. He remained a solid dose of unwelcome reality.

"Toni. You're a were—"

"I like cats. I have a large tabby named Orange."

He waited a moment, and then he shrugged, releasing her arm. "You can still like cats," he drawled. "I have a friend who really likes them with mustard."

It took a moment for his meaning to sink in. "That's not funny."

"No. No, I don't suppose it is."

Her stomach rumbled loudly in the awkward silence. She bared her teeth in hunger and he took a single step backward. She didn't even realize what she was doing until she pushed forward, her hands lifting, nails extended. Everything she did was unconscious. Her back seemed to lift up to her ears as her head dipped forward.

And that's when she saw it: her reflection in the bathroom mirror. She wasn't even sure what drew her attention. In truth, she looked just as she did before—spiky, dirty-blond hair, lightly freckled cheeks, oversized tee. Except for the fangs that were extending through her elongating jaw, she looked just like normal.

"AIIIIEEEEERRRRRRRRRRRRRR! Yiiiiiiiieeee! Yipp! Yip!" She was trying to say something. Truly, she was. But all that came out were the strange panicky sounds from a face that was both hers and not hers at the same time. And was that five-o'clock shadow? The idea of a beard freaked her as much as the muzzle. There wasn't enough wax on the planet to take care of that!

She raised her hands to her face and watched in revulsion as more hair grew there. A dog started whimpering somewhere—herself, obviously—but the thought couldn't displace the vision in the mirror. Hell, she didn't even like science fiction. Horror was not, not, *not* on her playlist!

She felt her muscles tense. Her thighs began to tighten, her bare feet gripped the cold linoleum floor, and she prepared to lunge straight at the mirror. It made no sense, but she was going to destroy that image if it—

"It's okay. You can handle this. Stay in control. It's okay." John's hand settled on her shoulder. She didn't feel it. She saw it in the mirror—a large white hand settling on a crimson T-shirt that stretched tight across her shoulders. Not *her* shoulders; a werewolf's shoulders.

"Stay in control," he continued, his voice a steady drone of sanity. "You can do it, Toni. You are in control."

Except, she wasn't. She wasn't that . . . that thing in the mirror. Except, she was. She started trembling. Her legs started to shake with the strain of her crouch. She wanted to lunge. She wanted to destroy that thing in front of her even if it was only her reflection. And yet it wouldn't help. She couldn't—

"Stay calm, Toni. You are in control."

"I am a goddamned werewolf!" she spat. And just like that, she lost and regained control. With speech came normalcy—humanity—and a fatalistic acceptance of total disaster. She'd turned away from the mirror to snap at John, but the moment she looked into his dark eyes and not her own freakish reflection was the exact moment that she began to find herself again.

His eyes seemed to hold her soul still, and a gentle warmth emanated from his hand, spreading into her like hot fudge on ice cream. She took a breath. And then another one. And then a long, deep gasp that ended in a shudder.

"What did you do to me?" she asked.

"I'm helping you stabilize your energies. I didn't think you really wanted to change to the wolf."

Her stomach rumbled again, bringing with it a surge

of primitive drive. She knew what it was and yet was powerless to deny her violent hunger. "I think I need to eat something."

"Chicken," he stressed. "You need to eat chicken. Over here." He urged her toward the kitchen.

She outdistanced him and fell on her food. She had enough control to not slaver over the plate, swallowing the stuff whole. She would like to say that was because she was in total command of her body and mind. She wasn't. The beast in her simply didn't like the *cooked* nature of the chicken. And that revulsion was enough to allow her to grab fork and knife and eat with some semblance of humanity. .

Normally, she loved mealtime. As a child, it was a cherished time when her family reconnected with one another. When she, her brother, and her parents had shared stuff from their day. Now, as an adult, she still kept mealtime sacred, either meeting with friends or simply enjoying her meals in solitary reflection and peace. A time to be grounded and simply enjoy. Not a time to slurp and gurgle and gobble, barely restraining herself from chomping the fork.

She ate her food and his. She practically choked on three glasses of milk. And she finished it all in five minutes flat. Then she licked her lips and sat back in her chair like a punk, like a preteen, underprivileged, crass punk with the manners of a . . . well, of a dog.

She stared at her empty plate—and his empty plate—and burst into tears. She didn't even stop when she heard John sigh and mutter to himself, "I think I need a beer."

At least he was a gentleman about it, offering her a box of tissues as he passed by. Then she heard him grab a bottle from the refrigerator and twist it open. She knew this not because she could hear it—her sobs were that loud—but because she could smell it. Or perhaps not smell, because her nose was stuffed up, but because she could taste it on the air. Beer on her tongue.

Without even thinking about it, she reached for the bottle. He lifted it away from her. "Not for you. Not until you learn some control."

"I'm not werewolfing right now!" she cried. She had no idea why the damned beer was so important to her. Probably because it was one of her favorite comfort foods. Whatever. She wanted it and she would get it now. She felt her hand extend, the bones lengthening into claws.

Aw, shit. She stared at her paw and burst into tears again. Apparently, werewolves had two moods: pissed off or weepy. This was so very, very wrong. So wrong that she looked at the knife on the table and seriously contemplated using it on her wrists.

He must have read her thoughts because before she could do more than stare, John grabbed it and tossed it into the sink—across the room and away from her. Then he sighed. "Toni, surely you've thought of this before. How many times have you been bitten in your career?"

"Bitten? A dozen times at least. By a werewolf? Never." She closed her eyes. "I handle dogs different."

She could feel his attention tighten on her.

"Different how?"

"I don't let them bite me! Damn it, John, this is ridiculous! Why didn't the SaniLyco work? Why didn't we know Victor was a werewolf? What freaking lunatic thought it would be a good idea to send an emerging werewolf into our school? Don't they have their own places for that?"

She continued on in that vein for a good long while.

She wasn't saying anything unusual, especially among public school employees, and yet as she ranted, she couldn't help but notice a sadness deep within John's eyes. He remained absolutely relaxed, sipping occasionally from his beer, mostly listening in respectful silence. He even got more comfortable and put his feet up on a nearby chair. And yet she knew in the core of her being that she was disappointing him. Or perhaps it was herself she was letting down. After all, hadn't she once professed to love all, regardless of race, creed, or color?

She sputtered to a stop, finally saying the one thing that she meant wholeheartedly. "I don't want to be a werewolf."

Silence fell, and she looked at her boss and, yeah, her lover, hoping for an answer. It took him a good five minutes before he arched an eyebrow at her. "I'm sorry," he said. "Is it my turn to speak now?"

She growled—yes, a full doggie growl—at him. "Try to be helpful, please."

Both of his eyebrows were now raised.

"Okay," she amended. "You've been great. You've fed me. You've . . ." *Given me the best sex of my entire life—fantasies included.*

He cleared his throat and looked down at his beer, his skin tinged with red. "No, I'm sorry. You've been hit with a lot all at once. Your reaction is completely normal."

She swallowed. "Do you think there's some counteractive drug? Maybe . . ." Her voice trailed away as he shook his head. But then he sighed, the sound coming from deep within his chest.

"Actually, I have a friend. Her name . . . Well, it doesn't matter what her name is. She could, um, unturn you if you want—"

"I want!"

"But she's tapped out right now. Her blood . . . I mean, it doesn't matter. She could unturn you eventually. Probably. But she's tapped out right now from when she closed the demon gate. It'll be a couple more months before she can do it."

Toni was slightly confused, but she looked at the large school calendar hanging on his wall. On it, she saw the next night of the full moon—a week away. A couple of months would be a couple of full moons—a couple of werewolf madness days. And that's if his friend came through.

Her heart sank like a lead weight as she continued to stare at the calendar. She saw not only the empty circle that indicated a full moon, but also all the school functions and . . . aw, hell . . . basketball practices that she was supposed to coach. A werewolf couldn't do any of that. Not at their school. Not really.

"I'm fired, aren't I?"

He quickly leaned forward, his feet hitting the linoleum with a loud thud. "No! No, you are definitely *not* fired."

"But you can't keep me. Even if you wanted to—"

"You're the best goddamned teacher I've ever had. . . ." He suddenly flushed, his words stopped cold.

"But the superintendent, the school board, hell, every single parent who has a child would raise bloody hell if I stayed. No werewolf teacher has ever kept her job. Ever."

He frowned at the table. "You were infected on the job. That's different."

"Yeah, because anybody cares about the wheres and whys of infection," she drawled.

He was silent. They both knew she spoke the truth. She was *so* fired.

"You're not fired," he repeated. "Because you don't have to be infected."

She paused. "Come again?"

He slowly raised his eyes to hers. "Fake it, Toni. The SaniLyco worked. Big sigh of relief. You're not infected."

"Lie? Forge an official document, lie to all my students and their parents, keep a serious medical *danger* secret."

He nodded. "Yup. I got doctor friends. They'll swear you're clean."

She took a moment to process that, then decided not to ask. "And what about during the full moon? Everyone knows I was bitten. Everyone will be watching me."

He nodded. "Yeah, I know. So that gives you . . ." He glanced at the calendar. "Eight days to get the wolf under control."

She glared at him, wondering if he was teasing her. Everyone knew that nobody controlled the wolf. Not during a full moon. All werewolves locked themselves up in the subways somewhere. Some of them had to stay there for a full week.

"It can be done," he stressed. Then he looked at her hard, a challenge in his voice. "You can do it."

"Because I have a magic powder that makes me impervious to the moon," she drawled. "Because I'm so sweet and beautiful that nothing bad will ever happen to me. Because—"

"Because you have a lover who will teach you the secrets of the wolves."

She blinked. He couldn't possibly mean him and her as an ongoing . . . as a boyfriend . . . as . . . One look at his face told her he was deadly serious. She just blinked.

"Yes, Toni, I will teach you the secrets of the universe." Then he abruptly grinned. "And even better, they're really, really fun."

Was he blushing?

Chapter Three

First say to yourself what you would be;
and then do what you have to do.
—*Epictetus*

Joey walked slowly home from the park, kicking at the weeds and trash while still dribbling his basketball. The ball was too big for his hands, but that didn't stop Joey from playing street ball every day after school until well after dark.

Drying sweat chilled his thin back and chest, but that's not what made him so cold. Vic was a werewolf. His older brother had hit puberty and bam, his life was over. Sure, Mom had warned them both that it was a possibility. Their dad was a wolf, but Mom wasn't. So that left a fifty-fifty chance for her kids, right? Looked like Vic had come up tails.

He caught the ball and held it against his hip, his chest burning with the unfairness of it all. Vic was a good ballplayer and smart at math. He did his homework without Mom yelling at him, and there was a girl down the street who had been coming around. But she wouldn't be visiting anymore. Not since Vic had bit a teacher and been dragged out in handcuffs and a muzzle by B-Ops, the fuckers.

Joey sniffed as some dust flew in his eyes. Then before he could wipe it away, the ball was punched from under his arm. He tried to grab it, but it had already been caught by a high school boy. He didn't know the kid's name, but he recognized the gang colors in the two bandanas twisted around his arm. Same with the other one—no, two . . . no, four—other guys who were surrounding him now. He only knew one of the boys: Kumars, from middle school with Vic. That creep's face gleamed sickly gray in the glare from the streetlight.

Joey swallowed, knowing he was about to get beat up. Still, he tried to put a brave face on it. Jutting his chin at the basketball, he grinned. "I'll take you on, one on one. We can play for the ball."

"You want to play me?" mocked the guy with the ball. He was a tall kid with a good reach, but he wasn't coordinated. Just walking, his movements seemed to jerk, as if he wasn't exactly sure where his body stopped and started. He'd still kick Joey's ass, but maybe he'd respect Joey's efforts. And that might just save him from a different kind of ass-kicking.

"Yeah," Joey said, putting a confidence he didn't feel into his strut as he pointed back toward the park courts. "Then when I'm in the NBA, you can say you played me, Joey Walters."

"They don't let no dogs in the NBA," growled a boy from behind.

Joey spun around, his fists tightening at his side. "I ain't no dog!"

"You're Victor Walters's brother," sneered another. "That makes you a dog."

"No, it don't!" Joey screamed, praying it was true. "I'm no dog! I'm gonna play for the Lakers and get a big ole house with a swimming pool up in the mountains. They're gonna pay me millions and I'm gonna drive a—"

The first blow crushed his skull. Even plastic pipes can break bone when swung with enough force.

"The Lakers don't take no dogs," spat Kumars, wiping his prints off the pipe then tossing it to the ground.

Off to the side, Rashard looked away from the huge pool of blood as it expanded then poured into the street. But that brought his gaze to the thick-jawed man at his side, the one who was peering at the body on the ground. "He dead?" the man asked.

Kumars and his friends shrugged.

The man grunted. "Well, better get goin', then. Come on, boys."

Rashard didn't dare look down, so he kept his eyes on his brother as they both fell in step behind their father. The others had already scattered.

"The Lakers." Kumars giggled as they turned the corner toward their apartment. "What a dumb dog."

"You said this was going to be fun," Toni drawled after her fourth, jaw-cracking yawn. "You even blushed. I saw it and thought . . ." Uh, best not to talk about what she'd thought. "Anyway, I think you lied."

John squirmed. He sat in the lotus position across from her on the floor—and wasn't that an odd sight on such a large guy? She lay sprawled on her back staring upward out a window. Somewhere behind the clouds was a three-quarter moon. She was supposed to somehow mentally connect with the moonlight and find her inner wolf. Ha! Her inner wolf—and outer woman—

couldn't stop thinking about how great it would be to become one with John again. And again. And again.

She slanted a glance at him, then hastily looked away. He looked adorable. Okay, so a broad-shouldered, chiseled-jawed, hunka-hunk shouldn't look adorable, but he truly did. He wore long athletic shorts and a triple-x sweatshirt, and he smelled like a hard-bodied guy with manly toes. Yes, manly toes. And her belly was quivering at the thought.

"Have I mentioned that I'm bored stiff here?" she lied. The truth was that she had a really bad case of lust, and frankly, she hadn't the will to force her thoughts elsewhere. "So are you really a Hell's Angel?"

She wasn't looking at him, but she could feel him start in surprise. She frowned and twisted so that she could see his whole blank expression. How exactly could she "feel" him?

"I am not a Hell's Angel," he responded in low, meditative tones. Clearly he was trying to impress a Zen-like "pay attention, Grasshopper" attitude on her. It wasn't working. She rolled onto her elbow to watch him closely.

"I know you were startled and I wasn't even looking at you. How can I know that?"

He frowned briefly before the expression was completely wiped away. "Our energies are mixed right now as I help you to control your wolf nature. Perhaps you are sensitive enough to feel my energies."

She mulled that over in her mind. The concept wasn't entirely foreign to her. She lived in California, for God's sake. *Everyone* knew about personal energy and mixing fields and . . . She felt her lips curve in a smile. Perhaps she should test this theory. She was, after all, lying in a pool of moonlight . . . or streetlight . . . or whatever.

She slowly rolled onto her back, making sure the motion was long, luxurious, and incredibly sexy as she arched her back into a stretch that—she hoped—beautifully outlined her rather modest breasts and accentuated her muscular legs.

Bam! Lust slammed into her like a summer storm. It roared through her thoughts and puckered her nipples. Her legs were already slipping open before she thought perhaps this wasn't a good idea.

Ah, hell . . . it wasn't a bad idea either, right? She tilted to give him a come-hither look.

"Stop that!" Sweat popped out on his forehead. Apparently, their energies were so entwined that she could feel that wetness at her own hairline. "I'm trying to teach you control!"

"It's not working," she said with absolute sincerity. Then she rolled to all fours, liking the way her breasts swayed without a bra.

"Try and concentrate!" he snapped, his expression one of complete and total disapproval. Mr. Principal at his most stern. And yet, she felt a thickening in her groin, a hunger that she knew was his.

"I'm going to eat you." Then she blinked, her rational mind pushing to the fore. "Damn," she whispered. "Who knew werewolves were this horny?"

He groaned, a sound of despair coming from deep within his soul. "You are not going to make me do this again!"

Despair? She froze. *Despair!* He was devastated that he had the hots for her? She sat back on her heels. "Well, jeez, it's not like I have the plague or anything." Then she gasped. Because, she suddenly realized, she *did* have the plague. The modern, lycanthropy plague, and one little bite, one little blood-drawing nick, and he would be baying at the moon right beside her. "Oh my God," she whispered as she scanned him from head to toe. "I didn't hurt you, did I? I didn't—"

"I am not afraid of infection."

His calm tones eased her panic. But then her rational mind kicked into high gear, chewing on his words rather than getting lost under mindless . . . well, mindlessness. What rational man wasn't afraid of infection? Especially given the explosiveness of their . . . Okay, rational mind veering away from that. Back to logical thought. Why oh why wouldn't he be afraid?

Oh. My. God! "You're a werewolf, too! That's why you knew the SaniLyco hadn't worked. That's why you couldn't resist me this afternoon. It was a doggie conversion frenzy or something." She scrambled backward away from him to huddle against the wall. "We're moon mad!"

"Calm down!" he said, scooting forward into the moonlight. "I'm not a werewolf—"

"Are too!" Okay, so maturity was not her strong point just now.

"Am not!" Then he grimaced. "I am not a werewolf," he enunciated clearly. "I am a druid."

She blinked. "A what?"

"A dru—"

"Druid," she finished for him, searching her mind for what possible relevance that could be to anything. "A tree worshiper and . . . um . . . justice-of-the-peace-like guy for the ancient Celts." She frowned, just now noticing the huge number of plants and green things about his home. "Um . . . werewolves aren't ancient Celts or something, are they?" Lord, that made no sense at all.

"What? No!" He rubbed a hand across his face. "I shape energy. I shift it, move it around. I can pull out the wolf in you or dampen it down to nothing."

She blinked, struggling to understand. In her brain, his words sounded something like "wakka wakka wakka."

"Here," he finally said, as he extended a hand. It was large, it was strong, and it hung in the air between them like a challenge.

She took hold of it. Even if he was a psycho crazy tree worshiper, he was still a solid base of reality for her in a rapidly shifting world. Besides, she'd had fantasies about holding John's hand for a long, long while. Well, maybe not just his hand. In any event, she grabbed him and held on.

"I'm going to shape your energies to dampen the wolf."

Bam. She was Toni, middle school SPED teacher and seventh grade basketball coach. And she was absolutely not in lust with anything. "Yuck. My laptop has more personality."

She felt his surprise ripple through their joined fields, but then he dampened that, too. "I'm going to push the werewolf now. Concentrate. I need you to keep control."

Terror rippled through her. She did not want to become that beast again. She was not a dog. Not a . . .

It didn't matter. The creature was coming, the animal was surging to the fore, complete with raging anger and grief and lust and fury and violence—

"Control yourself!"

Anger-management issues, much? She made an attempt. Truly. But it was as if her human mind was sitting in the backseat of the Toni-bus, watching while a rabid animal grabbed hold of the steering wheel. Human Toni watched her hands extend, becoming paws with claws. She felt her hips shift and her spine adjust. Her face—okay, that hurt—formed jaws and pointy ears. She didn't even want to think about where the hair was sprouting. And all that pain poured straight into a snapping fury especially as John body-slammed her back against the wall.

Thankfully, he was large. Okay, thankfully, he was Mack-truck large and she was petite, even in werewolf form. She might squirm and slaver—yes, slaver—but there was nowhere for her to go beneath the suffocating blanket of maleness.

And then she felt the change. The energy shifted, dampened, adjusted. Werewolf Toni was forcibly evicted from the driver's seat while robot Toni stepped in. Not real Toni—the woman with emotions and drives and her own share of pissed-off crankiness—but the totally professional, wouldn't-know-a-real-feeling-if-it-bit-her Toni.

The werewolf receded. The robot woman emerged. And as soon as John lifted up enough that she could breathe, she fixed him with an annoyed look. "Compartmentalize, much?"

He shifted back onto his knees. "Huh?"

"Get off me." Her tone was flat. Robot Toni was still in control.

He looked at her, sprawled against the wall. Then he looked down at his knees. He sat a good foot away from her. They weren't even touching. "Huh?"

"Your energies. Get off me." Then she made a conscious effort to mentally push him away. "Go. Away!"

Whoosh. His vital, hunky man energies withdrew. Wow, she hadn't even realized how alive he was until he left her. Then, while she was still puzzling over that, she felt robot Toni step away, and real Toni took the wheel. Except, apparently real Toni was still ticked.

"So, what the hell was that?" she snapped. "Let's

play with Toni's personality? Bam, she's a werewolf. Whoosh, she's a robot! Do you do sex kitten, too?"

"Toni, try to gain control."

"I am in control, goddamnit!" Except, of course, obviously she wasn't. She was screaming at him, shifting to her knees, and all of a sudden werewolf Toni had a hand on the wheel.

"Stop it!" she growled.

"I'm not doing anything!" he retorted, hands upraised in surrender.

"I know that!" she snapped. "I'm pissed. Real Toni is ticked off, and I damn well don't have to be a werewolf to express my rage!" She was screaming at werewolf Toni, who immediately retreated to the back of the bus with a whimper. She sat back, her hands on her hips, her breath heaving in and out with great gasps. "Oh, shit. What the hell is wrong with me?"

"You're trying to control a whole new aspect of yourself. That's got to be hard," he said, his voice once again taking that soothing Zen tone.

"Shut up, Grasshopper," she growled.

He arched an eyebrow, but didn't speak.

She ignored him. "I'm not trying to control myself. I'm trying to . . . to . . ." She bit her lip, suddenly hit with the horrible truth. She felt her shoulders slump as tears blurred her vision. She was a werewolf now. She wasn't trying to control herself. She was trying to . . . "Integrate," she whispered. "I have to integrate the wolf into me." Which meant she would have to accept it, to embrace it, to . . . to . . . "I have to learn to love the wolf."

She looked up, searching John's face for reassurance, denial, some show of emotion at all. Instead, she found cautious surprise. "That's . . . um . . . very druidic of you," he finally said.

"Bite me." She stood up and walked away. She'd already seen her keys, so she snatched them off the table and was out the door before he could say anything else.

Anger carried her all the way home. Anger and an acute sense of lost sexual gratification, which only made her angrier. Damn the man.

She stomped into her condo, only to be met by her very sweet, very confused large tabby, Orange. He was named by her niece who hadn't understood why anyone would name a cat Crookshanks. Toni turned on her favorite pet, barked—yes, barked—and chased Orange through the living room, around the kitchen table, and then into the bathroom where her cat hissed and spat from his place wedged behind the stool.

Toni stared at the terrified pet and burst into tears. God, this day just sucked.

Ten minutes later, she gave up on trying to soothe her cat and slumped her way into the kitchen. Halfway through a quart of chicken salad, she noticed her butt was beeping. Well, not her butt, actually, but her cell phone. Pulling it out, she saw she had twenty-five voice messages and ten texts. She started scrolling through, mentally cataloguing the list.

Friend. Friend. Mom. Friend. Nurse. Mom. Brother. Other brother. Friend. Dad.

Perhaps she ought to call her family. She started listening to the voice messages, which consisted of a lot of concerned calls from family and friends—oh, joy, her story had hit the news—and a zillion different media outlets and a Web-zine called www.oncebitten-twiceshy.com. She texted her mother.

Hey, I'm fine. SaniLyco works great! Love you!

So, yeah, she had lied to her mother—a big fat whopper—but the last thing she needed was her mom wondering what type of kibble to serve at Thanksgiving dinner. She had no fear of being tossed off the family tree; they were a progressive family. Her brother had once dated a vamp, after all. But still, she didn't really want her mother looking at puppies and thinking about grandkids.

Thoroughly depressed, she tossed aside the empty chicken salad container and reached for the chocolate chocolate chip ice cream. While microwaving some hot fudge, she flicked on the TV and clicked to *Headline News*. Surely the latest Mideast stories would put her little hair-growth issue into perspective.

"Crimson City faces yet another round of race wars. Special ed teacher and coach Toni Freedman was bit by an adolescent werewolf today." And there was her beaming face straight from last year's basketball team picture filling the screen. "The incident sparked a frenzy of outrage from parent and antiparanormal groups alike."

A wide-eyed mother complete with apple-red cheeks and a soft bun spoke earnestly to a camera. "It's appalling that our kids should be exposed to such things! And poor Miss Freedman . . ." She shook her head. "I put her name in my church's prayer chain. Principal Wong, too, since he's going to have to fire her. It's awful, but we just can't have werewolves in our schools."

The announcer came back on. "And in breaking news, nine-year-old Joey Walters was assaulted just a few hours ago. The brother of werewolf Victor Walters, Joey apparently suffered a blunt head trauma. A plastic pipe was recovered at the scene. He is listed in critical condition at . . .

Toni felt her stomach start to heave as the school picture of a dark-eyed Latino boy filled the screen. His face was thin like Vic's, but still had the roundness of an elementary school boy.

"We ain't no dogs!" sobbed his mother on the screen. "He was gonna be in the NBA. He weren't no dog!"

"Authorities declined to comment," continued the reporter, "except to maintain that an investigation is ongoing. Similarly, Principal Wong has been unavailable."

Toni made it to the bathroom just as her chicken salad made a reappearance. Her cat streaked out from behind the stool to disappear somewhere into the back of her closet.

Her next stop—after she'd cleaned up—was the bedroom window. It looked right out on the street. No strange cars yet. Everything was quiet, but she knew it wouldn't last. It was standard policy for teacher addresses to be kept very quiet, especially after an incident like this. It was one of the few protections offered to cops, teachers, and Mafia witnesses. Unfortunately, the city's survival rate for witnesses told her she had maybe an hour before some enterprising Jimmy Journalist found her.

She scrambled into her closet—sending poor Orange running again, this time under the couch—and hauled out her suitcase. She was packed in four minutes flat, purse and keys in hand, before she realized she had nowhere to go. How long before the media found her parents or her friends? Hell, they were probably calling her old basketball coach. She thought briefly of running back to John's, but he was under as much fire as she. More, since she was just the soon-to-be-fired victim. He was the principal who had allowed a violent werewolf into his school. As it was, she was a bit shocked to realize how much time he'd spent with her today without even a hint of the principal-survival-instinct showing through.

So, she couldn't run to John and couldn't go home. Just where, exactly, did she intend to go? She dropped onto her couch with a whoosh of disgust, barely noticing when Orange streaked out of the room for the kitchen.

"You're going to have to get used to me sometime, kitty," she drawled. Which is when she realized that her cat hadn't run because she had dropped onto the couch; Orange had taken off because four werewolves had suddenly appeared in her living room. Which would have been strange enough, but then came the commandos bursting through the door.

World War III began in her living room, and all she could think was that poor Orange would never be the same.

Chapter Four

You can't have everything. Where would you put it?
—Steven Wright

John heard the crash, but the sound didn't immediately compute. He'd expected a scream, maybe a frantic dash to the back door where he now waited to catch Toni when she fled in panic from the werewolves. But he didn't expect the thud of furniture or . . .

"B-Ops! Everybody down!"

He didn't wait. He'd intended to keep a low profile: She need never know that he'd followed her home and watched over her from a hedge in her backyard. That gave her space to come to grips with her situation without the added complication of . . . well, of him. And her. Together doing . . . In any event, that had been the plan: secret bodyguarding.

But fake B-Ops agents bursting through her front door demanded a whole new plan. One that involved busting down her back door and coming to her rescue. And they *were* fake agents. He knew something about how that organization worked. Real B-Ops did not slam through a woman's home in the dead of night without (a) securing the back or (b) attempting a sneak attack. These yahoos were making enough noise to rouse the entire neighborhood.

He pushed through the back door, nearly tripping over an orange streak—a cat?—as it bolted out the door. Reaching out with his druid senses, he sensed—

Too late. A fake agent—jeez, a teenager?—went for Gavix with a sawed-off shotgun. The werewolf had naturally seen it coming and ducked out of the way, but that just made the pseudocommando angry. With surprising speed, the bastard reversed his stroke and got Gavix in the face with the butt end, and the battle was on. Four werewolves against five fake teenage commandos with Toni in the middle.

Abandoning his druid senses—they were useless in a fight anyway—he plunged into the melee. He'd sensed enough to know that Toni was on the couch. His plan was to stand over her and protect her from whatever came near until he could drag her safely out of the mess. But when he rounded the corner, he realized that particular plan hadn't factored in Toni.

He should have known. He'd pictured her in terror on the couch. She was leaping into the fray instead, already swinging her tiny fists. She went for the nearest werewolf. Unfortunately, that was Keeli, the alpha werewolf who was turning to face the fake officers.

"Get out of my home! Get out! Get out!" Toni screamed as she blocked Keeli's upraised arm and shoved the werewolf toward the back door. Then Toni went for the leather-clad thug with the shotgun. Since the thug was dealing with a very pissed-off Gavix, she had no trouble chopping his wrist hard enough that the shotgun clattered to the floor. While Gavix scrambled out of the way, she shoved the idiot into the wall hard enough that his face landed with a wet splat.

In different circumstances, John would have enjoyed watching Toni take out her frustrations on the guy. But to her left, another body-armored teen was aiming a pistol at her head. John leaped forward with his own bellow, body-slamming the guy against the couch. They both flipped over the back, but not before John made sure the pistol went flying far, far away. That left three fake officers on three werewolves. But how many more guns?

Bam! Bam! At least one.

"Are you fucking crazy?" Toni screamed. "This is my house!" She'd obviously chosen fury over rationality. Not a bad decision given the situation. A normal person would be a gibbering idiot by now, but Toni continued to curse while John struggled to get to her side. He knew the werewolves would protect her, but he had a gut-deep need to kill anyone who threatened her.

Meanwhile, he was busy struggling with his own opponent. The guy wasn't bright, but he was wiry and strong. And he fought dirty; John was barely keeping the kid down. He needed just one good grip and then he'd deliver a consciousness-ending blow, but the guy would not stay still as he angled for neck cuts and groin kicks.

"Retreat! Retreat!" squeaked a nervous teen. The cry faded as the pretend officers took off out the door.

"Yeah. Get—" A thud cut off the last of Toni's taunt, and icy fear froze John's thoughts.

He turned to see what had happened, and in that moment, he lost control of his attacker. The guy twisted free and scrambled for the door. John lunged for Toni. He wasn't fast enough to stop her from landing hard against the wall—thrown there by one of the escaping "commandos"—but he was at her side before she crumpled.

Twisting past Keeli, who was lunging after the last teen, John caught Toni just before her head hit the floor. Then he waited in anxious silence as her dazed eyes eventually—finally—blinked and focused.

"John?"

"Take it easy. You were thrown pretty hard." He swallowed, trying to calm his anxiety enough to connect with his druidic senses. They would give him a general feel for how bad her injuries were, but his heart was beating too fast for him to clear his mind.

"How is she?" asked Keeli, her gravelly voice rising into a higher register as she shifted back to her human form.

"I don't know," John responded, anxiety degrading his focus even more. Why couldn't he calm his emotions around her?

"I'm fine," Toni groused as she frowned past John's shoulder at the werewolf leader. "And why are you in my house?"

"I let them in," John responded. "They just wanted to talk to you."

Toni took a moment to absorb his comment; then she abruptly pushed herself upright, out of his arms. "You? But . . ." She cursed and shook her head. He reached out to steady her, but she batted his hand away. "Okay. Start at the beginning—like, at the point where you explain how you got here and why you guys couldn't knock."

She wouldn't let him touch her, but he kept his hands at the ready, his body tensed to . . . he didn't know what. It didn't matter. He was ready to help her if she needed anything. But in the meantime, she lifted her head to glare at him.

"Well?"

He glanced around him at the werewolves who now stood in a defensive circle around them—all except for Keeli, who gestured for him to take the lead. Great.

He sighed. "I was worried about you. So I followed you after you left."

"Do you always stalk your teachers?" she snapped.

"Only the ones I've—" He abruptly cut off his words. He could see by the way her eyes widened that she knew what he meant. Only the ones he'd had hot, sweaty sex with. He scrambled to cover. "The ones who have been bitten by a werewolf."

She didn't comment, but he could see the gratitude in her eyes; she wasn't interested in advertising their relationship yet. Mentally, he agreed. But that deep pit in his gut—that place where his most primal instincts held sway—was vastly displeased by her reaction.

"Anyway," he continued, forcing himself to stay with his brain, not his inner Neanderthal, "when I got here, Keeli met me in your backyard." He glanced at the young were-woman by his side. She raised a hand. "She just wanted to talk to you. Before the press showed up. Before—"

"Before things got more explosive," Keeli cut in. Then she glanced ruefully at the bullet holes in the near wall. "Sorry we were late."

Toni followed the woman's gaze and abruptly paled. John steadied her immediately, but he hadn't needed to; she swallowed and stiffened her spine.

"Why would B-Ops shoot at me?" she whispered.

"That wasn't B-Ops," John said.

"Definitely posers," growled Gavix, whose face was a mess of red and blue from the shotgun butt to his face.

"But who . . ." Toni made a frustrated sound high in

the back of her throat. "I don't understand any of this."

John stroked her arm, pleased that her skin no longer felt clammy, thrilled that she didn't push him away. "They were probably haters—people who wanted to grab you in a really public fashion."

"They claim they're B-Ops," Keeli continued. "That keeps anyone else from interfering. They surprise you by bursting in, guns at the ready, then shoot you when the wolf emerges. Then it's cleanup and one less wolf, and everyone blames B-Ops . . . or thanks them, depending on their personal attitude."

Keeli's voice was gentle, but her words were devastating. Toni started to tremble.

"But I'm not a werewolf." She bit her lip. "I mean, how could they know?"

There was silence all around as everyone looked at Toni. Finally, John gently lifted her arms so she could look at her hands . . . or rather paws. She gasped in shock as she stared. Then he slowly pressed her hands to her mouth—her wolf jaws and sharp jagged teeth.

"Oh God," she gasped.

"It's okay," Keeli quickly rushed to say. "You're doing really well. You just have to remember to shift back to human. Just think human."

"I *am* human!" Toni shot back. And just like that, her hands appeared and her face returned to normal. "I am," she repeated in a whisper.

John felt his throat choke at her obvious pain. All around them, the werewolves shifted uncomfortably. They all knew the difficulties of life as a wolf—the automatic prejudice, the constant fear, not to mention the difficulties of living one's life by the phases of the moon.

"We'll get through it," he promised as he squeezed her arm. "I'm right here."

She slanted him a look. "Apparently you're right here letting werewolves into my home."

He felt his face heat. "You remembered that part."

"Yeah—," she began, but Keeli interrupted.

"We did knock. We just didn't do it very loudly."

"I didn't hear you . . ." Toni's voice trailed off as she frowned.

"I picked your lock," John confessed. "I figured you were hiding. And I know Keeli personally. She just wanted to talk."

Toni nodded. "I was hiding. From the press." She swallowed. "Did you see the news?"

He shook his head, but he knew about little Joey. He'd had a spate of messages from the press. He opened his mouth to respond, but was interrupted by a quavery voice from the doorway.

"Toni? Are you all right? Toni?"

They all looked around to see an elderly woman in a nightgown and sweatshirt with a broom gripped defensively in her hand. Behind her peeked an eight-year-old boy.

"No, Mrs. Hernandez, I'm not," snapped Toni as she pushed to her feet. "Not with people shooting off guns in my home!"

Mrs. Hernandez's eyes widened at the holes in the wall. "But they said they were B-Ops."

"They lied," Toni said as she stepped forward. "They were haters coming to . . . to . . ." She shook her head. "Anyway, if it weren't for John and his friends, I don't know what I would have done."

The older woman straightened, her eyes narrowing as she stared at Keeli. "I know you. . . ."

Keeli straightened, every inch the alpha. "I'm the leader of the werewolves. You've probably seen me on the news."

"Oh. Oh no!" Then her gaze cut to Toni. "That means you're—"

"No, it doesn't," Toni rushed. "I'm fully human. The SaniLyco worked. But the wolves know what kind of danger I'm in. After that attack on the news, they came to help. And a good thing, too." Her voice was strong and clear, but John could tell she was merely putting on a brave front. It couldn't be easy for her to lie like that to a friend and neighbor.

He walked to her side. "I think we need to call the police. They need to know you've been targeted by haters."

Toni nodded, but it was Mrs. Hernandez who suddenly took charge. Bustling forward, she gripped Toni's arm and led her to the couch. "You poor dear. You just sit right here while I make some tea. Frankie, get on home and call the police. I'll take care of you, Toni, while your young man lets his friends go. I'm sure they don't need to be here." The implication was clear: humans stuck together; the werewolves weren't wanted. The attitude was mild compared to the commandos, but still it grated. John was about to respond when Toni gently set her neighbor aside.

"They certainly do have to stay, Mrs. Hernandez, to give a police report if nothing else. Plus, I feel a lot safer with them here." She looked hard at the old woman. "They were protecting me. They're the good guys."

"But . . . But—"

"I'm fine, Mrs. Hernandez. Why don't you go make sure Frankie calls the police? I'll be safe here."

The old woman hesitated, obviously confused by Toni's attitude and still nervous around the werewolves, even though all of them were in human form looking as normal as anyone else. "But—" she tried again.

"They're the good guys," Toni stressed again. Then she firmly ushered the woman to the door.

John watched her defend the wolves, pride surging through his veins. What made it all the sweeter was that he knew Toni believed everything she said. Even before today's crisis, people were just people to her. She never saw wolf or vamp or human. They were all just people, and that's what made her great.

Keeli waited until the old woman was gone before addressing Toni in a low firm tone. "We'll stay and give our police report, but then you're coming with us. Whether you like it or not, you are a werewolf. There are things you have to learn before I let you out in public."

"Wait a minute—," Toni began, but Keeli cut her off.

"I'm the alpha werewolf. You're a wolf and therefore my responsibility. Like it or not, you belong with me."

Toni would have argued; John could see it in her face and her stance. But at that moment, a sudden bright light from a ready-cam flooded the room.

The press had found them.

Chapter Five

Some people see things as they are and say why?
I dream things that never were and say why not?
—*Robert Kennedy*

"Get angry, damn it!" John punctuated his demand with a hard backhand across her cheek.

"I am angry!" Toni shot back, but with more weariness than anything else. Her cheek stung, her arms and legs were bruised, and her entire body felt heavy with exhaustion. It was Sunday afternoon in the werewolf tunnels. Tomorrow morning was school, and they both needed to be sure she could control her werewolf side no matter how annoyed, frustrated, or just plain tired she got. Unfortunately, for all John's violence, she knew he was pulling his punches. He flinched every time he hit her, and his eyes apologized with every look.

Truth was, she didn't feel the least bit threatened by the man and so, painful or not, she really couldn't get all that stirred up. On the upside, though, her lips were getting that nice red bee-stung look.

"This isn't working," John groused as he dropped down on the cracked blue mat. "You're not changing."

She plopped down beside him, then couldn't stop the motion. She ended up lying on her back looking up at the ugly concrete ceiling. The werewolf population was not known for its nice digs. "That's the whole point, isn't it? To *not* change into a wolf?" She asked the question out of habit. In truth, they'd had this discussion more than once.

"You need to learn to control your emotions. The wolf lives on that, it feeds on your fear, magnifies your rage—"

"Ruins my pedicure."

He twisted, glaring down at her. "I'm serious."

"So am I! Do you know how hard it is for me to find the time to get my nails done? Forget the expense, not to mention deciding on a color that will match your clothes for the next couple of weeks—then, bam, one wolf moment and the paint's all chipped, the design ruined." She glanced down at her big toes where once had been a lovely pink and white floral design. Now they looked like . . . well, like ugly toes with a jagged pink stripe down one side.

"How do you endure?" John drawled.

"Badly," she moaned while contemplating buying an industrial-sized box of nail files.

"Actually," he said after a moment, "I think you're doing amazingly well. Are you sure you want to go to work tomorrow? School will still be there next week."

"Yeah, but my job won't be."

He twisted so that he sat cross-legged, facing her— Mr. Lotus, once again. "I'm not going to fire you."

"You won't have a choice." They'd both seen the news. Parents were pulling their children, a half dozen pro-segregation groups were already picketing the school while pro-paranormal groups jeered from behind plastic fangs. "The situation is just too inflammatory for you to keep a werewolf teacher on staff. I have to show tomorrow, otherwise they'll assume I'm a wolf. Especially since someone is going to figure out I spent the weekend down here."

He didn't argue, because they both knew she was right. If she wanted a prayer of keeping her wolf nature secret, she had to show tomorrow at school. She had to look straight at the cameras, the parents, and her coworkers, and lie through her not-pointed teeth claiming that the SaniLyco worked wonders.

"Okay, then," he said, as he pushed to his feet. "Let's get back to it."

"Oh, give it a rest. I'm not wolfing out. I'm too pooped."

He paused, his gaze quiet and intense. She looked back, wondering what he saw. She was in basketball shorts and a sweat-soaked tank. Her hips probably looked like Mount Saint Helens next to the flatlands of her tiny, minuscule, nearly absent breasts. On the other hand, his basketball shorts nicely outlined his sculpted tush above corded thighs. His waist was narrow—of course—and she already knew his shoulders were steady and broad. And if she hadn't, her view from the floor made his chest look like Mega-Man's.

"God, you're gorgeous," he said.

She blinked and responded with a sultry, "Huh?"

He dropped down on his knees beside her. "You are perhaps the most beautiful woman I've ever seen."

"You're high. Subway fumes or something."

"No, I'm not," he answered. His voice was flat, almost mechanical, but the intensity in his eyes mesmerized her as he leaned forward. Their mouths barely touched. He teased the edges of her swollen lips, then extended his tongue to soothe their hotness. She let her mouth open, extending her tongue to toy with his. She felt him smile and knew she echoed the expression . . . especially as she felt his hands on her belly, burrowing beneath her tank.

Her stomach quivered, and she sucked in her breath at the exquisite feel of large hands spanning her waist. She felt small and delicate next to him. Feminine. The sensation was extraordinarily rare in her tomboy life, and so wonderfully arousing.

She arched into his hands, wanted to feel his grip more fully. She was offering him her breasts, and she grinned when he greedily slid higher, pushing the tank up and away, even lifting her sports bra as if the heavy elastic were nothing. She helped him, angling so he could strip her top completely off. Then she fell backward again, shivering in delight as his hands returned to her breasts, shaping and lifting in long full strokes.

She purred happily, then opened her eyes to see his face. He had a childish expression of delight as he petted her. On the left, he thumbed her nipple; on the right he pinched and twisted. She gasped as fire slipped into her blood, beginning with the tips of her breasts and flowing steadily outward until her entire body grew hot and wet.

And then it happened. Just as he was leaning down, just before he took her nipple into his mouth to do that wonderful thing he did. Right then, she sprouted hair. Her body arched, her hands extended, and her face contorted. She howled with as much pain as frustration, and within moments she was a snapping, wriggling, horrified wolf, writhing on her back like some flea-bitten mongrel.

He shifted his grip quickly, pressing his hands into her shoulder joints to hold her still. She whimpered, unable to find herself enough to verbalize her humiliation. The wolf had taken control.

"Look at me, Toni. Look!" His voice was commanding, filled with a power that echoed long after the sound faded. And she could not refuse.

She turned her face to him, caught his dark gaze, and felt him slip inside her energy field: She had no other word for it. She'd never even been aware of her energy field, any more than she would acknowledge her kidney or her liver. And yet, abruptly, she felt everything that was her—her being, her soul, her existence—as if it were an electrical field suffusing her entire body. And he had joined with it.

She felt his vibration—his field—trembling at the edges of hers. Like two musical notes, different and yet harmonizing perfectly, they quivered beside one another. Until his expanded, merging with hers, entwining and echoing. She felt his humanness echo through her field. And she knew her own wolfness affected his.

"This is my gift," he growled at her. Growled? "As a druid, I shape energy, I merge with it, I become it." He leaned forward, and she watched his face shift, his bones becoming more wolflike—longer, darker, and yes, he even became hairier. "I can become one with you."

She stared at him, shock making her body lax and accepting. Part of her reeled in horror. He could *not* become a dog for her. He couldn't! And yet, he obviously could. For her. With her. Her heart swelled with an emotion she didn't dare name.

She felt his hips move. He'd taken away one hand to

shove down her shorts, then his. She waited in stillness, still caught by his steady gaze as he gently spread her legs and positioned himself between her thighs.

"And one more thing," he said, his words becoming more indistinct as his mouth elongated. "I can only do this . . ." He tucked his knees beneath hers, lifting her up enough to manage the angle. "It is only possible with someone I love."

Then he thrust. He filled her totally, more fully than she had ever thought possible. And it was all the more incredible because she felt his energy too—still completely merged with her own. She experienced it—she *knew* it—as his excitement grew. She savored his swelling and the rough, erotic glide of flesh inside flesh. It filled her body and her mind. She howled in delight and his voice merged with hers.

She felt his belly tighten, and his mind flood with ecstasy. Her muscles began to quiver, then shake, then tighten in mind-blowing eruption. It was him. It was her. It was them.

And it was love.

Crazy.

"You sure you're ready for this?" John asked, his voice robotically even.

Toni took a fortifying gulp from her latte before she answered. They were climbing into her car Monday much too early in the morning. But neither of them could sleep, and so they had taken one last shared moment of peace at a café before braving the media circus in front of the school.

Sunday afternoon—after The Amazing Sex Event—had been spent in mutual discovery, not completely of the physical kind. She'd learned that John and his fellow druids had been instrumental in closing the demon gate, and that he had lost his best friend in the process. He'd learned that she grew up on a farm in southern Illinois and ran all the way to L.A. to escape the small town life, only to discover that she really missed the quiet intimacy of little communities. Both of them lived in the hope of making a difference in kids' lives, and gleefully recounted their many successes and mourned their failures.

In short, they'd learned about one another, and Toni very much feared she was deeply in love with her boss. But in the landscape of her life, fraternization with her superior was the smallest of her problems. The largest, of course, was school day number one after becoming a werewolf.

Meanwhile, John was still speaking, his voice irritatingly monotonous. "Keeli's been talking about a new werewolf school, exclusive, a place where were-kids would feel safe."

Toni set down her coffee with a jerk, splashing herself and her dashboard in the process. "Segregation? Sure, that's a good idea. And while we're at it, let's block out the vamps, too. And the blacks. Why not the Asians? Oh, but then what about the mixed kids? Hmm, we might be getting some vamp-wolf hybrids soon. And God forbid if they're black or yellow or purple with dots. Let's get individual schools for each, with individualized ED and SPED programs—"

"Calm down! Toni, calm down! I was just—"

"Just being pigheaded and bigoted and narrow-minded! What we need is a way to integrate everyone safely, not marginalize them into some wolf ghetto school! Damn, John, how could you think . . ." Her voice trailed away as she stared at his expression. He was calm, his eyes patient, his body language completely relaxed. She frowned. "You were testing me."

He shook his head. "Not testing, just giving you another option."

"You don't think there should be an exclusive werewolf school?"

"No," he said firmly. "We're all people, and our kids need to know how to live in a world with werewolves and vamps and humans." He sighed. "I just hope—"

"That we can realize that dream," she finished for him as she started the engine. "I'm going to school, John. I can make a difference."

"Even if it means lying to everyone you know?" he pressed.

She sighed. "It's the only way." She was hoping he would give a different answer than he had the last four times they'd had this discussion. He did—by giving her a sad expression that was more eloquent than anything he could have vocalized. He really didn't believe she could continue to work if her were-status was known.

"You know, it's not your job I worry about," he said, almost as if he read her mind. "Do you really think Joey was an isolated incident?"

She swallowed. There had been no progress in the investigation, and none was likely to come. Even if B-Ops were willing to delve into an assault on a werewolf, they were terribly understaffed and had been crippled by finger-pointing and restructuring since the recent uproar.

"Sue me, Toni, but I don't really want to see your body on the six o'clock news."

"Sue me, John, but I don't really want to hide who and what I am from everyone I know."

He sighed. She did, too. They both knew he was right. No way would she be safe once the truth got out.

And on that depressing thought, she turned the ignition key.

"I'd much rather be riding up on your motorcycle," she said in an attempt to lighten the mood.

He grinned. "Soon. I swear. We'll ride up into the mountains and make love under the . . ." His voice trailed away.

"Moonlight? Yeah, that'll happen." She'd had a two-hour-long lecture from Keeli about the dangers of even the smallest moon for a werewolf. Until she was sure she had the wolf completely under control, she was to avoid being out at night completely. They even had a special cage in the tunnels especially for new and adolescent werewolves. Yippee.

"You can learn to control it. I can help you . . ." John would have said more, but they were three blocks away from the school and the protesters were already clogging the streets. She had to slow her car to a crawl that became a dead stop the moment the press caught sight of her. She wasn't sure if she was terrified or relieved when police in riot gear showed up to clear a path to the teacher parking lot.

"Did you know they were going to be here?" she whispered. John had been checking his cell phone messages regularly over the weekend, but had declined to explain. And she had been too cowardly to ask, having ignored her own zillion messages.

"I didn't think it would be this bad," he confessed. "I thought they were just being overly protective." He shook his head. "I'm sorry. I should have guessed—"

"It's okay. I mean, who wouldn't want to be the center of Crimson City's media attention just at the moment I have a deadly secret to keep?" She was being sarcastic to cover her own nervousness.

He didn't touch her, but she felt his energy, warm and comforting as it surrounded her. "You don't have to—"

"We've already been over this." She finally, blessedly, was able to park her car. "I'm going in."

Chapter Six

He's no failure. He's not dead yet.
—Lloyd George

She made it as far as the front step. With the police escort, she managed to duck cameras and microphones. John shoved away the few protesters who managed to evade the police. But no one was able to stop Rashard. An underprivileged African-American boy with an extremely erratic father, Rashard had been in her ED program and John's after-school program since sixth grade. His father was one of those angry men with an axe to grind against the whole world for no obvious reason. His older brother, Kumars, was a punk in the worst sense of the word, and one of the reasons she was in this current fix. He was, after all, one of the boys who'd been beating the crap out of Vic. But Toni had bonded with Rashard, and after two years together she loved him in the best sense of the word.

He'd obviously slipped away from home early to wait at school for her. All of her kids could be protective whenever she got hurt, but he seemed frantic as he barreled out the front doors into her arms.

"Miss Freedman! Miss Freedman!"

One of the cops moved to stop him, but John motioned him back. He knew how important her kids were to her, and that she would take down anyone—cop or not—who interfered between her and one of them. She took all of Rashard's weight with a muffled "umph" while cameras flashed from all angles.

"Wow, kiddo," she said when she could breathe again. "What's up?"

He shrank back into the shadows, abruptly self-conscious as he realized he'd just been caught in a nonmacho moment. Then he looked down at his shoes and mumbled. She wouldn't have heard the words if she didn't have wolf hearing.

"You're not a wolf, are you? *Are* you?"

Then he looked up, his eyes desperate with fear as he ignored all the noise and chaos around them. For him, obviously this question ran so deep that he couldn't wait. He needed to know now.

"Why don't we go inside, Ms. Freedman?" John urged. "You can talk . . ." His voice faded as she shook her head.

Maybe this is the way it's supposed to be, she thought with a tiny portion of her brain. In front of all the cameras asked by one of her kids. Now was the choice: lie or not?

She glanced over at John, an apology in her eyes. She had been prepared to fib to everyone—the authorities, the media, the parents. But not to one of her kids. She'd never lied to her kids, and she couldn't do it now. Even though Rashard probably wanted her to. She just couldn't do it.

She straightened, took a deep breath, and pitched

her voice so all those microphones could hear. "I'm fine, Rashard," she said more calmly than she felt inside. "I'm strong and healthy and nothing is going to stop me from doing my job." She flinched as the boy blanched, already guessing what she was about to say, but she had to do it. Clean and clear—like pulling a Band-Aid off a cut. "But the SaniLyco didn't work. I am now a werewolf."

She didn't dare look at John's reaction. Besides, her focus was completely centered on Rashard as his entire body tightened with horror. In truth, his whole energy seemed off to her, but that was only to be expected. They were being watched by the whole freaking world.

"But you're not sure," Rashard whispered. "I mean . . ."

"I'm sure," she said. "Just as I'm sure that I have it completely under control." Or at least with John beside her she did. So, just to erase Rashard's false hope, she closed her eyes and consciously brought out the wolf. It still hurt. According to Keeli, the change would always hurt some. Still, it was manageable as she allowed her face to shift, becoming as much wolf as woman, both dog and human staring down at a boy who couldn't stop the tears running down his cheeks.

With a sudden dash, he ran away—not into the school, but into the crowd. Toni twisted, calling after him. "Rashard! Rashard!" No go. The kid was fast and well hidden by the mob of screaming reporters and protesters. Meanwhile, John and the police were rapidly dragging her inside the building and slamming the doors shut on the tidal wave of bodies trying to get through.

Once in the front hallway, she turned to face the stunned expressions of her coworkers. Muttering a curse, she consciously forced her face back into full human. It was harder than expected until she felt the warm presence of John's energy, helping her to magnify the human, to suppress the wolf.

She turned to thank him just as her police escort dropped her arm with a curse. "Well, you're B-Ops's problem now." Turning to John, the cop narrowed his eyes in clear anger—whether at her or the situation, Toni couldn't tell. But there was no mistaking his words. "My people will help out today. We're here and it's gonna be nasty. But as of tomorrow, this is a paranormal problem and B-Ops's jurisdiction."

"You can't do that!" John shot back, his voice hard and clipped. He had shifted completely into principal mode, and the shift was rather chilling, especially as he left Toni's side to argue with the officer. She knew he wasn't abandoning her. He was, in fact, doing everything he could to protect her and the kids in the school. And yet, the loss of his warmth, coupled with the embarrassed and pitying stares of her coworkers, left her bereft.

So she did what she always did when she felt completely lost. She straightened her spine and went to Her Place. In this school, that meant her office. Unfortunately, her office was on the second floor down the north wing, all the way at the end. Which meant she had to traverse part of the sixth-grade hallway and all of the eighth.

God, it was a *loooooooooong* walk. She forced herself to move at a normal pace. It was just another day, she reminded herself, just like all the others. Except, there were news crews at the windows trying to get another shot of her. Clusters of teachers whispered, their words picked up by her supersenses. They glanced at her, then nearly fell over each other to get out of her way. In their defense, they didn't seem afraid of her. They feared becoming her: infected by a student, forced into a stigmatized way of life through no fault of her own.

Then she caught sight of the nurse and health teacher, Linda . . . the vampire. It was enough to stop her dead in her tracks. Linda, too, who glanced over from where she was drawing the food pyramid on a blackboard. Toni stared. Linda paled. No, Linda was always pale. Because she was a *vampire*. Toni's wolf senses had become more at tuned in the last few days. She could now pick up subtleties in scent, movement, and the cold blood of a vampire.

"Oh my God," Toni whispered. "You're . . . You're . . ." That's why Linda never took outside playground or bus duty. She was a vampire.

"Really, really sorry about what's happened," Linda said loudly as she rushed into the hallway. She moved so fast one might even say she *flew*. Then she grabbed Toni by the arm and dragged her inside her classroom.

"B-but," stammered Toni. "You're a . . . a . . ." She couldn't actually say the word *vampire*. Not out loud.

"Yeah," Linda answered as she pushed her classroom door shut. "I didn't know how fast you'd figure it out. Guess your wolf senses are in full form."

"But . . ." Of all the strange things that had happened to her, this somehow ranked as the most bizarre. She'd known Linda for years. *Years.* And had never, ever guessed that the woman was a vamp. But that explained why she'd resorted to *Tan-in-a-Can* rather than join their annual Beach-side Bake. "How? *When?*"

"Always," Linda answered. "Born this way. There are a lot more of us than you think. And we don't all hang out with the hoity-toity vampire elite."

"But . . . but nobody knows. I mean, you've kept it a secret for . . ."

"My whole life. Yeah. And anyway, lots of people know. Lots of *paranormals* know. Fortunately, we all know how to keep a secret." She glanced sternly at Toni. "Something we *thought* you'd be good at. Did you really have to announce it on the front step? In front of cameras? Do you know what that's going to do to this school? To all of us?"

"Us?" Toni was having a hard time thinking of herself as an "us" now. "You mean as in 'us' versus 'them'?"

Linda grimaced. "As in 'us'—me, Tom, Janie, Angela, Howie . . ."

Toni's eyes widened in shock. "They're all vamps?"

Linda pursed her lips in disgust. "Please. Can you see Howie as a vamp? *Hairy* Howie?"

Werewolf, then. She started mentally flipping through the staff. "Juan and Marcil too," she whispered. Linda didn't need to answer; Toni knew she was right. In fact, she abruptly realized, there were a huge number of paranormals on staff at all levels: teachers, coaches, office staff—even one of the janitors. That's why bus and playground duty was so weird. Because some of them couldn't go outside without a ton of special sunblock. "Kieera."

"Naw. She's just naturally pale."

"But she knows, doesn't she?" Toni realized. After all, she was the head organizer for John's special afterschool program. A program that taught "personal values and self-control" to the school's at-risk kids. In reality, the teachers called it Principal Wong's Were-Idenitification Class where suspected werewolf kids were given extra attention and watched for paranormal abilities. All the people she'd just listed had also taken special interest in the program, volunteering their time and talents with the kids. "You're teaching them how to control their abilities," she said.

"Yeah, we are. And it was working, too, as long as nobody knew." She wandered over to the window and grimaced at the crowd outside. "But now it's toast. No way we're gonna get away with it now."

"Get away with what? Teaching kids?"

Linda pointedly turned her back on the crowd, snapping the blinds shut with a quick flick of her wrist. "With *integrating* the school. With showing the world that all kinds of kids can go to school together without incident, especially here."

"But there *was* an incident. *I* was infected." She thought she'd gotten past that particular anger. She'd had three whole days to adjust, but the bitterness in her voice told her she was still harboring resentment. A large moon-sized load. But Linda wasn't letting her get away with any self-pity just then.

"Yeah, and we're all really sorry about that. Really sorry. But John had a plan, one that could change the world. And now it's all jeopardized because you had to shoot off your mouth in front of the cameras."

"What plan? What jeopardy? All I did was tell the truth."

"And shine the media spotlight right on us. We're not ready, Toni. Principal Wong figured ten more years at least. Long enough for some of his students to graduate from college and go into the workforce. For his wolves and vamps to integrate into society and live normal lives."

"*His* wolves? *His* vamps?" Toni's head was spinning. To think all of this was going on right in front of her and she hadn't noticed any of it.

"His *kids*. I gotta tell you, Toni, his druid thing is incredible. I've learned a lot about controlling the vamp. I can even tolerate short stints in sunlight. And I've been able to pass on that knowledge. That's the key, you know. Control."

"You can't seriously think you could have kept this going for years. For *ten* years without anyone knowing? Some kid somewhere is gonna break. He'll be found out as a vamp or a werewolf, and then *bam,* he'll spill who knew what. It's all going to come out."

"*You* didn't figure it out. You were right here. Some of your ED kids were in the program, and you didn't notice."

Toni paled. She hadn't known. She'd supported the program because it taught good values. She'd seen the difference in her kids after they'd started attending. They'd grown more confident, less erratic. They'd become *more comfortable in their own skin.* Toni felt her knees give way and she dropped heavily on a student desk. "Three years," she whispered. The program had been in place for three years, and she'd never guessed the truth. "You're running an intentionally paranormal school."

"Yes, I am," came a low voice from the doorway. John, of course. Slipping into the classroom, he quietly shut the door behind him. It wouldn't last. Kids would be banging on the door any minute now, but for the moment Principal Wong was facing her as if he were facing down a firing squad. "We're all people, Toni, we're just variations on a theme. And we should all be able to live together in peace."

Toni swallowed, the magnitude of what was going on slowly seeping into her brain. John had created an environment where paranormals interacted in harmony. He taught control and discipline, good values and personal responsibility. It didn't matter that no human really knew the whole truth. The fact was, until her, there were no unusual problems and a great many successes.

"Remember how I was trying to get Vic into my program? Remember how—"

"You knew!" she accused. "You knew Vic was a wolf and you let him bite me?"

He shook his head. "I didn't *know*. Nobody knows until they get into puberty and the wolf asserts itself. But, yes, we suspected."

"And I got infected."

He nodded, his expression grim. "I didn't think he'd break. I didn't know he'd get beaten up in the cafeteria. And I didn't know you would be the first there, as opposed to Howie or Juan." He stepped forward. "Toni, they're the first responders. You're supposed to be backup, remember? You're supposed to *call* for backup."

She remembered. She also remembered that she'd ignored protocol and waded right in. Oh God, could this whole thing be her fault? Could she have done this to herself? Yes. Of course, yes. She'd known that from the beginning. She'd known what she risked when she'd thrown herself into that fight. Hard to feel victimized when it was her own fault.

And then it got worse.

"And now, thanks to you, the whole program's at risk," Linda groused.

Toni frowned. "What? Why?"

"Because the program won't work under a microscope," John answered. "The only reason the kids come at all is that we've promised to keep their special nature a secret. It's just another after-school program."

"But with reporters everywhere, examining everything we do, it's going to get out," Linda finished for him.

"Not necessarily. . . ." Toni began, but both of them knew it was a false hope. She could call the media a lot of names right now, but "stupid" wasn't one of them. And on that sad thought, a couple of early students burst into the classroom. They didn't knock. Eleven-year-olds weren't known for their respect for closed doors. They filtered in, full of youthful angst and whispered gossip that immediately silenced the moment they saw the adults. Or, more specifically, the moment they saw Toni. They stared at her with mixed expressions of fascination and horror, like she was a fifteen-car pileup on the Hollywood freeway.

But there were only five kids. And the hallway, which should have been packed with little bodies, was only half-full.

"How many kids are coming to school today?" she asked.

John sighed. "At last count, at least a third have called in sick."

Linda groaned. "Because what these kids need is another day stuck in front of the TV playing video games."

"Or out on the street getting into trouble," Toni added.

"Or at home getting high," John finished, his voice heavy.

And that was the moment she decided. The determination had been gathering since she'd first accepted she was a werewolf, but the strength hadn't crystalized until she told Rashard who she was. The rest was simply an extension of that act, and the knowledge that something had to change. Some*one* had to change

Crimson City's steady downgrade into ignorance and despair. The partisan in-fighting. The stupidity.

"Secrets are bad," she said loudly. Like that was a big revelation to anyone. "Secrets cause misunderstandings and invite problems. Secrets need to step out into the light and be an example to others."

"Uh, Toni . . ." Linda began. "What are you doing?"

"I'm taking a stand. I'm stepping into the light." She walked to the window and threw up the shade, then slid open the window so that she could lean right out and address the media. Behind her, she heard John rush forward, his energies tight with anxiety.

"Toni?" he said. In his defense, he wasn't stopping her. He was just worried.

She reached out a hand behind her, and he immediately grasped it. Yeah, she was determined, but that didn't mean she wasn't nervous. Still, it was too late to change her mind as cameras all over the lawn immediately focused on her.

"Hello, everyone," she called. She knew that with today's high-powered microphones, they would have no problem picking up her voice. "You already know I'm a werewolf. You probably know that a large percentage of our students have stayed home because they're afraid I'm going to wolf out and kill someone." She straightened. "Well, I'm not. And you know why I'm not? Because I have learned special techniques on how to control myself." Nothing new there. In fact, she could already see reporters getting that glazed "whatever" look in their eyes. She had to up the stakes fast.

"So I'm going to prove it." That caught their attention. "I'm going to sit in the school gym on the night of the full moon. I'm going to sit there and chat with anyone who wants to talk to me—reporters, parents, even concerned citizens. I'm going to be there under the full moon and I'm going to be absolutely human. If I can do that, then you can bet that I'll stay completely calm during the school day."

"What special techniques?" called someone.

She paused, unsure how to answer. Just because she'd chosen to live the revealed life didn't mean John did. But before she could say anything, John squeezed her hand and stepped up beside her. "Druidic techniques," he said calmly. "Ways to control energy. Ways to manage a person's animal or . . ." He swallowed. "Or even vampiric energies. I'll explain everything in a press conference this afternoon. For right now, we have to start classes. Thank you for coming, everyone. Good day."

And with that, he stepped back and slid the window closed.

"You didn't have to do that," Toni said softly.

"Yeah, I did," he said as he met her gaze. "You're right. Secrets are bad." Then he shook his head. "I just wish you'd picked a few moons from now. This is your first full moon. I don't know that you'll be ready."

"I'll be ready," she returned firmly. Then she leaned in and, in front of Linda and now eight gawking students, planted a kiss right smack dab in the center of his mouth. "You'll make sure I'm ready."

Chapter Seven

The grand essentials of happiness are: something to do,
something to love, and something to hope for.
—Allan K. Chalmers

Their secrets came out. All their secrets.

Two days before the full moon the *Post* published a tell-all article about Crimson City's most diverse middle school. It wrote that Nurse Linda was a vamp. That security officers Howie and Juan were wolves. That Principal Wong—named Crimson City's Man with a Plan—was a high-ranking druid who specialized in energy manipulation. His after-school program had been training paranormal kids how to use their skills in secret.

And the Man with a Plan was sleeping with the Teacher Turned Werewolf. How bizarre was it that out of everything, the press seemed most interested in that?

The guilt could have been crippling. Toni hated knowing that everything was happening because of her. By accident, of course, but still because of her. If life had gone more typically, she would have slunk around the school, an apology in her every expression and action. She would be at her friends' houses and with their families, doing everything she could to make amends. That would be the normal course of her life.

But nothing was normal these days. She spent her nights training for the full moon and her days under guard. Yes, under guard. John had refused to fire her, but he had been forced to make some compromises. He'd hired a security team armed with B-Ops guns—the kind that shot silver or UV bullets. The official orders were to shoot Toni dead if she lost control, but their real job was more as her bodyguard, protecting her from protesters and loonies alike.

On the upside, none of her ED kids were messing with her. She and one guard, J.B.—an ex B-Ops officer—were developing quite a routine. All Toni had to do was hunch her shoulders and look mean, and J.B. would pull out a tazer—and train it on the kid saying, "Don't piss her off. I don't know if I can control *her,* but you I can handle. . . ." The kids fell right into line. Laniqua was being so studious, she might even pull a B in science.

Yet they were all living on borrowed time. Everything depended on tonight's full moon. Toni's intent had been simply to keep her job, to prove that she was safe around children. But the whole thing had grown to massive proportions. If she couldn't prove that John's druid techniques controlled the wolf, then obviously the techniques were flawed. There went John's after-school program. And all those newly exposed teachers would be fired.

The next step would be segregation and ghettoization. The werewolves were already persona nongrata, but now there was talk of walls and perimeter guards around Wolftown. The whole world was watching what would happen tonight and—based on Toni's actions—would decide the entire future of the surrounding community.

But no pressure.

Fortunately, most people wanted her to succeed. The paranormals wanted to believe they could control themselves, and the normals wanted to feel safe around the paranormals. And no one—or almost no one—wanted a full scale riot in a middle school gym. So whereas there might be guns all over the freaking place, most of the cops wouldn't be trigger-happy. Or so she hoped.

Damn, the lights were hot. Toni was sitting in the gym pretending to eat dinner. In truth, she was picking at her spinach salad. She didn't want wimpy green leaves. She wanted steak, raw and dripping with blood. The very thought nauseated her. Or rather, she wished it did. But the truth was, the wolf was *hungry*. And it was very, very close to the surface. Given that she was this twitchy three hours before moonrise made her even twitchier.

For the first time, she began to realize exactly what she was attempting. To her knowledge, no werewolf—none—had ever done such a thing on a full moon. Keeli had said that some—most—could exert some control of the wolf. But control and total suppression were two different things, especially on a full moon. And no one had ever tried to do this while being prodded and watched and harassed by everyone in freaking creation to the point that even normal humans would want to rip their necks right out and feast on the steaming remains. And if she failed, she knew she would be neutralized. Whatever form that took.

Toni forced herself to swallow another two spinach leaves. No problem here; she had everything under

JADE LEE

control. Thank God John was around. She hadn't a prayer without him standing beside her, keeping her energies under his control.

She looked up from her salad and glared at Keeli, who was looking all official and gorgeous. She was talking to the press, spouting garbage about how werewolves were an asset to any community and *blah, blah, blah*. Her vamp lover—some Vendix or something—was hanging in the background like a demon of death. The two exchanged a look—one filled with love and admiration and all that crap—and a surge of jealousy started a growl deep in Toni's throat. Not because some wolf and vamp had decided to get it on, but because John was right there too, standing next to Keeli in a pin-striped suit that made him look like a god.

And where was John looking? At Keeli. At the cameras. At everyone but where he ought to be looking: right at Toni. Right by her side. Wasn't she doing everything here for him? For . . .

"Are you all right?" Vic's high voice cut through her glower. She blinked and turned to the boy who had started this particular nightmare. She hadn't a clue how he'd managed to worm his way around to her side. He'd had to crawl through snarls of wires and slip beneath the barrier of guards.

"Miss Freedman? Can you hear me? I came with Keeli, but . . ." His voice faded away as he stared at her.

Toni realized that her lips were curled back in a snarl. She was a teacher, damn it. What was she doing snarling at a kid—any kid? Even if he was the little bastard who deserved to . . .

She blinked and looked down at her hands. It wasn't obvious to anyone else, but she knew her bones had lengthened. She knew that she was a single breath away from total moon-madness.

264

"I can't do this," she whispered. "Oh God. I've got to get out of here."

"You can't!" Vic growled. "It's too late!"

"Yes, she can," John interrupted, slowly moving into Toni's peripheral vision. At least, he started that way. She could never just watch him sideways. Even before all of this happened, she'd tried to watch him out of the corner of her eye only to find herself staring straight on at him. He was just that magnetic.

"John," she whispered. "I don't know if I can do this."

"Do you want to cancel?"

"She can't! They'll lock us up for sure!" Vic cried.

"She can. If she wants to." John stroked her cheek with his thumb. A single caress, but it reminded her better than anything that she was human. That *they* were human. That no matter what, she was a rational, thinking being, and she could control herself.

"It's hard," she whispered. "A lot harder than I expected."

"If you can't do it, Toni, we need to end this now. The last thing we need is bad press." This came from Keeli, her very feminine voice showing no hint of strain.

Toni turned to the alpha. "You're not having problems at all." It was half accusation, half jealousy.

"I've been doing this a lot longer. And besides . . ." She glanced at John. "He's helping." She turned and grabbed Vic's arm. "That's why we're leaving."

"But I'm staying." That was from the vamp, Michael. "Just to help keep things cool." His eyes were unnerving as he drilled her with his hard stare. "Are they going to stay cool?"

Too many questions. Too many people. Toni wanted to howl in frustration. She turned instinctively to John instead. "Can I?" She hadn't meant to ask. But he was the teacher here, the druid with the mojo. Shouldn't he know if she was capable of . . .

"I haven't a clue," he responded evenly.

Alarm shot through her. "You said I could! You said I was capable!"

He nodded. "And you are *capable*. I don't know if you will. Do you want to control the wolf? Do you want to—"

"Oh, just shut up!" she snapped. She'd been getting his druid mind control double talk all week. In truth, she knew he was right. At a certain point, she simply had to decide to be human, and then force her mind if not her body to stay human. No big deal. But right now, with moonrise steadily approaching, she was beginning to have doubts. Mental games were all well and good when the sun was out. But in moonlight? And if she failed . . . ?

She sighed. She dug deep into her heart, stared at all the people staring back at her. She also noticed the guns. Everyone was here: cops, B-Ops, national and international press, pro-paranormal groups, human preservationists, wolves, vamps, and Vic. Little Vic.

She focused on his young face. "I'm sorry about your brother," she said. "Have you had any trouble?"

He shook his head. "Not when I'm with Keeli."

"We've got him and his mother in the tunnels. They're safe now."

Toni nodded, her decision made. She didn't give a damn about her job, about John's program, or even changing the world. It all came down to Vic for her— one kid and his little brother. "I'm staying," she said firmly. Because if she didn't prove that werewolves were safe, then Vic would spend the rest of his life hiding underground.

"You go, girl!" Keeli answered with a grin. Then she glanced at John. "So, we'll get out of here. The last thing you need are three wolves under the moon." With one last loving glance at her vamp, she and Vic made their way through the crowd. It wasn't easy for them—especially once past the press and into the protesters. Cheers and curses filled the room as they passed. But a moment later, they were gone and all that nervous attention was focused on Toni, who resolutely took another bite of salad.

"I hate spinach," she groused.

John reached over and grabbed a bite for himself. "Me too," he answered. But they both resolutely chewed while everyone waited for moonrise.

Toni was sweating. She supposed that was a good thing since dogs didn't sweat; they panted. And her mouth was resolutely clamped shut. Still, the sweating wasn't all that pleasant.

Two hours past moonrise. She was sitting cross-legged on the floor. She wasn't doing that stupid lotus thing—her legs just didn't go that way—but she was busy concentrating on her breathing. And, apparently, sweating. The room was dead silent—or at least it had started that way.

From the moment someone had bellowed, "Moonrise!" the room had gone quiet as a grave. Toni had simply dropped to the floor and begun meditating on her breath. Frankly, her navel would have been more exciting. But breathing in and out was keeping her sane—and in human form—so who was she to knock, "Breathe in, Grasshopper, breathe out." Yawn.

An hour after moonrise, the whispers had begun. A half hour later, the whispers became chatter. Then,

full-out background noise like at a café. Toni didn't
care. As long as no one spoke to her, she could allow
the noise to roll right past. It was all part of the eternal
present. Yada, yada, yada.

A few hours later, her back began to hurt. She
stretched her legs out in front of her, then allowed herself to roll backward until she was lying flat on her
back. The room made an audible gasp as cameras suddenly riveted on her. She lifted her head enough to grimace at all of them. "Jeez, I'm just stretching out. All
that sitting hurts."

No response. She got the feeling they were disappointed she wasn't a slavering beast.

"Whatever," she drawled.

John came up beside her under the guise of giving
her a glass of water. "Don't fall asleep," he murmured.
"Your subconscious might take over and—"

"I got it, I got it." It's not like he hadn't said the
same thing a dozen times.

"You're doing great, you know. I haven't had to do
much at all."

She looked up at him, surprised. "Really?" Might
she possibly get through this thing unscathed?

"Really." Then he winked at her. "But don't let your
guard down."

"Never!" she swore.

But she did. It was three in the morning. She was lying on her back. Even the reporters were falling asleep
on their folding chairs. Her concentration faded.
Dreaming began. Running through the fields, baying
at the moon, beautiful, open, *wild* feelings. She had
never felt so free.

And someone opened the windowshade. Or perhaps
it wasn't the shade that moved; maybe the moon slid
into view. All she knew was that one moment she was

lying on her back wishing for her soft mattress, and the next moment she was arching for the dark silver disk and howling—yes, howling—not in fear or even hunger, just the pure joy of being alive.

"Arrrrooooo!" The sound echoed eerily in the subway tunnels outside. She couldn't really hear the response, but she felt it in her bones, this absolute joy in being alive. It was something her human side had never felt. Not moon-madness, but moon love, earth love, joy, and life as it had never before been—immediate, detailed, and so much more than a mere human could understand.

She smelled the sweat of fear and tasted the anticipation on the air. She heard a hundred heartbeats accelerate, and she saw the primal response from . . . John? How could he . . . ?

Of course. She felt his energy merge with her own, felt his very human existence call to her human side. But the wolf was so strong, so vital, why would it cede its existence to him? To anyone?

It wouldn't. It didn't. Instead, it brought out the instinctive in John, the animal out of the man. She howled again and he echoed her call. There was no anger in the sound, only love and lust, and acknowledgment that they were mated.

"No! Ms. Freedman, no!"

There was a child here. Rashard. And in her wolf mind, he was one of her cubs, a part of her pack, as much in her heart as John. His energies were different than she expected, but she didn't really care. She turned and grinned at him—a big doggie grin that made him tremble.

She knew he was afraid of her, and that terror made her sad. She ducked her head, searching for the words, finding something else instead. She stepped slowly for-

ward, extending her tongue to lick him, a big doggie
kiss that would make him giggle. She had seen him
with puppies before. He would like that.

"Shoot her! Shoot her!" a man was screaming.

Her wolf senses were aware of the man—Rashard's
father. She also could sense the straining, anxious
mass of people around her, some of them whipped into
a frenzy by Rashard's dad. She knew also Vendix,
Keeli's vampire, was at the ready and the cops had
their guns drawn. But she heard their hearts slow, their
eyes telling them she was no threat to anyone. Even so,
she twisted her head to look at the vampire in silent
communication. He nodded. He would hold the people back. This was about her and the boy—letting
Rashard know and accept the wolf in her.

She stepped forward and extended her tongue, licking the child's cheek. She felt his surprise, knew the
moment his tight shoulders relaxed.

"She's eating him!" Then there was an explosion,
loud and echoing. Gunfire. A shotgun blast. The shot
hit the ceiling, the barrel knocked upward by the vampire. Toni absorbed these things in a flash and reacted
just as quickly.

She knocked the boy behind her, out of danger, to
stand over him with teeth bared, senses straining. Beside her, she felt John dive forward as well, protecting
both her and Rashard. But the war had begun, and
they were dead center.

"Kill her! Kill her!" screamed the man.

"No! Dad, no!"

It was chaos, too confused for even her enhanced
senses to follow. There were too many guns being
drawn, too many people scrambling every which way.
Teenage boys—the fake commandos?—abruptly drew
silver knives and small handguns. They were blocked

by the cops, beaten back with nonlethal force, but she smelled the blood and pain as a wrist was broken, a shoulder dislocated. She tried to push Rashard into a corner, but he was straining forward, screaming at his father, who was still bellowing back.

"Kill her!" Rashard's father pulled a small handgun and aimed at her—or his son, she couldn't tell which. It didn't matter; she slammed the boy sideways to step between him and the weapon. Then she felt John push her aside. The gun went off. The bullet missed, but he caught another from the opposite side. She watched him spin and fall, and then she smelled blood—John's blood—and he fell before her.

Rational thought faded. Her love—her mate—was dying and the danger was still present. She twisted, following the acrid scent of gunpowder. A boy—a teen—was taking aim again but she was on him before he could do more than grimace. Her teeth sank deep and hard, blood hot and vital shooting into her mouth.

The boy screamed, but she held him down, her jaws locked on the kid's forearm. The gun went flying. The body armor beneath the boy's clothing only made him less flexible, so she easily knocked him down.

"Stop it! Stop it!" screamed Rashard, crawling on his knees toward his father. John grabbed the child and held him down, blood seeping thick and dark from his shoulder.

"Stay down!" he ordered.

"Stop it!" Rashard continued, his voice a half sob, half plea.

Which is when Toni at last understood. She saw it clearly in the eyes of the boy she had pinned to the floor. He was looking at Rashard's father seeking help, begging for guidance. Rashard's father was the leader of these children with guns.

She released the boy's arm; he was weaponless now and little threat. Rashard's father was still screaming, still urging everyone to kill. Because of him, John had been shot, children were being hurt, and his own son was in danger. He was the source of all threat.

Therefore, she need only finish him and the danger would pass. The others would quiet, the turmoil cease. Their eyes locked from opposite sides of the room, and she read soul-deep hatred coiled inside him—not just for her, but for everyone and everything. He was anger and bitterness in search of a target.

"Toni! Stop it! Change back! Toni!"

Her muscles tightened to spring. John was in danger. She would end it.

"Toni! Marry me! I love you, I want to marry you. We've got to get married, Toni. I love you!"

Of all the sounds, of all the noises that surrounded her, those words jarred. The rest were simply variations of anger and fear, hatred and violence. She heard them, catalogued them, and then let them slide into the unimportant category in her mind. But these words were different. These words needed her human mind to understand.

She paused, torn between the human need to comprehend and the lupine desire to protect.

"I love you, Toni. Please, marry me."

She hesitated, her human mind breaking through her wolfish focus. She swung her head to face John.

"That's it, Toni. Listen to me. Find yourself."

"I never lost myself," she snapped—in her human voice—as the instinctive lost ground to the cerebral. "And who the hell proposes in the middle of a fight?"

He grinned. "You need to be fully human, Toni."

She turned her gaze back to Rashard's father. He

was still screaming, spittle spraying from his mouth. The boys that followed him had already been handled by the cops, but he was still inciting the protesters. But then Vendix was there, expertly twisting the man down to the floor and silencing him with a single hand pressed hard into his back. The man went silent.

Toni remained crouched, her eyes scanning the crowd for further danger. Nothing. As expected, with Mr. Gray silenced and her calm, the rest of the room began to quiet. That, plus all the screamers had run out of the building.

The threat gone, Toni forced her heart to slow, her senses to reel back in. She made herself look human again. Meanwhile, Rashard crawled out from under John, his face streaked with tears. "I couldn't let him kill you," he stammered to Toni. "I couldn't."

She knew the truth then. She'd been Rashard's SPED teacher for two years now, and she could read the boy like no other. "Your father was the one who attacked Joey, isn't he? That's why you were afraid for me."

Rashard looked away, unwilling to speak. But she could see the truth in the hunch of his shoulders, the defeated cast to his face.

"It's okay, Rashard. We'll get it all sorted out. I promise." She paused a moment, waiting for a response from the boy. Nothing. But then, that was the best she could expect at the moment.

Her gaze traveled back to John. Even in wolf form, she'd known the wound wasn't mortal. She'd been more concerned with keeping him from getting shot again. But now—back fully human—the sight of the blood still seeping through his shirt made her sick with worry.

"John—"

"I'm okay."

"I know—"

"The news feeds are live. Someone has got to have called an ambulance."

Sirens were cutting through the air. "I know—"

"It's just a shoulder wound. I'm not going to die."

"Damn it, John, I know! So shut up already!" Her bellow effectively silenced him, and everyone else. And in the suddenly echoing room, she dropped to her knees beside him and planted a big wet kiss right on his lips. Then she drew back. "Yes."

He blinked. "Huh?"

She sighed. "If you were serious about marriage, then I'm serious about accepting."

He frowned. "I was trying to break you out of wolf mode, reach your human side."

"Oh."

They stared at one another, the awkward moment stretching, extending, getting really, really annoying. And just when both of them opened their mouths to speak, the paramedics shoved their way into the conversation.

"Excuse me. Excuse me. Has he been infected? Is this a were-wound?"

Toni lifted the pad off John's shoulder and pointed. "That's a bullet hole."

"No lycanthropy, then. Good."

"It's a bullet hole! As in, a bullet is in there. As in, he got shot!"

"I'm the one who was bit!" bellowed the kid from behind.

Toni didn't even give him a glance. "There's Sani-Lyco in the med kit. Go at it."

"Excuse me, miss, we need to get to work."

She was shoved out of the way. And while cameras continued to roll, John was bandaged up and driven off. The kid she'd bitten went, too. Rashard's dad had already left by way of cop car. She wanted to go. She stood to follow, but Vendix stopped her. Of all the people there, he was the one who still remembered the whole point of this night's vigil.

"You can't go out there. Not until sunrise."

"He's been shot!" She tried to jerk away from him, but his strength far outstripped hers, especially since she was still in human form. He didn't answer, and in the end, she quieted, knowing the truth. The wolf was perilously close to the surface. She could not risk going outside without John there to hold her in check.

"Are you okay without him here helping?" the vampire asked.

Toni bit her lip, her eyes taking in the remaining half dozen reporters, plus a few sullen protesters still watching her, still waiting to decide the fate of all nearby werewolves. "We've already lost," she muttered. "I bit someone."

"You were protecting me," Rashard muttered. Then, with a tug, he pulled her down to the floor. She settled beside him with a sigh, her thoughts still on John. Unfortunately, there was nothing she could do for her mate now. That was for the doctors. Right now, there was a child to protect, and an entire werewolf community hoping she could salvage this debacle.

She crossed her legs and glanced at Rashard's tight face. He would have to be interrogated by the cops, but the Children's Advocacy Center wasn't open yet. The police said they could wait until morning. In the meantime, they left two officers behind to finish interviews and nab video copies.

And oh yeah, there was still that full moon.

Toni felt twitchy all of a sudden. She hadn't realized how much John must have been helping her control the wolf. With him gone, it was all up to her. Unable to stop herself, she looked up at the window and the dark sky. Her bones were lengthening again, her body straining. With a disconnected horror, she realized she couldn't control herself without John there to help keep these energies in check. She couldn't . . .

"Ms. Freedman? Are you okay?"

Rashard. She tore her gaze away from the window to look into his young face. If ever there was a reason to get a grip, it was sitting right here beside her. He'd implicated his father for her. The least she could do was be worthy of his faith.

"I'm feeling a little ragged," she confessed.

"You need to focus," he answered, in a weird kind of role reversal. How many times had she said something like that to him? "We'll do it together."

She nodded, then glanced at his folded legs. Could everyone do the lotus but her? "My legs don't go that way."

"That's okay. Just sit normal and look at me." He flashed her a grin. "Just like when we do my math."

"Oh, goody. Fractions." But she did as he asked, and there, holding his hands and staring into his young, earnest face, she found a way to stay human for the rest of the night. Ten minutes after sunrise, she was on the way to the hospital.

Chapter Eight

*From what we get, we can make a living; what we give,
however, makes a life.*
—*Arthur Ashe*

"So, you made it through the night okay?" John was
looking like death warmed over, with pale, sunken
skin, and a hospital gown that couldn't hide the swath
of bandages around his shoulder.

"I bit a kid, John. Yeah, he was trying to shoot me,
but there'll be a brand-new werewolf in the tunnels
now because of me."

John shrugged, completely unfazed, though the
movement made him grimace in pain. "Doesn't matter. He was going to shoot Rashard. You were protecting a kid."

"He was going to shoot me."

John grinned. "That's not the way I saw it. Or the
guards."

"Your druid buddies? Those guards?"

"They weren't all druids, and that doesn't matter.
That's what we saw, and that's what the papers will re-

port. In fact, the superintendent was impressed enough to let the after-school program continue."

Toni glanced around his spare hospital room, mentally counting hours. "You got out of surgery three hours ago, you've been unconscious for another two—"

"Hour and a half."

"Whatever. How the hell—"

"He called and left a message."

"Bullshit."

John grimaced and waved at his cell phone—now listing fourteen new voice messages—resting on the bedside table. "Okay, so I called him and threatened to sic you on him if he didn't. Doesn't matter. You've got a job; I've got a job. All of our work can continue."

Understanding slowly crept into her sleep-deprived mind. "He couldn't find a replacement. For either of us."

John grinned. "And he expects to be invited to the wedding."

She blinked, too fogged to truly hope. And yet, he was smiling at her, his eyes dark and druggingly handsome.

"Do I need to get down on one knee?" he drawled. "Tell me now, because I think it'll take me a moment to get there. I was shot a few hours ago, you know. Trying to save my true love."

Toni bit her lip, trying to keep focused, trying to calm the rampaging emotions zinging around inside her. "Are you just trying to keep me in human form?" she asked.

"I love you, Toni. Dog or human, you're all woman to me."

She felt her mouth shift, pulling into a grin. "That was the corniest proposal I have ever heard."

"Give me a break here. I'm drugged. Plus, did I mention that—"

"You were shot a few hours ago. Trying to save your true love. I remember." She abruptly sobered. "No excuses, druid. Do you really, truly—"

He kissed her. He used her shirtfront to pull himself up to her and then took possession of her mouth. He was serious. And she was in love, too.

Long happy moments later, they finally separated. She clung to his lips as long as she could before she allowed him to settle back on his pillows. "You know we're going to have to adopt Rashard, don't you? I mean, with his father and brother in jail, he'll have no one."

John was quiet a long moment before he finally nodded. "Okay. We'll make it work."

She grinned, completely and totally in love with this man. "Of course we will. Just like we'll make the school work. And your program work. This city is a mess, but we can be an example. From here we can show the world how human and wolf can live peacefully together."

"And vamp." He tilted his head and smiled at her, and she was momentarily lost in the beauty of his face. Then his next words hit: "You did know that Rashard's a vampire, right?"

For Melissa Lynn Copeland, my fabulous writing buddy. Reading this story fresh off a plane from Europe is above and beyond—you're the best, Mel!

I'd like to thank:

Susan in California who e-mailed me one day and asked for Kimi and Nic. I hope you think their story was worth waiting for.

The Lunatic Café gang who came up with dozens of title ideas.

And a big thank you to Joely Sue Burkhart who suggested the name that was used for this story.

Dark Awakening

by
Patti O'Shea

Prologue

Augustin sneered at the human woman sleeping beside him. She was so much less than he deserved. He was Bak-Faru, the strongest and greatest of the demon branches—all should bow before him. Trailing a finger over her cheek, he imagined transforming it into a claw. It would be easy to shred her delicate skin, to cause exquisite agony, and his palm itched with the desire to tear into her flesh. But he could not. At least not yet. He breathed deeply until the urge passed.

For the present, Augustin needed the human. There was a *kijo* in the city; he was powerful enough to have felt her presence but had been unable to identify her. His bedmate, however, knew who the kijo was and had agreed to assist him—for a price. His contempt rushed back.

He must remember the plan. Later he could kill this woman who would betray not only the kijo, but thought to break faith with him as well. He'd read her thoughts, discerned her scheme to use him to steal the kijo's powers for herself. Such would not happen. As soon as the traitor was expendable, she was dead.

With another deep breath, he forced his fingers to relax. He needed the kijo and her magic. Immediately. None were yet aware that his strength had begun to wane, and although he still held power far beyond any other, he'd not be able to conceal his loss indefinitely. He had enemies, demons who would think nothing of ripping out his heart were they able to do so, and each eve he woke a shade less robust. Whether it was because the portal to Orcus had closed or some other reason, he knew not, but he had to act while he remained potent. Fate had chosen to side with him.

One kijo was born every five or six centuries. That he should find her now was an omen, especially since she had only begun her lessons. He would be unable to take her magic if she were fully trained. Yes, fortune had smiled upon him. He leaned back against the pillows and linked his hands behind his head. Soon his powers would exceed anything even he had known, then he would rule the Overworld and all would serve him.

The previous attempt by the Bak-Faru to take control of this realm had failed because of poor leadership. Most had been killed or banished. Augustin would not make their mistakes. Still, his efforts to organize the remaining demons had largely failed, and he had but one servant—a weak Ciretham who'd enslaved himself in exchange for protection. If they were in Orcus he could bend stronger demons to his will, but it was not so easy here in the human world. Once he took the kijo's powers, however, and blended them with his own, few would have any choice save to obey.

He had the spell committed to memory, but in order for it to extract her magic, he had to take the kijo's body by force. Augustin smiled. He preferred nonconsensual sex. In the two hundred years of his life, nothing had ever compared to the release he found as he ravished another—demon, human, werewolf, or vampire; it mattered not.

The memories left him aroused. He shook the blond woman awake, pushed back the covers, and grabbed her hair to pull her to his erection. At first she resisted and his blood surged, but to his disappointment, she quickly complied. As she serviced him, Augustin fantasized about the kijo struggling against his domination. It didn't take him long to find release.

Chapter One

Kimi put the folder in its place and shut the cabinet drawer before grabbing the next file. She couldn't believe a big-time ad agency like Smith and Copeland didn't have all its old campaigns stored digitally. Paper was archaic, and besides, she was supposed to be interning as a copywriter, not a clerk.

She knew why she'd been given this boring job—it was punishment for coming back late from lunch. Could she help it if Santos was having a huge shoe sale? Was it her fault they didn't have enough employees on duty? Of course not. But those black heels she'd tried on had done spectacular things for her legs and she wasn't leaving them behind to hurry back to work. Kimi went still and her lips curved as she imagined how Nic would stare when he saw her in a short, formfitting black dress and those pumps.

Her smile faded and, huffing out a long breath, she yanked open the drawer. He probably wouldn't care what she wore. After all, he'd been avoiding her since shortly after they'd been introduced at Mika and Conor's wedding. That had been eight months ago and now Kimi didn't even know where Nic was—San Francisco? Or had he returned to the Underworld?

With a scowl, she grabbed the next file. Of course, she hadn't realized when they'd met that he was a demon. Kimi hadn't even been aware at the time that Mika was half demon, and Mika was her cousin. Uncle David had been keeping one hell of a secret— Grandma Noguchi was still miffed about it.

Not that Kimi blamed her; she was kind of irritated too. For more than a year while her mom had been undergoing cancer treatment, she'd lived with Mika and Uncle David, and Kimi had never had a clue. The only one in the family who'd taken the news calmly was her dad, and Kimi couldn't help wondering if he'd been in on it. And she wondered if her dad knew something else. He'd been the one who'd arranged her internship at this firm. At the time her guess was that he'd done it because she'd changed her major three times and was waffling about her current choice— English. She'd believed he was trying to show her the job possibilities if she stuck with it, but now she questioned that. He was a big-shot in the San Francisco advertising community, so why had he pulled strings with a Los Angeles agency? That was something she planned to ask when she went home this weekend, and she wouldn't let him off the hook.

When she'd met Eleanor Inaba, the president of Smith & Copeland, Kimi had learned that the agency was filled with human women who had powers—her boss called them majo, though she always referred to Kimi as kijo and refused to explain why. According to Grandma Noguchi, both words roughly translated to *witch,* but then her grandmother didn't speak Japanese any more than Kimi did.

Kimi moved to the next set of filing cabinets. The

three weeks she'd spent at this agency had been interesting. Despite the fact that her job so far consisted largely of getting coffee for people, Kimi decided she liked advertising. It was intense, fast-paced, involved creativity and she actually enjoyed coming to work. Mostly. If only things were that exciting with the magic end of the deal. Oh, sure, it was way cool to have powers awakening, but she wanted to actually use them. Her training so far had consisted mostly of meditation, learning ethics and hearing about the history of the majo: They were children of the stars, they'd been persecuted throughout history and had subsequently gone underground; they believed, *Harm none*. Blah, blah, blah. Who cared?

Kimi stuffed a folder in a drawer. She already did no harm! She even put spiders outside when she found them in her apartment instead of squishing them, and she loathed those things. Kimi was trying to be patient, but all these endless lessons seemed like a waste of time. Why couldn't she learn to use her magic now instead of at some nebulous future date?

Being the youngest of a boatload of Noguchi cousins wasn't easy. Everything she'd tried—both good and bad—had already been done more successfully by someone else in the family. Not this time, though. For once, she had something all her own. Kimi grinned. She was a kijo. This was something she intended to be really good at. She wouldn't do anything stupid like use her abilities to clean the apartment or to interfere with others' free will. All she wanted was the chance to work with it, to feel her power.

Her smile dimmed. Maybe once she could actually do magic, Nic would be interested in her. She didn't understand why he kept avoiding her. She'd been sure the attraction was mutual. There'd been something in his eyes as he'd taken her hand the night they'd met that made her heart start to thunder, that had caused feelings she'd never known to awake, and she was certain he'd been flirting with her—until Uncle David came over and practically pushed Nic aside.

Because she'd been away at Berkeley, she hadn't been able to see Nic often, but the few times she was home, she'd sought him out. He hadn't run from her in the beginning; in fact, there was one occasion where he'd spirited her away and Kimi had been certain he was going to kiss her—until Uncle David had shown up again and ruined the moment.

She couldn't remember him interfering this way with Mika, his own daughter, and short of reading minds, there was no way her busybody uncle could know that Kimi had decided Nic was going to be her first lover. Yeah, she'd fooled around some with the boys she'd dated, but she always drew the line. She'd decided a long time ago that when she had sex, it was going to be with someone who meant something to her, someone she wanted so much, she couldn't say no. Nic got her that wound up, and considering he hadn't even kissed her yet, it had to mean that things were going to be explosive between them.

Yet it was more than that. Their few conversations had left her intrigued. He was fun and fascinating and smart, and everything else she'd ever dreamed of finding in a man. That had made her more determined that he be the one.

Maybe Nic had read her mind—she'd heard some demons could do that—and he'd begun avoiding her because he didn't want to waste time on a virgin. If she could find a way other than shouting it at his back as he fled from her, she would have told him she wasn't ignorant or skittish or shy. But the last time . . . Kimi rested her arms on top of the open drawer and grimaced. The last time she'd seen him, the message that Nic wanted her to stay away had been clear.

It had been the day the family celebrated the marriage of Nic's mother to Uncle David. Mika had been elated that her parents were finally together, and she hadn't been able to talk about anything else for weeks, but Kimi hadn't thought she'd be able to attend the party because she had a test. Luckily—or unluckily, depending on how she looked at it—she'd made it. What had happened that evening was indelibly imprinted on her memory:

She'd looked around the room, trying to find Nic. She'd seen him a moment before she'd offered Uncle David and her new aunt her best wishes, but then he disappeared. She frowned. He'd been avoiding her lately, but—There he was!

She tried to follow him out of the room, but Grandma Noguchi stopped her, and it seemed to take forever before her mom joined them and Kimi was able to excuse herself. Of course, she'd lost Nic by then, but Kimi wandered the way he'd been headed, hoping she could catch him. When she spotted the open game room door, she picked up her pace. Maybe he was shooting pool or something.

"You promised me she wasn't going to be here!"

Kimi came to an abrupt halt in the hallway outside the room. That was Nic's voice and he sounded angry.

"She was supposed to stay at school; I wasn't lying." Mika replied.

They were talking about her. Nic was pissed off that she had come home. Kimi twisted her fingers together, part of her wanting to walk away, another part wanting to hear what was said.

"It doesn't matter. I'll have to leave." Nic was resigned now, and that was worse than him being mad.

"Mom will be disappointed."

"I know, but Kimi chases me, Mika. I've gone out of my way to avoid her and she's yet to get the message."

Kimi felt as if someone had reached inside her chest and twisted her heart. His words hurt almost beyond bearing.

"It's that Noguchi stubbornness." Kimi thought Mika sounded both amused and sad. "And she feels—"

"I'm aware of what she feels, and that only makes it more difficult for me. You know what it's like for a demon, and I can only take so much."

There was a long pause. "I'll explain your absence to Mom. She'll understand."

Nic laughed. "No, she won't. You know how she is."

"One hundred percent Mahsei," Mika agreed.

Kimi realized Mika and Nic were headed for the door, and that shook her out of her paralysis. Moving as quietly as she could, she high-tailed it back down the corridor and away from them; the only thing that could make this night worse was getting caught eavesdropping and seeing the pity in their eyes.

Nic had disappeared after that. Yet, Kimi was haunted by one thing he'd said. *You know what it's like for a demon, and I can only take so much.* Did that mean if she kept after him, he would cave in? Maybe she would put on that dress and her new shoes and summon Nic anyway; then she could find out what exactly he'd meant. She had the power to call demons forth, and she'd been practicing for months, long before she'd come to the agency; so, why not? What was the worst that could happen?

Kimi immediately envisioned Nic laughing at her. She put away the final folder and slammed the drawer shut. The last thing she wanted was Nic rejecting her. She'd made it obvious she was attracted each time she'd seen him, and yet he stayed as far away as possible. And the vanishing act was an insult in itself. Everyone knew demons were free and easy when it came to sex. Nic apparently just wasn't with her.

Kimi left the file room and worked her way out of the bowels of the office building. Her stride faltered, though, when she reached the dimly lit atrium. When had darkness fallen?

Mika's warning about going out alone at night in Crimson City echoed through her head and Kimi shivered before she shook it off. Her cousin was overprotective, that was all, and it wasn't like Kimi was outside—she was in her office building. But it was summer, and for it to be this dark, it either had to be close to 9:00 p.m. or there had to be a total solar eclipse. Since the only astronomical event the news stations had been hyping was some kind of meteor shower, it had to be option one.

How had she lost nearly eight hours?

Her sleeveless black and white polka-dot dress suddenly seemed insubstantial, and Kimi wrapped her arms around her waist, trying to warm herself. "Hello?" she called.

No answer.

Maybe this was some type of test.

Kimi took a few hesitant steps forward, the tap of her low heels sounding incredibly loud in the emptiness. If this was an evaluation, one of the majo could have affected her perception of how much time had passed while she'd been filing—they had that ability— but what would they want to test her on?

The hair on her nape stood on end, and Kimi came to a halt. There was no reason to think something evil was lurking; any deserted office building this late at night would seem sinister. She reached for her comm before she remembered it was in her purse, damn it. She'd left that behind when she'd gone to file because someone had made a crack about her talking instead of working, but she wished she had it with her right now.

Lowering her hands to her sides, Kimi ran through what her dad had taught her about self-defense and chose her best options for a few of the more likely scenarios. It didn't hurt to be prepared just in case this feeling of dread was more than her imagination getting the best of her.

Illumination came from a few scattered emergency lights, and the deep shadows had her jumpy. She bit her lip. Anyone or anything could be concealed within them, and Kimi had to force her feet to move.

"Get to your cubicle," Kimi told herself. "Get your purse, and call for security to escort you to your car. Simple."

Pulse pounding, she quickened her pace, wanting to get out of here. Later, she'd laugh over how silly she was being, but that would be when she was in her apartment and safe.

Kimi was halfway across the atrium when someone stepped out of the dimness. She nearly shrieked before she recognized one of the agency's creative directors. "Brittany," she said, putting her hand over her racing heart. "You scared me."

Brittany ignored her. Turning her head to address someone hidden in the darkness behind her, the woman asked, "Is she powerful enough for your needs, Augustin?"

"Quite. She is exquisitely strong."

The man's voice was a rich baritone, and it made him sound pleasant, even attractive, but it raised goose bumps on Kimi's arms and she backed up a step.

"And as young as I promised," Brittany said.

"Beautiful as well. I'll delight in taking her body as much as I enjoy seizing her magic."

He edged forward just far enough for Kimi to see his silhouette, and she took another step back before she realized she couldn't run. She was only five and a half feet tall and this man towered over her by nearly a foot; if she attempted to flee, he'd catch her in a few strides. Fighting face-to-face gave her more options than being grabbed from the rear. Kimi shifted to balance her weight evenly.

This couldn't be happening, though. She had to be misunderstanding what was going on. Had to be. Brittany was majo; she wouldn't sell Kimi out. "Brittany? What's the deal?"

"The deal?" The woman finally looked at Kimi. "The deal, Kirstie, is that humans are falling behind, and that's only going to get worse as the alliance grows between the fangs and the dogs. I'm doing what I have to in order to ensure that I'm not among the losers."

Kimi fisted her hands, then relaxed her grip. "Kimi. My name is Kim-mee," she enunciated clearly, wanting the older woman to know exactly whom she'd betrayed. "And your explanation doesn't really tell me a whole lot."

"She is young," Augustin commented. He finally came into view.

The first thing Kimi noticed was his eyes. The irises were so pale, she couldn't guess their color in the dim light. He was a demon, then. The next thing she noticed was how obscenely handsome he was—Hollywood would love his face. He had waist-length, dark blond hair, and at both temples he had a tiny braid, each interwoven with shiny thread. Bak-Faru.

Mika's admonition to never use the name of that branch rang in her mind, and immediately on the heels of that thought came the dozens of warnings her cousin had given her about the Dark Ones. Kimi's gulp was audible in the silence.

Augustin smiled at her fear and held out his hand. "Come to me," the demon ordered.

Kimi shook her head. There was no way in hell she was going to make it easy for him. He was big, he was muscular, and he had the power of the darkest of the demon branches, but she would fight him with everything that she had.

"Excellent," he said. "The more you struggle against me, the easier it will be to wrest your magic from you."

He'd read her mind and that scared her, but not half as much as the fact that she was getting information from him and didn't think Augustin was sending it on purpose. A demon acquired a kijo's powers through sex, and he planned to rape her to get it. Like hell. She wasn't letting anyone take what was hers.

Making the decision calmed her somewhat. Kimi felt her heart begin to slow, and her respiration became deeper, more even. She'd only had a few weeks of training and hadn't used her magic yet, but she knew she could protect herself with a shield of light. Calling it forward, she surrounded herself, letting it thicken and grow until it would be impenetrable.

"Think you that such a meager defense will stop me?"

It took all her will, but she forced a smile and shrugged, trying to appear unconcerned. Her dad said if she didn't have a full house, to bluff 'em into think-

ing she held a royal flush. The dark demon threw back
his head and laughed. Damn it, he was still picking up
her thoughts.

Brittany shifted then, and Kimi looked to her, hoping the other woman was having second thoughts and
would help her. In a glance, she knew she was on her
own. So be it. Kimi had one advantage—the demon
wanted her alive—and she'd exploit that as much as
possible.

"Come to me," Augustin ordered once more. This
time, there was a mental compulsion behind it that
Kimi could feel, but it had no effect on her. The second
push was far less subtle.

"I think you're out of luck," she said with a smirk.

To her great amazement, her near-serenity remained even when Augustin started toward her. As
he tried to grasp her left arm, she slammed his face
with the heel of her right hand. She missed his nose,
damn it, but she got his eye. Her action left him momentarily stunned, and she kicked out, catching him
solidly in the knee with her foot. He remained standing and she kicked again, only this time he dodged
the blow.

"I could prevent you from moving your arms and
legs," Augustin said, "but I won't. I like it when a female fights." He smiled, his eyes so cold that Kimi
shuddered.

He tried to snare her again, but she whirled—a big
mistake. Her hair fell into her face, partially obscuring
her view, and she fought the long tresses, trying to get
them out of her way. Augustin took advantage of her
difficulty and seized her wrist.

Kimi turned her arm, and with help from her opposite hand, yanked herself free of his grip. She backed

away, using the time to shove her hair out of the way so she could see.

Another lunge by the demon and Kimi found herself fighting in much closer proximity to her attacker than she'd expected. She hit him in the kidney with an elbow, then rammed him on the opposite side with the other one. Her knee connected firmly with his groin and he slapped her. Hard. That froze Kimi. No one had ever hit her before.

Augustin caught her and spun her around, pinning her against his body. All she could manage was some weak backward kicks that caused no damage. He put his mouth against her skin and bit her exposed shoulder.

The pain woke her up. She knew he believed that he'd won. She struggled, twisting and writhing, trying to break his hold. And as she fought, she felt him grow hard against her. He began chanting in a language she didn't understand.

No! This wasn't happening. It wasn't.

Kimi felt someone playing with magic and she shook her head, moving her hair enough to see Brittany. The woman's eyes were half closed and she was working some kind of spell. Augustin finally noticed too, and raised his head. "Her power is mine! You will not touch it."

Brittany ignored him and the demon took one arm from around Kimi and threw a fireball at the woman. The creative director hit the floor, her body convulsing. Before it went still, Kimi took advantage of her assailant's lack of attention to fight free.

She should be afraid, but she wasn't—there was no fear left anywhere inside her. Instead, Kimi was furious, more furious than she'd ever been in her life. First

some damn demon thought he was going to rape her
and take her powers; then a majo had tried to steal her
magic. Enough.

When Augustin started toward her, she held her arm
out, palm facing him, and directed the rage building
inside her at him. What came out of her hand looked
like a bolt of electricity. It affected the demon the same
way. This time, he was the one who was knocked to
the floor. He didn't get up.

Kimi saw he wasn't dead, only injured; she caught
the movement of his chest and was relieved. It would
make things easier if she'd killed him, she knew, but
she wasn't quite sure how she'd feel about taking a
life. Sidestepping him, she scurried to Brittany, but the
other woman's life force was gone.

The demon stirred, so Kimi ran. She went to her cubicle first; she had to have her purse to get her keys to
drive her car. As she yanked the bag out of her desk
drawer, she realized she needed help. She didn't know
what she'd done to Augustin or how exactly she'd
done it, which meant she couldn't count on repeating
the act when needed. She had to have someone who
could help her fight a Dark One.

Mika! Mika was a demon. Gasping for breath, Kimi
clawed through her purse, trying to find her comm and
the number for the hotel—the number she was only
supposed to use in an emergency.

She located both, but the few seconds it took made
her realize she couldn't call her cousin. Mika was in
Tahiti on a belated honeymoon; by the time she and
Conor got back to Crimson City, Kimi would be long
dead. And demons who had human blood couldn't be
summoned, either. Kimi needed someone here now
who was strong enough to protect her.

Nic.

It didn't matter if he were in Orcus, San Francisco, or Timbuktu, a summoning would bring him instantly to her side. All she had to do was make it to her apartment safely, find her grimoire, and call forward the demon named Nicodemus.

Chapter Two

Nic sat at a scarred wooden table in the corner of the diner and waited for his change. Although he was restless, edgy, he was in no hurry to leave the air-conditioned building and face the oppressive West Texas night.

The place was nearly empty; he could have lingered without difficulty and he would have except his waitress had made it clear she'd like to take him home with her. It irritated him beyond measure that he wasn't interested. Darla was an alluring, curvaceous redhead, and he should have flirted in return, not discouraged her. Sex had always been easy for demons: If there was a mutual desire, they sated it; it was no different than drinking water when thirsty or eating when hungry. Things, though, had changed for him, and Nic knew exactly who was to blame: Kimi Noguchi.

Though the time he'd spent with her could be measured in minutes—a handful of meetings and several short conversations over a two-month period—the bonds had begun to form. For him. They weren't fully developed, not yet, but they were strong enough that he was averse to having sex with other women.

Not that he'd been celibate these many months away from California, but his encounters had been few and far between, happening only when his need for physical release was greater than he could deny. The corners of his lips quirked up. If he did the bonding rite with Kimi, there would be no others at all. Perhaps, though, mating with those women had been for the best. He'd been very careful with each of them, and his confidence in his ability to maintain control had increased.

Nic sighed, tapped his fingers against the table and thought about the day he'd realized he couldn't have Kimi—not in the near future. It had been yet another Noguchi family party, and he'd been standing in the corner, his eyes never leaving her. His half-sister, though, had seen the way he'd been watching, and had dragged him out of the room. What she'd said still worried him.

"Stay the hell away from her, Nicodemus," Mika growled the instant the door closed behind them.

"You know what there is between Kimi and me," he countered. Demons read energy; Mika should discern it readily.

"I know," his half-sister replied, "but she's too young. Kimi won't turn twenty for another month yet. You need to give her time to grow up, to finish college, to mature."

"But—"

"No buts." Mika made a slashing gesture as if she needed to stop his arguments with more than words. "It's not just her age. You could hurt her."

His temper flared, no doubt making his eyes glow red. He'd never hurt Kimi, and Mika should know that. He started to stalk past her, to leave the room, but she grabbed his arm.

"Not intentionally," she said quickly, emphatically. "I know you'd never knowingly harm her, but you're a demon and she's human."

This was Nic's first time out of Orcus, and he knew there was much he didn't understand about humanity. "How?" he asked, hoping that Mika was wrong, but fearing that she wasn't. She was half-human and understood this world in a way he did not.

"Demons are stronger than humans—much stronger—and we're not necessarily gentle when we have sex. We bite, we claw and we like hard thrusting—our females as well as our males. But if you mated with a human the way you do with another demon, you'd severely injure her."

Nic stood there, stunned. Were humans so very fragile?

Mika misinterpreted his silence. "If you don't believe me, ask Conor what it was like for him before we met. Ask him about how much self-command he had to exert to have any kind of sexual contact with a human, and he's a lot more controlled than you are. I don't think you could rein yourself in tightly enough, Nic, particularly not with Kimi."

"Because of the bond?"

"Yes." His half-sister nodded. "Even if you managed restraint with other human females, you know what the vishtau does to demons, and if you slipped, even for a moment . . . Well, I don't want to think about that."

Neither did he. "Why even mention her age then?" Nic asked bitterly. "With our physical differences, it's a moot point."

She squeezed his arm. "Because I don't believe it's hopeless. In five or ten years, when Kimi is old enough to deal with you, you'll have learned how to hold back. I know you, big brother, you'll be working hard to master your nature."

He mulled that over. Could he do it? Demons were emotional and tended to lose themselves in sex. And they did like it rough; Mika was right about that as well. Could he overcome his own genetics and be careful with Kimi?

"I want a promise from you," Mika said.

Nic tensed. Once a demon gave his word, he'd die to keep it, and his half-sister knew this. What was she going to ask of him? Was she going to demand that he—

A playful caress of his arm yanked Nic from his memories. "You were a million miles away, sugar," the waitress drawled. Her voice was sultry, enticing, and he tried again to work up some interest in going home with her. It wasn't there.

He reached for his rucksack and stood, slinging it over a shoulder. That broke her hold, but after he handed Darla a generous tip, she reached for his arm again. "You have incredible eyes," she told him. "I like—"

One instant Darla was stroking the inside of his wrist, the next he was standing in a small room with white walls and battered furniture. He sensed a human standing behind him and it only took a second to realize he'd been summoned. His hands clenched, but Nic didn't turn—he needed to get his rage under control first.

"Nic!"

Though it had been months since he'd last spoken with her, he recognized her voice and forgot his anger. Immediately, he pivoted and his breath caught. Kimi Noguchi was beautiful—more than beautiful. She was only about average height for a human female, but she'd fit against him perfectly; he was certain of that. Her legs were long, her body lithe, and although her curves weren't overly generous, she was sexy. He took in her stubborn chin, imagined kissing her full lips, then began to raise his gaze to the dark brown eyes that had haunted his sleep. Something, however, stopped him midway.

Dropping his pack to the floor, Nic closed the distance between them and gently ran the backs of his fingers over the handprint on her cheek. "Who did this to you?" he demanded.

She pulled away from his touch. "My face isn't important."

"Someone caused you pain; nothing is more important."

She stepped nearer, pressed her body against his, and put her arms around his waist, holding him tightly. Nic returned her embrace, hoping this wasn't another dream, that he wouldn't awake again to find himself alone, his body aching for hers. Closing his eyes, he inhaled deeply, filling his senses with her scent. Everything about Kimi aroused him—the warmth of her skin, the swell of her breasts, even the soft sound of her respiration—and he steeped himself in her, wanting to memorize each sensation.

"Nic," Kimi whispered, her breath tickling his ear, "I'm in trouble. Will you help me?"

He suspected that the summoning wouldn't offer him a choice, but it didn't matter; Nic would willingly give his life to protect this woman. "Of course," he said simply.

"You don't know what the problem is yet." Kimi leaned back far enough to meet his eyes, but she didn't release him.

"No doubt it has something to do with the man who

left his mark on your skin. Or werewolf. Or vampire."
And Nic would gladly kill any such bastard for daring
to cause Kimi even a moment of pain.

"Not a man. A demon. A Dark One."

His blood turned to ice at the thought of his woman
facing a Dark One on her own. The Bak-Faru scared
all other demons, most of whom refused to even use
the name of that branch for fear of catching their notice. A human would be wholly at their mercy. "What
happened?"

Kimi told him, the words tripping out. Her story
was nearly incoherent, but Nic didn't interrupt with
questions. She was shaken and he let her talk, allowing
her to share what she wanted in her own way. Her chin
wobbled a couple of times, but her eyes remained dry,
and when she finished she buried her face against his
throat again and clasped him firmly.

He let the silence stand, content at this point to offer
comfort. Stroking his hand over her hair, Nic felt an
odd sense of satisfaction—though he'd gone to great
lengths to keep his distance from her, Kimi had called
him when she needed help. She must sense the connection between them even though she was human.

"I'm glad you came to me instead of Mika," Nic said.

"I couldn't go to her for help; she and Conor are
halfway around the world and would never get here in
time."

Nic smirked at himself. He'd asked for that one. Of
course Kimi would think of Mika first; the two women
were close. That was why his half-sister had faced him
down and demanded he keep his distance from her
cousin. Proximity made the ties strengthen, and Mika
knew that.

He sighed silently. Kimi Noguchi was his vishtau
mate. Humans would call her his soul mate, but that

was inaccurate because this bond went far beyond. It encompassed every level of being for demons, involved an overwhelming sexual desire, and it was only with such a mate that they could conceive children. Kimi wouldn't feel it as strongly as he did because she was human, but it would affect her to some degree as well. That was what Mika had pushed to avoid for a few years longer.

Nic's hand went still. His promise to his sister had been that he'd do his best to stay away from Kimi, and he'd kept his word; it was she who'd summoned him to her side. Which meant all bets were off. The circumstances were lousy and Nic hated the thought of his woman in danger, but the die was cast.

The time had come to claim his vishtau mate.

Kimi couldn't believe Nic was holding her. She'd half-expected him to push her away or walk out before she could tell him that she needed him, yet he'd done neither of those things.

"You're really going to help me?" she asked.

"Of course. Why would you doubt it?"

She levered herself away from his chest so she could glare into his eyes. "Maybe because of the way you've treated me. How many times did you disappear when you saw me coming?"

To her surprise, Nic laughed. The sound was deep, melodic, and made her tingle. He was gorgeous. Nicodemus no-last-name-because-demons-didn't-have-them was the best-looking man—make that male—she'd ever seen. He was just over six feet: tall, but not too tall for her. The close-fitting jeans and black T-shirt he wore showed off his killer muscles, and Kimi wanted to run her hands over them. His dark hair was cut short enough that it stood up in places, and his eyes were laser blue—darker than most demons', but lighter than normal for a human and they were so piercing she could swear they saw deep inside her to places she'd never shown anyone.

It was his face, though, she found most appealing. His features were rugged, and while he wasn't as pretty as the dark demon she'd fought tonight, Kimi preferred Nic's rougher looks. The slight depression in his chin made her want to lean forward and press a kiss to that spot. It wasn't a cleft—it wasn't deep enough for that—but it added character. His cheekbones were high and sharp, his eyelashes were long, and with his dark brows, his eyes stood out more. Without thinking, Kimi stroked his stubbled jaw.

She thought she saw a flash of red in his eyes, but when she looked closer, she detected nothing out of the ordinary. Kimi lowered her hand and cleared her throat.

"Why did you go out of your way to avoid me? You even disappeared after your mom's wedding party and no one would let me know where you were."

Tension came into his body: she felt it, and she knew Nic wasn't going to tell her the truth—at least not all of it.

"No one knew where I was," he said. "I'd told Mika and her father that I was going back to Orcus, but I changed my mind and decided to explore the human world."

"And you dodged me because . . . ?"

Nic shook his head, as if amazed she had to ask. "Because of your age. You were too young when we met. You're still too young."

"I'm twenty. Not that much younger than you are."

He grinned and stepped away. "How old do you think *I* am?"

Kimi almost moved back into his arms, drawn by something she couldn't explain, but stopped herself and considered his question. He was Mika's older half brother, so that gave her a frame of reference to work with, but she took a moment to study him. "Twenty-eight? Twenty-nine?"

Nic shook his head.

"You can't be thirty yet!"

He laughed again, and it was only then that Kimi realized she'd said that as if it were ancient. She blushed at her rudeness. Maybe he was thirty, but that was only ten years older than she was. "Sorry."

"No need." Nic sobered and, eyes locked with hers, he said, "I'm forty-six."

"No way!" He was lying or teasing her or something. Her uncle David was that age, and her dad only a few years older. Nic didn't look anywhere near as old as either of them.

"Yes way," he said with a grin. "Demons age differently than humans, and we're much longer-lived. Our average life span is a few hundred years."

Kimi mulled that over. It had to be true. Nic's mother didn't look old enough to have grown kids. She'd chalked that up to plastic surgery, but it made sense that demons aged more slowly. She hadn't thought about it. "I guess that means *I'm* too old for *you,* since I'll be dead a couple hundred years before you."

Nic looked startled, and then his lips curved. "An interesting perspective, but not entirely accurate."

She nodded. From watching her cousin, Kimi knew demon children grew to adulthood at about the same rate human kids did, so what he meant was that he had more life experience. A lot more. But even if he were closer to her age, they wouldn't have a common frame of reference anyway, since he'd lived in Orcus almost his entire life. As far as she was concerned, that meant the gap between them wasn't really an issue.

No, she had a different problem. She'd just learned she had power, that she was a kijo, and having sex with a demon would give him her magic. Kimi wasn't ready to lose what she'd barely begun to explore. Not that Nic had indicated he wanted to take her to bed, but there was something in his eyes that made her think he was done keeping his distance. Be careful what you wish for!

Taking a deep breath, Kimi reached up and ran both hands through her hair, pushing it behind her shoulders and out of her way. Nic's growl had her jerking to attention. His eyes were definitely glowing red. She backed up until she hit the wall.

The urge to flee as he stalked toward her flooded Kimi, but she fought it. Nic wouldn't hurt her—Mika would kill him if he did—but he looked inhuman with his eyes that color. She almost squeaked when he reached for her, but all he did was lightly touch the mark on her shoulder.

"He bit you."

"Yes."

"Bastard," he said coldly. Nic lowered his hand. "Demons bite when they're sexually aroused."

"Are you warning me or informing me?"

"Both." As if sensing her unease, he moved away and Kimi drew a deep breath. "Are you up to answering some questions about the Dark One for me?"

"I told you what happened."

Nic dragged a hand through the top of his hair, making more of it stand on end. "Let me ask you something else. Have you been allowed free entry into Mika's home?"

"Do you mean, did she give me a key? No, she

didn't." Kimi smiled. "I don't think she wanted to chance me walking in on her and Conor. They *are* newlyweds."

He didn't return her smile. "When I said entry, I meant does Mika invite you in or can you enter on your own?"

"They invite me in. Why?"

That answer didn't appear to make him happy. "Because McCabe has some damn formidable protection around his home and no one can enter without an invitation. I was hoping, though, that you had permanent permission. If you did, you could hole up there while I hunt the dark demon and I wouldn't have to worry about protecting you."

Kimi wasn't sure how she felt about his desire to get rid of her. Part of her never wanted to see the Dark One again: that side wanted to allow Nic to make it all better. Another part of her, however, rebelled at the idea of letting him fight her battle on his own. She belonged at Nic's side no matter what.

"I won't be a liability," Kimi said.

"You're human."

And human equaled hindrance in Nic's mind. "I put him on his ass once—don't underestimate me."

"How did you do that?" he asked.

With a shrug, Kimi moved away from the wall. "I'm not sure. If I knew, I wouldn't need to ask for help."

"You said that—"

"I don't want to talk about it again," she snapped. She turned to go.

Before she could leave the room, Nic was there, his hands gentle on her shoulders as he faced her toward him. He hesitated only a moment before gathering her against his body and soothing her. "Hush, *tes,*" he said as he ran his hand over her hair.

She growled. "My name is Kimi, not Tess."

Nic laughed. He didn't make a sound, but she felt his chest shaking. "'Tes' is a demon word, not a name."

"Oh." And she felt stupid and young. "What does it mean?"

He ignored her question. "Would you trust me to read your thoughts? Only about the demon attack; I would delve no further. I give you my word on that."

Kimi hesitated, then agreed. He stopped stroking her hair and put his hands on either side of her head. She swore she could feel him in her mind, but he was as careful as he'd said he'd be and she relaxed against him. It was Nic who went rigid.

"What is it?" she asked when he stepped away. "Nic?"

"I know the one who assailed you." He began to pace. "He's very powerful and very dangerous. Fortunately, you hurt him severely—not just because you were able to get away, but because we'll have some time before Augustin will be recovered enough to come after you again. That's the good news."

"And the bad news?"

"There might not be any demon capable of defeating him."

Chapter Three

Of all the Dark Ones loose in the Overworld, why did it have to be this one after Kimi? Nic would move heaven and earth to protect his vishtau mate, he'd die so that she might live, but if he didn't take Augustin out with him, Kimi would be left to face the demon alone.

She moved, putting herself in his path as he paced the length of her apartment. "Nic, please. Talk to me."

"What do you want me to say? I'll defend you to the best of my ability, but that might not be enough."

"Is he really that dangerous, then?"

Her hands were clutched in front of her and Nic reached out, taking them in his. The iciness of her fingers told him how nervous she was. "Let me put it in perspective for you," he said quietly. She had to understand the gravity of the situation. "Many residents of Orcus wish the Bak-Faru didn't exist. They feel that all demons have been given a bad reputation because of the actions of this one group. Many of the Bak-Faru wish that Augustin never existed."

"Because they feel he gives them a bad name."

"Bingo," Nic said. He didn't quite know what the word meant, but he'd picked up plenty of slang since he'd come to the Overworld and he'd used the term correctly.

"How terrible is he?" Kimi asked. "Honestly?"

Nic debated. "Evil. I don't use that word lightly, either. He's twisted inside. The Dark Ones have done vile things, but Augustin has surpassed them to the point that his own branch shuns him."

"Why don't other demons do something about him? Arrest him or whatever?" Kimi asked, clasping his hands tightly.

Despite how serious things were, one side of Nic's mouth quirked up. How did he explain to her what his society was like? Their caste system was rigid and based on which branch someone was born into. Weaker demons regularly enslaved themselves to stronger demons for protection, and the alliances among branches were an intricate tangle that even the oldest of their people couldn't unravel. This would have made pursuing Augustin difficult enough, but when the innate fear most demons felt for the Dark Ones was factored in, it became impossible.

"The Bak-Faru live separate from other demons, and it would have been left up to them to handle Augustin. For whatever reason, they've opted to let him roam free."

Kimi took a step closer. "Could they just be scared of him too?"

"It's unlikely it's that simple, but I don't know. The Dark Ones seem irrational, and I can't begin to guess their logic."

She continued to gaze up at him, and Nic found himself sinking into her beautiful brown eyes. He wanted to reassure her, to make her believe that everything would be okay, but he couldn't. Instead, he leaned forward and brushed his lips over hers.

He meant to do nothing more than offer comfort, but their kiss was more perfect than he'd imagined—and he had expected it to be damn good. Unable to stop himself, he took it deeper. Kimi opened her mouth beneath his and Nic groaned as he finally tasted her: his vishtau mate. At last, he was kissing his vishtau mate. Pulling his hands free of hers, he reached for her hips and drew her body against his. Nic had to feel her, and he wanted her to know how she affected him, wanted her to know that even this simple kiss left him excited.

Kimi broke away. "I don't want this," she told him, and her lips trembled.

"Really? Eight months ago you wanted more from me than a few kisses." He hadn't meant to say that, even if it was true, but he didn't get a chance to apologize.

"That was then," Kimi shot back, and with a toss of her head, she flipped her hair behind her shoulder.

Reluctantly, Nic smiled. He liked the fire, and it was that which prompted him to push her. "So you no longer want me to slowly undress you, kissing each inch of exposed skin as I go? You don't wish me to bare your breasts, to roll your nipples between my fingers and take them in my mouth?" She blushed and looked away. Nic's grin broadened and he kept going. "That's not the only part of you I want to use my tongue on. I've imagined putting your legs over my shoulders and going down—"

"Shut up," Kimi snarled. She glared into his eyes, but he read more than anger and embarrassment. There was also arousal.

"Why?" he asked, trying to sound innocent. "I was just getting to the interesting part."

"I don't want to hear it."

"What have *you* fantasized about doing to *me?*" he asked, although he didn't expect an answer.

"Right now, I'm imagining punching you—hard."

Nic grinned. Kimi had grown up. He couldn't visualize her holding her own with him when they'd first met, and he liked the change. His smile faded. No doubt he should allow her more time to mature into the person she'd be one day and take more time to work on gaining the control he'd need to safely bed her, but he already sensed the bonds between them tightening—for him, not for her. Yes, she felt the attraction, but it wasn't the driving need to mate that he had. Everything would have been easier between them if she'd been a demon herself, or even part demon.

From time to time in his life, he'd idly wondered about his vishtau mate. Would he find her? What would she be like? How would it feel to be that closely connected to another? He'd never, not even once, imagined her to be a human.

He'd known it wasn't outside the realm of possibility. His mother had found a human vishtau mate after the death of his father. His sister's mate was half demon, another proof of a vishtau bond between the species. And he'd heard of others of mixed blood, but he hadn't thought he'd be one of those with a mate outside Orcus.

Maybe it was the Mahsei side of his nature, but to a large degree, Nic believed in going with the flow. He'd met Kimi, felt their bond, and developed new dreams. She'd been one of the reasons he'd chosen to stay in the Overworld. Since she couldn't live in his home, it was up to him to learn to fit into hers.

He said none of this, though. If Kimi were skittish—and he couldn't blame her if she was—it was up to him to win her, not scare her further.

"When I probed your memories," he said, getting back to what was crucial, "there was a part that wasn't clear. You held up your hand and Augustin was knocked to the floor?"

Kimi nodded, the motion making her dark hair slide in front of her shoulders again. It was long enough to fall below her breasts and Nic found himself distracted, picturing only her tresses hiding her naked body from his gaze. He fought it off.

"I don't know what happened, not exactly," she said, and he dragged his attention back to her face. "All I remember is being furious, so enraged that my fear was gone. I put my hand up and boom! That lightning or whatever it was came out and he dropped to the floor. I'm not sure how it happened."

Nic frowned, trying to come up with an explanation for what she'd done. If Kimi were a demon from one of the stronger branches, it would be simple, but she was human—there was no question about her heritage. "And that was the first time anything like that has happened?"

"Yeah. Why are you so interested in that?"

"Because if I die," Nic said grimly, "you'll have to fight Augustin alone. I want you to be able to defend yourself."

"What do you mean, if you die?" Kimi demanded.

"It'll be a battle to the death, tes. Do not doubt it."

She strode toward him, and if he hadn't stood his ground, he felt sure she would have backed him against the wall. "Listen up, Nicodemus," she said, and poked a finger into his chest. "I didn't call you forward to get killed. I called you forward to kick some ass. Are we clear?"

"And I'll do my best, for only with Augustin's death

will you be safe, but you need to understand that he's Bak-Faru and stronger than I am."

"I've been told you're dangerous."

Nic flattened her hand against his chest and rested his own over it. "I am. I'm half Grolird—the second darkest of the demon groups—and have the powers of this branch, but my Mahsei blood weakens them to a degree."

"How wide is the power gap between first place and second?"

Her question confused him for a moment, but then he understood. "It's unclear how much stronger the dark demons are than the Grolird. There've been few confrontations between members of the two branches."

"So, you could very possibly be more powerful than Augustin," Kimi said, sounding satisfied. "You'll win and I'll be safe."

"I'm not more powerful."

"You just said—"

"I know what I said, but I've fought Augustin before. I'm the one who got his ass kicked."

Kimi was momentarily stunned speechless. "And you're just telling me this now?"

He growled, a sound that wasn't human. "I haven't been here half an hour yet. Shit," he muttered, and Kimi was startled to hear such a human curse word coming from a demon. "Pack a bag," he ordered. "We can't stay here."

"It's packed. I was planning to go home tomorrow morning to spend the weekend with my parents."

Without a word, Nic disappeared into her bedroom and returned with her stuffed overnight bag. He retrieved his own backpack and, heading for the door, said, "Let's go."

"First tell me about what happened between you and the Dark One. Please," she added when he stared stubbornly at her. "Nic, you said he beat you. I need to know what we're facing."

His sigh was loud and Kimi figured that meant no dice. She'd grabbed her car keys and purse, slung the strap across her body, and was headed toward him when Nic began to talk.

"I was hiking with my father outside Biirkma—that's a city in Orcus—when we heard a child crying and went to help her. You have to understand that children are considered precious. No demon would walk away without helping one in need, nor would any of my people dream of harming a child—or almost none of us."

"Augustin being the exception to the rule," Kimi guessed. Nic grimaced and she saw something in his eyes that made her heart start to pound. Suddenly, she wasn't sure she wanted to hear this, but she braced herself and waited.

"She couldn't have been more than eight or nine, little more than a baby." Nic's hands clenched around the handles of the bags so hard that his knuckles went white. "When we topped the rise and saw what was occurring, my father bade me hide."

The choppy way he delivered the story was so unlike Nic that Kimi started to reach for him. He stepped back out of her range, and she let her hand fall to her side. Although his expression remained carefully blank, she could feel his torment. Almost against her will, she asked, "What was happening?"

"Augustin was raping her."

Kimi gasped and said, "Oh God."

"My father pulled him off and told the girl to run, and then he and the Bak-Faru fought." Nic's hands clenched harder around the straps of the bags. "My father was pure Grolird, but he was no match for Augustin, and though he told me not to show myself, I did. He needed help. Likely, the wiser course of action would have been to summon aid, but I could not imagine us not besting the Dark One." She heard Nic swallow. Then he said, his voice flat, "Augustin killed my father and left me for dead. I would have died, too, had the girl's father not come to murder the Dark One himself."

Kimi felt sick. Nic must, too. Though she hadn't been there, she'd never be able to get the image out of her head of that huge man raping a child. How much worse must it have been for Nic, who had not only seen it happen, but had seen his father killed before his eyes, and had nearly lost his own life.

Outrage filled her. "And no one did anything to that animal?" she demanded.

"The dark demons did something—he never forced himself on another child—but I don't know what."

"They should have killed him," she growled.

"I agree," Nic said, "and so did many others. There was a lynch mob outside the Bak-Faru enclave for weeks after the incident, and it was thousands strong. Or so I was told."

"How badly hurt were you, and what kind of recovery period did you have?" She knew Nic, and Kimi had no doubt in her mind that he would have been outside the enclave himself had he been able to make it.

"I told you," he said, voice still expressionless, "Augustin left me for dead. It took the healers months of work before I was able to stand. The recovery went faster after that."

Kimi moved closer to him, and taking his face between her hands, she stood on her toes to kiss him.

"You did what you could, Nic. You can't blame your-self."

"You're wrong, I can. But yes, I did what I was able. That's the point. I fought Augustin with all my strength and I lost." He leaned forward and there was nothing blank about his eyes or face now; he burned with intensity. "You have to be able to—"

The sound of crashing glass broke him off midsentence. Kimi whirled, but before she could see anything, Nic put her behind him, placing his body between her and the windows of her unit. "Stay back," he warned. He himself moved forward.

Then she saw what stood in her apartment. This was the demon of human nightmares. Its body was black and covered in thick scales. It had black wings, and its eyes were so dark, they were like a void—except for the red glow. It stood eight feet tall and towered over Nic. At least, it did until he shifted form to match it. Kimi gulped. Maybe demons weren't really just people, too.

Chapter Four

Nic circled with the other demon—a Ciretham, and clearly Augustin's minion—looking for an opening to attack. He'd heard Kimi's reaction as he'd shape-shifted, and that concerned him. This was a talent of his he'd been hoping not to share with her. Not immediately. He'd had no choice, however; he'd be at too big a disadvantage if he didn't equal the other's size.

The demon lashed out with his taloned right hand, but Nic easily blocked the blow and struck out with his tail, whipping the creature across the upper thigh. The groan he received made him smile.

Leathery wings slapped toward him, and Nic jumped out of range. He couldn't afford to fight long. Although he believed his presence had been unexpected, he couldn't dismiss the fact that there could be a second attacker waiting to swoop in while he was occupied. Kimi was next to the door and vulnerable.

He kicked out, catching the demon in the center of its chest and raking it with the claws of his feet. While the assault drove his opponent back a step, its scales prevented true injury.

"You will not protect the kijo," his foe said.

Kijo. The word sounded familiar, but Nic couldn't place it. There wasn't time to think, though, before his enemy went on the offensive. He tried to block the strikes, but a few landed and one ripped the black scales off Nic's shoulder. Pain tore through him, but he pushed it from his mind, and with a growl, leaped at the demon. Their exchanged blows came fast and furious as each tried to pummel the other into submission.

Nic noticed a shimmer—a weakness in the body armor directly beneath the sternum of his foe—and he sank his talons into the spot, gouging as deeply as he could. He felt skin and muscle give, and dragged his hand down, trying to cause maximum damage.

The demon threw back his head and roared. Nic lunged, sinking his teeth into the exposed neck. He'd been on the edge of control from the instant he'd heard glass break; now, with the taste of blood in his mouth, rage surged. This demon had thought to take his mate. A red haze filled Nic's brain and there was no reining in his Grolird nature—he ripped out the creature's throat.

He returned to his senses—and his humanoid form—as he knelt panting over his kill. Nic bowed his head, uncertain if he could stand to see Kimi's revulsion for what he was. If Kimi were demon herself, it would be one thing, but . . . A bead of moisture trickled from the corner of his lips, and Nic wiped at it. His index finger came away red. As his vision cleared further, he scanned the area and breathed a sigh of relief. At least he'd had the presence of mind to make a clean kill. Most of the blood had been contained behind the other's scales, and there was little splatter. Perhaps that had prevented Kimi from being too repelled.

Knowing he had no choice except to face her, Nic

pushed to his feet and turned. Her eyes were enormous and her face so ashen that, when she swayed, he feared she was going to pass out. He nearly rushed to her side. Nic needed to cuddle her, to reassure her, to drive that appalled, dazed expression away, but if he offered any sympathy, she'd fall apart. They didn't have time for that.

"Human women are weak," he sneered, putting enough contempt into his voice that she couldn't miss it.

"I am not weak," Kimi protested. There was a spark in her words, but the response was more contrary than fiery.

"Do you think any demon female would stand frozen with shock, feeling remorse over the death of an enemy?" Nic shook his head with mock sadness. "Pitiful."

Kimi lost some of her pallor as anger took hold. "I am not pitiful! I've never seen anyone killed before, you know. Not with teeth and claws and"—she waved a hand helplessly—"things like that." Her chin wobbled.

"Block it from your mind." He allowed his voice to soften a bit, but not much; she was still too close to the edge. "If you want to fall apart, you do it after this situation is over. And I do mean completely, totally finished. Do you understand me?"

She nodded and, with a sense of relief, Nic watched her lock down her emotions. Confident now that she wasn't going to become hysterical, he closed the distance between them.

"You're bleeding," Kimi said. "How bad is it?"

Looking down at his shoulder, Nic assessed the damage and decided it was minor. "It's nothing, it'll be healed in a couple of hours."

"Good."

The near-desperation in her voice told him she was searching for distractions to keep from thinking about what had happened. He could help her with that. Nic ran a hand over his chest and down his belly, drawing her attention.

"You're naked!" she squeaked.

He smiled at her reaction—his Mahsei side was as much a part of him as the Grolird, he decided, because only a Mahsei would find something humorous at this moment. "I had to get rid of the clothes when I changed form or they'd have been shredded."

"At least put some pants on," she snapped.

She hadn't commented on it, but not only was he naked, he was hard. It was demon physiology at work—a strong adrenaline charge always left them aroused after the danger passed, and Nic was fighting it for all he was worth. If Kimi were demon, he'd have her on her back and already be inside her. Hell, if she were demon, she probably would have been on top of him before he reached her because of her own adrenaline spike.

"Are you sure you wish me to cover myself? You don't seem to want to look at anything but this." He stroked his shaft a couple of times, and her gasp had him smothering another laugh.

"Nic," she growled in warning.

"What?" He tried to look innocent. "Did you want to take care of it yourself?"

"Not now. Ask me again in ten or fifteen years."

Relieved she was past her shakiness, he magicked his clothes to him and reluctantly donned them. As hard as he was, the last thing he wanted was to confine himself, but he gingerly zipped up anyway. This was the price for having a young human mate, but as Nic gazed at Kimi, he knew he could live with the frustration as long as he had her.

When he finished dressing, she asked, "What do we do with Augustin's body?"

"That isn't Augustin," he told her.

"Of course it is," Kimi insisted. "He's the only demon after me."

Nic took a deep breath and released it slowly. "Demons form alliances," Nic explained. "The male that attacked was from a midrange branch called Ciretham. My guess is that he was working for Augustin and was sent to capture you."

"The threat isn't over, then," she said, sounding subdued.

"Sorry, but no. Why do you think I made you promise to hold it together?" He didn't wait for her to answer. Gathering up their bags, Nic said, "We have to leave. Let's go."

She looked dazed again, but this time he put an arm around her shoulders and steered her down the hall to the stairs. "I'll do everything within my power to protect you, tes. Trust me."

"What does tes mean?"

He'd ignored her the last time she'd asked that question, and Nic didn't answer this query either. Kimi wasn't yet ready to learn that tes was the demon word for *beloved*.

When Nic said he wanted to find a motel, Kimi had imagined some seedy dive with winos and derelicts. Instead, he'd chosen the kind of place families would stay while they were in Crimson City to visit Disney. It was a pleasant surprise.

Kimi arranged the pillows against the headboard

and leaned back. She'd forgotten to throw pajamas in her bag, so Nic had loaned her a T-shirt. It felt . . . sexy to be wearing only panties and one of his tees. He was half a foot taller, and broad through the shoulders and chest, so while this was hardly immodest, the idea that she was nearly bare beneath *his* shirt made her shiver.

Thinking about her physical reaction to him helped her keep other thoughts at bay. She didn't want Nic to consider her weak, but every time she closed her eyes, she saw him slay the other demon. There'd been no choice, Kimi knew. It had been kill or be killed, but she wasn't acquainted with violence beyond what they showed on the news or what she saw at the movies. The idea of killing another was nearly incomprehensible to her . . . and yet, Nic had done it without difficulty.

Her body trembled and she pushed the images away. She'd promised she wouldn't fall apart until they were safe. Mika had told her that demons always kept their word to the letter, and that they looked down on humans who didn't. Kimi refused to give Nic another reason to prefer a demon female over her.

The shower shut off and she sighed with relief. When he was around, it was easier to forget. Kimi focused on visualizing Nic bare and wet, imagined licking water droplets off his warm skin. He'd made it clear he'd welcome her touch. She was trying to wrap her mind around that. For months she'd believed he wasn't interested in her, and it was heady stuff to learn otherwise. Too damn bad that she had to stay away from him now.

Nic came out wearing nothing except a pair of jeans, and Kimi fought the need to squirm. He'd shaved, and as hot as he was with stubble, he was more striking without it. He must have towel-dried his hair because

it was standing up worse than ever, but it was his muscled abs, chest, and arms that she couldn't take her
eyes off. Something clenched inside her, not between
her thighs, but in the vicinity of her heart.

"You're staring," he said with that usual damn smirk
of his.

"I'm trying to see how your wound is healing,"
Kimi lied.

That brought him over to the bed. All she had to do
was lean over and she could put her mouth on him
through the denim. She wanted to do it so badly, her
body almost shook, and Kimi had to remind herself
that it wouldn't stop there. He'd want to be inside her
and she'd want him there too, but she wanted her
magic more than an orgasm—even if she'd bet he
could make her scream.

"That wasn't where I was injured," Nic told her,
laughter in his voice. Kimi jerked her gaze up to his
shoulder.

"There's only a few pinkish lines left," she said, then
cleared her throat to lose the raspiness.

"We demons heal fast. You should know that."

Nic walked to the other side of the bed, propped his
pillow next to hers, and got in. As he leaned beside
her, his shoulder brushing hers, Kimi swallowed a
sigh. He'd asked for one king-size bed. She didn't care
that he'd claimed it was the best way to protect her;
she knew better. He wanted to seduce her, and he was
counting on his nearness undermining her resolve.

Too bad for him that she was a Noguchi and her
family prided itself on their stubbornness. It wouldn't
hurt either of them to wait ten years or even fifteen to
have sex—she was young and he was a demon with a
long life span. By then, she'd have fully explored her

powers and maybe she wouldn't mind losing them . . . much. At least at that point, she'd know what she was giving up.

There was a bead of water he'd missed, directly below his left pec, and the temptation to take care of it for him was eating at her. Didn't he realize it was there? Or was he deliberately teasing her?

"So," Kimi said, trying to distract herself. "You've been exploring the human world. What do you think of it?"

He shrugged. "There are things I like and things I don't, just as there are in Orcus. Overall, though, the informality of the Overworld suits my personality, and everyone who means something to me is here. I plan to stay."

Kimi decided she was reading too much into his words. Just because he'd stared hard at her as he'd said *everyone who means something to me* didn't mean he was referring to her. He just was a standard demon: easily aroused.

"What are you going to do?"

"Do?" he asked, sounding confused.

"For a job—to earn money to live on."

That drew another shrug. "I've been hustling pool to pick up cash." He grinned. "I'm good."

"There's a great career aspiration." She laughed. "I can just picture Uncle David introducing you now. 'It's nice to meet you. I'm David Noguchi, president of a brokerage firm, and this is my stepson, Nicodemus, the pool hall hustler.'"

"That would be barroom hustler," Nic corrected her. "I've never played in a pool hall."

With a growl at his flippancy, Kimi tried to jump out of bed, but Nic drew her back. "You don't like my career? For you, tes, I'll find another. I live to make you happy."

"I didn't realize demons were such smart-asses."

"I wasn't joking," he said.

Kimi shook her head. He'd bullshit her all night, but she wasn't going to buy it. Instead of arguing, she thought about how Nic spoke. At times his speech had a formality to it that seemed out of place for this century. Other times, he sounded as laid back as any Southern Californian surfer. Something about the mixing of styles kept her off balance, and she didn't like that.

A lot about Nic had her reeling, though—just the brush of his arm against hers was making her insane. What was it about him that made her want him so much?

There was a mirror opposite the bed and Kimi watched Nic in it. She couldn't stop gazing at him, but she didn't want him to know the effect he had on her. After a few minutes, she realized his head was canted at an odd angle. "What are you staring at?" she asked. He smirked and she turned from the reflection to look at him. "Nic?" she prompted, warning in her voice.

"You're wearing white cotton panties."

He couldn't know that. Could he? She dropped her gaze and winced. The T-shirt had ridden up, exposing her choice of lingerie. Kimi knew she should be embarrassed, that she should push the shirt down and clasp her legs tightly together. Instead, she turned and leaned into him, unable to fight herself.

From the night she'd met him, Kimi had felt desire. It had grown each time she'd seen him, each time she'd spoken with him, and the months she'd spent without contact with him hadn't stopped it. She'd spent hours dreaming about Nic—about the way she'd touch him, the way he'd caress her, but especially about his kisses. Those had been even better than she'd imagined. She wanted more.

His mouth was a breath away, but he didn't close the gap. Frustrated, Kimi put her arms around his neck and pulled Nic to her. The kiss zoomed out of control. Before she was aware of moving, she was on top of him, her legs on either side of his.

Nic. She devoured him. This was the male she'd longed for and fantasized about for months, the demon she'd believed didn't want her.

He didn't touch her. She lifted her head, noticed his hands were knotted in the bedspread and his eyes glowed red. This time, the sight didn't scare her, it built her fever higher and she swooped down for another kiss. This was right. She knew it, felt it, trusted it.

Using her hands and mouth, she explored his jaw, his throat, his arms, chest, and belly. His growls were as inhuman as his eyes, but something about those sounds set her on fire and she wanted to hear more. Kimi lightly bit the skin below his navel, and the instinctive action surprised her so much, she paused.

"Take the shirt off," he suggested thickly, and since that sounded like a brilliant idea, she did. Maybe she couldn't have everything with Nic—not yet—but there was no reason why they couldn't pleasure each other without actual sex.

While she'd undressed, he'd opened his jeans. Wearing only her panties, Kimi knelt beside him, dipped her fingers into the gap, and sucked in a sharp breath; she'd touched the moist head of his erection. As soon as she recovered, she grabbed his waistband with both hands and tugged. Nic laughed at her impatience, but he raised his hips and pushed off his pants.

Kimi had never been so brazen before, not with any other guy, or this casual about baring herself, but it was different with Nic. It was if something inside her could relax because he was The One, the male she was meant to share all of herself with.

Before she could say anything emotionally revealing, though, his hand cupped her breast and she looked down. The sight of his tanned fingers against the paleness of her skin made her shiver. Then he rotated his palm, teasing her with the callused center. Kimi arched her back, silently pleading for more, and after another kiss, Nic bent and took her nipple into his mouth.

He didn't use only his tongue and lips, he bit at her too, little nips that made her gasp and moan and hang on to him. Her breasts were fairly small, but she didn't feel self-conscious about her size with Nic—he left no doubt in her mind how much he appreciated what she did have.

With another of his sexy growls, Nic eased her down on her back and pressed his thigh between hers. He wasn't on top of her, not quite, but it would only take a shift of inches to change that.

As he explored her mouth more, Kimi rubbed against his chest, enjoying the friction. She moaned in protest when Nic moved his leg, but it turned to a gasp as his hands reached for the waistband of her panties.

Kimi was ready to help him get rid of her last article of clothing when she realized just how far this had gone, how far things would continue if she didn't stop them. Nic wasn't going to be the voice of reason.

"No," she said firmly, despite the huskiness of her voice. "Those are staying on," she added when he lifted his head.

"As you wish." Nic didn't sound any calmer than she had.

He shifted and his hand slipped under the waist-band of her panties to settle between her legs. Kimi sucked in a sharp breath and waited to see what he'd do next. Staring into her eyes, he began to lightly stroke her.

"Not like that," she complained, and put her hand over his to guide him. When he had it, Kimi let go and just enjoyed. It didn't take her long to start coming, but she didn't scream—she didn't have enough oxygen for that.

Slowly, she regained awareness and saw that Nic had his jaw clamped so tightly shut, a muscle was jumping in his cheek. She pulled his hand out from between her thighs and got to her knees. It wouldn't be fair to leave him this hard, not after he'd taken care of her. Kimi reached for him.

He was big and thick and seemed to pulse in her hand, but she didn't hesitate. She loved the feel of him, loved his heat and told him that as she ran her hand up and down his shaft. His eyes locked on hers. Kimi knew when he was close and stroked faster. And with his most demonic growl yet, Nic found his own climax.

Chapter Five

Nic watched Kimi sleep. She'd pulled the T-shirt back on while he'd cleaned up, and when he'd expressed his disappointment, she'd told him too bad. He grinned. The more he got to know her, the more he liked her. Demon females tended to be independent and fiery— an equal match for their mates—and he'd been concerned about Kimi, since she was human. He needn't have worried; she held her own.

She could have fallen apart after being attacked by Augustin, but she'd fought back and escaped. She could have been repulsed by his kill of the other demon, but while she'd been shaky, she'd handled that well. He returned his gaze to his vishtau mate.

Damn, his woman was sexy. Nic relived the way she'd acted during their sex play. He'd allowed Kimi to set the pace, and she'd given more than he'd expected—though not as much as he'd hoped. Unlike many human women, she hadn't been hesitant to show him how she liked to be touched. He'd loved that. The feel of her hand over his as he'd caressed her so intimately—that alone had almost made him come.

There was a bruise on her collarbone where he'd bitten her, and Nic now brushed his fingers over that spot. It was primitive as hell, but he liked seeing his mark on her skin. Maybe next time he could get her to bite him back.

That was something else he'd think about later. Right now, his focus had to be on keeping her safe. Augustin was fixated, and once a dark demon became obsessed, he never swerved from his goal. He'd continue to come after Kimi until he died. It was up to Nic to ensure that happened sooner rather than later.

Grabbing the edge of the blanket, he pulled it over Kimi's arms and lay back down, his hand tucked behind his head. Why had Augustin sent his minion? A Ciretham was a weak demon, and Kimi had already knocked the master to the floor. Was he betting that she couldn't do it twice, or had Kimi hurt Augustin worse than Nic had seen in her mind? Of course, it could be some other reason altogether, one he wouldn't guess.

You will not protect the kijo.

Something about that word nagged at him, as if the knowledge he needed existed somewhere in his head but was just out of reach. The way the sentence was structured, it had to refer to Kimi—she was of Japanese descent and the word itself sounded Japanese. And Nic didn't think the demon had just been insulting her.

Their room had online service available, and lately humans seemed to have compiled a lot more information on demons—especially since the attack. Not all of it would be accurate, but maybe he could find something that would point him in the right direction.

Carefully, Nic slipped out of bed and went to the desk. He winced at the fee they charged and hated adding more debt to Kimi's card, but this was too important not to get some answers. Sitting down, he selected yes to start the service.

As far as Nic was concerned, one of the best things about the Overworld was instant access to an incredibly large knowledge base. Yes, there was garbage, but a bit of discernment and some additional checking weeded that out easily enough. In Orcus, information was not as easy to come by and the ruling council hoarded books, keeping important facts from their people.

He searched for *kijo* and pulled up thousands of results. Sometimes, he thought, there was too much knowledge available.

Browsing down the page, he discovered that many of them were names, belonging to either a person or a place. That wouldn't make it easy to eliminate hits. With a silent sigh, Nic continued to scan the screen, but he didn't find anything he considered helpful.

After forty-five minutes with nothing to show for his work, Nic added *Japanese* to the search parameters. One of the results he received this time was for an online dictionary. Curious, he selected it and read the definition.

Kijo meant *witch, demoness, ogress.*

Demoness?

A vague recollection came to him, something that he'd heard in a tale from his mother. When he'd been a small child, she'd frequently told him demon legends as bedtime stories.

Think. He had to think, he had to remember.

Could a demon legend have made it into human lore? Nic returned to the search screen and entered some new terms. He didn't get many results, but one of them yielded what he was looking for. The information he found on the site prodded his own memory, but he kept reading anyway. "Well, shit," he murmured, "this explains a lot."

Half awake, Kimi heard Nic's voice and reached for him, but all she touched were cool sheets. Propping herself up on her elbows she let her gaze sweep the room and found him at the desk. "What are you doing?" she asked around a yawn.

"Some research, tes. Go back to sleep."

Kimi pushed back the covers and padded over to him. If he was checking something out, she wanted to know about it. As soon as she reached him, she glanced at what Nic was reading. The picture on the screen made her shiver. It showed a hideously ugly woman with blood dripping from her hands. "What is that?"

"This," Nic said, turning to smirk at her over his shoulder, "is an artist's rendering of a kijo."

With a sniff of disdain, Kimi straightened. "I'm insulted. Even on a bad hair day, I've never looked that terrible."

Nic swiveled to face her. "You heard the Ciretham demon call you kijo?"

"He did? No, I didn't hear that."

Nic scowled and his eyes took on a faint red glow. "You've been keeping secrets, then. Start talking, Kimi."

"I have not kept any secrets," she insisted. "I told you right away that Augustin wanted to steal my magic."

He shook his head. "No, you didn't. You told me only that he'd attacked you. Damn it, you never even mentioned that you have power. Didn't you think that was critical information?"

"Oops." No wonder Nic seemed pissed off. "Sorry."

She heard him growl, and his eyes grew brighter. "Maybe you'd like to begin explaining now."

Not really, but considering how volatile he looked, she didn't think that was the best answer to give at the moment. "I really don't know that much. About three weeks ago, I got an internship in Crimson City. I didn't realize until after I started, but the ad agency is filled with women of power. Majo, that's what they call themselves. Except for me. They refer to me as kijo. Grandma Noguchi said both translate to witch."

Nic held out his hand, inviting her to take it. Reluctantly, she did, and he tugged her onto his lap. He backed up to an earlier screen and pointed to the definition of kijo. "Demoness?" she asked.

"There's a demon legend," he said, "one I didn't remember until I found a site that retold much of it. It talks of a human female born to a line of sorcerers who possesses much more power than the others around her. Such a woman is rare, and many demons will never hear of one within their lifetime."

"The kijo?" Kimi asked. She held her breath.

"Yes." Nic shifted, settling her more comfortably on his lap, and Kimi fought to stay focused on the conversation. All he had on was a pair of boxers, and they seemed awfully thin.

"Sometimes," he continued, "she's never found. Maybe she wasn't born or maybe she died before coming into her powers. Unlike demons, the kijo doesn't develop her talent until about five years after the onset of menstruation."

Nic didn't blush at the word, but Kimi did. In her family, this wasn't discussed in front of men, but he seemed unperturbed. "That means I had my magic then for almost two years before I learned of it." She considered. "Well, I did figure out I had the ability to summon demons about six months ago, but the rest I didn't know about until I came down here for that job—and I'm still not sure what I can do."

He frowned. "It would have been useful if you'd had those years of education and practice. Augustin would likely leave you alone then, since it's nearly impossible to take the powers of a kijo who's far enough along in her training."

"Nearly?" she questioned.

"Nearly," Nic confirmed. "And once you're fully trained, no one will be able to touch them at all."

"How come—" she asked slowly, feeling safe next to him, she snuggled closer. "—demons have a legend about a human?"

"My guess is because she has powers similar to a member of one of the strong branches, and because enough kijo have bonded with demon males over the millennia to make an impact."

"But the kijo is human. What kind of bond can she have with a demon?"

"Any human can have a demon vishtau mate." When Kimi looked at him blankly, Nic explained what it was. Then he added, "But for the kijo it's different. When she performs the bonding rite with her mate, her physiology gradually changes from human to demon."

"Are you saying that Augustin is my vishtau mate and that he's trying to turn me into a Dark One?"

Nic frowned fiercely. "I doubt he shares the vishtau with you. It makes demons protective, and a male will die if that's what it takes to shield his mate. He's hurt you, and that would be next to impossible if you shared those ties with him."

Kimi had a sense Nic wasn't being completely honest with her. "What aren't you telling me?"

There was a long hesitation, and Kimi felt her stomach knot. "You're *my* vishtau mate," he admitted at last.

Kimi ran through what he'd told her about the vishtau thing again. That meant he had a biological imperative to sleep with her because she could give him children, and an instinctive need to protect her. Not too flattering. "And you have no choice whether or not you want me. Nice."

With a growl, he wrapped his arm around her waist and prevented her from hopping off his lap. "Damn it, Kimi, why is any male attracted to any female? What makes one beautiful woman uninteresting and another unforgettable? Just because demons know their mates on sight doesn't mean we have no choices. I could have kept my distance and nothing would have happened."

"But I took that option away from you."

"I'd already made the decision to find you when you were older and finished with college. You merely moved up the time frame." Nic shrugged. "I'm glad you did. I want to be at your side—I want to be at your side the next time Augustin attacks."

"Bull! You tried to avoid me," Kimi accused. "You even ducked out of your mother's wedding dinner when I showed up—after complaining to Mika about how I was chasing you."

For a minute he looked blank, then he gave her that infernal smirk. "It was only a complaint because I couldn't have you. I'd promised Mika that I'd keep my distance until you were older, and until I'd learned how to temper my strength enough not to hurt you. But from the start, Kimi, I wanted you. Never doubt that."

Kimi thought about things for a minute. She could

sit here and pout that Nic was interested solely because of some stupid demon bond, or she could believe him about only avoiding her because of a promise to Mika and that he would have chosen to come to her in a few years. Demons lied—she knew that—but she believed Nic was being honest with her.

But it was Augustin they needed to stay focused on. He was dangerous and he was after her. The idea of him stealing her powers and using them to further his own agenda was intolerable to her. No matter what, she couldn't let him succeed. Kimi made a decision, one she wished she didn't have to consider.

"Nic," she said, clutching his biceps, "if it looks like we can't defeat Augustin, I want you to take my magic. I'd rather you have it than him."

Nic scowled so ferociously Kimi straightened. "I will not take you by force," he snarled.

"It wouldn't be with force. I'd want you to do it."

He looked at her funny. "It has to be rape. No one can steal your powers any other way. Something about the act of violence opens a hole in your psyche, and that's what allows a demon male to use an incantation to steal your talent."

"Wait a second," she said, gripping him more firmly, "are you saying that if I willingly make love with you, I'll still have my magic afterward?"

"Yes." Nic's confusion cleared and he grinned. "Why, is that what you're thinking of doing? Have at me, tes."

"You're not lying, are you?" she asked.

"No, I'm telling you the truth. You have my word on it, and demons never break an oath."

Kimi thought for a moment. The demon male she'd wanted for eight months wanted her back, and she could have sex with him and still have her powers. Besides, if Augustin showed up they could both die, and she wanted to experience everything with Nic. "I was in charge last time," she said. "This time *you* have at *me*."

Chapter Six

With a low growl, Nic moved, putting Kimi on the bed and covering her with his body. She gasped, but he suspected that was because of his preternatural speed rather than any alarm over his actions. When he raised his head to check, she smiled at him and threw her arms around his neck.

Smoothing her hair out of her eyes, Nic took a moment to gaze at her: his vishtau mate. "You're gorgeous—*special*," he told her, wanting Kimi to understand that, even without this connection between them, he'd want her still.

Slowly he lowered his head to hers, kissing her softly. Her generous lips had sparked fantasies since they'd first met, and if he was lucky, Kimi would be willing to do some of those things he'd imagined. He nipped her bottom lip lightly and then soothed it with the tip of his tongue.

Her hands tightened around him, but he wasn't going to be rushed. He kissed one corner of her mouth, then the other. She turned her head, trying to get more of him.

Nic moved down, bit her chin and nibbled his way to the pulse point in her throat. Because his T-shirt was too big for her, it sagged at the neckline, exposing her collarbone; he kissed along one side. As he reached the center, he tugged the shirt lower and nuzzled the valley between her breasts. She inhaled softly and held her breath.

Nic wasn't done yet. Shifting to her side, he returned to Kimi's lips, delicately sucking on them. She opened her mouth for him, but he ignored her request.

"You're teasing," Kimi complained.

Raising his head, he let her see his eyes. As aroused as he was, he knew they glowed brightly—her gasp confirmed that. But Nic had himself on a short tether. It wouldn't take much to derail his intention to worship her before joining their bodies, so he had a plan. And there was need: Kimi was human, not tied to him the way he was to her—he had to convince her that there were advantages to keeping him around.

"I remember the first time I saw you," he admitted. "We were standing on the beach and the moonlight caught your face." He lightly traced her cheekbone with his finger. "You took my breath away, and my thoughts were only of you."

"Because of that vishtau thing," she said, and he heard a note of resentment in her voice.

Nic shook his head. "I didn't know yet that you were my mate—you were too far away from me. It was you and the way you shine that caught my attention. Not merely your beauty—you, Kimi."

"If you're so into me, why are you moving this slow? You were faster earlier."

He couldn't stop the smile. "You set the pace, then. This time, I am." And he'd take it as slowly as he could for as long as he could. "I'm past the impatience of youth and can take time to savor you, tes." Though it was a struggle.

She put out a hand, stopping him from lowering his lips to hers. "What does tes mean? Will you tell me now?"

The debate was brief; he wanted her to know. "It translates to *beloved.*" And without giving her time to reply, Nic kissed her, his mouth moving lazily against hers.

It only took a moment before Kimi's tongue trailed over his lips. Nic opened his mouth, let her in. She was trying to take over, and for now he was content to let her. She was exploring him. Earlier, when she'd encouraged him to taste her, she hadn't returned the favor; this time she was the aggressor.

Nic felt his emotions and lust start to slip the leash, and he fought to hang on. He needed more time before this swamped him. He ran his hand along her side, caressed her flank and moved down to the back of her knee. His finger circled there, and then he lifted her leg over his hip and pulled her closer. They both groaned at the feel of their bodies pressing together.

This was so right, was the perfection he'd been waiting for. Sweet Kimi with her big brown eyes and those lush lips was finally in his arms. He pushed her shirt up and traced the elastic waist of her panties.

She pulled out of his arms, but Nic didn't try to hold her. As she sat up, she yanked the shirt over her head, tossed it aside, and dove back down at him.

His control slipped further at the feel of her bare breasts against his chest. Kimi shoved him to his back, straddled him, and Nic fought hard to let her keep the superior position. It went against his nature. She kissed him wildly, demanding his surrender, which he gladly gave. He fisted his hands in the blankets, trying to hold out, trying to let her retain dominance. Then she shifted, her nipples grazed him, and Nic lost the struggle. He flipped her so that he was on top.

Giving her lips one last kiss, he moved down to her breasts. With a light touch, he traced one areola. Before he even reached them, her nipples were taut and Nic grinned—her responsiveness excited him so much. He nibbled at the underside of her breast, not stopping until she arched and twisted with ecstasy.

Instead of obeying her unspoken request, he moved to tease the other breast. Damn, he loved touching her this way, driving her as crazy as she drove him.

The tip of his cock protruded from his boxers, something he didn't realize until Kimi circled her fingers over its head. Nic growled in pleasure. She toyed with him, pushing him to his limits. Then she brought her finger to her mouth, looked him in the eye, and licked it.

His tether snapped. *Kimi is human*, he reminded himself as he pushed his shorts off. He couldn't thrust as hard as he did with demon females and he couldn't bite her. But desire flooded him and Nic knew he would have to fight to hold back.

The sight of her panties prevented him from ripping them off her and plunging inside. They were high cut, sexy in style, but there was something so damn innocent about that white cotton. Nic groaned, his body trying to overrule his mind. Intellect won at last.

Returning to her breasts, he finally took a nipple into his mouth, teasing her with his tongue, lips, and teeth. She was moaning before he moved to the other. "Beautiful," he murmured, and dipped his head.

Kimi's hands sank into his hair, holding him to her as if she was worried he'd stop before she was ready. She clutched at him when he slipped lower, but Nic ignored that—she'd thank him later. He kissed his way down her body to her navel, paused to trace it with his tongue, then went lower yet.

Using both hands, he carefully pushed the waistband of her panties down. She kicked free of them and then they both went still. Nic looked up her body at her face, met her gaze. His mate was aroused, her pupils dilated, and he smiled.

Nudging her legs apart, Nic moved between them. One was canted to the side and he nibbled at the hollow behind her knee. He kissed and licked his way up her inner thigh, pausing now and then to pay special attention to whatever spot made her moan. By the time he reached his goal, he had both of her legs over his shoulders and Kimi was open to his gaze.

Her moisture glistened inside her folds, and Nic bent his head to taste. He meant to tease her longer, but she grabbed his head and drew his mouth where she wanted it. That inflamed him further—he loved that Kimi made him aware of what pleased her.

He didn't deny her any longer. This was one of his favorite things and it was even more so with his mate. Breathless, she told him exactly what she wanted, and he realized from her voice and words that she was more aroused than he'd known. He circled the center of her pleasure, and in mere moments, brought her to the brink. Before she could come, though, he pulled away.

"Nic! *Damn* it!"

Using his thumbs to open her even more, he leaned forward and kissed her there. She gasped and arched her hips. With a small smile, he moved a bit farther down and sank his tongue into her. He thrust and withdrew until Kimi was pleading, her legs clenching and relaxing.

He didn't want her coming yet, and she cursed when

he stopped. The laugh escaped before he could stifle it. Her thighs tightened around him, trying to hold him where he was, but he easily broke away and returned to her lips.

Kimi rocked against him, and the head of his sex nudged her entrance. He froze; he had to or he'd thrust inside her—and he couldn't, not yet. This was his *mate;* he had to take care of her. Nic fought the instinct that demanded he join with Kimi, but he wasn't sure he was going to win the battle.

"Nic?"

He gazed into her face, saw her arousal—and he saw her trust. Kimi had put her faith in him.

Breaking free, he rolled off the bed. She groaned a curse that made him grin despite the way his cock ached. He found his rucksack and dug out a condom. He had the thing ready to roll before he returned to the bed.

As soon as he was sheathed, he rejoined her and kissed Kimi, his hand moving between her legs to bring her back to the level of arousal she'd felt before he'd left. "I need you, Kimi," he murmured against her lips. And not only for right now. Again and again. Forever.

After a brief hesitation, Kimi's hand curled around him and she guided him into her body. Nic struggled for control, struggled to keep his emotions in check. She was tight enough to squeeze him, and it felt good. So damn good. Warring against instinct, he kept his entry slow. He needed to ensure that Kimi found nothing save pleasure in his arms.

Once he was completely inside her, he paused, and as he looked into her eyes, something tightened around his heart. This was his vishtau mate, and though she was human, Kimi Noguchi was more than he'd ever dreamt.

Nic had to move—had to—and he fought to keep his strokes light. Kimi moved with him, her hips arching into his. She held him near and he loved that. He'd found where he belonged: in the arms of his mate. His thrusts became faster.

The urge to bite her slammed into him. He couldn't do it. Not while he was this aroused; he would hurt her. Nic levered himself farther away, but Kimi wrapped her arms and legs more tightly around him and drew him to her.

He let himself be dragged back. His body shook, not only from desire, but from the restraint he forced upon it.

Kimi's long hair trailed off the side of the pillow onto the bed. He wanted to feel it falling across his body, to have her tease him with her tresses. Next time. He could wait.

"Nic!" Kimi's voice was thick, her eyes heavy-lidded.

He knew she was close, that he'd need to do her harder to send her over the edge. Not too hard, he warned himself even as he moved more forcefully into her. The other women he'd been with hadn't excited him like Kimi did, and he hadn't worried about losing his self-command to the point where he hurt them. He had to be careful; it would take so little for his mate to push him into mindless hunger.

His body shook as he battled to hang on to awareness. And then she bit him. She sank her teeth into his biceps and Nic was lost. "Bite me again," he growled. Kimi did.

The world narrowed to encompass only one goal—reaching orgasm. He drove into her, pinning her to the bed with his hips. Nic was on the edge, a hairbreadth away when Kimi cried out. She clasped him tighter and her body bowed. It was too much for him. His soul reached for hers as he came with her—as he found the joy only his vishtau mate could give him.

"Kimi," he groaned.

When Nic regained his senses, he realized he'd let his mate take his full weight. Regretfully he eased out of her body, shifted to her side, and tugged her against him. "Are you all right, tes?" he asked, concerned that he'd done her injury.

Her smile was slow and satisfied. "Better than fine. Next time, though, I get to touch you more. Deal?"

"Deal." And as relief poured through him, Nic grinned. Not only had he maintained enough self-control to leave her unharmed, she wanted to couple with him again. He kissed her slowly and with the reverence she deserved.

Nic delayed the inevitable as long as he could. "I have to get rid of the condom," he said unhappily.

"Hurry back."

He did.

Nic knew he was lucky to have met Kimi, and he told her that once he'd climbed into bed again. Cuddling her close, he ran his hands lightly over her body and asked her questions. What was her favorite birthday? Had she had a pet as a child? Who was her best friend? Nothing earthshaking, but each small bit she told him about her life was a precious nugget, a glimpse into the heart of his vishtau mate.

The beep of her comm made Nic groan. "Ignore it," he said.

"I can't. What if it's important?" Kimi scrambled out of bed and, still naked, grabbed the phone from her purse. "Hello?"

Dropping his head back to the pillow, Nic tried to remember that he couldn't keep Kimi to himself forever. He wished, though, that they'd had this one night.

"You son of a bitch, I want to talk to her!" There was a brief pause. "Mom! Mom, are you okay?"

Nic sat up fast. Their idyllic encounter had just come to an end.

Chapter Seven

Kimi gripped the steering wheel tightly as she drove to the rendezvous point Augustin had named. Nic sat beside her, finally out of advice about her magic. He hadn't heard much about humans who had talent, so he'd gone through that information quickly. Next, he'd told her what he'd recalled about the kijo from Orcus legend, and then he'd explained the basics of how demons used their powers.

With every mile, though, he seemed to become more and more tense. She could feel it radiating off him, and it made her own anxiety increase. She'd never seen him like this, not even when he'd fought that demon in her apartment.

"Nic, are you okay?" she asked when she stopped at a light.

"Yes." He put his hand on her thigh and gave her a squeeze. "I only wish I could have left you at the hotel."

She nearly snarled, but swallowed her words. How could he consider fighting alone? But there was no point in arguing about something that hadn't happened. Back in their room, Nic had claimed it might be a setup to leave her unguarded. Either way—as if she wanted to remain behind!

The light turned green and Kimi stepped on the accelerator. "Do you really think he's bluffing about having my mom?" she asked.

"Yes, I do," Nic said, and even though this was the fourth or fifth time she'd asked, he sounded as patient now as he had before.

"But if he doesn't have her," she countered, as she had earlier, "how did he get my comm code? And I talked to my mom—that was definitely her voice."

"There are demons with the ability to mimic," Nic said, already knowing what her next argument would be. "The comm code? Maybe he picked that up from the coworker who betrayed you."

Kimi wanted to believe Nic. There was nothing she wished for more than this to be a simple ruse, one to ensure that she showed up to face the Dark One. As far as she was concerned, even if there was only a one percent chance that Augustin was holding her mother hostage, she had to meet him. She couldn't lose her mother, not now and not like this. Memories swamped her. Kimi had been in grade school when her mom was diagnosed with cancer. That had been the worst year of her life, the most frightening, and she'd vowed never to take her mom's presence for granted. Yet she'd done just that. It had happened gradually, when she wasn't thinking. How easy that was.

As if sensing her unease, Nic gave her thigh another squeeze. "Do you want me to try reaching her again?"

Kimi nodded, and he fished the comm out of her purse. That's what had her most scared—she'd called and called her parents and no one had answered. It was nearly three o'clock in the morning. Where the hell could they be if they weren't at home?

"Voice mail again," Nic reported and returned her comm to her bag. Kimi felt her gut twist tighter.

It wasn't only her mother she worried about; her father wasn't picking up the comm either. Augustin hadn't mentioned anyone except her mom, though. Was her dad hurt?

Then there was Nic. Kimi glanced over at him and the ache in her chest increased so much, it felt as if someone had reached inside her and was trying to crush her heart. His jaw was set, his expression resolute, and she saw an intangible emotion there that added to her fear. She wished this whole thing were already over, her family safe, Nic unharmed, and Augustin out of the way. Why did she have to be a kijo?

When they reached an area of Crimson City that looked as if it had been firebombed—the lower, a place she never went—she decided they had to be getting close. A few minutes later, Nic said, "Park here. We'll walk the remaining distance." She prayed they'd be safe from things other than just Augustin.

He stopped her as they stood on the sidewalk next to her car. "You need to stay hidden from Augustin for as long as possible. Once he knows you're there, he'll be focused on reaching you. What I want you to do is to stand behind me, always keeping my body between you and the Dark One. And if it looks as if he's going to win, leave."

"No!"

"Yes. If your mother is there, take her and go. I'll do what I have to in order for you to rescue her and get away."

She didn't say anything, just stared at him. He could issue all the orders he wanted, but she didn't have to listen. Of course, if her mom really was there, Kimi would take her to safety, but then she was heading right back to help Nic. There was no way in hell she'd just leave him to die.

"Ah, tes, that stubborn look says much." He framed her face between his hands and leaned down to brush his lips over hers. "Don't you understand? I want you safe. Nothing matters more."

"How much longer do you want to stand here and argue?" Kimi asked. She wasn't giving in, and she wasn't going to lie to him.

With a groan, he stepped back. "Didn't you summon me to fight for you?"

Kimi had, but things had changed. Nic wasn't just some demon she was attracted to; he'd become important to her—every bit as critical in her mind as the safety of her family. How was that possible? It just was. "We're a team, Nic."

"I assume that means you're not going to see reason no matter what I say." Kimi smiled weakly and he sighed. "We might as well go, then." He pointed to his right. "This way."

As they started off, Nic ran his hand down the length of her braid. The caress seemed almost adoring, but his face revealed nothing of his thoughts.

Running her palms over her thighs, Kimi tried to wipe away some of the clamminess. She was dressed in her yoga clothes because they were the only things packed in her bag that were appropriate for this showdown. The Lycra pants, cropped red T-shirt, and tennis shoes gave her freedom of movement, and that was more important than style right now.

One thing kept echoing in her thoughts: Nic nearly died the last time he fought Augustin. From what he'd said, she assumed he'd been much younger, but did that make a difference in demonic power?

Something odd drew her attention away from the

dread building inside her, a sense of surrounding magic. "What are you doing?" she asked.

"Trying to cloak us both from Augustin. No point announcing our imminent arrival if we can avoid it." He turned down a narrow alley, and the odor of rotting garbage made her gag. She covered her nose and mouth with her hand. Fortunately, the smell didn't last and they reached the next block quickly.

Nic's hand brushed hers and Kimi reached for him, linking their fingers. She didn't know what, exactly, Nic meant by cloaking, but she didn't ask. Instead, she took a few deep breaths now that the air was more pleasant, and tried to center herself. Her stomach, however, was doing barrel rolls.

He drew her to a halt in the middle of a block. Augustin stood on the cross street, kitty corner from where they were, and he leaned indolently against the front of a blackened brick structure. Even at this distance, he appeared bored.

Bending down, Nic put his mouth against her ear and whispered, "This is the best we could hope. I sense no presence except Augustin's."

Kimi nodded. It was dark and the streetlights cast a dim glow, but she knew demons could read energy. On the other hand, what if Augustin had cloaked an ally or her mom's presence the way Nic had concealed theirs? She couldn't assume anything.

"Stay here," Nic ordered, tucking her into a recessed doorway, and without giving her time to respond, he left. She could barely see him as he covertly made his way to the corner.

It was an attack of mind-numbing speed: Nic drew his hand back and hurled something. As it raced toward Augustin, the fireball grew in size and became more intense. Kimi held her breath, hoping that this one shot would take care of their enemy, but at the last instant, the Dark One jumped clear. The missile struck the building behind him, blasting a hole that had to be fifteen feet across. Kimi's eyes bugged out. As pieces of brick and mortar rained down around him, Augustin roared with fury. His return blast struck where Nic had been standing, and the entire side of an apartment collapsed. Fortunately, Nic had already moved.

Shifting from foot to foot, Kimi remained in the shadows of the derelict building and tried to figure out what she should do. While she didn't want Nic to fight alone, neither did she want to get in his way or distract him.

She was in over her head, she knew it and she was scared—not only for herself, but for everyone. If she had a clue how she'd created that one lightning bolt, maybe she could assist him, but as it stood, she couldn't count on producing it again. Why had she been so proud of this power? It was useless without training! And why had the majo insisted she have the background and ethics before learning to do actual magic? She needed more than philosophy, damn it!

Nic let loose with two more fireballs in quick succession. The first crashed into the same structure, making the hole bigger, but the second caught Augustin.

It had no noticeable effect.

Running toward the Dark One, Nic dodged a string of blasts. Rubble fell onto the sidewalk, but both demons seemed oblivious.

It developed into a scene like some kind of Old West shoot-out with two gunslingers standing in the middle of the street, firing at each other. Kimi could only guess they had some kind of invisible shield that protected them, because neither Nic nor Augustin seemed injured despite a number of blasts that connected.

Twisting her fingers, Kimi tried to come up with some idea how to help him. She couldn't just stand here. She couldn't! But what the hell could she do that wasn't stupid? Both Nic and Augustin had impossible abilities.

One of the dark demon's blasts winged Nic, but it was different: it spun him halfway around. Kimi put her hand over her mouth to block her gasp. Nic! She could sense rather than see that he was hurt and she crept closer, wanting to tend to him.

"You are weak," Augustin said with a sneer. "But then, so was your sire. I'll kill you as I killed him."

It was a ploy to rile Nic, but despite the fact that demons were emotional by nature, Nic didn't visibly react. Instead, he summoned magic again and leapt out of the way of the Dark One's continued assault.

From the effort Nic was putting in now to avoid Augustin's blasts, Kimi guessed that he no longer had any magical shield. She twisted her fingers harder, wanting so badly to help him, but knowing that delivering a solid thigh kick wasn't going to do much to slow down Augustin. And what else could she do? This method of fighting left her daunted. Paralyzed. She was useless, no help at all. The realization made her sick.

Nic took another blast, this one dead-on, and he staggered. Kimi choked back a cry. *Not Nic,* she pleaded. *Please don't let anything happen to Nic.* The thought consumed her.

He let loose with a volley of fireballs, and Kimi took a deep breath. Maybe that meant he was okay. Some of the salvos were deflected by the Dark One, and more brick fell into the street. Others hit Augustin, but they seemed to do little harm.

The Dark One sent a wave of fire at Nic. It was like nothing Kimi had ever seen before, and her lover had no way to avoid it. As it crashed over him, magic shimmered around her. It was the cloak he'd put over her, faltering. For an instant, it sparked back to life, and then she felt it disappear for good.

Augustin turned his head and stared directly at where she stood. A shudder went through her. He smiled. "Kijo," he said, his voice barely audible. "You picked a poor champion."

She tore her gaze away and looked at Nic. He was on his feet, but swaying precariously. He appeared dazed.

Something Nic had said came back to her then—a male demon would die to protect his vishtau mate. And *she* was Nic's mate. For the first time, Kimi understood that he hadn't been exaggerating. He really would die for her.

As the dark demon started to close the distance to where Nic was, Kimi knew she couldn't stand there like a mannequin. She had to do something, anything. Heart in her throat, she raised her hand and tried to picture the lightning shooting out of her palm. Nothing happened.

Come on, Nic! Come on!

Nic managed to summon another blast of energy, but it was noticeably weaker—even to her—and it went astray. Far astray. With a smile that made him look deranged, the Dark One blasted Nic. Nic fell to his knees as the other demon strolled closer.

"Kimi, flee," Nic called, and her heart leapt into her throat. He believed he was going to die.

She shook her head. Nic couldn't see her. Maybe she couldn't shoot fire and maybe she didn't know how she'd let that lightning loose, but she wasn't abandoning him. She had the power to do magic, and she'd had some rudimentary explanations from Nic. She tried to draw energy from the planet the way he'd told her he did, and she raised her hand again. Still nothing. Damn it!

Augustin released another shot and Nic collapsed.

Chapter Eight

Up until now, Kimi had stood in the shadows, obeying orders and hoping Nic would take care of it all for her. That had been easier than dealing with her fear, easier than risking herself, and easier than trying to come up with something to counteract Augustin's firepower, but there was no longer any choice.

Nic wasn't dead yet. Kimi felt it, though she didn't understand how, but if she didn't step in and do something, he would die and her cowardice would be to blame. She couldn't let anything happen to him—she *couldn't*—and Kimi knew Augustin wouldn't hesitate to finish off his downed adversary.

Taking that first step away from the building was the hardest thing she'd ever done, but she couldn't run and desert Nic, not if she wanted to look at herself in the mirror ever again. "Leave him alone," she said, voice wobbly. The dark demon stopped in his tracks.

"You think to defend him?" Augustin asked.

"I put you on your ass once—I can do it again." Kimi thought her bluff sounded convincing, but the Dark One shook his head and laughed.

"It was a fluke, you know that as well as I. With no real training, you're little more than human."

And no match for him. He didn't say that, but he didn't have to. It was the truth. She'd just kind of hoped that he hadn't realized that her coup had been accidental.

"You said you had my mom," Kimi said, changing the subject.

Augustin smiled. "I lied."

That's what Nic had told her. She was surprised the dark demon was admitting it now, but then Kimi guessed it didn't matter. She was here, wouldn't be able to outrun him, and if he needed more, Nic was on the ground and vulnerable.

"Come here, kijo," he said, and held out his hand.

Kimi shook her head. She sought a solution. If she thought it would help, she'd give the Dark One her damn powers, but she knew that wouldn't change anything. He'd kill them both once he had them. And the method of extraction . . .

She had to do something, had to come up with a brilliant plan soon, because Augustin wasn't going to stand there forever waiting for her to walk over to him. The only advantage she had was that the demon didn't want her dead yet. How could she use that?

Before any ideas occurred to her, he started toward her. Kimi shifted, moving closer to Nic.

"Think you that he will defend you yet?" Augustin laughed again, sounding genuinely amused. "Even were he at full strength, he'd be no match for me. He fell easily beneath my onslaught." He shook his head. "His Grolird sire never should have allowed a Mahsei female to weaken the bloodline."

There was such contempt in his voice that Kimi stiffened. The slur wasn't only on Nic, but on his parents as well. Kimi liked Nic's mother—she was fun and sweet. She thought of Augustin's reaction if he knew that Nic had a half-human sister—it would be beyond contemptuous. Kimi felt her fear begin to seep away and become anger.

She fed that, built herself into a fury. This demon had hurt Nic badly, he'd terrified her by claiming he had her mother, he had every intention of raping her if he could get his hands on her, and he had raped a *child*. Her remaining fear burned away beneath her outrage.

When she'd faced Augustin last time, the lightning had appeared when she'd gotten mad. *Third time's the charm,* she thought; and drawing energy from the earth, she raised her hand to strike.

Nothing.

Except, her action angered Augustin. He raised his own hand and a ball of fire exploded toward her. Kimi tried to evade, but she wasn't fast enough. Pain crashed through her, but she was aware that the energy was considerably weaker than what Nic had endured. The only thing that kept her upright was knowing Augustin would be on her before she could regain her feet.

Majo are children of the stars.

Nic had told her that demons took their power from the planet. In her recent lessons, she'd been taught that the majo were connected to the earth yet were children of the stars. She looked up and saw a few bright pinpoints of light through the city haze.

Could it mean—? But that was too easy. Wasn't it?

As Augustin closed in on her, Kimi reached for the universe and drew energy from that. Something felt different than the earth energy—this resonated with her. But if it didn't work, she was going to have to fight hand-to-hand. She shifted to balance her weight evenly, yet didn't stop seeking power.

When she was almost within the Dark One's reach, Kimi raised her hand again.

"You're a slow learner," Augustin commented.

She released all the power she could.

The demon flew back a good ten feet. This time, Kimi was the one who advanced. She attacked again.

His body slammed into the side of a building. She blasted him again and again. At last, when Augustin fell, she stood over him and added a couple more bolts of electricity, not stopping until she knew he was dead.

"Berkeley doesn't admit slow learners," she said, and then she realized she was talking to a corpse.

Kimi began to shiver. Yeah, Augustin deserved to die, but she'd killed him. She was a killer. *God. Oh God. Oh God.* She closed her eyes, but she could still see his face. Bile rose and she swallowed hard to keep from puking.

Nic groaned, and she grasped the distraction gratefully. She didn't have time to think about what she'd done to Augustin; she had to check on her mates.

Her body shook so hard that Kimi could barely walk, but her legs didn't give out until she was beside him. She scooted closer and then reached out to touch his face. The warmth of his skin calmed something inside her, but she still didn't know how badly he'd been hurt.

"Nic—" She had to clear her voice and try a second time. "Nic, are you all right?"

He groaned again. They were in the middle of the street, but Kimi eased closer and rolled him carefully onto his back, arranging him so that his head was in her lap. Leaning over him as if to shield him from any further danger, she lightly stroked his face, needing to touch him more than anything.

Kimi didn't realize she was crying until the first tear splashed onto Nic's cheek. She wiped it away, and the one that followed it, and the one after that.

"I killed someone," she whispered. "How do I live with that?"

"The same way as any warrior, tes," Nic said, his voice weak and raspy. "You accept that there was no other choice."

"Are you okay?" she demanded, her tears drying.

"I'll live, but I won't be able to move for a while." He laughed wryly, then groaned.

Kimi nodded, hoping he felt the movement. His eyes remained closed. "I don't have to be back at work till Monday." She kept stroking him—his hair, his cheeks. She couldn't touch him enough. After a long silence, she asked, "What do we do with Augustin's body?"

"Leave it where it's at."

"If someone doesn't find it, rats will get him."

"He deserves no better." Then one side of Nic's mouth quirked up. "See? It's as I told you—human females are weak."

He still believed she was weak? After everything she'd done tonight? Pain lanced through her, but Kimi pushed it aside. "Why don't you just stay quiet?" she suggested, hiding her emotions with a laugh. "If you keep talking, I might be tempted to hurt you myself."

Epilogue

Kimi smoothed her hands down the sides of her black dress—the skirt was short, the halter plunged in front, and the back was nonexistent. With it, she wore the black high-heeled shoes she'd bought on sale two months ago. The ones that had started the whole mess.

Nic hadn't seen her in this yet—she'd picked up the dress yesterday on her lunch hour—and she was nervous about sauntering around in an outfit that blatantly screamed *Take me to bed*. It wasn't that she didn't initiate sex between them—she did almost as often as he—but this was different; it required all her courage to walk out of the bedroom. The living room was empty, Nic nowhere to be found.

She slumped against the wall and stared morosely at the boxes and bags piled in the middle of her floor. The summer had flown by, and tomorrow she'd drive back up to Berkeley. Kimi wasn't ready to leave Crimson City, though. Not yet.

It had nothing to do with her magic. Eleanor, the majo wise woman, had made arrangements for her training to continue while she was in college. Kimi didn't want to go because she was afraid that it meant the end of her time with Nic.

The words he'd spoken the night they dealt with Augustin wouldn't leave her head. *Human females are weak.* He'd never repeated them after that, but it had eaten at her, made her wonder if he would prefer a demon woman. They'd never talked about the future; he'd simply stayed.

Kimi liked waking up beside him and sharing the household chores. And it wasn't just the sex or the things he did around the apartment—it was Nic.

She loved him. Even if he could be a pain in the ass sometimes.

Her mom and dad hadn't been thrilled about her living with him, but she was ecstatic that they were both alive to complain. Although Augustin had been untrustworthy, Kimi hadn't breathed easily until she'd talked to them. Of all nights for them to decide to drive to the country and watch a meteor shower, they'd picked that one! She'd never know if Augustin had been aware that they were out, or if he'd simply gotten lucky.

Of course, her parents had been in a panic about her when they'd returned home and seen her dozen middle-of-the-night calls listed. Her comm had been chirping when she and Nic had made it to her car at dawn.

Kimi wrapped her arms around her waist. That situation with the Dark One still gave her nightmares. Who would soothe her and distract her if Nic stayed in LA? Who would she curl up with on the couch and talk to into the wee hours? Who would she laugh and play with?

"Why the long face, tes?" Nic asked. She hadn't heard him come in, and sometimes the quiet way he moved made her uneasy.

"Because I came out in *this* and there was no one to seduce," she replied. She wanted to show Nic what he'd be giving up if he didn't come north with her. Maybe human females were weaker than demons, but she could offer some compensation.

Straightening, she stepped away from the wall and slowly pivoted so that he could admire every inch of bare skin. "Like?" She tossed him a glance over her shoulder.

The way his eyes were glowing, the question was unnecessary. He only stood and stared, though, and she gave him one last goad. "I'm not wearing anything underneath, either."

His eyes flared brighter, and Kimi barely had time to blink before Nic had her pressed against the wall. His hand slid under her skirt, checking out her claim, and she smiled at his stunned expression when he discovered she told the truth.

Reaching between them, she opened the button at his waist and slowly lowered the zipper of his jeans. He never moved his gaze from hers, not even when she stroked him. "Keep that up," he warned with a growl, "and I'll take you standing here."

"So?" She squeezed him exactly the way he liked.

Nic took that as a challenge. She'd known he would.

Kimi clutched at his shoulders as he lifted her into position and thrust inside her. This wasn't going to be one of those times where he brought her to the brink over and over. He had a goal. With a moan, she grasped him harder as she rode out her orgasm, then his.

It took a while to recover, and even after Nic set her on her feet again, he held on to her.

"You could have me like this any time you wanted," she said softly next to his ear, "if you came to Berkeley with me."

He pulled back to look at her. "That's what this is about?"

Kimi nodded tentatively, uncertain what his tone meant.

Nic began to laugh. He laughed so hard, he lost his balance, and because his jeans were down at his knees, he had to grab her to keep from falling. Then he laughed harder yet.

She pushed him strongly enough that he fell to the floor. Kimi didn't wait around to see the look on his face, she whirled and escaped into the bedroom. She couldn't let him see her cry. Here she'd been trying to sell him on staying with her and he thought her attempt was funny. Jerk.

But she should have known a locked door wouldn't keep Nic at bay. "Ah, tes," he said at her back, his hands gently clasping her shoulders. "I wasn't laughing at you." She went rigid. "Okay, I was laughing at you, but not for the reason you believe. If there was any need to convince me to leave with you tomorrow, this seduction would have done it, I'm certain of that."

"Then what's funny?" Kimi asked grudgingly.

"That you thought you needed to convince me." Nic turned her to face him and his expression went solemn as he wiped the tears off her cheeks with his thumbs. "I'm sorry," he said. "I didn't realize how deeply I'd wounded you. I told you that you're my vishtau mate—why would you believe I wouldn't go where you go?"

"You only told me that once, the night I summoned you. I thought maybe you were only saying it because you'd changed your mind about getting me in bed."

Nic choked, and Kimi thought he was fighting back the need to laugh again. She glared at him, but if he was amused, he managed to rein it in before she knew for sure.

"Besides," she added, "you said human females are weak." He looked at her blankly, so she prompted, "Remember? After you killed that demon working for Augustin, and then later, after the Dark One was dead and you regained consciousness."

He shook his head slowly. "The first time I said it was to prevent you from falling apart. We had no time for that, and I knew if I made you angry you'd regain control. The second was my attempt at a joke— apparently a poor one." He shrugged. "Since you'd taken out Augustin while I was prone on the street, I thought you'd understand."

Afraid to believe he meant it, she asked, "So, you don't want a demon female instead of me?"

"I want *only you*. Kimi, I love you. No," he said when she tried to interrupt. "Listen to me. Do you think I'd share the things I've told you with just anyone? I've only spoken of my father's death in detail once—with you. That should tell you something."

"You really love me?" she asked.

"I really do. You're more than I dared dream of. I know what your next argument will be—the vishtau bond does not promise any deep emotion will develop. But how could I not fall in love with you? You're special, so much more than I deserve. The most important thing, though, is how I feel when I'm with you. It's as if I'm complete, as if the part of me that I never realized was missing has been given back."

She relaxed enough to lean into him.

"If I didn't mention the vishtau again, it's because I worried over your reaction," Nic admitted. "I didn't want you to feel pressured by me, or to feel that you had no choice. You do."

"No, I don't. I love you too, Nic. I want no one else."

"Are you certain?" He looked impossibly hopeful.

She nodded and he leaned down to kiss her, his touch adoring but much too brief.

"There's a bonding ritual," Nic said, sounding cautious. "It's permanent. Normally, it doesn't affect humans, but because of your power, you'll be as tied to me as I am to you."

"And that's a problem because . . . ?"

"It isn't a problem, not as long as you're fully aware of what you'll be signed up for. There'll be no other mate for either of us for as long as we live."

As far as Kimi was concerned, she'd already made that commitment. She told him that.

His lips curved. "You're not getting the best end of the bargain, I know that, but you do get one benefit. Remember when I told you the kijo develops demon physiology after the rite?" He waited for her nod. "I've been doing some reading and your life span will lengthen to that of a demon's as well."

"Good," she said, leaning into his chest, "because sixty years with you won't be enough. I need at least three hundred." And going up on her toes, Kimi felt true happiness awakening inside her. She kissed him. Now she had what she truly wanted—the power to be forever with Nic.

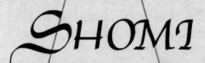

ATTENTION
BOOK LOVERS!

Can't get enough of your favorite **ROMANCE**?

Call **1-800-481-9191** to:

✴ order books,

✴ receive a **FREE** catalog,

✴ join our book clubs to **SAVE 30%!**

Open Mon.-Fri. 10 AM-9 PM EST

Visit **www.dorchesterpub.com**
for special offers and inside
information on the authors you love.

We accept Visa, MasterCard or Discover®.
LEISURE BOOKS ♥ LOVE SPELL